THE BEST SHORT STORIES OF

Lesléa Newman

Selected Titles by Lesléa Newman

Novels

In Every Laugh a Tear
Good Enough to Eat

Short Story Collections

She Loves Me, She Loves Me Not
Just Like a Woman (audiobook)
Girls Will Be Girls
Out of the Closet and Nothing to Wear
Every Woman's Dream
Secrets
A Letter to Harvey Milk

Poetry Collections

Signs of Love
Still Life with Buddy
The Little Butch Book

Anthologies

Bedroom Eyes: Stories of Lesbians in the Boudoir
Pillow Talk: Lesbian Stories Between the Covers (volumes I and II)
The Femme Mystique
My Lover Is a Woman: Contemporary Lesbian Love Poems

Children's Books

Heather Has Two Mommies
Too Far Away to Touch
Cats, Cats, Cats!
Dogs, Dogs, Dogs!
Felicia's Favorite Story
Matzo Ball Moon
Runaway Dreidel!

For a complete list of titles, visit www.lesleanewman.com.

THE BEST SHORT STORIES OF

Lesléa Newman

alyson books
los angeles

Manufactured in the United States of America.

This trade paperback original is published by Alyson Publications,
P.O. Box 4371, Los Angeles, California 90078-4371.
Distribution in the United Kingdom by Turnaround Publisher Services Ltd.,
Unit 3, Olympia Trading Estate, Coburg Road, Wood Green,
London N22 6TZ England.

First edition: June 2003

03 04 05 06 07 a 10 9 8 7 6 5 4 3 2 1

ISBN 1-55583-775-1

Library of Congress Cataloging-in-Publication Data

Newman, Lesléa.
[Short stories. Selections.]
Best short stories of Lesléa Newman.—1st ed.
ISBN 1-55583-775-1 (pbk)
1. Lesbians—Fiction. I. Title.
PS3564.E91628A6 2003
813'.54—dc21 2003040398

Credits

Cover photography by Diana Koenigsberg from the Stone Collection.
Cover design by Matt Sams.

for Mary Vazquez,
who brings out the best in me

Contents

Introduction

The adolescent narrator of "Right Off the Bat" is the product of "alternative insemination." Her mother insists on using language that respects her life and family, and she knows there's nothing artificial about her beloved daughter. The phrase "alternative insemination" not only characterizes one of Newman's many invented mothers but also summarizes the effect of this extraordinary short-fiction collection that spans a decade and a half. Whether chronicling the erotically ovarian escapades of a menopausal lesbian ("Eggs McMenopause") or the process by which the gift of Jewishness becomes one's own ("The Gift"), Newman uses the written word to inseminate her readers with alternative ways of thinking, loving, and living. The capaciousness of Newman's vision makes her a hard writer to pigeonhole; indeed, her works are significant contributions to overlapping traditions of queer, Jewish, feminist, romantic, and erotic literature.

This collection provides intimate and historical portraits of lesbian lives. In "A Letter to Harvey Milk," "The Butch That I Marry," "The *Babka* Sisters," "Homo Alone," and "Mothers of Invention," lesbian daughters cope with and resist their birth families' attempted enforcement of the "don't ask, don't tell" policy. Whether through an unplanned lesbian dance with Aunt Sadie on Thanksgiving or a carefully choreographed Jewish wedding complete with *chuppah,* best butch, dyke of honor, and shattered glass, these women proclaim their love for themselves and their life partners. Lesbian revisions of motherhood and diverse responses to "the gayby boom" are the stuff of "Mothers of Invention" as well as "Of Balloons and Bubbles." Indeed, the latter story brilliantly represents "baby time" as it simultaneously demythologizes motherhood *and* the state of being child-free. "What Ever Happened to Baby Fane?" and "With Anthony Gone" represent the bonds of kinship between lesbians and gay men that were cemented in response to the AIDS epidemic. Taken together, these moving stories constitute not only a literary event but also a queer cultural history.

At a time when discourses of woman-identification tended to desexualize lesbian bodies, Newman's writings joyfully reinscribed lesbian eroticism. In Newman's literary universe, great sex delights the body and sometimes transforms the world. For two nice Jewish girls, "the *babka* sisters," a kiss on *Shabbos* creates "a new world, a world so sweet, so fine, so holy and precious." And decades later when they find each other again, they prove that "old ladies do know from such pleasures." In "Keeping a Breast," the discovery of a lump, fears of mortality, and the relief provided by the word *benign* alter the rhythms of a couple's lovemaking. The "diesel dyke" narrator of "A True Story" repositions herself in bed for a "night that stands apart like it was a whole lifetime by itself." In "*Bashert*," an artist comes to understand that her sexual awakening on a *kibbutz* was also her aesthetic awakening. For Newman, the art of living and the art of loving are exquisitely interwoven.

Contemporary Jewish-American literature is not Israel-centered, and Newman's works are no exception; indeed, "*Bashert*" is the first and only Israel story in Newman's oeuvre. Jewish identity and culture, however, are a consistent presence in Newman's fiction. In the award-winning "A Letter to Harvey Milk," stories become the key to preserving and revising communal identity. Barbara, a young Jewish lesbian rejected by her birth family after coming out, tries to reconstitute a family by collecting life narratives from immigrants. Harry Weinberg first provides memories of Harvey Milk, the first openly gay official in U.S. history, and then relates a story that begins in the camps and ends in his own marriage bed; here, an old Jewish man becomes an ally in part by expressing fatherly pride in Barbara, in part by seamlessly interweaving gay and Jewish history. In "The Gift," Newman chronicles a journey from Jewish self-hatred often nurtured by seemingly progressive lesbian-feminist communities to the joyful realization that the Jewish lesbian is "twice blessed" (I borrow this term from Christie Balka and Andy Rose's anthology of the same name). Although "The Gift" was first published in 1988, its republication in this anthology is particularly timely given that anti-Semitism has become an invisible yet potent presence in many of today's progressive movements.

In Newman's later works, Jewishness becomes less of a thematic battle and more a cherished but assumed cultural context. Thus in "The Butch That I Marry," the narrator takes for granted Jewish wedding rituals and the officiating role of a rabbi, chopped liver is a part of the wedding feast that even the vegetarians enjoy, and an anniversary breakfast in bed naturally includes a red rose alongside "the bagel and lox." As the title first indicates, the sensual pleasures of Jewish food become a rhetoric of lesbian love in "The *Babka* Sisters." In that story, Evie's lips are described as being "sweeter than *challah*...sweeter than *babka,*" and a sexually sated Ruthie is "like a puddle of *shmaltz.*" The beloved friendship between Missy and Fane in "What Ever Happened to Baby Fane?" begins with a recognition of close doubling: Missy is a Brooklynite, Fane a survivor of the Bronx, and they had "both gone through a 'Jew-fro' stage at the exact same time." When Fane finally loses his battle against AIDS—and this *is* a battle, one movingly rendered—Missy begins to say kaddish, the prayer of Jewish mourners that praises God but does not mention death. Thinks Missy, "out of nowhere I began to chant ancient Hebrew words I thought I had forgotten long ago." Remembering Jewishness is part of Newman's literary project.

Newman identifies her native language as Yinglish, a form of English that makes generous use of Yiddish phrases and syntax; she credits Grace Paley for teaching her that Yinglish might have literary qualities of its own rather than merely being a bastardization of the queen's English. In "A Letter to Harvey Milk," Barbara says to Harry Weinberg, "when I hear old people talking Yiddish, it's like a love letter blowing in the wind. I run after it as fast as I can, but I just can't seem to catch it." For those of us who grew up in Yinglish-speaking communities, Newman's prose in such stories as "Harvey Milk" and "The *Babka* Sisters" is a love letter firmly grasped; indeed, with such lines as "you should only live and be well and find your own Evie," Newman masterfully reproduces the intonations, sentence structure, and vocabulary of such communities. Yiddish is known as the *mama-loshen,* the mother tongue, and it seems no coincidence that the Anglicized remnants of this feminine language become a vehicle for constructing Jewish lesbian identity.

Conservative critics of *Heather Has Two Mommies* have classified Newman as "one of the most dangerous writers in America today." Such critics are afraid of alternative insemination. Those of us who have no such fears, however, think of Newman as one of the most courageous writers in America today. She has the courage to expose the plagues of our culture and our domestic lives: unexamined anti-Semitism that passes as progressive discourse; entrenched homophobia that makes the daughter of a lesbian couple wary of potential friends; the heartless neglect of an AIDS epidemic that claimed and continues to claim the valuable lives of the best, the brightest, and the ordinary; the horrors of hate crimes that sometimes kill millions at a time and leave their mark on the psyches of generations; parents who disown their children for no good reason; lovers and partners who find themselves straying from each other and from their own desires. Yet these plagues are only part of the stories that Newman tells. Indeed, just as powerful are the moments when a loving lesbian couple claims and revisions Jewish wedding rituals; when a lump in a breast is pronounced benign and life is lived more mindfully; when love between women is consistently presented as being as sweet and as sticky as *babka;* when elders provide young students and teachers with hope and history; when love and kinship rather than blood relations define a family. This collection is coming out in a post–Matthew Shepard, post-9/11, post–Daniel Pearl world. Perhaps especially in such a world, we need writers like Newman, who bear witness to worlds of pain and yet never let us forget our capacity for compassion and for common decency. Jews call this capacity *menschlikhkeit* and consider it the consummate human obligation. As a writer of *menschlikhkeit,* Lesléa Newman offers gifts. May her readers joyfully accept them.

Helene Meyers
Professor of English
Southwestern University

FROM

A Letter to Harvey Milk

(1988)

A Letter to Harvey Milk

for Harvey Milk
1930-1978

I.

The teacher says we should write about our life, everything that happened today. So *nu,* what's there to tell? Why should today be different than any other day? May 5, 1986. I get up, I have myself a coffee, a little cottage cheese, half an English muffin. I get dressed. I straighten out the house a little, nobody should drop by and see I'm such a slob. I go down to the Senior Center and see what's doing. I play a little cards, I have some lunch, a bagel with cheese. I read a sign in the cafeteria: WRITING CLASS, 2:00. I think to myself, why not, something to pass the time. So at two o'clock I go in. The teacher says we should write about our life.

Listen, I want to say to this teacher, I.B. Singer I'm not. You think anybody cares what I did all day? Even my own children, may they live and be well, don't call. You think the whole world is waiting to hear what Harry Weinberg had for breakfast?

The teacher is young and nice. She says everybody has important things to say. Yeah, sure, when you're young, you believe things like that. She has short brown hair and big eyes, a nice figure, *zaftig* like my poor Fannie, may she rest in peace. She's wearing a Star of David around her neck, hanging from a purple string, that's nice. She gave us all notebooks and told us we're gonna write something every day, and if we want, we can even write at home. Who'd a thunk it—me, Harry Weinberg, seventy-seven years old, scribbling in a notebook like a schoolgirl. Why not, it passes the time.

Note: A Yiddish and Hebrew glossary appears at the end of this book.

So after the class I go to the store, I pick myself up a little orange juice, a few bagels, a nice piece of chicken, I shouldn't starve to death. I go up, I put on my slippers, I eat the chicken, I watch a little TV, I write in this notebook, I get ready for bed. *Nu,* for this somebody should give me a Pulitzer Prize?

II.

Today the teacher tells us something about herself. She's a Jew, this we know from the *Mogen David* she wears around her neck. She tells us she wants to collect stories from old Jewish people, to preserve our history. *Oy,* such stories that I could tell her shouldn't be preserved by nobody. She tells us she's learning Yiddish. For what, I wonder. I can't figure this teacher out. She's young, she's pretty, she shouldn't be with the old people so much. I wonder is she married. She don't wear a ring. Her grandparents won't tell her stories, she says, and she's worried that the Jews her age won't know nothing about the culture, about life in the *shtetls.* Believe me, life in the *shtetl* is nothing worth knowing about. Hunger and more hunger. Better off we're here in America, the past is past.

Then she gives us our homework, the homework we write in the class, it's a little *meshugeh,* but all right. She wants us to write a letter to somebody from our past, somebody who's no longer with us. She reads us a letter a child wrote to Abraham Lincoln, like an example. Right away I see everybody's getting nervous. So I raise my hand. "Teacher," I say, "you can tell me maybe how to address such a letter? There's a few things I've wanted to ask my wife for a long time." Everybody laughs. Then they start to write.

I sit for a few minutes, thinking about Fannie, thinking about my sister Freida, my mother, my father, may they all rest in peace. But it's the strangest thing, the one I really want to write to is Harvey.

Dear Harvey,

You had to go get yourself killed for being a *faygeleh*? You couldn't let somebody else have such a great honor? All right, all right, so you liked the boys, I wasn't wild about the idea. But I got used to it. I never said you wasn't welcome in my house, did I?

Nu, Harvey, you couldn't leave well enough alone? You had your own camera shop, your own business, what's bad? You couldn't keep still about the boys, you weren't satisfied until the whole world knew? Harvey Milk with the big ears and the big ideas, had to go make himself something, a big politician. I know, know, I said, "Harvey, make something of yourself. Don't be an old *shmegeggie* like me, Harry the butcher." So now I'm eating my words, and they stick in my throat like an old chicken bone.

It's a rotten world, Harvey, and rottener still without you in it. You know what happened to that *momser,* Dan White? They let him out of jail and he goes and kills himself so nobody else should have the pleasure. Now, you know me, Harvey, I'm not a violent man. In the old country, I saw things you shouldn't know from, things you couldn't imagine one person could do to another. But here in America, a man climbs through the window, kills the mayor of San Francisco, kills city supervisor Harvey Milk, and a couple years later he's out walking around on the street? This I never thought I'd see in my whole life. But from a country that kills the Rosenbergs, I should expect something different?

Harvey, you should be glad you wasn't around for the trial. I read about it in the papers. The lawyer, that son of a bitch, said Dan White ate too many Twinkies the night before he killed you, so his brain wasn't working right. Twinkies, *nu,* I ask you. My kids ate Twinkies when they was little, did they grow up to be murderers, God forbid? And now, since Twinkies are so dangerous, do they take them down from the shelves, somebody else shouldn't go a little crazy, climb through the windows and shoot somebody? No, they leave them there right next to the cupcakes and the doughnuts, to torture me every time I go to the store to pick up a few things, I shouldn't starve to death.

Harvey, I think I'm losing my mind. You know what I do every week? Every week I go to the store, I buy a bag of jellybeans for you, you should have something to *nosh* on when you come over, I remember what a sweet tooth you have. I put them in a jar on the table, in case you should come in with another crazy petition for me to sign. Sometimes I think you're gonna walk through my door and tell me it was just another *meshugeh* publicity stunt.

Harvey, now I'm gonna tell you something. The night you died, the whole city of San Francisco cried for you. Thirty thousand people marched in the street, I saw it on TV. Me, I didn't go down. I'm an old man, I don't walk so good, they said there might be riots. But no, there was no riots. Just people walking in the street, quiet, each one with a candle, until the street looked like the sky all lit up with a million stars. Old people, young people, black people, white people, Chinese people, you name it, they was there. I remember thinking, Harvey must be so proud, and then I remembered you was dead, and such a lump rose in my throat, like a grapefruit it was, and then the tears ran down my face like rain. Can you imagine, Harvey, an old man like me, sitting alone in his apartment, crying and carrying on like a baby? But it's the God's truth. Never did I carry on so in all my life.

And then all of a sudden I got mad. I yelled at the people on TV: For getting shot you made him into such a hero? You couldn't march for him when he was alive, he couldn't *shep* a little *naches*? But *nu,* what good does getting mad do, it only makes my pressure go up. So I took myself a pill, calmed myself down.

Then they made speeches for you, Harvey. The same people who called you a *shmuck* when you was alive, now you was dead, they was calling you a *mensch*. You were a *mensch,* Harvey, a *mensch* with a heart of gold. You were too good for this rotten world. They just weren't ready for you.

Oy, Harveleh, alav ha-sholom,
Harry

III.

Today the teacher asks me to stay for a minute after class. *Oy,* what did I do wrong now, I wonder. Maybe she didn't like my letter to Harvey?

After the class she comes and sits down next to me. She's wearing purple pants and a white T-shirt. "*Feh,*" I can just hear Fannie say. "God forbid she should wear a skirt? Show off her figure a little? The girls today dressing like boys and the boys dressing like girls, this I don't understand."

"Mr. Weinberg," she says.

"Call me Harry," I says.

"Okay, Harry," she says. "I really liked the letter you wrote to Harvey Milk. It was terrific, really. It meant a lot to me. It even made me cry."

I can't even believe my own ears. My letter to Harvey Milk made the teacher cry?

"You see, Harry," she says, "I'm gay too. And I don't know many Jewish people your age that are so open-minded. So your letter gave me lots of hope. In fact, I'd like to publish it."

Publish my letter? Again I couldn't believe my own ears. Who would want to read a letter from Harry Weinberg to Harvey Milk? No, I tell her. I'm too old for fame and glory. I like the writing class, it passes the time. But what I write is my own business. The teacher looks sad for a minute, like a cloud passes over her eyes. Then she says, "Tell me about Harvey Milk. How did you meet him? What was he like?" *Nu,* Harvey, you were a pain in the neck when you was alive, you're still a pain in the neck now that you're dead. Everybody only wants to hear about Harvey.

So I tell her. I tell her how I came into his camera shop one day with a roll of film from when I went to visit the grandchildren. How we started talking and I said, "Milk, that's not such a common name. Are you related to the Milks in Woodmere?" And so we found out we was practically neighbors forty years ago when the children was young, before we moved out here. Gracie was almost the same age as Harvey, a couple years older maybe, but they went to different schools. Still, Harvey leans across the counter and gives me such a hug, like I'm his own father.

I tell her more about Harvey, how he didn't believe there was a good *kosher* butcher in San Francisco, how he came to my shop just to see. But all the time I'm talking, I'm thinking to myself, no, it can't be true. Such a gorgeous girl like this goes with the girls, not with the boys? Such a *shanda.* Didn't God in His wisdom make a girl a girl and a boy a boy—boom they meet, boom they marry, boom they make babies, and that's the way it is? Harvey I loved like my own son, but this I could never understand. And *nu,* why was the teacher telling me this, it's my business who she sleeps with? She has some sadness in her eyes, this teacher. Believe me, I've known such sadness in my life, I can recognize it a hundred miles away. Maybe she's lonely. Maybe after class one day, I'll take her out for a coffee, we'll talk a little bit, I'll find out.

IV.

It's three o'clock in the morning, I can't sleep. So *nu,* here I am with this crazy notebook. Who am I kidding, maybe I think I'm Yitzhak Peretz? What would the children think to see their old father sitting up in his bathrobe with a cup of tea, scribbling in his notebook? *Oy,* my *kinder,* they should only live and be well and call their old father once in a while.

Fannie used to keep up with them. She could be such a nudge, my Fannie. "What's the matter, you're too good to call your old mother once in a while?" she'd yell into the phone. Then there'd be a pause. "Busy-shmizzie," she'd yell even louder. "Was I too busy to change your diapers? Was I too busy to put food into your mouth?" *Oy,* I haven't got the strength, but Fannie, could she yell and carry on.

You know, sometimes in the middle of the night I'll reach across the bed for Fannie's hand. Without even thinking, like my hand got a mind of its own, it creeps across the bed, looking for Fannie. After all this time, fourteen years she's been dead, but still, a man gets used to a few things. Forty-two years, the body don't forget. And my little *Faigl* had such hands, little *hentelehs,* tiny like a child's. But strong. Strong from kneading *challah,* from scrubbing clothes, from rubbing the children's backs to put them to sleep. My Fannie, she was so ashamed from those hands. After thirty-five years of marriage, when finally I could afford to buy her a diamond ring, she said no. She said it was too late already, she'd be ashamed. A girl needs nice hands to show off a diamond, her hands were already ruined, better yet buy a new stove.

Ruined? *Feh.* To me her hands were beautiful. Small, with

veins running through them like rivers and cracks in the skin like the desert. A hundred times I've kicked myself for not buying Fannie that ring.

V.

Today in the writing class the teacher read my notebook. Then she says I should make a poem about Fannie. "A poem," I says to her, "now Shakespeare you want I should be?" She says I have a good eye for detail. I says to her, "Excuse me, Teacher, you live with a woman for forty-two years, you start to notice a few things."

She helps me, we do it together, we write a poem called "Fannie's Hands."

Fannie's hands are two little birds
that fly into her lap.
Her veins are like rivers.
Her skin is cracked like the desert.
Her strong little hands
baked *challah,* scrubbed clothes
rubbed the children's backs
to put them to sleep.
Her strong little hands
and my big clumsy hands
fit together in the night
like pieces of a jigsaw puzzle
made in Heaven, by God.

So *nu,* who says you can't teach an old dog new tricks? I read it to the class and such a fuss they made. "A regular Romeo," one of them says. "If only my husband, may he live and be well, would write such a poem for me," says another. I wish Fannie was still alive, I could read it to her. Even the teacher was happy, I could tell, but still, there was a ring of sadness around her eyes.

After the class I waited till everybody left, they shouldn't get the wrong idea, and I asked the teacher would she like to go get a coffee. "*Nu*, it's enough writing already," I says. "Come, let's have a little treat."

So we take a walk, it's a nice day. We find a diner, nothing fancy, but clean and quiet. I try to buy her a piece of cake, a sandwich maybe, but no, all she wants is coffee.

So we sit and talk a little. She wants to know about my childhood in the old country, she wants to know about the boat ride to America, she wants to know did my parents speak Yiddish when I was growing up. "Harry," she says to me, "when I hear old people talking Yiddish, it's like a love letter blowing in the wind. I run after it as fast as I can, but I just can't seem to catch it."

Oy, this teacher has some strange ideas. "Why do you want to talk Jewish?" I ask her. "Here in America, you don't need it. What's done is done, what's past is past. You shouldn't be with the old people so much. You should go out, make friends, have a good time. You got some problems you want to talk about? Maybe I shouldn't pry," I says, "but you shouldn't look so sad, a young girl like you. When you're old, you got plenty to be sad. You shouldn't think about the past so much. Let the dead rest in peace, what's done is done."

I took a swallow of my coffee to calm down my nerves. I was getting a little too excited.

"Harry, listen to me," the teacher says. "I'm thirty years old, and no one in my family will talk to me because I'm gay. It's all Harvey Milk's fault. You know what he said before he died, 'If a bullet enters my brain, let that bullet destroy every closet door.' So when he was killed, I came out to everyone: the people at work, my parents. I felt it was my duty, so the Dan Whites of the world couldn't get away with it. I mean, if every single gay person came out—just think of it!—everyone would see they had a gay friend or a gay brother or a gay cousin or a gay teacher. Then they couldn't say things like 'Those gays should be shot.' Because they'd be saying 'You should shoot my neighbor, or my sister, or my daughter's best friend.' "

I never saw the teacher get so excited before. Maybe a politician she should be. She reminded me a little bit of Harvey. "So *nu*," I asked, "what's the problem?"

"The problem is my parents," she says with a sigh, and such a sigh I never heard from a young person before. "My parents haven't spoken to me since I came out. 'How could you do this to us?' they said. I wasn't doing anything *to* them. I tried to explain I couldn't help being gay, like I couldn't help being Jewish, but that they didn't want to hear. So I haven't spoken to them in eight years."

"Eight years, *Gottinyu.*" This I never heard in all my life. A father and a mother cut off their own flesh and blood like that. Better they should cut off their own hand. I thought about Gracie, a perfect daughter she's not, but still, your child is your child. When she married the *goy,* Fannie threatened to put her head in the oven, but she got over it. Not to see your own daughter for eight years, and such a smart, gorgeous girl she is, such a good teacher, what a *shanda.*

So what can I do, I ask. Does she want me to talk to them, a letter maybe I could write. Does she want I should adopt her, the hell with them, I make a little joke. She smiles. "Just talking to you makes me feel better," she says. So *nu,* now I'm Harry the social worker. She says that's why she wants the old people's stories so much, she doesn't know nothing about her own family history. She wants to know about her own people, maybe write a book, but it's hard to get the people to talk to her, she says, she don't understand.

"Listen, Teacher," I says to her. "These old people have stories you shouldn't know from. Hunger and more hunger. Suffering and more suffering. I buried my sister, over thirty years ago, my mother, my father, all dead. You think I could just start talking about them like I saw them yesterday? You think I don't think about them every day? Right here I keep them," I says, pointing to my heart. "I try to forget them, I should live in peace. The dead are gone. Talking about them won't bring them back. You want stories, go talk to somebody else. I ain't got no stories."

I sat down then. I didn't even know I was standing up, I got so excited. Everybody in the diner was looking at me, a crazy old man shouting at a young pretty girl. *Oy,* and now the teacher was crying. "I'm sorry," I says to her. "You want another coffee?"

"No, thanks, Harry," she says. "I'm sorry too."

"Forget it. We can just pretend it never happened," I say, and then we go.

VI.

All this crazy writing has shaken me up inside a little bit. Yesterday I was walking home from the diner, I thought I saw Harvey walking in front of me. No, it can't be, I says to myself, and my heart started to pound so, I got afraid I shouldn't drop dead in the street from a heart attack. But then the man turned around and it wasn't Harvey. It didn't even look like him at all.

I got myself upstairs and took myself a pill. I could feel my pressure was going up. All this talk about the past: Fannie, Harvey, Freida, my mother, my father, what good does it do? This teacher and her crazy ideas. Did I ever ask my mother, my father what their childhood was like? What nonsense. Better I shouldn't know.

So today is Saturday, no writing class, but still I'm writing in this crazy notebook. I ask myself, Harry, what can I do to make you feel a little better? And I answer myself: Make me a nice chicken soup.

What, you think an old man like me can't make chicken soup? Let me tell you, on all the holidays it was Harry that made the soup. Every Passover it was Harry skimming the *shmaltz* from the top of the pot, it was Harry making the *matzo* balls. *Nu,* I ask you, where is it written that a man shouldn't know from chicken soup?

So I take myself down to the store, I buy myself a nice chicken, some carrots, some celery, some parsley—onions I already got, parsnips I can do without. I'm afraid I shouldn't have a heart attack *shlepping* all that food up the steps, but thank God, I make it all right.

I put up the pot with water, throw everything in one-two-three, and soon the whole house smells like a holiday.

I remember the time Harvey came to visit and there I was with my apron on, skimming the *shmaltz* from the soup. Did he kid me about that! The only way I could get him to keep still was to invite him to dinner. "Listen, Harvey," I says to him. "Whether you're a man or a woman, it don't matter. You gotta learn to cook. When you're old and alone, nobody will do for you. You gotta learn to do for yourself."

"I won't live past fifty, Harry," he says, smearing a piece of rye bread with *shmaltz.*

"Nobody wants to grow old, believe me, I know," I says to him. "But listen, it's not so terrible. What's the alternative? Nobody wants to die young either." I take off my apron and sit down with him.

"No, I mean it, Harry," he says to me with his mouth full. "I won't make it to fifty, I've always known it. I'm a politician. A gay politician. Somebody will take a potshot at me. It can't be helped."

The way he said it, I tell you, a chill ran down my back like I never felt before. He was forty-seven at the time, just a year before he died.

VII.

Today after the writing class, the teacher tells us she's going away for a few days. Everyone makes a big fuss, the class they like so much already. She tells us she's sorry, something came up she has to do. She says we can come have class without her, the room will be open, we can read to each other what we write in our notebooks. Someone asks her what we should write about.

"Write me a letter," she says. "Write a story called, 'What I Never Told Anyone.'"

So after everybody leaves, I ask her does she want to go out, have a coffee, but she says no, she has to go home and pack. I tell her wherever she's going she should have a good time.

"Thanks, Harry," she says. "You'll be here when I get back?"

"Sure," I tell her. "I like this crazy writing. It passes the time."

She swings a big black book bag onto her shoulder, a regular Hercules this teacher is, and she smiles at me. "I have to run, Harry. Have a good week." She turns and walks away and something on her book bag catches my eye: a big shiny pin that spells out her name all fancy-shmancy in rhinestones: Barbara. And under that, right away I see sewn onto her book bag an upside-down pink triangle.

I stop in my tracks, stunned. No, it can't be, I says to myself. Maybe it's just a design? Maybe she don't know from this? My heart's beating fast now, I know I should go home, take myself a pill, my pressure, I can feel it going up.

But I just stand there. And then I get mad. What, she thinks I'm blind as well as old, I can't see what's right in front of my nose? Or maybe we don't remember such things? What right does she have to walk in here with that thing on her bag to remind us of what we've been through? Ain't we seen enough? Stories she wants. She wants we should cut our hearts open and give her stories so she can write a book. Well, all right, now I'll tell her a story.

This is what I never told anyone. One day, maybe seven, eight years ago, no, maybe longer, I think Harvey was still alive, one day Izzie comes knocking on my door. I open the door and there's Izzie standing there, his face white as a sheet. I bring him inside, I make him a coffee. "Izzie, what is it?" I says to him. "Something happened to the children, to the grandchildren, God forbid?"

He sits down, he don't drink his coffee. He looks through me like I'm not even there. Then he says, "Harry, I'm walking down the street, you know, I had a little lunch at the Center, and then I come outside, I see a young man, maybe twenty-five, a good-looking fella, walking toward me. He's wearing black pants, a white shirt, and on his shirt he's got a pink triangle."

"So," I says, "a pink triangle, a purple triangle, they wear all kinds of crazy things these days."

"Heschel," he says, "don't you understand? The gays are wearing pink triangles, just like the war, just like in the camps."

No, this I can't believe. Why would they do a thing like that? But if Izzie says it, it must be true. Who would make up such a thing?

"He looked a little bit like Yussl," Izzie says, and then he begins to cry, and such a cry like I never heard. Like a baby he was, with the tears streaming down his cheeks and his shoulders shaking with great big sobs. Such moaning and groaning I never heard from a grown man in all my life. I thought maybe he was gonna have a heart attack the way he was carrying on. I didn't know what to do. I was afraid the neighbors would hear, they shouldn't call the police, such sounds he was making.

Fifty-eight years old he was, but he looked like a little boy sitting there sniffling. And who was Yussl? Thirty years we'd been friends, and I never heard about Yussl.

So finally I put my arms around him and I held him, I didn't know what else to do. His body was shaking so, I thought his bones would crack from knocking against each other. Soon his body got quiet, but then all of a sudden his mouth got noisy.

"Listen, Heschel, I got to tell you something, something I never told nobody in my whole life. I was young in the camps, nineteen, maybe twenty when they took us away." The words poured from his mouth like a flood. "Yussl was my best friend in the camps. Already I saw my mother, my father, my Hannah marched off to the ovens. Yussl was the only one I had to hold on to.

"One morning during the selection, they pointed me to the right and Yussl to the left. I went a little crazy, I ran after him. 'No, he stays with me, they made a mistake,' I said, and I grabbed him by the hand and dragged him out of the death line. Why the guard didn't kill us right then, I couldn't tell you. Nothing made sense in that place.

"Yussl and I slept together on a wooden bench. That night I couldn't sleep. It happened pretty often in that place. I would close my eyes and see such things that would make me scream in the night, and for that I could get shot. I don't know what was worse, asleep or awake, all I saw was suffering.

"On this night, Yussl was awake too. He didn't move a muscle, but I could tell. Finally he said my name, just a whisper, but something broke in me, and I began to cry. He put his arms around me and we cried together, such a close call we had.

"And then he began to kiss me. 'You saved my life,' he whispered, and he kissed my eyes, my cheeks, my lips. And Harry, I kissed him back. I never told nobody this before, I...you know, that was such a hell, that place, I couldn't help it. The warmth of his body was just too much for me and Hannah was dead already and surely we would soon be dead too, so what did it matter?"

He looked up at me then, the tears streaming from his eyes. "It's okay, Izzie," I said. "Maybe I would have done the same."

"There's more, Harry," he says, and I got him a tissue, he should blow his nose. What more could there be?

"This went on for a couple of months maybe, just every once in a while when we couldn't sleep. He'd whisper my name and I'd answer with his, and then we'd, you know, we'd touch each other. We were very, very quiet, and who knows, maybe some other boys in the barracks were doing the same.

"To this day I don't know how it happened, but somehow, somebody found out. One day Yussl didn't come back to the barracks at night. I went almost crazy, you can imagine all the things that went through my mind, the things they might have done to him, those lousy Nazis. I looked everywhere, I asked everyone, three days he was gone. And then on the third day, they lined us up after supper, and there they had Yussl. I almost collapsed on the ground when I saw him. They had him on his knees with his hands tied behind his back. His face was swollen so, you couldn't even see his eyes. His clothes were stained with blood. And on his uniform they had sewn a pink triangle, big, twice the size of our yellow stars.

"*Oy*, did they beat him but good. 'Who's your friend?' they yelled. 'Tell us and we'll let you live.' But no, he wouldn't tell. He knew they were lying, he knew they'd kill us both. They asked him again and again, 'Who's your friend? Tell us.' And every time he said no, they'd crack him with a whip until the blood ran from him like a river. Such a sight he was, like I've never seen. How he remained conscious I'll never know.

"Everything inside me was broken after that. I wanted to run to his side, but I didn't dare, so afraid I was. At one point he looked at me, right in the eye, as though he was saying, *Izzie, save yourself. Me, I'm finished, but you, you got a chance to live through this and tell the world our story.*

"Right after he looked at me, he collapsed, and they shot him, Harry, right there in front of us. Even after he was dead they kicked him in the head a little bit. They left his body out there for two days as a warning to us. They whipped us all that night, and from then on we had to sleep with all the lights on and with our hands on top of the blankets. Anyone caught with their hands under the blankets would be shot.

"He died for me, Harry, they killed him for that, was it such a terrible thing? *Oy*, I haven't thought about Yussl for years, but when I saw that kid on the street today, it was too much." And then he started crying again, and he clung to me like a child.

So what could I do? I was afraid he shouldn't have a heart attack, maybe he was having a nervous breakdown, maybe I should get the doctor. *Oy,* I never saw anybody so upset in all my life. And such a story, *Gottinyu*.

"Izzie, come lie down," I says, and I took him by the hand to the bed. I laid him down, I took off his shoes, and still he was crying. So what could I do? I lay down with him, I held him tight, I told him he was safe, he was in America. I don't know what else I said, I don't think he heard me, still he kept crying.

I stroked his head, I held him tight. "Izzie, it's all right," I said. "Izzie, Izzie, Izzeleh." I said his name over and over, like a lullaby, until his crying got quiet. He said my name once softly, "Heschel," or maybe he said "Yussl," I don't know, but thank God he finally fell asleep. I tried to get up from the bed, but Izzie held on to me tight. So what could I do? Izzie was my friend for thirty years, for him I would do anything. So I held him all night long and he slept like a baby.

And this is what I never told nobody, not even Harvey. That there, in that bed where Fannie and I slept together for forty-two years, Izzie and I spent the night. Me, I didn't sleep a wink, such a lump in my throat I had, like the night Harvey died.

Izzie passed on a couple months after that. I saw him a few more times and he seemed different somehow. How, I couldn't say. We never talked about that night. But now that he had told someone his deepest secret, he was ready to go, he could die in peace. Maybe now that I told, I can die in peace too?

VIII.

Dear Teacher,

You said write what you never told nobody and write you a letter. I always did all my homework, such a student I was. So *nu,* I gotta tell you something. I can't write in this notebook no more, I can't come no more to the class. I don't want you should take offense, you're a good teacher and a nice girl. But me, I'm an old man, I don't sleep so good at night, these stories are like a knife in my heart. Harvey, Fannie, Izzie, Yussl, my mother, my father, let them all rest in peace. The dead are gone. Better to live for today. What good does remembering do, it don't bring back the dead. Let them rest in peace.

But Teacher, I want you should have my notebook. It don't have nice stories in it, no love letters, no happy endings for a nice girl like you. A best-seller it ain't, I guarantee. Maybe you'll put it in a book someday, the world shouldn't forget.

Meanwhile, good luck to you, Teacher. May you live and be well and not get shot in the head like poor Harvey, may he rest in peace. Maybe someday we'll go out, have a coffee again, who knows? But me, I'm too old for this crazy writing. I remember too much, the pen is like a knife twisting in my heart.

One more thing, Teacher. Between parents and children, it ain't so easy. Believe me, I know. Don't give up on them. One father, one mother, it's all you got. If you was my *tochter*, I'd be proud of you.

Harry

The Gift

To be a Jew in the twentieth century
Is to be offered a gift.

Muriel Rukeyser
"Letter to the Front"

Rachel is five years old. She is going out for a walk with her father. It is a windy day near the end of autumn, and Rachel is wearing her red wool coat with the real fur collar. Today is Sunday. Every Sunday Rachel's father takes her on an adventure so her mother can have a little peace and quiet. Sometimes they go to a diner for lunch, sometimes they go out for a little ice cream, and sometimes they just walk and walk through the streets of New York, with Rachel holding tightly to her father's hand.

Today they are walking through a part of Brooklyn that Rachel doesn't recognize. Her father stops to look at some books stacked high on a cart outside a bookshop. Rachel notices right away that these are grown-up books—not big and shiny like her picture books at home, but old and dusty. Her father picks up one to read. When he turns the pages, some of them crumble, and bits of them fall into the street and mix with the dry brown leaves whirling around their shoes.

Rachel's father picks up another book, holds it close to his nose, and begins to read. He reads and reads and reads. Rachel is getting bored. She starts hopping up and down, first on one foot and then on the other. She wants to keep walking maybe, or just go home.

All of a sudden, Rachel notices a man coming toward them. He is short, not tall like her father, and he is wearing all black—black shoes, black pants, black coat, funny black hat.

And swaying back and forth in the middle of all this black is the man's long white beard. Rachel gets more and more excited as the man draws near. She stops hopping up and down and grabs her father's arm. "Daddy, Daddy," Rachel says, pulling at her father's sleeve with one hand and pointing with the other. "Is that Santa Claus? Why is wearing those funny clothes?"

Rachel's father looks up from his book and sees the old Hasidic Jew coming toward them. He stares at the old man, and the old man stares at him. The old man moves slowly; Rachel's father does not move at all. Now Rachel is frightened. She watches the old man approach, and it is as if her father is watching himself in a mirror, growing older until he looks just like the old man; and it is as if the old man is watching himself growing younger until he looks just like her father. Then the old man passes them, and Rachel's father becomes himself again. He puts the book back on the cart, reaches down for Rachel's hand, and takes her home without a word.

Rachel is eight years old. She is standing in the kitchen with her back leaning against the counter, her arms folded across her chest, and her lower lip sticking way out. Rachel's mother is making soup, and Rachel is mad that her mother is paying more attention to the soup than to her.

"But why can't we have a Christmas tree?" Rachel asks again.

"Because Jews don't celebrate Christmas," her mother says in a voice stretched so tight it sounds as though it might break.

Rachel watches her mother's back, and her pout turns into a scowl. *That's no reason*, she thinks, staring down at the blue linoleum floor. *I hate you*, Rachel mouths silently as her eyes travel across the floor to her mother's feet. Rachel is so mad right now that she hates everything about her mother—her scruffy white slippers, her baggy stockings, her flowered housedress, her yellow apron, the *shmate* on her head, even the *knaydlach* she is rolling into a perfect ball between her two small hands.

Rachel tries once more. "How about a *Chanukah* bush then?"

"There's no such thing," her mother answers, turning around to face Rachel, the wooden spoon still in her hand. "Shush now. Your father will be home soon. Do you want to pick out the candles?"

"No," Rachel says, and she stomps out of the kitchen to sit on the hallway steps. It is the seventh night of *Chanukah,* and she has saved all the red candles—her favorite color—for tonight. But now she hates even them. Rachel doesn't want to light the *menorah* and recite the blessing. She wants to sing "We Wish You a Merry Christmas," and she wants a tree. A tree with tinsel and little colored balls and a string of popcorn hanging on it, and lots of presents underneath, and pretty lights blinking on and off, and a beautiful star on top. Like they have everywhere, Rachel thinks with her chin on her fist. Everywhere. At school, across the street at her best friend Kathy's house, even on TV. "Everywhere," Rachel whispers loudly so her mother will hear. "Everywhere but here."

✤

Rachel is ten years old. It is spring, and Rachel knows better than to ask her mother if the Easter bunny is coming to visit their house. Jews don't celebrate Easter, Jews celebrate *Pesach,* her mother has told her. Rachel doesn't like Passover very much. She doesn't get any presents like at *Chanukah,* and she can't eat any of her favorite foods, like tuna fish sandwiches or vanilla ice cream cones with chocolate jimmies or Sara Lee pound cake. Instead she has to carry peanut butter and jelly on *matzo* sandwiches to school while all the other kids get to bring pretty blue and pink and lavender hard-boiled eggs in their lunch boxes. Rachel's *matzo* sandwiches make her thirsty, and they're hard to eat. They get crumbly and make a big mess on the table and all over Rachel's lap.

Rachel is smart, though. She saves up all her milk money, and by Friday she has fifteen cents, enough to buy a package of chocolate chip cookies. She trades the cookies for half of Melanie Thompson's bologna and cheese sandwich. Right before she takes the first bite, Rachel looks around the lunchroom. She has a funny feeling in her stomach. What if God punishes her, or worse than that, what if someone tells her mother? Rachel takes a bite, chews rapidly, and swallows. She looks around again. Everything seems normal. Billy McNamara is still shooting spitballs at Marlene DiBenedito, and Alice Johnson is still sitting by herself, eating a banana with her nose in a book, pretending she doesn't care that nobody likes her. Lightning doesn't strike, and Rachel's mother doesn't rush in hysterically to snatch the forbidden food out of her daughter's hand.

Rachel finishes the sandwich feeling relieved and disappointed at the same time.

✤

Rachel is fourteen. She is getting taller. Her hips are getting wider. There is hair under her arms and between her legs, and now she has to wear a bra. She hooks it around her waist, swivels it around so that the cups are in front, and pulls the straps up onto her arms. Rachel misses her soft cotton undershirts. She keeps them at the bottom of her underwear drawer, and sometimes when she is alone in her room, she piles them on her lap and strokes them like a cat and cries.

Rachel is getting very pretty. Everyone says so: her mother, her father, her Aunt Esther, everyone except her grandmother. "*Oy*, such an ugly face you got. A face like a monkey," she says, pinching both of Rachel's cheeks. "What are we going to do with such an ugly monkey? Take her back to Macy's where we got her, that's what we'll do."

Rachel hates when her grandmother says that, though she likes to believe she was adopted. She also hates when anyone says she is pretty. I'm not pretty, Rachel thinks, staring at herself in the mirror. I'm too short and too fat and my hair is too frizzy. Rachel wishes she was tall and thin and blond, with hair the color of yellow crayons and eyes the color of the sky. She wants to look like the models in *Glamour* magazine. She wishes she would get taller, and her father offers to string her up on a rack. Very funny, she tells him. She wishes she could get thinner, and her mother tells her to go to Weight Watchers. Gross, Rachel says. But most of all, Rachel wishes her hair was straight.

Every other night Rachel washes her hair. First she shampoos it with Head and Shoulders and then she rinses it with Tame. She combs it out, and before she even steps into her bathrobe the ends start to frizz. Rachel scoops up a gob of Dippity-Do and smooths it onto her hair. She divides her hair into eight sections and wraps each one around a pink roller big enough to put her fist through. Then she ties a net around her head and sits under the hair dryer for forty minutes, until her hair is dry and her ears are bright red.

Now Rachel parts her hair in the middle and brushes it out, checking her reflection in the mirror for ridges or bumps from the bobby pins. Before she goes to bed, she gathers all her hair up in a ponytail at the top of her head and wraps it around an empty orange juice can. Rachel sleeps on her stomach with her head hanging off the bed, and before she falls asleep she makes a deal with God: I'll be good, she whispers into the darkness, if you promise that tomorrow you won't make it rain.

✣

Rachel is fifteen. She is going to the beach with her best friend, Kathy. Kathy is tall and thin and blond—everything Rachel would like to be. She even wears the perfect bathing suit: an itsy-bitsy pink bikini that Rachel would give her life to be able to fit into. Rachel wears a black one-piece suit she bought last week with her mother. Rachel hates going shopping with her mother. She always says things like: "I'm not buying you that. Your whole *tuchus* is sticking out." Or, "Too bad, kid, you got those famous Goldstein hips." Try as she might, Rachel can't make her hips any smaller, no matter how little she eats or what diet she follows. She has to admit, though she hates to, that the Goldstein family has indeed left its mark.

I wish I looked like Kathy, Rachel thinks, as the sun warms her skin. She is lying on her back on a big blue beach towel, with her arms over her head so her belly looks flatter. She squints into the sun and then looks behind her, past her arms. There is a man lying a little ways away from her, and he is wearing boxer trunks with nothing underneath. Rachel can see up his skinny, hairy legs, to his thing, which rests inside his bathing suit against his left thigh. The man is sleeping, and his thing seems to be sleeping, too. Rachel pokes Kathy on the shoulder.

"Look," she whispers, pointing with her eyes.

"Oh, my God," Kathy whispers back, and they giggle and turn away and then look again.

When Rachel gets home from the beach, her mother is on the phone. "She's fine," she says in a tone of voice that lets Rachel know her mother is talking about her. "She just got back from the beach and she's so dark, *vey iss mir,* she looks like a *shvartze.*" Rachel doesn't know what a *shvartze* is, but from the way her mother says it, she knows it's something Jewish and not very good to look like. Rachel runs upstairs to consult the mirror, but she doesn't look like anything much, except herself.

✤

Rachel is sixteen. She is sitting on the couch next to her father, looking at old photographs. The big album is spread across both their laps. Four black triangles, one in each corner, hold each picture in place, though some of them have gotten loose and stick together between the pages.

Rachel's father points to all the pictures and tells her who everyone is. "That's your Great Aunt Yetta," he says, pointing. "That's your Uncle Manny. That's your Grandpa Louie, who died right before you were born."

"Who's this?" Rachel asks, staring at a photo of a young girl about the same age Rachel is now. She wears a frilly white dress and black shoes with thin ankle straps. Her father lifts the album up on his lap and bends down closer to the picture.

"Who is that?" he repeats softly to himself. "Oh, for God's sake, that's your Aunt Esther with her old nose." Her father lowers the album and chuckles. "Look at that. God, that must be an old picture. Must be 1942, maybe '43." Now Rachel bends closer to see the picture. It doesn't look like Aunt Esther to her. The girl in the picture had her hands clasped tightly behind her back. She was wearing dark red lipstick, but she wasn't smiling.

"I didn't know Aunt Esther had a nose job," Rachel says to her father.

"Oh, sure she did. Both my sisters had one—your Aunt Selma and your cousin Robin too. Thank God you got your mother's nose. Look, there's you at the old house on Avenue J. Do you remember that house?" He lowers his own nose to get a closer look at the page.

✤

Rachel is seventeen. She takes the train into the city with Kathy to visit the Museum of Modern Art. Rachel pretends to admire the paintings, though she really doesn't think they look all that different from the crayon drawings of her five-year-old cousin Nathan, which her Aunt Selma has hanging on her refrigerator door with magnets shaped like orange slices and banana peels.

Rachel and Kathy go into the gift shop to buy some postcards, and then Kathy says she has to go to the bathroom. Rachel stands by herself, slowly turning the creaky postcard rack.

"Hey, lady, hey, mama," a man's voice calls, and without turning around Rachel knows he is talking to her. She ignores him, just like her mother taught her to, and stays right where she is, waiting for Kathy. The man comes right up to her and puts his hand on the postcard rack so it can't turn. He is wearing black pants and a brown corduroy coat, and he is short, about the same height as Rachel.

The man starts speaking to Rachel in Spanish. She shakes her head, holding up one hand. "Listen, I don't speak Spanish. I'm sorry," she says, and her voice is sorry too, as if she has done something wrong.

The man doesn't believe her. "C'mon. No kidding me. You speak Spanish, yes?" He smiles, and Rachel notices he has bright white teeth.

"No, you don't understand. I'm not Spanish. I'm Jewish," Rachel says, backing up a little.

Now the man's smile grows even bigger, as though Rachel has made a joke. "No," he says. "You are no Jewish. You are too pretty for Jewish. You speak Spanish, yes?" The man leans toward Rachel, and now she feels afraid. She leaves the gift shop quickly and walks swiftly through the lobby toward the bathroom, and much to her relief, she sees Kathy's face floating in her direction above the crowd.

✣

Rachel is eighteen. It is *Yom Kippur,* and today she does not go to school. She goes to services instead, with her mother and father. Rachel puts on her new plaid skirt, her soft red sweater, and a pretty gold bracelet. Then she laces up her red high-top sneakers and goes downstairs, where her parents are waiting for her.

Her mother looks her up and down. When her eyes reach Rachel's feet, she starts to scream. "What's that on your feet? Get upstairs and put on your good shoes."

"But Ma, you're not supposed to wear leather today. You're supposed to give thanks to the animals. Even the rabbi goes in sneakers." Rachel stares at her mother in defiance.

"Since when is she so religious?" Rachel's mother asks the ceiling. The ceiling offers no reply, so Rachel's mother turns back to her daughter. "I don't care if the rabbi is going barefoot, you are not wearing those sneakers to *shul*. Do you hear me?"

Rachel hears her. She changes her shoes.

✣

Rachel is still eighteen. She is going away to college. She has survived high school, much to her great relief and astonishment. She is in the backseat of the car with her pillow, two blankets, a suitcase, and a potted plant. The rest of her things are in the trunk, and her parents are in the front seat. They talk and talk while Rachel pretends to be asleep. They talk about the pretty

New England towns they drive through; they talk about where they will stop for lunch and how hungry they are and what they will eat; they talk about Rachel and how big she is, already going off to college.

They arrive at Rachel's college in mid afternoon. Rachel will be living in a suite with three other girls, and she is glad they have not yet arrived. Rachel doesn't want anyone to meet her parents. She is embarrassed by how loudly they talk and ashamed of her mother's shabby fake-leather coat.

Rachel's parents leave, and the three other girls arrive soon after dinner. Rachel sits on an overturned milk carton and watches them unpack. Their names are Debbie, Donna, and Marie. None of them are from New York. None of them are anything like Rachel. Soon they all sit in the bare living room, two on the orange couch and two on blue director's chairs. They talk. Debbie tells them she grew up on a farm in Vermont, Donna says she comes from Illinois, and Marie is from Pennsylvania. Rachel tells them she is from New York, only the way she says it, it sounds more like New *Yawk,* and the other girls laugh at the way she talks. Rachel vows to practice her *R*'s and doesn't hear what Donna is saying.

"Are you Jewish?" Donna asks her again.

Rachel thinks for a minute. "No," she says slowly. "I used to be, but I'm not anymore." And suddenly Rachel is talking and laughing with her new friends and feeling free—free as a downy bird that has just pecked her way out of a baby blue egg with a beak as sharp and pointed as her Aunt Esther's new nose.

✤

Rachel is nineteen and a half. She has a boyfriend named Eddie. Rachel and Eddie are in bed together. It is eleven-thirty in the morning and Eddie's roommate is at his biology class. After the class there is a lab, so he will be gone most of the day.

Eddie is smoking a cigarette. He leans back to grind the butt out in the ashtray on the floor. He has nothing on except a thin gold chain around his neck. Rachel is naked too.

Eddie lazily stretches his arms overhead and grins at Rachel. "I'm starving." He brings one arm down to stroke her hair. "I wonder what delicious delicacies they're going to bestow upon us in the dining hall today," he says in a pseudo-intellectual voice.

"Probably Spam sandwiches and Jell-O mold with floating fruit cocktail," Rachel answers, wrinkling up her nose.

"Hey, what's the difference between a Jewish-American princess and a bowl of Jell-O?" Eddie asks. Rachel doesn't answer. "One moves when you eat it and the other doesn't," he says, diving under the blankets. Rachel opens her legs wide and hugs Eddie's head with her thighs. I'll show him a thing or two, Rachel thinks, as Eddie goes to town. Rachel knows what is expected of her. She digs her nails into Eddie's back and moves for all she is worth.

✤

Rachel is twenty years old. Her dorm is having a Christmas party, and this year she is Donna's Secret Santa. She goes downtown to buy a little present to leave outside Donna's door. The trees that line Main Street are decorated with red and green lights that blink on and off, and the sidewalk is filled with people rushing about with packages of toys and wrapping paper grasped tightly in their hands.

Rachel turns down a side street, where it is quieter, and enters a store. The store is filled with Indian clothing made of one hundred percent cotton, costume jewelry, cards, posters, and knickknacks. An old man and woman sit behind the counter, eating. Rachel walks around, touching a mauve skirt, inspecting a wooden elephant, picking up a pair of white cloth shoes. She walks over to the jewelry counter and looks at a row of silver earrings.

"For something special you're looking, maybe?"

Rachel raises her head and looks at the old man who has spoken to her. He wears a *yarmulke* on his head, and the old woman next to him has a silver *chai* around her neck. They are sitting on little wooden stools with napkins on their laps, eating potato pancakes out of a plastic container between them. Rachel stares at the food.

"You want a *latke* maybe?" the woman asks, smiling at Rachel and holding out a pancake.

"No, thanks," Rachel stammers, aware now that she has been staring. "I just came in for a *tchotchke*." The Yiddish word, coming from nowhere, flies out of Rachel's mouth.

"A *tchotchke* she wants? *Oy*, do we got *tchotchkes*," the man says, coming out from behind the counter. "Little animals we got, and wooden baskets, paper fans maybe you like?" He gives Rachel a guided tour of the shop, and she picks out a hand-painted wooden giraffe.

Rachel pays the man and sees that now the old woman is eating some applesauce out of a jar with a plastic spoon. "Take, take a *latke* home, you'll have it for later," she says, handing Rachel a package wrapped in tin foil. Rachel picks up the *latke* and Donna's present and leaves the store.

When she gets back to the dorm, Rachel hides Donna's present under her bed and takes off her coat, hat, and scarf. She goes into the bathroom with the bundle of tinfoil and locks the door. The old woman has given Rachel not one but three potato pancakes. Rachel eats the *latkes* ravenously, then licks her fingers and searches the tin foil for any stray crumbs she may have left behind.

Rachel is twenty-one. This is her last semester of college. She has learned many things over the past three and a half years. She has learned about Art History and Abnormal Psychology and American Literature since 1945. She has learned about drinking sombreros and Singapore slings, smoking pot, and taking speed. But the most important thing she's learned is that she likes women better than she likes men.

Rachel has a girlfriend. Her name is Angie. They do everything together. They eat meals together in the dining hall, they study together on the top floor of the library, and they sleep together in Angie's tiny single room.

One Saturday, Rachel and Angie get dressed all in purple and walk downtown holding hands. It is Gay Pride Day, and this is the first year there is going to be a parade in their town. They stand in a schoolyard with about 300 people, and there are balloons, dogs wearing bandannas around their necks and chasing Frisbees, even a marching band led by a man and a woman twirling batons.

Now the march begins. Rachel and Angie get in line and start up the street. They feel very happy stepping to the beat of the drums. They walk up Main Street proudly, past all the little shops and restaurants they have gone into together many times before. People line the streets. Some raise their fists and cheer; others simply stand there staring.

At the top of Main Street the march takes a turn into a park. At one side of the park entrance, a group of people stand holding signs that say *God Made Adam and Eve, Not Adam and Steve* and *Jesus loves the sinner but not the sin.* On the other side of the park, two girls stand with a big sign made out of an old white sheet stretched between them. Their sign says NEVER AGAIN, and it is decorated with women's symbols, men's symbols, and Jewish stars. Rachel looks at the sign and feels tears well up in her eyes and flow down her cheeks. She turns her face away so Angie won't see and wipes her eyes with the back of her hand.

✤

Rachel is twenty-two. She and Angie live in an apartment in town. Angie is in graduate school and Rachel is working in an office and daydreaming about becoming a famous movie star or winning the lottery and getting at least a million dollars.

Rachel is grouchy when she comes home. She doesn't like working in an office, and she doesn't get to spend enough time with Angie. She's always at a meeting or studying at the library. Rachel eats dinner by herself, listening to the radio. The news is on. Otto Frank, Anne Frank's father, has died today in Switzerland at the age of ninety-one. Rachel puts down her fork. *The Diary of Anne Frank* was one of her favorite books when she was growing up. She walks over to her bookcase to see if she still has it. She does. Rachel takes it down and begins to read. She gets so absorbed in the book that she crawls into bed at ten o'clock with all her clothes on, still reading. Angie comes in at eleven o'clock and finds Rachel asleep, with the book on the bed upside-down beside her.

"Hi, honey," Angie whispers, kissing Rachel awake. She slips into bed beside her and gathers her up in her arms. "I missed you all day," Angie says, kissing Rachel's warm cheek. "Hey, you still have your clothes on. Let me undress you." Angie unbuttons Rachel's shirt and plants little kisses all across her chest. Soon her mouth finds Rachel's breast. Rachel cradles Angie in her arms, and together they are rocking each other gently and moaning together softly.

"You feel so good," Rachel murmurs as Angie unbuttons her pants and slides them down around Rachel's feet. Angie touches Rachel in the way Rachel likes best and just as she starts to come, Rachel bursts into tears.

"What is it, baby? What?" Angie holds her as she sobs and sobs.

"Never again," Rachel cries out, sniffling and gasping for air. "Never again," she repeats, crying uncontrollably now. Angie is puzzled, but she holds Rachel, stroking her hair and muttering, "It's all right, Rachel, it's all right."

Suddenly Rachel is furious with Angie. "It's not all right," she says sharply, pulling herself away. "What if they came tomorrow? What if they're coming right now? Would you hide me? Would you?"

"Who, Rachel? Who's coming to get you?"

"The Nazis," Rachel says, a fresh batch of tears falling from her eyes.

"Oh, Rachel, that's over. You're safe now. No one's coming to get you."

"What if they are? What if they're coming right now? Where would I go? Who would take care of me?"

"I would, honey. I would hide you. Of course I would. Rachel, I won't let anyone take you away from me. I'll hold you really tight. Just like this." Rachel lets Angie encircle her in her warm arms, even though she doesn't believe her.

✤

Rachel is twenty-three. It is April, and she has been invited to two feminist *seders*. She stands in the kitchen looking at the *Women for Peace* calendar hanging on the wall. Angie is sitting at the table drinking lemongrass tea.

"We can go to Amy's *seder* Thursday night and Meryl's on Friday. Okay?" Rachel asks.

Angie pours some honey into her tea. "Do we have to go to both?" she asks. "I'm getting a little Jewed out."

"What?" Rachel's body jerks itself forward. This is the woman who touches me in all my secret places, Rachel thinks. This is the woman I'm going to spend the rest of my life with. "What did you say?" Rachel asks, sitting down next to Angie at the table.

"Never mind," Angie says, letting out a deep sigh. "You have *seders* for Passover and the *menorah* is for *Chanukah,* right?"

"Right," Rachel says, leaning back in her chair. "And let's see. You have a tree for Christmas and a rabbit for Easter, and you put *shmutz* on your forehead for Ash Wednesday, and you give up something for Lent on Good Friday, and…"

"Okay, okay, I was only trying. You don't have to get nasty," Angie says, staring out the window, the clear sky reflected in her blue eyes.

"Sorry," Rachel mumbles, but she doesn't really mean it. She's sorry Angie hurt her and she's glad she hurt her back.

✤

Rachel is twenty-four. She and Angie aren't girlfriends anymore. It is December, and Rachel is out doing errands. She goes to the post office and asks for five stamps. The clerk hands her a strip of stamps, three with pictures of Christmas trees and two with a child's drawing of Santa Claus.

"I don't want these," Rachel says, handing them back. The clerk gives her five stamps with American flags. Rachel isn't crazy about these either, but they'll have to do. She pays the postal clerk and waits for her change. The clerk hands her some coins and says, "Merry Christmas."

"I don't celebrate Christmas. I'm Jewish," Rachel says as she drops the money into her wallet.

"Oh, I'm sorry," the woman says, and Rachel can tell by her voice that she's not sorry for the mistake she made; she's sorry for Rachel's misfortune. "Well, have a happy holiday then."

I'm not having a holiday, Rachel thinks as she shoves her wallet into her coat pocket. *Chanukah* was over five days ago. She leaves the post office wrapped in a cloud of angry silence.

Rachel is twenty-five. She has a new girlfriend named Bernie. Bernie's real name is Bernice and she's Jewish. Rachel is shopping for Bernie's *Chanukah* presents. She is going to get her eight presents—seven little ones and one big one for the last night.

Rachel walks around town and finds her way to the women's bookstore that just opened several weeks ago. She's sure she'll be able to find something there. At the front of the store there is a bulletin board with lots of buttons and Rachel thinks maybe she can find something funny for Bernie. Her eyes search the little shiny circles until she finds the perfect one: THIS BUTCH MELTS. Rachel reaches up to get the button, and her eyes follow the motion of her hand until they rest upon another button: I SURVIVED A JEWISH MOTHER.

Rachel looks away, then looks at the button again. *I Survived Kent State*, she thinks. *I Survived Three Mile Island.* But *I Survived a Jewish mother*? Rachel takes the button down and brings it over to the cash register. The woman behind the counter looks up from the invoice she is checking.

"This button really offends me," Rachel says, with her heart pounding against her chest.

The woman looks down at the button, then looks up at Rachel's face. "I'm Jewish too," the woman says.

So what? Rachel thinks. She says nothing.

"Those buttons are made by a feminist company," the woman says, as if that explains everything.

Rachel waits, but the woman says nothing else. Rachel asks, "How many of them do you have?"

The woman opens a wooden drawer and fishes around among buttons, key chains, and loose coins. She counts out eight buttons. "I'll take them all," Rachel says, handing the woman a ten-dollar bill. Her heart still racing, Rachel puts her change into her wallet and her wallet into her shoulder bag. Then she reaches into her shoulder bag again, removes a felt-tipped pen, and uncaps it. She scribbles on all the buttons and then asks the woman behind the counter if she has a trash can.

"Get out of my store," the woman says. Rachel and her beating heart leave.

✤

Rachel is still twenty-five. She is going shopping for *Chanukah* candles. She gets in her car and drives to Waldbaum's. She asks the man in the courtesy booth where the *Chanukah* candles are. "Aisle six," he says. "International foods."

Rachel is a little wary as she walks to aisle six. That same man told her last spring that the *matzo* was in the frozen food section, confusing *matzo* with bagels.

Rachel turns down aisle six, and her eyes scan the shelves until she comes to the Jewish food: borscht, applesauce, chicken soup in jars, potato pancake mix, *Shabbos* candles, *Yarzheit* candles, but no *Chanukah* candles. Rachel walks up the aisle until she sees a man in a red smock pricing boxes of fortune cookies.

"Excuse me," Rachel says, "but I can't find the *Chanukah* candles." She walks back up the aisle with the man following behind her. The man looks up and down the shelves and points to the *Shabbos* candles. "There," he says.

"No, those are *Shabbos* candles. I want *Chanukah* candles."

The man studies the shelf and picks up a *Yahrzeit* candle. "Is this what you want?"

"No, I'm looking for a box of forty-four candles, all different colors, little, to fit into a *menorah,*" Rachel says.

"A what?" The man puts the *Yahrzeit* candle back and picks up a box of *Shabbos* candles. "Look, these are very nice candles, seventy-two in a box. Can't you make do?"

"Never mind," Rachel says, and she leaves the store. How can Waldbaum's not have *Chanukah* candles, she wonders, as she backs out of her parking space and heads for another store. It is the same at Stop and Shop, Price Chopper, the Food Co-op, and Store 24. By the time Rachel gets home, she is exhausted. She calls the synagogue, and the woman who answers the phone tells her she can buy candles at the Goodman Pharmacy on Grove Avenue. Rachel hangs up the phone and cries for an hour.

The next night is *Chanukah*, and Bernie is coming over for dinner. Rachel gets home from work early and chops up apples for applesauce and grates potatoes for *latkes*. She is very happy, bustling about the kitchen and listening to *Fiddler on the Roof* on the stereo.

Bernie comes over at seven. She is tired from a hard day at work. Her head hurts. She asks Rachel to turn down the music. She tells Rachel she isn't very hungry. Rachel is disappointed. At least they light the candles together.

Then Bernie tells Rachel she can't stay very long. She's going to a Christmas party at Mary Ann's house.

"A Christmas party!" Rachel is astonished. "On the first night of *Chanukah*? I thought we were spending the first night of *Chanukah* together."

Bernie thrusts her hands in her pockets and shifts her weight. "Well, I forgot Mary Ann's party was tonight, and I promised I would come weeks ago. Besides, I didn't know the first night was such a big deal. *Chanukah* has eight nights. We can spend another night of it together."

"But this is the *first* night. Of course it's important." Rachel starts to whine. "And I made a whole dinner for you."

Bernie looks at the food on the stove. "I don't like *latkes* very much anyway. They're too greasy," she says. "Look, why don't you come with me to Mary Ann's? I just have to stop at my house and get her present."

"You bought her a Christmas present?" Rachel is practically yelling now.

"Yeah." Bernie thrusts her hands deeper into her pockets and fingers her change.

"But Bernie, you're Jewish."

"I know I'm Jewish."

"Then why would you buy someone a Christmas present?"

"Mary Ann's not *someone*. She's my best friend."

"So did she buy you a *Chanukah* present?" Rachel asks, folding her arms and leaning back against the sink.

"No." Bernie stares at Rachel's feet.

"Then why did you buy her a Christmas present? And why are you going off to celebrate her holiday with her instead of staying here to celebrate our holiday with me?"

"What's wrong with doing something special for a friend you love?" Now Bernie is yelling too.

"Then why doesn't she do something special for you and buy you a *Chanukah* present?"

"Because she's not Jewish."

"And you're not Christian."

"Rachel." Bernie sighs. "Christmas isn't a Christian holiday. It's a universal holiday."

"That's bullshit."

"Rachel." Bernie sighs again. "Do you really think Mary Ann is celebrating the birth of Jesus Christ?"

"Yes."

"Well, she isn't." Bernie is pacing around the kitchen floor. She stops in front of Rachel. "She just likes having a tree and a party because Christmas was the best day of her lousy childhood every year and..."

"Well, it was the worst day of mine," Rachel yells, flinging up her hands. "Go, then. Have a great time. Kiss someone under the mistletoe for me."

"I will," Bernie yells into the night as she yanks open the door. Rachel closes it behind her and sits down to eat the *latkes* by herself, salty tears running down her cheeks.

✣

Rachel is twenty-six. She needs some new clothes. She goes downtown to a used clothing store called Clothes Encounters and begins to browse. Usually Rachel finds something she likes at Clothes Encounters, but not today. On her way out she stops at the fifty-cent bin to look at some scarves. She squats down and rummages around. Her eyes fall on something white and shiny, trimmed with blue. It is a *tallis*. Rachel can't believe it. She rubs the shiny material against her face. How did it ever wind up here, she wonders. Rachel buys the *tallis* and brings it home. She sits in her rocking chair, braiding the strands of the *tallis* together, just like she did when she was a little girl sitting next to her father in *shul*. Rachel is lonely. She and Bernie aren't girlfriends anymore. Rachel wants a new lover. Being a lesbian is lonely, Rachel thinks. Being a Jew is lonely. Being alive is lonely, she reminds herself. A tear slips down her cheek, and Rachel wipes it with the corner of her *tallis*.

Rachel decides to call a friend, but the line is busy. She calls someone else and gets an answering machine. Rachel takes a warm bath and drinks some chamomile tea. She sleeps with the *tallis* under her pillow, one hand stroking the shiny cloth the same way she used to pet the shiny part of her baby blanket to put herself to sleep twenty-five years ago.

Rachel is twenty-eight. She has just moved in with her girlfriend, Nina. Rachel loves Nina very much, and Nina seems to love Rachel too. Nina is not Jewish, but she knows some things about Judaism, like why the Jews were driven out of Egypt and who Miriam the Prophet was and how you're supposed to kiss the *mezuzah* when you go in and out of the house.

Nina tells Rachel that even though she can't be Jewish for her, she can be supportive. She says maybe she'll take a Hebrew class or a Jewish history class. Rachel doesn't like this idea. She doesn't want Nina to know more about being Jewish than she does. She tells Nina so and Nina gives her a big hug. "It's okay, Rachel," she says. "I won't if you don't want me to. But it would be neat to know Hebrew so I could go to temple with you."

Rachel doesn't tell Nina she hasn't been to *shul* in ten years. Today they are going to an all-day lesbian conference. There are lots of workshops and activities to choose from. Rachel decides to go to a writing workshop in the morning and a cross-cultural relationship workshop with Nina in the afternoon.

Rachel enjoys the writing workshop. The leader is full of ideas and very encouraging. The women write for half an hour and then go around the room sharing their stories. Rachel is very moved by what she hears.

As they go around, a few women decide not to read their writing. The leader says that's okay; there's no pressure. One woman apologizes. The workshop leader says, "It's really all right. Nobody's going to force you to do anything you don't want to do. This isn't a Nazi concentration camp."

Rachel is stunned. She looks around at the faces of the women in the circle, all of them paying rapt attention to a woman in a green jumpsuit who is reading a poem about her grandmother. Rachel slowly scans the room. I am the only Jew here, she thinks as tears begin to rise.

After the workshop, Rachel approaches the teacher. Her heart beats in her throat. "What you said..." she falters and looks down at her hands. This is a very famous writer, Rachel reminds herself. "What you said," she begins again, "about this workshop not being like a concentration camp." She pauses again and then bursts out, "How can you compare not sharing your writing with being in a Nazi camp? Do you have any idea what went on there? This is nothing," Rachel says, gesturing around the room with one hand. "Nothing."

The famous writer is very sorry. She apologizes a hundred times. She supports Rachel. She says she's glad Rachel brought it to her attention and that Rachel is very brave.

Rachel doesn't feel brave. She feels tired and apprehensive about the next workshop. She and Nina go to Room 307 and sit down. There are already about a dozen women there. The leader of the workshop smiles. She is a white woman.

"Welcome to the workshop on interracial relationships," she says. Rachel and Nina look at each other. "I thought it was cross-cultural relationships," Nina whispers. "Should we stay?"

Rachel shrugs her shoulders. "I guess so."

The workshop leader has the group break into pairs and talk about the first time they met someone from a different racial group and what that was like. Then they talk about an interracial relationship they are having right now and what they're learning from it. Then they talk about what barriers prevent them from having more interracial relationships.

After the third question, the women regroup into a big circle for discussion. Rachel smiles at Nina when she comes back to sit next to her. They listen to the discussion. A white woman talks about how difficult her parents make it when she brings her black lover home for a visit. Another white woman raises her hand. She tells the group that she is involved with a Jewish woman whose parents are Holocaust survivors.

"It's really hard to be around them," the woman says, "especially when they act in that stereotypically obnoxious Jewish way."

Rachel's body stiffens for the second time that day. She looks around this group of faces, asking herself again, *Am I the only Jew here? Doesn't anybody else have ears?* Now everyone is listening to a black woman who is speaking. Rachel is afraid to look at Nina. She sits in silence until the workshop is almost over. When there are only about five minutes left, she rises slowly and walks to the front of the room to stand next to the workshop leader. The woman turns. "Yes?" she asks, putting her hand on Rachel's shoulder. Rachel bursts into tears.

Rachel is twenty-nine. It is *Rosh Hashanah.* She stays home from work to go to *shul.* Nina offers to go with her, but Rachel says no, this is something she needs to do by herself. Nina says, "Good *yontiff,*" the way Rachel has taught her, and kisses her cheek. Rachel tells her that later they will eat apples and honey together so the new year will be sweet. Nina tells Rachel she has a little present for her. "Do you want it now or later?" she asks.

"Later," Rachel says. "I don't want to be late for *shul.*"

Nina leaves for work and Rachel gets dressed. She puts on black pants, a fuzzy white sweater, and a pair of turquoise earrings.

She laces up her red high-top sneakers and wears a labyris and a Jewish star around her neck. She buttons her coat, thrusts her hands in her pockets, and starts the long walk to temple.

As Rachel walks she thinks about all the things that have happened to her over the years. She thinks about being a little girl who wanted a Christmas tree more than anything in the world. She thinks about how ashamed she was to take peanut butter and *matzo* sandwiches to school, and all the years she spent trying to diet and straighten her hair. Rachel walks quickly through the streets of her town, not paying much attention to the cars that pass her, all the while thinking. She thinks about marching with Angie at Gay Pride and she thinks about fighting with Bernie about Christmas. And she thinks a lot about Nina: how she offered to go to *shul* with her that morning, and how sometimes she asks Rachel to sing her to sleep. "Sing me a Hebrew song," she says. "Your voice sounds so beautiful when you sing in Hebrew."

Rachel walks and walks. Tucked under her arm is her *tallis* in a little blue velvet bag she has sewn herself. She wonders what her mother would think to see her daughter carrying a *tallis*. Rachel remembers how happy her mother was last year to receive a New Year's card from her. The card had a picture of a woman with a shawl on her head, chopping apples in her kitchen, and Rachel had written inside, "Thank you for never letting me forget who I am."

Rachel also remembers her first day of college, when she told her three roommates that she wasn't a Jew and how she hadn't said anything to Eddie when he told his awful Jewish-American princess jokes. Rachel is thinking about all of these things as she turns onto Elmwood Avenue and the synagogue comes into view. She notices a young couple across the street and smiles at them, knowing where they are going. The young woman calls to her son not to run so fast and to wait for his father before he crosses the street.

Rachel enters the *shul* and takes a prayer book from the shelf in the lobby. She is too shy to put on her *tallis*. She goes inside and sits down, holding the prayer book and the *tallis* on her lap.

The rabbi is reading in Hebrew. Rachel looks around to see if she can find anyone she knows. Her friend Aviva is sitting two rows in front of her with a bunch of women Rachel doesn't know. One of the women is wearing a *yarmulke* on her head. When the Ark is open, Rachel tiptoes down the aisle and squeezes in next to Aviva. Aviva smiles, happy to see Rachel in *shul*. Aviva is wearing a gray sweater and a black skirt with little gray elf boots. She has a gold labyris with a Jewish star cut out of one its blades around her neck.

The rabbi begins to sing, and the congregation sings with him. Rachel sees that Aviva can read Hebrew. She is moving her finger right to left across the page. Her voice is loud, strong, and beautiful. Rachel cannot read Hebrew, but she sings along, surprised that she remembers all the words and melodies. Rachel feels like a little girl again, and she half expects to see her mother and father sitting in front of her in the next row.

The rabbi and the cantor sing the *Sh'ma* in loud, clear voices, and Rachel feels her heart swelling inside her chest. She repeats the *Sh'ma* along with Aviva and the hundred or so other people in the small synagogue, letting the tears run down her cheeks like rain. Aviva turns to face Rachel, and Rachel does not turn away. They smile at each other, and Aviva squeezes Rachel's hand. She understands. Rachel has come home.

FROM

Secrets

(1990)

Right Off the Bat

My mother's a lesbian. That's the first thing I want you to know about me. I know it's not really about me, but it sort of is, and anyway I like people to know right off the bat so they don't get weird on me later when they find out.

Like Brenda, for instance. Brenda used to be my best friend at my old school and then one day she just stopped talking to me. For no reason. I mean we didn't have a fight or anything, like the time she told Richard Culpepper I liked him. Which was a lie. We didn't speak for almost a whole week that time. But this time there was no reason. I mean, she crossed the hallway when she saw me coming and everything. I finally cornered her in the bathroom between homeroom and first period and asked her what was wrong. She said, "Go away, my mom says I can't talk to you anymore. Your mother's a dyke."

"Dyke" is a bad word for lesbian, like "Yid" is a bad word for Jew. I'm Jewish too, which is another thing that makes me different. Being Jewish means I go to temple instead of church, only we hardly ever go anyway, and we have *Chanukah* and Passover instead of Christmas and Easter. Being a lesbian means my mom loves women instead of men. Not everyone knows these words. Sometimes my mom says "dyke" when she's talking to her friends on the phone or something, but she says that's okay—lesbians can say "dyke," but straight people can't. I don't really understand that. I don't understand a lot of what my mom says or does. She's not like anyone else's mother I've ever met.

Like even what we eat. My mom won't let me eat school lunches, though sometimes I save up my allowance and buy one and throw out the one she packed for me. At my old school I liked macaroni and cheese the best, with chocolate pudding for dessert.

My mom's not the world's greatest cook, and we always fight because she wants me to eat weird stuff like tofu, which is this white square that looks like soap and tastes like nothing. Just to get her to make me a Swiss-cheese sandwich is a big deal, because she always has to give me a lecture about dairy products and how they clog you up.

If I'm lucky, Linda will be around and tell my mom to lay off. I like Linda. Linda's the reason we moved here in the first place, so my mom and Linda could be together. Linda's like, well, she's part of the family. She's my mother's, well, they use the word "lover," but it's not like she's Casanova or anything. Lots of kids have single parents and lots of kids' moms have boyfriends. My mom has a girlfriend.

We have two bedrooms in our new house. My mom and Linda have one, and I have the other. When we moved here my mom said I could paint my room any color I wanted. I said pink. She said any color except pink, but Linda said that wasn't fair and anyway I'd grow out of it sooner or later. We have a kitchen and a living room and a big yard, and a cat named Pat-the-cat. Pat-the-cat sleeps with me, and Linda sleeps with my mom.

Linda found us the house and then we moved here. I like it better than my old house. My old house was really an apartment, and I didn't have a room. My mom had her room and I had half the living room and my clothes were in the hall closet. I slept on a futon that we folded into a couch during the day. A futon is a weird kind of mattress my mom says is good for your back. Anyway, I like the new house better—it's bigger and I have my own room but I kind of liked it when it was just me and my mom. Except Linda was there every weekend anyway. Once in a while we'd go to her house, but I didn't like that so much. I couldn't see any of my friends, and even though I packed things to do like books to read and records to listen to, it always worked out that I left what I really wanted to do at home. I mean, how should I know on Friday afternoon when I'm packing up my stuff that on Sunday morning I'd be just dying to hear my new Whitney Houston album? My mom would just tell me to stop *kvetching*—that's a Jewish word for complaining—but I never dragged her off to spend a weekend with one of my friends. Then she'd see what it was like.

Anyway, now we all live together, and I know your next question, you don't even have to ask it—where's my father, right? Well, this will probably shock you, but I don't have a father. I have a donor. A donor is a man who gives sperm to a sperm bank so a woman can have a baby. Oh, I know all about the birds and the bees. My mom told me.

You see, twelve years ago, no, make that twelve years and nine months ago, my mom decided she wanted to have a baby. And she'd been a lesbian for a long time, so she certainly wasn't going to do it the old-fashioned way. That's what she calls it, you know how they do it in the movies and stuff. So she used alternative insemination.

She's into all kinds of alternative stuff—that's what people call her lifestyle, but that makes her kind of mad. "How come straight people have a life and gay people have a lifestyle?" she asked Linda. Linda said, "I don't know, maybe because gay people have hair and straight people have hairstyles." My mother thought that was hysterically funny. Personally, I didn't get it at all.

Anyway, what I was going to say was some people call it artificial insemination, but my mom gets really mad at that. She gets mad pretty easy. She says it's not artificial, it's alternative. And there's nothing artificial about me. The way it works, see, is my mom got the sperm from the sperm bank and put it into a turkey baster and when her egg popped out, she popped the sperm in, and the rest, as they say, is history.

Only my mom would say "herstory". She's always changing words around so they're not sexist, but I forget sometimes. Anyway, I don't think it's all that important, but my mom gets mad when I say that. Like I told you, practically everything makes her mad. Like the fact that I want to wear makeup, for example. I'm not really ugly or anything, but I'm not exactly Whitney Houston either. It's bad enough being different in all the ways I've already told you about. It would really help to at least be able to look halfway normal. So just a little makeup and some blush, I asked her. I mean, I don't want to look like a tramp.

But my mom, as usual, had a fit and went on and on about women's oppression, one of her favorite topics. She ranted and raved about how a woman's body is supposed to look a certain way, and if we took half the energy we spend on our bodies and spent it on our brains, we could probably overthrow patriarchy (whatever that is) and really change the world.

Well, you know, by that time I was sorry I asked. It would have been a lot easier to just buy the stuff, put it on in the girls' room at school, and wash it off before my mom got home from work. But Linda was great. She's the only one who can calm my mother down in these situations. "But darlin'," she said—that's what she calls my mom—"darlin', you're just laying your own trip on her, the way your mother laid her own trip on you. Leave her alone. She's got to make her own decisions about things. And besides, you wouldn't look so bad with some lipstick on yourself."

"Yeah," I said, "and anyway, you're always saying that oppression is not having any choices, so if you don't let me wear makeup, you're oppressing me."

I knew my mother wouldn't be able to argue with that one, and I felt pretty proud of myself for thinking of it, but she just shook her head and said that was different and I didn't understand. Anyway, it doesn't really matter because she finally gave in, and Linda even showed me how to put eyeliner on straight.

My mom doesn't know about things like that. She never wears dresses or anything, but Linda does—just on special occasions. Like last year they got all dressed up to celebrate their anniversary at a big, fancy restaurant. I wanted to go too, but my mom said it was a special night for just the two of them. She promised to bring me home a treat from the restaurant. I asked for something chocolate. Anyway, Linda got all dressed up in this royal blue dress with a big black belt around the waist. She even put all her hair up on top of her head and wore these really cool silver earrings with three loops and a ball in the middle, kind of like an atom with a nucleus and protons and electrons orbiting around. She looked awesome.

My mom, on the other hand, well, she's not the world's greatest dresser. All she ever wears is jeans and flannel shirts. And not designer jeans either—nerdy jeans from Kmart. And in the summer she wears T-shirts with sayings on them like I AM A WOMAN. I CAN BLEED FOR DAYS AND NOT DIE. That's a white T-shirt she has, with red splotches on it that stand for blood. She made it herself. It's gross. Anyway, you get the picture. I mean, her wardrobe is completely pathetic. So that night she wore a pair of black jeans, a white jacket, a red shirt, and a white tie. You probably think that's really weird, a woman wearing a tie, but lots of my mom's friends do. I'm kind of used to it, I guess. Anyway, I can't imagine my mother in a dress. First of all, she has these really hairy legs she refuses to shave, and second of all, what would she wear on her feet? She only has work boots, sneakers, and green flip-flops for the summer.

So Linda and my mother got all dressed up that night. I took their picture, and off they went to have a good time. Only they didn't. Here's what happened: I guess they were in the restaurant eating their dinner and everything and some punks figured out they were lesbians. They were probably doing something dumb, like holding hands. Anyway, while they were eating, I guess the punks scoped out which car was theirs, which wouldn't be too hard to do, since my mother has all these bumper stickers that say things like "My Other Car Is a Broom" and "You Can't Beat a Woman" and one with purple letters that just says "We Are Everywhere." It's kind of embarrassing when she takes me someplace, but I'm not sure if I'm more embarrassed by the bumper stickers or by the car. It's not even a car really, it's a truck, a beat-up old pickup because we aren't exactly rich or anything. So I bet my mother's pickup wasn't too hard to find in that parking lot full of Mercedes-Benzes and Cadillacs and whatever other kinds of cars rich people drive.

Anyway, by the time these punks or whoever it was got done, my mom's truck had four slashed tires. My mom was so mad she wanted to kill somebody. Linda just got really sad and started to cry. That's what always happens—my mom gets mad and Linda gets sad. I get both, but this time I got mad, just like my mom. I mean, it was their special night, and they weren't hurting anybody or anything; they were just going out to have a good time. But then something happened inside me and I got really mad at my mom. I mean, if she would just shave her legs and put on a dress, or quit holding Linda's hand or something, these things wouldn't always be happening to her.

Me and my big mouth. As soon as I said it, I knew I shouldn't have. My mom always tells me to say how I feel, and then when I do, she always gets mad at me. "Haven't I taught you anything?" she yelled. Then she started pacing up and down the living room and delivering one of her famous speeches about oppression and blaming the victim. And then all of a sudden, she just stopped. Maybe she saw I wasn't really listening because she came over to the couch, sat down next to me, and took my hand.

"Roo," she said, and I knew she couldn't be too mad if she was calling me Roo. That's my nickname from Winnie the Pooh. See, when I was a baby, my mom carried me around in a Snugli and she felt like Kanga with her baby Roo. My real name's Rhonda, after my grandma Rebecca, and my nickname's Ronnie. Anyway, my mom said, "Listen, Roo. I know it's hard for you to understand why I live my life the way I do. You think if I just put on a skirt and shaved my legs, everything would be okay. Well, your Great-Aunt Zelda and your Uncle Hymie thought the exact same thing with their fancy Christmas tree on their front lawn and still, their neighbors in Poland turned them in to the Nazis for a buck fifty a piece. Remember Brenda, Ronnie? You don't need friends like that. Listen, Roo," she said again. "If I only teach you one thing in your whole life, it's be yourself. Be gay, be straight, be a drag queen in heels or a bull dyke like your old ma, but be whoever you are and be proud of yourself. Life's too short to pretend you're someone you're not and then spend all your time wondering what's going to happen if you get caught. I spent too many years in the closet, and no tire-slashing jerks are going to push me back."

She made a fist and smacked it into her hand, hard. But she didn't hurt herself or anything. My mom studies karate, which is another weird thing she does. I watched her in her class once, where we used to live. It was pretty cool to see her punching and kicking and everything. My mom's small and kind of skinny, but she's a lot stronger than she looks. Her teacher was a lesbian too. I could just tell by her short hair and the way she shook my hand.

Which leads me to the next question I know you're wondering about—do I think I'm going to be a lesbian when I grow up? I don't know. Kissing boys seems really gross and kissing girls seems really weird. Maybe I'll be a nun, except my mom says Jews can't be nuns. I don't know. I guess I'm kind of young to worry about it too much. That's what Linda says anyway. She says, "Just be yourself and see what happens." I asked her, who else would I be—Whitney Houston?—and she laughed. Linda laughs at my jokes most of the time, unlike my mom.

But really, I kind of know what she means, because I used to pretend I came from a normal family. I even made up a father and pretended he was away on business trips a lot just so the other kids wouldn't tease me for being so different and all. I never told my mom that. I can just imagine what she would say.

So anyway, that's all about me. I wanted you to know right off the bat, so I wouldn't have to worry about you pulling a Brenda. Do you think your mom will let us be friends?

What Happened to Sharon

When I dropped my contact lens into the kitty litter, I knew it was going to be a bad day, but even that didn't indicate how bad. I mean, it could happen to anyone, right? One minute I was standing in front of the sink and the lens was balanced on the tip of my finger, and the next minute I was on my hands and knees searching the bathroom floor with a flashlight. I didn't want to admit, even to myself, that my hands were shaking, but they must have been, and why the hell do I keep the kitty litter under the sink anyway? I shone the flashlight all around the floor, illuminating dust balls, a stray marble, and other such interesting items, until it dawned on me to look into Pan's box, and sure enough, there, shining like a diamond on a black velvet cushion, was my ticket to twenty-twenty vision, perched on a piece of poop.

Well, there was no way I was going to pop that piece of plastic back into my eyeball. I'm not a Virgo for nothing, you know. I barely managed to fish the lens out of there and drop it back into its little plastic case without losing my breakfast. Yeah, I was nervous all right. The day before I had put both contact lenses into the same eye and that hurt like hell, you better believe it, sister. But after about an hour I'd been able to wear the little buggers. Not today, though. I'd have to sterilize them first. Nope, today I'd have to wear my glasses, and damn, today of all days, I wanted to look good. This was the day I was going to see Sharon.

Hell, maybe I didn't really wanted to *see* her. You don't have to be a shrink to figure out the significance of all this contact lens jazz. Sharon. How could one little word, six little letters, hold so much emotion for me? When I think about seeing her, I get angry and sad and excited all at the same time.

I guess that's what happens when you've been with someone for seven years. Seven years! We even used to joke about the seven-year itch, how it would never happen to us, or if it did, we'd just scratch it. Ha ha, very funny. Well, the joke's sure on me, because it was exactly three days after our seven-year anniversary that Sharon said she wanted out. She said she'd been thinking about it for a while, but she didn't want to spoil our anniversary. She wanted us to have one last good time to remember. And didn't I feel like a fool.

That night was so awful—not our anniversary; that night was fine, or so I thought. I'd been sensing that Sharon felt a little off lately—she'd been a little distant, she hadn't been feeling very sexual—but I wasn't worried or anything. You know how it is after seven years, these things come and go and it's no big deal. But still, I wanted our anniversary to be really special. So I told her to get all dolled up and I'd take her out to Sam's, this very fancy place complete with a piano bar, where we happened to go on our very first date.

Every year on our anniversary we'd go to Sam's, ask the gay boy at the piano to play "As Time Goes By," drink too much champagne, eat too much food, and go home and make love and fall asleep. I'd buy Sharon red roses and she'd wear this little black miniskirt that still fit her the same as it did seven years ago. She'd worn it on our first date and that just about knocked me out—that this dyke would have the nerve to do something like that. I think that's when she got me. It was love at first sight with Sharon. She said what got her was the way I held the car door open for her and how I lit her cigarette. She'd thought chivalry was dead. Hell, I would have laid my jacket across a puddle for her if I'd had to. I'd have done anything. I was so taken with her. And I still felt the same way.

So imagine my surprise when three days later, Sharon said she wanted to break up. And before I could turn around, she was gone. Just like that. Now, I may be a fool, but one thing I do know is that you don't find an affordable apartment in a safe neighborhood in three days. Not in this city. She must have been planning this for a long time. Shit. You'd think after seven years I would deserve a little more respect than that. She wasn't even willing to go to therapy like any self-respecting dyke would. She just didn't want to be with me anymore and that was that.

Maybe it was my gray hair. I looked in the mirror and started fussing with it. I look a lot older than Sharon, even though we're only a couple of months apart. Maybe my looking older reminded her that she was getting older too, and who wants to be reminded of that? Maybe she wanted to be with a young chick, some suave hipless butch who mousses her hair or something. I doubt it, but then again, who knows? You think you know someone pretty well after seven years and then they pull a fast one on you.

Speaking of fast, I had to move my butt along so I wouldn't be late. That would really piss Sharon off. Punctuality is not my strong point, but Sharon sure changed that. I was on time for our first date, of course, and for a couple of weeks after that. But then, well, you know how it is. You try to get out of the house and then you remember the fish have to be fed and then the phone rings and you spend ten minutes telling whoever it is you can't talk because you have a date, and right as you're leaving you pass the hallway mirror and decide the shirt you're wearing doesn't really go with the pants you have on, so you pick out another shirt and of course it needs to be ironed...you get the picture. Sharon wouldn't stand for it. She got me a watch for our one-month anniversary and wrote on the card, *Happy anniversary from your new girlfriend who doesn't like to be kept waiting.* She can be tough, my Sharon. My ex-Sharon, I mean.

Getting dressed, though, is easier said than done, because everything I own has some memory of Sharon attached to it. I hate buying clothes, but Sharon was born to shop. Sometimes she goes shopping just for the fun of it, if you can even believe that. When I had absolutely nothing left to wear, I'd let her drag me to the mall, and before I could even say "Visa," I had a whole new wardrobe.

I wanted to wear something she hadn't seen, hadn't picked out, hadn't fucked me in, for Chrissakes. I wanted to show her I have a life without her. Hell, six months is long enough to get over anyone, right? Wrong. Anyone but Sharon.

All right, basic white shirt, jeans, and sneakers—what the hell, it's not like this is a date or anything. I'll go casual, like what do I care what I look like, I only have a few minutes anyway. We were meeting downtown for coffee in a "neutral" place. Christ, what did she think, I was going to rant and rave like a blithering idiot? I didn't even do that when she left. I didn't even cry. Not in front of her anyway. Except when she took Cakes.

See, for our three-year anniversary we got these two kittens, and we named one of them Pan and the other one Cakes. Separately they were okay, a pan and some cakes, but together they were fabulous—Pancakes! Just like us. So when Cakes left, it really got to me. I've always been a sucker for animals. I tried to explain it to Pan, but she just moped around the house looking up at the door every ten seconds like she was waiting for Sharon and Cakes to come back. At night she slept in bed with me, under the covers even, like she was afraid I'd run out on her too if she let me out of her sight for even one second.

That was tough. God, I really feel for people who have children. Must be really hard to explain to them why Mommy or Daddy isn't coming home. At least Sharon and I never had kids. We talked about it some. She used to bring it up more than me, all that stuff about our biological clocks ticking away. We were both pretty ambivalent about it though. I mean, if we could just have gotten pregnant by making love, we probably would have done it. But it was too complicated to figure it all out—known donor, unknown donor—it was just too much. And besides, we didn't have the money. And besides that, I wasn't too wild about the idea of having a boy. We decided we really wanted to be aunts, you know, enjoy a kid but not be totally responsible for her. Though it was a pity that Sharon never had a daughter—she'd be beautiful just like Sharon, with long brown hair, big brown eyes, gorgeous full lips, and a body that just won't quit.

Okay, enough of that. I'm out of here. And no more crying. I took my glasses off to wipe a tear on my sleeve. I didn't know how I'd feel when I first saw Sharon. The *first* first time I saw her, my legs started shaking, my knees got weak—it was love at first sight, like I told you. And sometimes I would still feel that way when I'd come home from work and she'd be sitting at the kitchen table talking on the phone, or standing at the sink doing dishes, or even sprawled on the couch pouting because I was late. I still got all trembly knowing she was mine.

Was. What a lousy word. Oh, well, nothing lasts forever, I guess. I sure thought these past six months would. This no contact stuff was all Sharon's idea. I mean, how could we go from seeing each other every day for seven years to not seeing each other at all for six months? At first we tried getting together once a week and then we tried talking on the phone, but according to Sharon it didn't work because the conversations always turned into a fight about why we broke up. I mean, what did she expect me to talk about—the weather?

So six months ago, we decided we'd meet at the Eggshell Diner today at three o'clock. It was unlikely we'd bump into anyone we knew at that hour, so we'd really be able to talk, though what we had left to really talk about was beyond me. It was bizarre to think I literally hadn't laid eyes on Sharon in six months. I mean, we live in the same city, even though she works in Westbrook, which is about half an hour away, and I work right downtown. I hadn't seen her at any dances or dyke events, not even at the Alix Dobkin concert, and everyone who was anyone was there. I'd even taken this woman, Dana, who I knew had a crush on me, but the only reason I went out with her was to make Sharon jealous. But Sharon wasn't even there. What a waste of twenty-four bucks.

I'd asked around a little, but no one seemed to know what happened to Sharon. No one had seen her at the bar or at the bookstore—hell, she hadn't even played softball this year. Maybe she was really depressed over our breakup and was just lying low. That's what I'd hoped anyway. It's not like I'd been Ms. Social Butterfly myself. Maybe Sharon had come to her senses over the past six months and realized that no one would ever love her like I did. Maybe she was going to beg me to take her back.

Well, there was only one way to find out. I got to the Eggshell early for a change, slid into a booth way in the back, and ordered myself a cup of coffee, which I hoped would dissolve the lump in my belly by the time Sharon got there. Boy, was I nervous. After about ten minutes I felt Sharon come in. *Felt,* I say, because the whole energy of the place changed. Every single guy stopped what he was doing to turn around and gawk at Sharon. Like I said, she's quite a looker. Guys were always staring at her when we were together, and it used to make me mad, but she'd just laugh and toss her head and tell me I was too serious. Politics were not exactly Sharon's forte. Even now, I could swear she just winked at one of those guys.

I watched her make her way over to my table, and I slid my hands onto my lap to hide their shaking. She looked gorgeous. She was wearing these white pants and a baggy red sweater with a black and gold scarf around her neck. Her hair was pulled back, and she had some makeup on, of course—Sharon would rather be caught dead than without makeup on in public. She looked, though I hate to say it, happy somehow. Happier than I'd seen her in a long time.

"Hi."

"Hi." I half rose out of my seat, then thought better of it. What were we supposed to do—kiss on the mouth, kiss on the cheek, hug, shake hands? Why hadn't anyone written the *Emily Post Guide to Lesbian Ex-Lover Etiquette* yet? Sharon, who never loses her composure, simply slid into the booth, planted her purse on the table, and stared at me.

"New glasses?"

"No, I dropped..." I stopped myself, remembering that when we were together, the only times I'd ever worn my glasses in public were when we'd been up all night long making love and I was too tired to put my contact lenses in the next morning. "I just couldn't put my lenses in today," I said, staring at my coffee. Let her wonder.

We didn't say anything for a few minutes, until the waitress came over to take Sharon's order, and of all things she asked for herbal tea. I looked up at her, puzzled, and she shrugged.

"Don't you drink coffee anymore?" I asked, as the waitress brought her tea and poured me a refill.

"No, I stopped." She picked up the honey bear from the table, turned it upside down, and let a smooth golden stream flow out of the top of the bear's head.

"I suppose you've given up cigarettes too." Sharon, who, like Bette Davis, was usually enveloped in a cloud of smoke, hadn't lit up yet.

"Yep," she said, still dribbling honey into her tea.

"Got enough honey in there?" I wondered if she had turned into a clone of Winnie the Pooh.

She put the honey bear down and made a face. "Actually, I hate tea." She picked up a spoon to stir with, and it was then I noticed something new on her finger.

"What's that?" I asked, leaning forward to stare.

"What's what?"

"That." I pointed to her right hand.

"This?" She turned her hand toward her and studied it as though she'd never seen it before. As if out of nowhere some fairy godmother had magically plopped a diamond ring on the fourth finger of her right hand.

"Yeah, that."

"Just a ring." She said it as if I couldn't see her hand in front of my face. My vision isn't that bad, even without my glasses. Sharon continued stirring her tea, and I knew by that something was up. To Sharon, nothing is "just" a ring or "just" a coat or "just" an anything. Everything Sharon owns has a story. Take that black and gold scarf she has around her neck, for instance. I remember the day she brought it home and told me over supper, "Well, it was hanging in the window of this secondhand store, and I made the salesclerk get it out for me, and she had to climb over all these mannequins, and she got really miffed because there was this long line of customers waiting, and then it wasn't really the style I wanted exactly, but I couldn't not buy it after she'd gone through all the trouble, and anyway it was only a dollar, so I thought I'd give it to my mother, but then I remembered she hates anything black, it makes her feel old, she says, so I guess I'll keep it, I kind of like it, actually…" Etcetera. So I knew this diamond ring had a story. A story Sharon didn't want to tell me.

"Family heirloom?" I asked.

"No." She took the spoon out of her tea and put it on her napkin.

"Is it real?" I wondered why I insisted upon knowing what would probably kill me.

"Is what real?" She picked up her spoon and licked it.

"The honey," I said, my voice dripping with sarcasm.

She put the spoon down and looked at me then, and I wished she wasn't so damn pretty. I knew I still wanted her back, and I knew I'd never tell her.

"Well, if you must know," she gave her head a little impatient shake, "it happens to be an engagement ring."

"An engagement ring?" All of a sudden the piece of toast I'd eaten for breakfast that morning felt like a cinder block in the pit of my stomach. Very, very cautiously I asked, "Sharon, why on earth are you wearing an engagement ring?"

"Because I'm engaged."

"You're engaged?" Ask a stupid question, get a stupid answer, I reminded myself. My eyes started blinking, and I took off my glasses to rub them. Be cool, I told myself. I put my glasses back on and shoved them up my nose. "So, uh, not that I really care, but who's the lucky girl?" I tried not to let on that I was dying of curiosity.

"Jo..." She hesitated for a split second. "Jo, it's not a girl. It's a guy. His name is Rick."

I just stared at her, feeling the fist in my belly clench even tighter. Sharon was with a man? A person with a dick? A dick and a beard and a hairy chest and no tits? My Sharon? My Sharon who had buried her face between my legs more times than I could count, who had licked my breasts for hours, *hours* on end, who...but I didn't want to think about all that now.

"Hello?" She was waving her hand, her ringless left hand, thank God, in front of my face. "Earth to Jo, earth to Jo." I shook my head and she came back into focus. "So, aren't you going to congratulate me?"

She always did have nerve.

"Hell, no," I said, staring at her. She looked like Sharon. She sounded like Sharon. She even smelled like Sharon, and I should know; I'm the one who used to buy her perfume. Maybe this was her evil twin sister from another planet? This couldn't possibly be the same woman whose hair I braided every night, who'd slept right next to me for seven years, as if her head were Velcroed to my shoulder. "No," I repeated, almost to myself. "I can't believe this. What'd you do, get it out of a bubble gum machine? Ha ha, very funny, Shar. You almost fooled me."

"It's not a joke, Jo." She took her purse, which is the size of a small valise, off the table and dug around in it until she fished out her wallet and flipped through her license and charge cards. Sharon was probably still paying for a couple of my shirts, maybe even the one I was wearing, but hell, I wasn't going to say anything. She held something out toward me. "Here."

I took the picture and looked. It was a guy all right, an old hippie type, complete with beard, drawstring pants (turquoise or purple, no doubt, though I couldn't be sure because the picture was black and white), aviator glasses, and a dog.

My belly lurched, and I knew it wasn't from the coffee. "You're not kidding," I said, barely managing to get the words out. "Where did you meet this guy?"

"At work. You remember, I told you about him. We had lunch a few times when I was still living with you."

Oh yeah, Rick. Another hippie-dippy-do-good-social-worker-save-the-world type. God, how could this be happening? I handed her back the photo, wondering if she still carried around a picture of me too. I still had one of her in my wallet, but not for long, that was for damn sure. "So what's so special about this guy, this Dick?"

"Rick." She corrected me like I was three years old. "You don't have to get nasty."

"I don't have to get nasty? You get fucking engaged to a guy six months after we split up and I don't have to get nasty?" My voice was rising and people were starting to stare, so I got a grip and spoke lower, my words coming out like a hiss. "Sharon, that was seven years of my life, remember? Seven fucking years. And since your memory is so short, let me remind you, I wanted to get married too."

She sighed and shook her head. "Jo, what good is it? A

bunch of lesbians sitting in a circle passing a flower or a feather around talking about how wonderful commitment is, and two years later they're all broken up and sleeping with someone else."

"How dare you?" I slammed my hand down on the table with more force than was really necessary, since unfortunately what she said had more than a ring of truth to it. "Straight people don't have such a great track record either, you know. One out of two break up. That's fifty percent..."

"You always were a whiz at math," Sharon said dryly. Now I knew she was mad because Sharon hardly ever gets sarcastic. It's too unladylike.

"How's Cakes taking all of this?" I asked, trying to change the subject for two seconds anyway, to get some comic relief.

"She's fine. She just loves Rick. It took her a while to get used to Rufus—that's Rick's dog—and pretty soon..." Her voice trailed off.

"Pretty soon what?"

"Oh, nothing." She didn't meet my eye.

"Don't 'oh, nothing' me." All of a sudden I felt like we were a couple again. "Are you living together?"

She nodded, and it's a good thing the table was bolted to the floor or I would have knocked the whole damn thing over. I swear, I felt my blood beginning to boil, as the saying goes, and I hoped I wasn't turning beet-red all over, though why I should care about the way I looked now was beyond me. Sharon was living with this guy? Damn it, she had made me wait two lousy years before she'd move in with me—two whole years of "Whose house should we sleep at tonight?" Two whole years of "But we *always* sleep at your house." Two whole years of never knowing where half my shit was, at home or at Sharon's house. And she was living with this guy after only being with him for six months? Or...suddenly I felt a little sick.

"Sharon." I was holding on to the edge of the table for dear life. "Tell me the truth now. Did you start seeing this guy"—I still couldn't bear to say his name—"before we broke up?"

"No." She looked me right in the eye. "Only a few lunches and I didn't hide them from you." I knew she was telling the truth by the way she looked at me, and the knot in my stomach dissolved a little bit.

I loosened my death grip on the table. "Just tell me why."

She shifted her weight and started playing with the scarf around her neck. "I don't know, Jo. I always considered myself bi."

"That's a lie," I interrupted her. "You know I would never go out with a bisexual."

"I know. That's why I never told you."

I tightened my grip on the table again until my knuckles turned white. "You lied to me? For seven years?" I stared at this stranger sitting across the table from me, who I thought I'd once known, as my whole world crumbled.

"Not exactly." She kept playing with her scarf, untying it and retying it and tucking the ends in just so, until I wanted to strangle her with it.

"Sharon." My tone of voice said I meant business.

"Well." She finally took her hands away from her throat. "Listen. I never lied to you. I felt like I was a lesbian. I mean, coming out was so wonderful, you know, I was with Sal for four years, and when we broke up I didn't think about going out with a man at all. I thought about going out with you."

My heart raced. I wished she hadn't said that. "So?"

"So, I didn't think it mattered, because I thought we'd be together forever. You know I always got upset when the Lesbian Alliance didn't want bisexual women in it. But I never said anything about it because I knew it would make you mad."

"Sharon, you said a lot of things you knew would make me mad."

She shrugged. "Look, Jo, I know you're not going to like this, but something happened to me. For, oh, I don't know, about the last eight months of our relationship, I kept dreaming about men. You know, it wasn't that different from coming out. I just felt my heart opening in that direction, and I knew I needed to explore it." She laughed a little and shook her head.

"What?" I asked, though I couldn't imagine what on earth could possibly be funny at this particular moment.

"You know before, when you said, 'Who's the lucky girl?' Well,

I felt the same way as when people used to ask if I was seeing anyone and I'd say yes I was, and they'd say, 'What's his name?' and I'd say, 'Jo. Short for Joanna.'"

She smiled, but somehow I failed to see the humor of the situation. The irony, however, was not lost on me.

Sharon went on. "Don't you see, Jo, it works both ways. You remember how exciting coming out was—everything you felt for the first time, like you were being born all over again. Well, this is the same thing. I hadn't been with a man for almost thirteen years. I forgot what it was like to be held by a man, to look up at a man, to..."

"Spare me." I leaned back and crossed my arms. I couldn't stand to see her look so...so goddamn dreamy about it. It wasn't the same thing at all, but I wasn't going to start that argument with Sharon. I didn't have to say anything, though. It was like Sharon could read my mind. After all, even though it was hard to believe at this particular moment, we had been together seven years.

"Joanna," she said, and I knew something important was coming, because no one ever uses my full name. "I know you're upset, but I wish you would try to understand. I'm not like you. I wasn't satisfied with women's this and women's that and half the world hating me and not even being able to walk down the street holding your hand."

That was the last straw. "Do you hold Rick's hand on the street?" I asked, amazed that I didn't choke on his name. It had always been an issue between us. I didn't give a shit what people thought, unless we were in some dangerous situation like walking by a bunch of skinheads or neo-Nazis or something, which wasn't too likely in this town. Sharon, on the other hand, hated even the thought of people staring at us. So we compromised by walking side by side, touching arms from the shoulder down to the elbow. Sharon even felt funny about that. She wouldn't even hold my hand at night on a deserted street or even in Provincetown, where you could hold hands with an octopus and no one would notice.

Sharon was very busily not looking at me, so I answered the

question for her. "So you walk around holding this guy's hand." I didn't wait for her acknowledgment. "And you kiss him hello when you meet him downtown and you let him put his arm around you at the movies and you're going to marry him and share health insurance and tax breaks and you expect me to be happy for you?" I unfolded my arms and leaned forward, as if I were about to make a speech. "Sharon, do you know, for seven years I worried about what would happen if one of us got hurt? I worried about how I'd get in to see you if you were lying in a hospital somewhere? Seven years of that, and now all you have to do is say 'I do' and this man will be your next of kin?"

I sat back and then leaned forward again. "I bet your mother is thrilled, isn't she? We lived together for five years, and every time I answered the phone she'd say, 'Hello, is Sharon there?' like she didn't even know who I was."

"Jo, I'm not denying anything you're saying." Sharon was playing with that damn scarf again. "You're right. You're absolutely right. You have no idea what it feels like to be able to tell the women at work about Rick and have them get excited for me. I finally feel like I belong, and to tell you the truth, it's a big relief. They're even giving me a bridal shower, Jo. I feel so..." she thought for a moment, "...so *normal.*"

"Excuse me, I'm about to be sick," I mumbled, sliding out of the booth. I headed for the woman's room, where I did in fact lose my breakfast. It never fails. Whenever I get upset, it goes right to my stomach. When my grandmother died, I cried so hard I puked, and Sharon was really good about it, stroking my hair, holding a cold washcloth to my forehead. God, why did I have to have so many good memories about her? And I felt so weird about what she was saying. I felt relieved and normal and like I finally belonged when I came out, and for Sharon it was just the opposite. My head was beginning to ache, so I stayed in the bathroom for a while, washing out my mouth and trying to get it together. If there had been a back door, I would have exited then and there, but unfortunately this wasn't the movies. This was my life.

Slowly, and against my better judgment, I made my way back

to the table. Somewhat to my surprise, Sharon was still sitting there, her hands cupped around her tea, which she still hadn't touched. Just as well, since it probably had enough honey in it to curl her hair anyway. I slid into the booth and sort of smiled. "Did you think I fell in?"

She smiled back, because despite herself Sharon always did appreciate my junior-high sense of humor. "Are you okay?"

"Better now. I did get sick, though."

"Poor baby." She almost reached for my hand. Out of habit, I suppose. Her right hand, the one with the ring on it, edged toward my end of the table, stopped, and then retreated. "I got sick this morning too."

I was touched. "Were you that nervous about seeing me?" I asked, and this time it was my hand that started creeping across the table, as though it had a mind of its own.

"Well..." She hesitated, and my intuition told me to brace myself. "Not exactly. Jo, I'm pregnant."

"Whoa." I lurched back as if I'd been punched in the face. Pregnant! She was really going the whole nine yards with this guy. "You're pregnant?" I stared at her face, and then my eyes traveled down her body, which still looked exactly the same to me, though of course a good part of it was hiding under the table. Maybe I was on a bad acid trip. I hadn't taken drugs in over fifteen years, but still, could this possibly be a flashback? I couldn't seem to comprehend the fact that there was not one but two people sitting across from me, one inside the other.

The one who was visible to the naked eye (behind my glasses of course) was now really smiling. I could see she'd been holding back, because happiness was just oozing out of her now. That pregnant glow, I suppose.

"You're having a baby?" I asked, like an idiot, since that is, after all, what being pregnant implies. "I never knew you were that serious about having a baby."

"I wasn't. It just happened."

"It just happened?" All I could do, at this point, was repeat everything she said.

"The rubber broke." She sort of giggled, and I could have killed her. I couldn't believe the words that had just come out of her mouth. Rubber meant dick. I could not, for the life of me, bear to imagine Sharon's beautiful pink insides being hammered away at by some prick. Not to mention all the dykes I knew who spent months, years even, trying to get pregnant. And then to Sharon it "just happens."

"Aren't you happy you're finally going to be an aunt?" she asked. Out of the corner of my eye I saw our waitress approach the table and then think better of it. You probably could have cut the vibe between Sharon and me with a knife.

"An aunt?" I still couldn't manage more than being Sharon's echo.

"Of course." Sharon leaned forward, pushing her tea aside so she wouldn't drag the end of her scarf through it. "You were the most important person in my life for seven years. Of course I want you to be an aunt."

Were. There it was again, that lousy past tense. *You were*. Boy, did that hurt. I couldn't believe she thought we could just let bygones be bygones and live happily ever after, her and the kid and the husband, and good old Aunt Joanna.

"What about what's-his-face? Does he approve of his child having a lesbian aunt?"

"Of course." Sharon chose to ignore my temporary memory loss concerning names. Or rather one name. His. "I've told him all about you."

I groaned. I could just see the two of them lying in bed side by side, with Sharon telling him all about me. All about us. Guys get turned on by stuff like that, you know. Sharon would probably tell him what we used to do, and then he'd get a hard-on, and then... Oh, God. I felt like I was going to get sick again.

"He's very understanding, Jo. In fact, he had an affair with a man once."

"He's bisexual too?" My voice and eyebrows shot up. "Has he been tested for AIDS?"

"Of course." Sharon waved her hand as if she were shooing away a fly. "That was right after high school, when he was just playing around. But yes, he did get tested and everything's fine."

Just playing around? Is that what Sharon considered the last seven years of *her* life?

"Jo." Now her hand was definitely seeking mine. I slid my hands off the table onto my lap, safely out of reach.

"Shit," she mumbled under her breath. "Jo," she said again. She always was persistent. "Listen to me. I'm still the same person. I'm still woman-identified. I still love women. I still think women are smarter, more creative, more passionate, more…more everything than men. You don't have to be a lesbian to be a feminist, you know. It's just…" She let out a deep sigh. "Never mind. You wouldn't understand."

"Sharon." I decided to try the voice of reason. "If you think women are better than men in every way, how can you have your most intimate relationship with someone you think is inferior to you?"

"I never said inferior. Men are human beings, you know." I knew it. I was just waiting for her to start in with that men-are-people-too crap. "Besides," she went on, "it's not what I *think,* it's what I *feel.*" She pointed to her heart with the hand that had that damn ring on it. "When you were a teenager, you thought you had to be with men, right, but you *felt* you wanted to be with women. No one made you change. You couldn't *force* yourself to be attracted to men. Well, it's the same thing. During our last year together, I knew I should want to be with women, but I felt myself changing, being drawn toward men. And I couldn't stop it or deny it. I wanted to be with a man."

"It's not the same thing." My voice was coming out low and even. "It's not the same thing at all." I looked down at my lap and ran my fingers through my hair. For a second I felt like Sharon had been brainwashed by some cult, and I was the hired deprogrammer, out to save her. I knew logic wasn't going to work, but I had to try it anyway. "Sharon," I looked up at her. "Everyone tried to make me change. My parents, my teachers, hell, even some of the women I slept with."

"Exactly." She looked triumphant. "You see, Jo, you're different from me. I'm not a fighter. *You pays your money, you makes your choice.* That's what my father used to say. You made your choice,

I'm making mine, and each one has its price." She looked down at her hands then, which were folded on the table. "The price of being a lesbian was just too high for me," she said, and I swear I thought I saw a tear leak out of her eye.

"Sharon." I leaned forward, resting my elbows on the table and trying to meet her eye. "Don't you see?" I asked gently. "If the world didn't make it so hard for lesbians, you'd still be with me." I even reached across the table and stroked her arm. "We can make it, babe. Sure, it's tough, but if we love each other enough, it doesn't matter. Just because the world hates lesbians is no reason to deny your own happiness. That's way too high a price." I squeezed her arm and waited. Two fat tears definitely streaked down her face. I decided to go all out. "Hey, listen. Ditch the guy and I'll be your co-mother."

"No." She jerked her arm away. "I'm not going to have my kid go through this. I can just see her bringing her little friends home, and they'll ask a few questions and the next thing you know, it'll be all over her school and no one will be allowed to play with her. No, Jo," she shook her head, "I made my choice."

Well, at least I had tried. I studied her face, tempted to wipe the tears from her cheeks, as I had done so many times before. "But won't you miss women?" I asked.

She shrugged. "I'm bi, not straight, remember? Maybe I'll have an affair. Married people do all the time."

Now I was confused. "Didn't you say a minute ago that you weren't attracted to women anymore?"

She shrugged again. "Things can change, you know."

"But what about your husband?" I asked, pronouncing the two syllables distinctly.

She waved her hand, brushing aside that invisible fly again. "Rick lets me do whatever I want."

"He *lets* you?" God, she was even talking like a straight woman. "Sharon, Sharon, Sharon." Oh, I just wanted to shake her. "What are you going to do, put an ad in the classifieds: 'Married woman seeks same for afternoon delight'? What do you think, Rick's going to watch the baby while you trot off to the Michigan Womyn's Music Festival next summer to have an affair?

You're getting *married*. That means a lifetime commitment."

"So? You think lesbians have cornered the market on non-monogamy?"

"Sharon, you can't have everything. You can't live a straight life and have one foot in the lesbian world too."

"Jo, you're just as bad as my straight friends who dumped me when I came out, you know that? It's the exact same thing."

"Will you stop saying that? It's not the same thing." My voice rose and this time I didn't care. "Sharon, do I have to give you a crash course in Oppression 101? You are joining the dominant culture. Are you still going to fight for gay rights? No. Are you going to make a statement at your wedding about straight privilege? No. Are you going to take your child to gay pride marches? It sure as hell doesn't sound like it. So have a nice life." I rose to go, but I was stopped by Sharon's hand on my arm. I hate to admit that even now the touch of her skin sent electric shocks through me, but it did.

"Don't leave," she said and I made the mistake of looking into her eyes. "Jo, I miss you."

My heart started pounding, and I slid back into the booth. Once a fool, always a fool, I suppose.

"Sharon, for the last time, listen to me. I still love you. I'm still in love with you. I would take you back in a heartbeat. You and the baby." I'd never felt so vulnerable in my life.

She looked at me and our eyes filled at the same time. She reached for my hand and I let her take it. Her skin was so soft and warm, I almost kissed her palm. Bi, my ass, I thought to myself. Sharon was a woman's woman through and through.

"I can't, Jo," she said, her voice barely a whisper. "But I'd like you to be my baby's godmother."

I sighed deeply. That's some consolation prize, I thought, taking my hand back and standing to go, for real this time. I fished around in my pocket for some cash and tossed a buck on the table for my coffee, hearing Sharon's words echo in my brain: *You pays your money, you makes your choice.*

"Jo?" She looked up at me.

I held out my hands, palms up, and lifted my shoulders, as if

I were pleading for mercy. "Sharon, how in the world can you expect me to answer that question right now?"

She didn't give an inch. "Jo, it's important to me."

I lowered my hands in defeat. "I don't know, Sharon. Maybe. I have to think about it. Hey." A lightbulb went off over my head.

"What?"

"What if you have a daughter and she grows up to be a lesbian?"

Sharon's eyes filled again. "I'd be awfully proud," she whispered. And I tell you, I left a mighty big piece of my heart sitting at that table as I turned and walked out the door.

A True Story (Whether You Believe It or Not)

This is a true story, and it happened to me, Zoey B. Jackson, on the twelfth of May, whether you believe it or not. And to tell you the truth, it's kind of hard for me to believe it myself. It's the sort of thing someone would make up to impress a girl they just met at a party or something. But believe me, I could never make this up. I could never even imagine such a thing happening, and least of all, happening to me. But it did, sure as I'm standing here telling about it.

Well there I was in the Famous Deli (which isn't famous for much, except maybe its slow service) waiting for Larry, the kid behind the counter, to make me two BLT's on rye. I was just standing there minding my own business, studying the different cheeses in the deli case, wondering how do they make one cheese taste different from the next and why do they bother? I mean, cheese is cheese as far as I can tell. Cheddar, Muenster, Monterey Jack—do they use different kinds of cows for different kinds of cheeses, or what?

I guess my mind was a little fuzzy, sort of like a TV that's out of focus. I had just spent two hours trying to get a cat down from a tree and I wasn't in the greatest mood of my entire life. When I'd joined the fire department two years before, cats stuck up in trees weren't exactly what I had in mind. I'd wanted to be a fireman ever since I was a little girl, only my mama said I couldn't—little girls don't grow up to be firemen or policemen or businessmen or garbagemen or any other kind of men at all.

But I didn't care what my mama said. I used to dream about riding in a fire truck with all the lights flashing and the sirens screaming, wearing a big red hat and racing through town with a black-and-white dog wagging its tail on the back. I got a piggy bank shaped like a fire truck for my birthday once, and I used to sleep with the thing. Still have it too.

So when I turned forty, two years ago, I decided to come work for the FD as a present to myself. I didn't want fame or glory or anything, but I did have visions of myself on the front page of the *Tri-Town Tribune,* all dirty and sweaty, having worked all night putting out a fire and saving a couple of lives. I was in the paper, actually, not for any heroic deeds or anything, but because of my size. I don't know whether it's something to be proud about or something to be ashamed about, but I'm the smallest person in the history of the whole state to ever join the fire department, and only the second woman. Probably the first lesbian too, but you know they didn't put that in the paper. I'm just about five feet tall when I'm not slouching, and I weigh about a hundred pounds soaking wet, but it's all solid muscle. I can whip that hose around like nobody's business when I have to.

But that night I didn't have to do anything fancy. I mean, whose idea was it to call the fire department to get a cat down out of a tree anyway? People watch way too many cartoons, that's what I think. When we got there (we meaning me and Al) old Mrs. Lawrence was standing under that tree crying and carrying on like it was her husband or one of her kids up there instead of her stupid old cat Matilda. She had Matilda's dish out there full of food and all her favorite toys—a whiffle ball, a sock full of catnip, and a tangle of yarn, and she was practically on her knees begging that animal to please, *please* come down. Mrs. Lawrence was promising her all sorts of things: She'd feed Matilda fresh fish every day, and she'd let her sleep in bed with her, and she wouldn't yell anymore when Matilda sharpened her claws on the living room furniture if only Matilda would just *get down.*

I guess old Matilda had been up there for most of the day yowling, and by this time it was ten at night and the neighbors were trying to get some sleep. Half of them were out there in their PJ's in Mrs. Lawrence's yard trying to figure out what to do. It was probably the most exciting thing that's happened in that part of town for about ten years.

So me and Al made a big show of getting the ladder out and

climbing up there and getting Matilda down. Ornery thing she was too—sunk her claws deep into that branch, fluffed out her tail until it was fat as a coon's, and hissed at Al fiercer than a rattlesnake. He finally grabbed her, getting his face scratched in the process, tucked her under his arm, and climbed down the ladder with everybody cheering except poor Mrs. Lawrence, who couldn't even bring herself to look.

Once Matilda was safe in Mrs. Lawrence's arms, everyone went back home to bed, and me and Al got into the fire truck to come back to the station and make out a report. We stopped at the deli first, though, for something to eat, like we usually do. For some reason, most food tastes better at midnight than it does in the middle of the day. We usually get sandwiches, sometimes coffee and a piece of pie. Al likes strawberry, I go for apple or banana cream.

So Al was sitting in the truck outside waiting, and I was standing by the counter inside waiting, and I was beginning to think Larry was standing behind the counter waiting too, for the bacon to be delivered maybe, or for the pig to grow old enough to be slaughtered or something, it was taking so goddamned long. But then in walked this woman and all of a sudden I didn't care if those sandwiches didn't get made until half past next July.

She sure was pretty. More than pretty. Beautiful. Gorgeous. A real looker. Awesome, like the kids on Mrs. Lawrence's block would say. I knew she was a stranger around here because I know every woman in this town—those who do, those who don't, and those who might. This one would, I was sure of it.

She was wearing jeans that fit her just right—tight enough to give a good idea of what was under them, but loose enough to keep you guessing just a little bit. She had on this red shirt that was cut straight across the shoulders so that her collarbones were peeking out a little bit. And I could just see the edge of her bra strap, which was black and lacy. She had on these little red shoes that damn near broke my heart and a mess of silver bracelets on her right arm that made a heck of a noise sliding down her wrist and all crashing into one another when she reached into her purse for her wallet. There must have been fifty of them or more.

Her pocketbook was red too, and so were her nails and lipstick. Not too red though—not cheap red or flashy red. There's red and there's red, you know what I mean, and this red looked real good. She had silver hoops in her ears, to match the bracelets maybe, and she was a big woman, which suited me just fine. I like my women big, you know, like those old painters like Renoir used to paint. None of this Twiggy stuff for me. I like a woman you can hold on to. A woman you're not afraid you're going to break if you squeeze too tight. A woman with a little meat on her bones.

Well, I took all of this in in about two seconds flat, and then I looked away, because I didn't want her to think I was being impolite. I know my manners. My mama taught me it's real rude to stare, but I just couldn't help it, and before I knew it I found myself looking at her again. Mind your manners, I said to my eyeballs, but they just wouldn't. I watched her unzip her little blue change purse and take out four quarters for a soda, and then before I could say *boo* she was looking right at me with her deep brown eyes the color of a Hershey's Special Dark, which happens to be my favorite candy bar. She smiled at me slow, a real sexy smile like she knew she was looking good and I knew she was looking good and she knew that I knew that she was looking good and that made her look even better.

"Hey, Zoey, here's your chow."

Wouldn't you know it? Just when things were starting to get interesting, Larry got my order done. I took my sandwiches, paid for them, and would have tipped my hat, but I'd left it out in the truck with Al. I just kind of nodded my head at her or made some such gesture that was meant to be gallant but probably looked foolish. I walked past her, catching a whiff of perfume that almost made me dizzy, and left the deli with another vision to add to my fantasy life, which is about the only action there is around here for an old bull dyke like me. I don't know why I stay in this town giving all the PTA ladies something to gossip about. I could tell them a thing or two myself, but that's another story.

Well, we weren't back in the firehouse for more than ten minutes when the phone rang. I let Al get it since my mouth was full of sandwich and he had downed his in about three seconds flat.

"It's for you," Al said, and I don't know who was more surprised, him or me. I never get calls at work. We're not supposed to tie up the phone in case there's a fire or another cat stuck up a tree or something, and anyway I keep my personal life, what little there is left of it, pretty much a secret, though it's crystal-clear I'm queer as a three-dollar bill even if I don't wear purple on Thursdays. I think it was the first phone call I'd gotten in the whole two years I'd worked there. I wiped the mayo off my chin with the back of my sleeve, took the phone, and spoke in my most official-sounding voice. "Hello?"

"Hello. Is this Zoey?"

I knew it was her. I couldn't believe it, yet I wasn't surprised. A little startled, a little shook-up, even shocked maybe, but not surprised. She sounded like she looked. Good. Sassy. Sure of herself. And hot.

"Yeah, this is me." God, what a dumb thing to say.

"My name is Natalie, and I was just in the deli a little while ago. I don't know if you noticed me or not," (yeah, right) "but I noticed you and I was wondering if you'd like to go out and have a cup of coffee with me sometime."

How about right this second, I wanted to say, but I didn't. Get a grip, Zoey old girl, I said to myself. Don't rush into anything now.

"Uh, yeah, sure, that'd be great," I said, sounding about thirteen.

"How about tomorrow then, around four?"

"Sure," I said, "you know where Freddy's is?" Freddy's is the only place in town that sells a decent cup of coffee and doesn't have a million high school kids throwing spitballs at each other in the middle of the afternoon. It's a little out of town, not sleazy or anything—it's not far from my place, as a matter of fact—but not smack-dab in the middle of town either. I told her how to get there and then there wasn't much left to say.

"See you tomorrow, sugar," she said, and I swear I could feel her tongue licking the inside of my ear right through that telephone.

I hardly slept at all that night, I tell you. I was more than a little curious and more than a lot flattered, and hell, I figured that any woman with that much sass deserved at least an hour of my time and hopefully more. I wondered where she had come from and what she was doing out there by herself all spruced up like that in the middle of the night. But to tell you the truth, I didn't really care. I was just glad she was where she was when she was and that I was there too.

I tossed and turned, too full of BLT and lust to sleep, but I must have dozed off sometime because the next thing I knew it was ten o'clock and the sun was coming in through the windows, heating up my eyes like they were two eggs cooking on a grill. My bedroom is tiny—one wall is mostly all windows, and the bed takes up almost the whole room. I don't mind, though; in fact, I kind of like it like that. Feels sort of like a nest, though why I have a double bed at this point is beyond me. Nobody's been in it since Sally left over two years ago. Hard to believe it's been two years already. Time sure does fly, I guess. But it must have been because she left right before I turned forty, right before I signed up at the fire department. That's one of the reasons I did it. With Sally gone there was this empty space in my life, this aching in my belly I didn't know how to fill, and I just couldn't face all those awful lonely nights by myself. So now I sit in the firehouse two, sometimes three nights a week, playing poker with Al.

I sure didn't want to be thinking about Sally this morning, so I got up, plugged in the coffeepot, and went into the jane to splash some cold water on my face. "Looking good, old girl," I said to myself in the mirror over the sink ,which I noticed was speckled with old toothpaste. "Who says Zoey B. is over the hill, huh? Women are still beating down your door, old gal." I winked at my reflection—I am a pretty good winker, if I do say so myself. I can also raise one eyebrow at a time; it's not as hard as it looks if you practice. I looked at myself and wondered what Natalie—God, even her name was sexy—had seen last night standing in the deli that made her give me a call. Your basic brown eyes, an ordinary nose, average lips, nothing special.

Maybe it was the uniform. Some girls really go for that sort of thing. Or maybe it was the gray hair at the temples, makes me look kind of distinguished. Some girls like older women. I wondered how old Natalie was and if she did this sort of thing often. Maybe her buddies, whoever they were, had put her up to it. Maybe a whole gang would be waiting at Freddy's to laugh their heads off at the old bull dyke who'd been taken in by the first pretty face that's shown up in this pint-size town since 1959. Or worse, maybe there'd be some guys waiting with chains and billy clubs ready to kick ass. Like I said, it's no secret who I am and it's no secret that some folks in this town don't exactly like it either.

That was really hard on Sally, one of the reasons she left, I think. Nothing ugly's ever happened, but we were always thinking it might. Sally took herself to San Francisco, where she says the streets are paved with queers and she can even hold hands with her new girlfriend all over town and nobody bats an eye. Not even the cops, because even most of the goddamn cops are queer themselves. Now, that's something I'd sure like to see.

I drank my coffee and messed around most of the day, cleaning up the house and doing chores. My place is small, just the bedroom, the kitchen, the living room, and a small spare room where I keep all my stuff—my tools and papers and stuff. Used to be Sally's painting room—that's what she does, paint—watercolors mostly. She even had a show of them in San Francisco, sent me a postcard about it.

About three o'clock I started getting nervous. First of all, what the heck was I going to wear? Not that I had much choice. It was either jeans or jeans. Jeans with a ripped knee, jeans speckled with white paint, or jeans with two belt loops missing. I could wear my black chinos, but that would look awfully funny, me so dressed up in the middle of the day. I put on the jeans with the belt loops missing and a white shirt I thought about ironing and my sneakers. By the time I'd finished fussing with my hair, which is only about two inches long and not all that much to fuss about, it was time to get my ass out the door. I sure didn't want to be late—something told me Natalie wasn't the kind of woman who liked to be kept waiting.

It only took me ten minutes to walk to Freddy's. I got there at four o'clock on the nose, and she wasn't there. Well, fine, I told myself. I don't care. Wouldn't be the first time old Zoey B.'s been stood up, not the first time she's looked like a fool. I sat myself down in a booth toward the back, ordered a cup of coffee, and looked at my watch. Four minutes after four. Oh well, I thought, ripping open a packet of sugar and dumping it into my cup. I knew it was too good to be true. These things don't really happen. Not in real life anyway.

At exactly ten past four, the door to Freddy's swung, and I mean *swung,* open and in walked Natalie like she owned the whole goddamn place. She was looking so good I almost dove right straight into my coffee. I held on to that cup for dear life as she stuck her hands on her hips and looked around like she had all the time in the world. When she spotted me, a slow smile crept across her face that said, *I knew you'd be waiting for me.* I smiled too, thinking to myself, *Fool, of course she'd be late.* She didn't just want to meet me here. She wanted to make *an entrance.*

I watched Natalie walk across Freddy's slowly, giving me plenty of time to admire her as she weaved her butt in and out of tables and chairs on her way over to where I was sitting. She was wearing this white, blousy kind of thing with a belt at her waist and these pink pants that had little black designs on them all over the place that reminded me of slanty tic-tac-toe boards. She had on little pink shoes too, which knocked me out, round pink earrings that looked like buttons, and hooked over her arm, a shiny black purse. It's those little things that separate the femmes from the butches, you know. Sally taught me that. *Accoutrements are everything,* she used to say, and of course I had to ask her what the heck accoutrements were. They're just a fancy word for accessories, which is just a fancy word for earrings and pocketbooks and stuff. Sally was always throwing those fifty-dollar words around when was angry at me or frustrated at being stuck in this peanut-size town.

Anyway, I don't know a thing about accoutrements. I have an old leather wallet I stick in my back pocket, two pairs of sneakers, and earlobes as unpunctured as the day I was born. But Natalie, boy, I bet she has a jewelry box the size of Montana and a closet full of pretty little shoes that could just about break your heart. She was wearing those same silver bracelets that clattered down her arm in a fine racket practically every time she moved. It was like each one of those bracelets wanted to be the first to get down to her wrist and maybe win a prize. Her lipstick was one shade lighter than yesterday, her smile one shade darker.

"Hi, honey, sorry I'm late," she said in a voice that let me know she wasn't sorry at all. "Have you been waiting long?"

All my life, I wanted to tell her, *just to hear a woman like you call me honey.* "Nah, I just got here myself," I lied. Both of us knew I had been waiting and would have kept waiting forever and then some if I'd had to.

She slid into the booth, put her purse beside her and leaned back against the seat looking at me.

"Want some coffee?" I asked.

"I'll have tea," she said, and leaned toward me with her elbows on the table as if deciding to have tea was an intimate secret just the two of us were in on. Her blouse moved when she leaned forward, revealing the top of her cleavage, and I almost forgot how to breathe.

"Hey, Freddy, bring this lady a cup of tea," I hollered over my shoulder. Natalie smiled and settled back in the booth and her blouse settled back over her skin and her cleavage disappeared to wherever it is cleavages go to when they're not out there in the open calling to you practically by your own name.

We kind of looked at each other again, with me grinning like a fool because I just couldn't believe I was sitting there in Freddy's with this absolute doll who had come out of nowhere, and she smiling that I-know-what-you're-thinking smile and playing with one of her bracelets.

"So, uh, here we are," I said, always brilliant at making conversation.

"Yes," she said. Not *yeah* or *yep* or *uh-huh,* but *yes.* "Thanks for coming out with me."

"My pleasure," I said, and I hoped she could tell I meant it. "I was very flattered that you asked me."

Now she smiled a real smile and I could see her beautiful white teeth. She even blushed a little bit, which only made her prettier because I saw that maybe she wasn't as sure of herself as she thought she was.

"I didn't know if you'd be glad or not. But when that boy behind the counter at the deli called your name, I knew it would be easy to find you. How many Zoeys could there be at the fire department of a town this size?" She waved her hand around like the whole town was sitting in Freddy's, and that sent her bracelets rushing back down toward her elbow this time, sounding like a million tiny little bells.

"I'll have to remember to thank Larry next time I see him," I said.

"Yes," she said again. It sounded almost like a hiss, like she had just run into the room and was a little out of breath when she said it. "I wanted to meet you."

"Why?"

"Because," she said, staring straight into my eyes, "I've always been interested in fires. Ever since I was a little girl."

"Really?" I couldn't believe it.

"Yes. And when I saw you in your uniform," she lowered her eyes and lifted them again. "I knew I could ask you some questions about fires and maybe you'd have the answers." She leaned forward. "Now, why, for example, do you sometimes fight fire with fire, and why is it sometimes better to soak the flames until everything for miles around is wet through and through? Then I've heard that some fires," she paused like she was really thinking this out, "some fires burn even hotter when you try to put them out. And some fires can burn for days, weeks, months even, and there's just no stopping them." She started stroking my arm, which felt like it was on fire itself, and her fingertips were soft as feathers. "I thought maybe you could explain," she went on, "why some fires are just warm enough, some burn so hot they destroy you, some go out in a minute, some need to be stoked to keep them going, and some will just burn and burn on their own forever."

"Let's go," I said.

We stood up, and I threw two bills down on the table. Freddy was just coming over with Natalie's tea, but we just walked right by him without saying a word. We didn't say anything to each other either as we walked down the street. I just listened to

Natalie's little heels clicking and my heart beating and thought about the fire burning deep inside my belly and wondered how in the world it could ever be put out. I never wanted anybody the way I wanted Natalie right that second, and I didn't care if the whole town knew who she was and who I was and what I hoped we were just about to do. It was all I could do not to take her in my arms right there on the street. But hell, this isn't San Francisco. The six blocks between my house and Freddy's seemed like five hundred miles.

Finally we got to my place, and my hands were shaking so bad I could barely get the key in the lock. There goes my suave bull dyke image, I thought, if I ever had one to begin with. I kept fiddling with that door for what seemed like forever until it finally gave way and we stumbled inside. Or rather I stumbled. I don't think Natalie's ever stumbled a day in her life. Natalie *entered* my place. She sauntered, sashayed, swished, and swung those big luxurious hips from side to side, checking out the place like it was something special, like Buckingham Palace. We were standing in the living room, and she had her back to me, looking at this painting of a sunset that Sally had done.

I didn't want to tell her about Sally. I didn't want her to know I had ever been with another woman before or ever would be again. Nothing mattered but this moment. Nothing mattered but her. She filled my house with all the longing I had ever known in my whole life, and I knew if I didn't have her that second, I would burst and maybe even die. With my heart beating in my throat like a big bullfrog, I walked up behind her and cupped my hands under her gorgeous behind. She leaned back slightly, letting her weight settle into my palms, like she was sitting in them, and I thought of that song for a minute, "He's got the whole world in his hands." But just for a minute, because Natalie turned her head and whispered into my neck, "How about showing me where you live, baby?"

I turned Natalie around and put my mouth down on hers for an answer. She was about the most kissable woman I ever met in my whole life. And even though I'm hardly a Casanova or Don Juan, I've known a few women in my time. None of them kissed like Natalie kissed. Natalie sucked, nibbled, bit, chewed, licked, rubbed, stroked, caressed, and damn near danced with those lips. And the things she did with her tongue I don't even have words for. I was dying. My knees got all rubbery and I thought they'd give out on me for sure. Finally she, not me, led us to the bedroom, like the tough femme she was.

But once we got there, she knew her place. She kicked off her shoes, slid all those damn bracelets off her arm, lay back on my bed, and let me undo her buttons one by one, setting loose her glorious body an inch at a time. Her breasts were round and full as the moon, the perfect size for me to get my mouth around. She pressed my head into her knockers harder and harder ,and I made love to her breasts for hours, weeks, years, it seemed, and that woman just couldn't get enough. Finally she took my hand and put it where it belonged.

I took off her pants and her pink lace panties gently, and slid four fingers inside like a diver hitting the water in one clean, easy motion. She took me in all the way, and inside there it was soft as...soft as...hell, she gave a whole new meaning to the word *soft*. Soft and sweet and wet and wonderful. Oh, I tell you she was all woman from those deep dark chocolate eyes down to the soles of her pretty little feet, and I should know because I explored every single inch of her. I felt like a kid in a candy store—my eyes just got bigger and bigger and bigger and I wanted *everything*. And each kiss I gave her, each touch, each lick, would make her catch her breath in the sweetest little gasp, like that was the first time anyone had ever touched her in that spot before. I tell you, some women are just made for loving, and Natalie was one of them, that's for sure.

Before I knew it, it was dark outside, with the windows all filled up with black and a little sliver of a moon peeking in. I could barely see Natalie's face, though I could feel it an inch away from mine. Maybe that's why I let what happened happen. It's almost like I didn't even know what was going on until we were in the middle of it, but before I knew anything, there I was flat on my back with Natalie up above me, unbuttoning my shirt and sliding my jeans down.

Now, I'm usually clear about who's the butch and who's the femme, and I like my women to just lie back and enjoy themselves while I give them what they want. That's how I get my pleasure—from giving pleasure. That's the way it's always been and that's the way it's always going to be and that's the way I like it. But Natalie had me under some kind of spell. My whole body just wanted to leap into her mouth—breasts, belly, legs, elbows, you name it. So when she finally reached for me down there, I didn't give her my usual, "No, thanks, babe." I let her.

Listen, I sure don't want this getting around the PTA or even to my friends who are queer like me, because it's a known fact, in certain circles anyway, that Zoey B. Jackson is a proper, old-fashioned stone diesel dyke who doesn't flip for nobody. I've never been a rollover butch, but that night stands apart like it was a whole lifetime by itself, or a dream maybe, or a visit to another planet. No one I knew had ever met Natalie or ever would. My instincts told me that. And I was safe with her. And for some reason beyond what I could understand, I needed her to do to me what no one else had done, though more than a few had tried.

"Silky," she whispered as her fingers stroked me. "You're as soft as silk, see?" And she took her pink lace bra, which happened to be real silk, and rubbed it all over my body. I went wild, I tell you. Then she kissed her way down from my breasts to my belly and beyond, and when her mouth landed down there, I thought they'd have to pick me up off the floor in a million little pieces. I wondered why it had taken me forty-two years to lay myself down for a woman. I sure hoped all the women I ever made love to had felt that good. Just thinking about it got me even more excited, and before I knew what was happening my whole body exploded like the fireworks they set off down by the high school on the Fourth of July and I was gasping and moaning and carrying on like a banshee.

I felt a little shy after that but Natalie just laughed and came up to kiss me. I tasted myself on her lips, and I tell you, that got me going all over again. I'm usually a once-a-night girl—I don't need all that much to keep me satisfied—but that night I lost track of how many times I did it to Natalie and she did it to me and we did it to each other.

What a night. We didn't even think about getting any sleep until about six in the morning, when the windows were a pale pink and the birds were singing their wake-up song in the trees. I held Natalie tight and she laid her head against my chest and filled up my arms with all the sweetness in the world. I fell asleep with one of her legs braided between mine and her soft breath tickling the base of my neck.

When I woke up hours later, the sun washing my face with heat, she was gone. Gone. I couldn't believe it. Lock, stock, and pocketbook, gone. I got up and paced around the house, fooling myself every two minutes. Oh, she must be in the bathroom, I'd tell myself, and go looking. Or maybe she's in the kitchen making coffee. Nope. Maybe she's in the spare room looking at my stuff, spying on me. I wouldn't mind. But it was useless. She was gone. I climbed back into bed, forlorn as a big-pawed puppy whose owner just hollered at him to go on home.

I stretched out flat on my back with my hands behind my head, thinking. I could still smell her—hell, I could practically still taste her in my mouth. I wanted her again so badly I almost touched myself. I don't want this going any further than you, me, and the lamppost, but I even cried a little bit—just a tear or two leaking quietly out the corner of my eye. I buried my face in her pillow then, the pillow she slept on, which still smelled like her fancy perfume. And when I turned over and reached my hands up under my head again, I felt something cold, round, and hard. One of Natalie's bracelets. She'd either forgotten it or left it under the pillow on purpose, for me.

I put it on and a second later took it right off. It looked silly, like an ankle bracelet on a dinosaur. I've never worn a bracelet or a ring or a necklace in my whole life. But when I got dressed later, I surprised myself and put it on again, just to keep her near me. I pretended like we were going steady, and I liked the feel of that bracelet sliding up and down my arm like a kid on a water slide. I wished I had given Natalie something, and I probably would have if she'd stuck around a little longer. Or maybe what I had given her was enough.

So that's what happened to me, Zoey B. Jackson, on the twelfth of May. It's a true story, and here's the bracelet to prove it. Funny, I feel almost naked without it, wear it all the time now, in case she comes back. Well, that's not really why. I guess I know Natalie isn't going to pass through this town again, except in my dreams maybe. Hell, who knows how long I'm going to stay in this town anyway? Been thinking I might get myself to San Francisco one of these days, see what Sally's up to. Bet I could get myself a job there, and wouldn't that be something, riding up and down those San Francisco hills in a big red fire truck? I'm not really a city person, but I don't know, these past few weeks this town has felt too small all of a sudden, like a sweater that shrunk in the wash one day and doesn't fit right anymore. Al says there's something different about me too, but he doesn't know what. Oh, he noticed the bracelet right off—said it looked real fine, and was I going to start putting out fires in high heels and skirts now? I must have blushed real red when he said that. If only he knew what I know. And don't you dare tell him.

FROM

Every Woman's Dream

(1994)

Of Balloons and Bubbles

I am not a mother by choice, meaning I have chosen not to be a mother, unlike Maria, who is also not a mother by choice, meaning she is a mother though she did not intentionally choose the position. Maria merely fell in love with Stephanie, who three years down the road announced she was going to have a child. And so she did.

Now it is two and a half years since Frannie came into the world, and Stephanie has had to take a part-time Saturday job in a music store to help pay for Frannie's day care. Which means Maria has to watch Frannie on Saturdays. And it's not that Maria doesn't love Frannie to pieces, you understand. It's just that having a child was never in her scheme of things, and every once in a while Maria longs for a luxurious Saturday afternoon when she could practice her violin in peace (she and Stephanie met in a music theory class) or hang out with a friend downtown over a cup of cappuccino, or even go grocery shopping without her two-and-a-half-year-old angel taking every box of cereal off the bottom shelf to see what's inside.

And that's where I come in. You see, as my biological clock continues to tick away like that obnoxious stopwatch on *60 Minutes,* I've been reconsidering my decision. Lately, every once in a while (I suspect when I have PMS) I experience a strange longing to hold a baby in my arms, to rock a child to sleep, to bake cookies and pour tall glasses of milk. Lately I've been wondering what my daughter would look like (she's always a daughter in my fantasies). Lately, visions of me sitting peacefully in a rocking chair with a cup of tea, my little bundle of joy blissfully asleep beside me, have been dancing through my head.

Usually when I am in this particular mood I pop over to Maria and Stephanie's house and Frannie obliges me by sitting on my lap and hearing my latest rendition of *Green Eggs and Ham*. Today, though, my hormones must really be going wild, for I have spent the entire morning at Kmart, not buying the plastic and window caulking I need to get my apartment ready for winter, but oohing and aahing and even shedding a tear or two over the tiniest, sweetest pair of black patent-leather Mary Janes you've ever seen. Then I went home and called Maria with a daring proposal: I offered to take Frannie off her hands for an entire Saturday afternoon. It's time for me to really try out this motherhood business once and for all, I told her. And she agreed.

It is a gloriously sunny, crisp New England afternoon, the kind we Vermonters remember on subzero January days when we're wondering why in the world we live in this state. I'm taking Frannie to a farm stand to pick out a pumpkin and then we're off to the park for a rollicking afternoon on the swings. Or at least that's the plan. I arrive at one o'clock, as prearranged with Maria. "Hello," I call as I push open the front door. "Anybody home?"

"Nomi! Nomi!" Frannie comes tearing into the front hallway wearing nothing but a yellow T-shirt that says GIRLS ARE GREAT on it. "Nomi!" she shrieks again, quite pleased with herself, as she has just learned to say my name two weeks ago.

"Hi, Frannie-pie. Ready to go?" A rhetorical question, as Frannie obviously can't go out in the October air, glorious as it may be, without her pants on. I squat down and give her a hug. "Where's Maria?"

"Ria! Ria!!" Fannie races through the living room, which is scattered with building blocks, the colored rings of a stack toy, several picture books, a teddy bear, and Frannie's bottle.

"Hi, Naomi." Maria emerges from the bedroom waving a pint-size pair of panties. "Frannie, you ready to put these on, or do you want to try the potty again?"

"Potty." Frannie runs into the bedroom and disappears, presumably to perch her tiny, cellulite-free bottom on the potty.

"Excuse us." Maria goes in after her. "We're running on baby time here."

"That's okay." One of my shortcomings as a lesbian is always being on time, or worse yet, arriving early. I can see having a child would certainly cure me of that nasty habit. "I'll just make myself at home," I call, flopping down on the couch, right on top of a graham cracker smeared with strawberry jelly.

I clean my jeans and sit down again, more carefully this time, just as Frannie gallops back into the living room in her T-shirt and underwear. Progress is definitely being made. "Nomi, I pooped!" she announces, flopping down on the floor and picking up a block. "I build house."

"Frannie, here's your overalls, honey. Let's get dressed so you can go get a pumpkin with Naomi."

"Pumpkin! Pumpkin!" Frannie dances around the room with Maria following her, miniature overalls, socks, shoes, and sweater in hand. I am dazzled by all this constant motion. Finally Frannie is ready and Maria's face sags with relief.

"Why don't you just take my car?" Maria asks, grabbing her keys from a hook on the wall. "The stroller's in the trunk, and the car seat's all set up." She hands me the keys and a huge blue bag. "There's a set of clothes in there, a bottle of apple juice, some books, her stuffed piggy, whatever. I think there's some toys in the car too. I'll walk out with you." She turns to Frannie. "Ready?"

"Up." Frannie raises her arms and Maria lifts her, for her two-and-a-half-year-old legs aren't quite long enough to navigate the back stairs yet.

We get to the car and Maria buckles Frannie into her car seat, tucking a bottle, a plastic set of car keys, an elephant puppet, a small Kermit the Frog, and a Sears catalog around her, even though the farm stand is a mere five minutes away.

"Isn't she a little young to be thinking about washing machines?" I ask as Frannie immediately goes for the Sears book.

"She loves the pictures," Maria replies, putting the blue bag next to Frannie. "There's a hat in there in case it gets windy, but I don't think you'll need it. Bye-bye, Frannie-love. Here's a kiss." Maria gives Frannie a hug and a kiss and starts to back out of the car.

"Kiss Goofy," Frannie says, kicking her foot up and extending the plastic Goofy bow-biter on the edge of her shoelace.

"Bye, Goofy. I'll blow him a kiss." Maria kisses her own palm and blows in Goofy's direction. "Here's one for Son of Goofy." She blows a kiss toward Frannie's other foot, straightens up, and closes the car door. "Bye, you two. Have fun." Maria stands on the edge of the driveway while I start the car and shift into reverse.

"My painting hurts," Frannie calls from the back.

"What, sweetie?"

"My painting hurts."

"Your painting hurts?" What can that possibly mean? I put the car back into park and swivel around in my seat. Maria, smelling trouble, walks back to the car.

"Her painting hurts," I inform Maria.

"Your painting hurts?" she asks, opening the car door again.

"My painting hurts," Frannie repeats loudly, frustrated I imagine by the nonintelligent life forms she is dealing with here.

"Your painting hurts," Maria says to Frannie. "Show me where."

"Here." She points under her bottom and squirms in her seat.

"Let's see." Maria lifts Frannie to reveal a crumpled-up piece of scratchy artwork. "Did I put you down on your painting? Silly me. I'm sorry." She removes the painting and buckles Frannie in again. "There, that's better. Everything hunky-dory now?"

"Yeah." Frannie settles in and puts her bottle into her mouth.

"Bye." Maria waves as I back out of the driveway without incident. It is one-forty-five, according to the clock on the dashboard. Not bad, I suppose, for baby time.

"Look at the leaves, Frannie. Aren't they pretty?" I say, pointing out the window.

"Yeah," Frannie answers, dropping her bottle. *Yeah* is her favorite word. "My bottle. My bottle, Nomi." I look in the rearview mirror to see her reaching for it, straining against her seat belt.

"Hold on, Frannie. I'll get it." I reach behind my seat, keeping one hand on the wheel, feeling for the bottle with the other. Thank God Maria has an automatic, I think as my fingers brush the bottle, sending it further out of reach. I contemplate pulling over, but with a little twist I manage to retrieve Frannie's bottle and undo fifty-five dollars worth of chiropractic work at the same time. "Here you go, Ms. Frannie." I extend the bottle to her and make a wide right turn. Now we are on Route 57, a beautiful country road.

"We're almost at the pumpkin patch," I sing out, opening my window a little. "Umm. Doesn't the fresh air feel good, Frannie?"

"Yeah," she says, this time both hands holding fast to the bottle.

"Here we are." I pull the car over to the side of the road, where a long line of cars have parked. "Look at all those pumpkins, Frannie." I point out the window. Orange spheres are everywhere, large and small, as far as the eye can see.

"Pumpkins! Pumpkins!" Frannie pushes at her seat belt with both hands. "I want out. Out!"

"Just a second, honey." I get out of the car and walk around to the side away from the road to free Frannie. She's off like a shot, yelling, "Hi, pumpkins! Hi, pumpkins!" and waving her little hand with me trotting after her. The place is swarming with kids and adults, all buying pumpkins, gourds, and gallons of apple cider.

"I can't." Frannie is pulling at the stem of a pumpkin twice her size, next to a sign that says DO NOT PICK UP PUMPKINS BY THEIR STEMS. "Nomi, help. Nomi, up."

"That pumpkin is a little too big, Frannie. Let's go look at the ones over there." I point to a large area of kid-size pumpkins, and Frannie runs over, with me at her heels.

"This one. This one." Frannie points with excitement at a huge orange plastic garbage bag with a jack-o'-lantern face printed on it, stuffed to the gills with leaves. "I want this pumpkin." She flings her arms around it and tries to pick it up.

"That's not real." An older and obviously more worldly little girl speaks solemnly to Frannie. "That's not a real pumpkin," she repeats, this time to me.

"Thank you for pointing that out," I say, my voice just as serious. I squat down and pick up a fat little pumpkin. "How about this pumpkin?" I ask Frannie, holding it out to her.

"No."

"How about this one?" I offer another.

"No."

"Ooh. Look at this one. See what a nice curvy stem it has?"

"No."

"All right." I'm no fool. This could go on all day. I straighten up, my knees cracking. "I guess we won't get any pumpkins then," I say, sounding more than a little like my own mother.

"Pumpkins!" Frannie trots across the farmer's yard to an old-fashioned wagon filled with gourds. "Up," she says, lifting her arms to me.

I pick her up, praying that my chiropractor will have an opening this week, and point to the gourds. "See, Frannie, these are gourds. There's green ones and yellow ones..." I pick up one to show her. "Sometimes there's seeds left inside and you can make a sound with them." I shake the gourd but nothing happens. No matter, though, as Frannie is not the least bit interested in my music lesson. "Pumpkin!" she yells, shattering my eardrum and squirming out of my arms. "My pumpkin. Mine." She reaches toward a small, round orange gourd.

"That's not a pumpkin, honey. That's a gourd. It looks like a pumpkin, though, doesn't it?" I grab it off the wagon and hold it up. "See, it's round like a pumpkin, and it's orange like a pumpkin..." I gesture toward the zillions of pumpkins surrounding us, and Frannie snatches the gourd out of my hand.

"My pumpkin," she croons happily. "My pumpkin."

"But, Frannie." I don't know what to say. Obviously the child is in love, and who am I to spoil it for her? But then again, am I screwing her up for life by letting her believe something is what she wants it to be rather than what it really is?

"Okay. Let's go give the farmer a quarter." I put Frannie down and we walk over to a man in a plaid shirt and overalls with a white cloth money bag tied around his waist. After all, she isn't hurting anyone with her little delusion, I reason with myself. And life is full of disappointments as it is.

We make our purchase, get back in the car, and turn around to head for town, our destination being the schoolyard, also known as the park.

"Oh, look, Frannie. A fair." I nod my head out the window toward the town common, where autumn festivities are in full swing. There are craft booths set up and a band and a big food tent. A banner stretched across the road proclaims AUTUMN FESTIVAL, SATURDAY, OCTOBER TWELFTH. "Want to check this out, Frannie?" I ask.

"I want a balloon," Frannie says, reaching toward a bunch of orange, yellow, and red balloons tied to a tree bordering the commons. "My balloon, my balloon," she calls as we drive by.

"One balloon for Ms. Frannie, coming right up." I take a left and look for a place to park. The street is jammed and I finally find a space three blocks away.

"We'll have to take the stroller, Frannie-Pie," I say, shutting off the ignition. "This is a big walk." And I know for a fact my back cannot possibly withstand lugging an extra thirty-something pounds up this hill.

I leave her in the car while I open the trunk, take out the stroller, and try to figure out how to uncollapse it. It somehow works on the accordion principle, I know, like those old-fashioned wooden drying racks, but I can't seem to get the sides straightened out and even. I'm working up quite a sweat here, so I take off my jean jacket and fling it into the backseat next to Frannie. "You're being so nice and patient," I say, giving Frannie, with that one remark, more positive reinforcement than I received in my entire childhood. "Just one more second and Aunt Naomi will get it together." I wrestle with the stroller again, to no avail. Finally I see a man and a woman with a Frannie-size child in a similar contraption coming up the street. I swallow my butch pride and ask for help.

"Here." The man pushes a lever on the side of the wheel, snaps the stroller open and locks everything in place. "Just pull this to fold it up," he says, flicking the little lever.

"Thanks," I say. I was kind of hoping for the woman's assistance as a good role model for Frannie, but oh, well. Instead of fussing with the stroller, she walks over to the back of the car, pokes her head in, and pokes it back out.

"How old is she?"

"Two and a half."

"What's her name?"

"Frannie."

"Hi, Frannie. Are you going to the fair?" She reaches into the car and strokes Frannie's hand. "Oh, what nice soft skin you have. What a nice soft hand." The woman straightens up and says to me, "God, remember when we had skin like that?"

We. Not only can I not remember my skin ever being butter-soft like Frannie's, but I also cannot remember the last time a straight woman lumped me together with herself into a collective pronoun. Maria says having a kid is like being let into this secret club; straight women talk to her all the time now. Until, of course, they hear Frannie call her "Ria" instead of Mommy and ask her why, and Maria explains that she is Frannie's co-mother, her lover Stephanie is Frannie's birth mother. They usually just nod politely, and, clutching their own child, quietly slink away.

"Let's go, honey." Father and son are impatient, though I sense Mom would be happy to stand around and chat all day.

"Bye-bye Frannie." The woman waves, and Frannie waves back. "She looks just like you," she says, ambling away with her family. Strange, Maria says people say that to her all the time too. I laugh and take it as a compliment as I duck into the car to remove Frannie. Before she can demand to walk, I buckle her into the stroller and off we go.

The fair is mostly local craftspeople selling patchwork quilts, stoneware pottery, wooden pull toys, crocheted booties and sweaters, and fresh honey along a narrow midway of tents and booths. There's a bluegrass band playing over by the food tent, and three black dogs of various sizes, all with bandannas around their necks, are frolicking in the grass. People mill about, looking at the crafts, eating hot dogs, and generally enjoying what is undoubtedly one of our last truly warm days for at least six months. I crouch down to unbutton Frannie's cardigan, for in the sun it is almost hot.

"I want out. Out, Nomi," Frannie says. "My balloon."

"Okay, honey. Let's go find your balloon." I take her out and we walk along, pushing the empty stroller together. "There's the balloons," I say, pointing to the far end of the crafts aisle, where a bouquet of balloons wave in the air. We make our way over to them, steering the stroller around people, dogs, tent poles, and table legs.

"What color do you want, Frannie?" I ask, looking up at a bunch of balloons in the sky. "See, there's red, yellow, green, purple, blue..." I turn from the balloons toward Frannie, but she is no longer at my side. "Frannie? Frannie!" I turn around, my heart thumping wildly, my imagination already picturing her dear little face on the side of a red and white milk carton:

FRANNIE MATTERAZZO-HARRIS. LAST SEEN OCTOBER 12...

"Frannie!" I yell again, relieved to spot her not ten feet away, her hands covering her ears. I desert the stroller and go to her. "What's the matter, honey?" I squat down, my knees cracking again. "Are you scared, sweetie-pie?"

"Yeah." She doesn't take her hands away from her ears.

"Are you scared the balloon will make a big noise?" Maybe she accidentally popped a balloon once.

"No." Frannie shakes her head vigorously.

"What then, honey? Should we forget about the balloon?"

"My balloon." She reaches one hand out tentatively, then clasps it back over her ear again as a woman with green frizzy hair and a big red nose comes over to us. She is wearing a pink and yellow checkered clown suit, with enormous purple sneakers on her feet.

"Hi there, little girl. Would you like a balloon from Emma the Clown?"

"No!" Frannie shrieks, puncturing my other eardrum. She collapses in a fit of sobs, and I sit cross-legged on the grass, pulling her into my lap.

"Whoops. Sorry." Emma the Clown backs away toward her helium tank, where a young customer is waiting.

"Are you scared of the clown, Frannie?" I ask, holding her tight.

"Yeah." She punctuates her answer with a howl I'm sure Maria hears back in the apartment. I rock Frannie on my lap, wiping her face gently with the edge of my sleeve, since of course I don't have a tissue or a hankie on me. She continues to cry softly as I ponder the situation. I could say to her, *It's all right, Frannie, clowns are fun, they're not scary,* but that wouldn't help her trust her own instincts, now, would it? So maybe it would be better to agree with her and say, *Yes, Frannie, that's a very scary clown.* But would that make her even more fearful and ruin her chances of ever enjoying a trip to the circus or a parade? I sigh and stroke her fuzzy head. What's a mother to do? I decide to go the route of my own mother and sidestep the issue of Frannie's feelings in favor of offering a practical solution.

"You wait right here Frannie, and I'll get you a balloon, okay? You sit here, and I'll deal with the clown. All right?"

"Yeah."

"I'll be right over by the balloons, see? I'm only three steps away, okay?"

"Okay."

I ease her off my lap and hobble over to the balloons, as my right foot has fallen asleep. "What color do you want, honey?" I call.

"Red."

"Okay. Stay right there." I keep an eye on her while the clown fills a red balloon with helium and ties it to a long white string.

"Here you go." Frannie takes the balloon's string from me. "Come, let's go to the park." I start pushing the stroller and she scoots under my arm.

"Frannie push," she says, holding on to the stroller. Immediately her balloon takes flight, soaring skyward toward balloon heaven.

"My balloon. Bye-bye balloon." Frannie waves, fascinated for an all-too-brief moment. Then her lower lip starts to tremble and her eyes fill.

"I'll get you another one," I say quickly. "Let's go back to the balloons." Again I leave her and the stroller three steps from the clown, who is handing a green balloon to a little boy's mother. She takes it, ties a slip knot in the string, and loops it around the little boy's wrist. Oh, right, I think as I order another balloon. Of course you don't hand a helium balloon to a child. You attach it to them. Fortified with this new knowledge, I take the balloon to Frannie and tie it to her wrist. "All set?" I take a few steps with the stroller.

"Frannie push." She butts her head under my arm and takes over. We proceed until she crashes into the tent pole of a woman selling wind chimes and stained-glass window ornaments. The collision creates quite a musical racket, but nothing breaks, thank God.

"Frannie, it's too crowded for you to push the stroller by yourself." I put my hand on the stroller which she promptly pushes away. "Do you want to ride in the stroller?"

"No. Nomi ride. Frannie push."

"I'm too big to ride in the stroller, honey," though at this point I do appreciate the offer.

"Balloon ride."

"You want your balloon to ride in the stroller?"

"Yeah."

"Okay." I slip the string off her wrist, secure it around the stroller and set the balloon in the stroller seat. "There, how's that?" I let go and the balloon, being full of helium, bobs up, straining at its string.

"Balloon ride," Frannie insists, reaching up for it.

"Sweetie, the balloon can't ride. It's full of helium," I say, wondering what in the world that can possibly mean to a two-and-a-half-year-old-child. "You want to hold the balloon again?"

"Yeah."

I untie the balloon from the stroller and, noticing Frannie's wrist is a little red, I tie the balloon to the strap of her overalls. A vision of Frannie floating up to the treetops like Winnie the Pooh crosses my mind, but she stays firmly rooted to the earth.

"How's that?" I ask. Frannie looks up. "Hi, balloon," she sings out, waving. We push the stroller together, and she doesn't move my hand away until we have taken five whole steps.

"Frannie, I have to help you push the stroller. It's too crowded for you to do it by yourself."

Frannie lets out a wail. "No, Frannie push. Nomi go away."

I am cut to the quick. Rejected by a two-and-a-half-year-old?

"What's wrong, Frannie-pie?" I wonder if she's still a little flipped out over the clown. Maybe there's a load in her pants? Nope. Could she be hungry? "You want a hot dog, Frannie?" I ask, wiping her nose with my sleeve again.

"Yeah."

"Let's go then." Two more steps, and again Frannie slaps my hand from the stroller.

"Frannie." My voice is firm yet loving, I hope. "Here's your choice: You can either ride in the stroller or let me push it," I say, not giving her a choice at all, a handy trick I picked up from Maria. Frannie continues to scream and cry as I buckle her into the stroller, acting like the countless parents in supermarkets I have always glared at with disapproval.

We make our way over to the food tent, Frannie's balloon hitting me in the face with every other step. She continues to howl, and I ignore the stares, real and imagined, being thrown our way. I park her at the entrance to the food tent. "Hang on, honey. I'm right here. One hot dog coming up." As soon as I take two steps up to the table, Frannie quiets down.

"You want ketchup or mustard?" I say over my shoulder as a woman hands me a hot dog.

"Ketchup," Frannie says. I squirt a thin red line down her bun, sidestep a swarm of bees, and stuff my back pocket with paper napkins before returning to her, pleased with myself for finally catching on. "Here." Frannie takes the hot dog and I retreat behind the stroller, ready to head out. Two steps later a howl reaches my ears.

"What now?" I lean down toward Frannie.

"Bumblebee." And there is her hot dog on the grass with two bees crawling around the bun.

"Let's just go to the park," I say. "I'll buy you something to eat on the way." I reach into my back pocket for a napkin, marveling at the fact that even though Frannie was unable to take a bite out of her hot dog, she did manage to get a glob of ketchup in her ear. I wipe her face and steer her back to the car, stealing a glance at my watch. How can it possibly only be two-thirty-five? I can't take her back to Maria's yet. We haven't even been gone an hour.

I open the car door, and a gust of heat hits me in the face like hot air from a blow-dryer. I buckle Frannie into her car seat, untie her balloon, retie it to the handle of the back door, open the window of the driver's side, collapse the stroller, stash it in the trunk, pop Frannie's bottle into her mouth, slide behind the wheel, start the car, and head for the park.

"Window up," Frannie says from her perch in the back.

"You want the window up, Frannie?" I roll it up, then crack it, as the air in the car is really stifling.

"Window up. Window up." Frannie's high-pitched voice is reaching new heights.

"Honey, I have to have the window cracked. It's ninety-eight degrees in here."

"Up! Up!" Frannie is screaming.

"Are you afraid your balloon will fly away again? I tied it." Frannie is screaming too loudly to hear me, but nevertheless I continue. "Are you afraid a bumblebee will get into the car?" Frannie yells even louder. I roll the window down a little more to let the sound out. "I'm sorry, sweetie, you can't always have things your way." Now I sound exactly like my own mother. Oh, well. She always did say when I had a child I would understand.

I drive by the schoolyard, also known as the park, only to find half the grass dug up and a noisy yellow tractor moving along on its gigantic wheels. I am a little disappointed and a lot relieved. "Looks like the park is closed today, Frannie. We'll have to go home."

"Swings. I want swings." Frannie points out the window.

"Sorry, toots. Not today. We'll have to go another time."

"Swings. Swings." She continues to cry as I steer the car back to Maria and Stephanie's, one hand on the wheel, one hand stroking her little leg. Finally, one block from home, when I think my head is just about to implode, Frannie falls asleep.

I pull into the driveway and open the car door as quietly as possible. Frannie is dead weight in my arms as I lift her out of her car seat. I close the door with my hip just at the moment that Frannie's red balloon decides to peek its stupid little head out of the car. Of course the door shuts right on it. I hold my breath as the noise startles Frannie's eyes open. Quiet prevails for one lovely second and then all hell breaks loose.

"Go ahead and cry, Frannie," I say, hoisting her onto my hip. My own eyes fill too, for it is not only Frannie's balloon that has burst, but my own bubble as well. Being a mother isn't all it's cracked up to be, I realize, but much, much, much, much more, and I'd only tried it for an hour. I ring the bell to Maria and Stephanie's apartment. No answer. Stephanie is still at work, I know, and Maria is probably out enjoying the precious freedom I once took for granted.

I walk with Frannie over to a little patch of grass beside the driveway and sit down to wait for someone to come home. I am absolutely exhausted. I guess my decision not to have a child is the right one after all, I think, looking down at Frannie, who has just fallen back asleep with her head on my shoulder and her arms around my neck. I stroke her back and she sighs with contentment, clinging to me as my own heart turns over, heavy with the dearness of her and the weight of my choice.

With Anthony Gone

I didn't mean to do it. It wasn't premeditated or anything, and it wasn't exactly a crime. It was just incredibly politically incorrect and totally weird besides. I'm not sure what it means, if anything, except this: Death sure does some really strange things to people, including me.

I didn't want to go to Anthony's memorial. Hell, does anyone ever really want to go to a funeral? First of all, he died at a really inconvenient time: I had used up all my sick leave and had to take an unpaid day off work. Second of all, I had to drive into Manhattan, which in my opinion is about as much fun as jumping off the Brooklyn Bridge, not to mention just as dangerous. And third of all, if I went, I'd have to admit that Anthony was dead, something I'd been avoiding for two months, ever since Mark left that message on my answering machine: "I'm calling to tell you what you think I'm calling to tell you." Thanks a lot, Mark. You could have put it more gently: "Hi, Joanne. Anthony passed away this morning." Or "Hi, Joanne. Anthony's no longer among the living." Or even "Hi, Jo. Anthony's gone." Oh, hell, I guess it doesn't really matter how he said it, and even I know it's pretty lame to be mad at Mark for his choice of sentence structure. Anthony's dead, and that really pisses me off. But what can I do about it? Nothing. And that makes me even madder. If I ever stop being so goddamn angry, I'll probably be incredibly sad and that's just not my style, so I just kind of blocked out the whole thing, which is exactly my style. And besides, it's not very hard to do, since no one up here knew Anthony; he was part of my former life. A life that was very different than the one I'm leading now in several important ways. First of all, back then I was straight, which I know is hard to believe since I could easily win the Ms. Dyke America contest these days with my crew cut, nose ring, and leather jacket. Second of all, back then, AIDS was spelled with a "Y" and came in caramel cubes that were sold in stores and were supposed to make you lose weight. And third of all, Anthony was very much alive.

Anthony. When I met him, I was awed by him. He was easily the most beautiful person, male or female, I had ever seen, with his huge dark Italian eyes framed with masses of lashes, his olive skin, his black shiny hair, snow-white teeth, and that body that was built to last with mile-high legs, a smooth torso, and biceps that rippled in the sun. Anthony was attractive, all right, but I wasn't attracted to him. At that time, I had simply accepted the fact that I was a completely nonsexual creature. I knew men didn't do it for me, and I didn't yet know that women were an option. So I was never in love with Anthony, but I was definitely drawn in by his charm and I knew I wanted to be his friend.

We met in Boulder, Colorado, in the summer, two native New Yorkers totally out of place amid the cowboys and the mountains. Ironically, we met in a place called the New York Deli, which was anything but. I was waiting on line (out there they say "in line") when I heard a voice with that unmistakable accent declare, "An egg cream. No, it has nothing to do with eggs. Three squirts of chocolate syrup, two fingers of cream, and top it off with seltzer, all right, lady? Don't bust my chops. And an order of fries. It's not for nothing I'm from Staten Island." My heart leapt at the sound of someone from home. "Hey," I said, "I'm Joanne Bergman. From Brooklyn."

"*Oy vey,* a *landsman,*" he said, proving you don't have to be Jewish to be Jewish, as long as you're from New York. "Anthony Scarnici from Staten Island. You want an egg cream, *mameleh*? Make it two," he barked to the woman behind the counter. We sat and talked for hours, eating what I soon learned was Anthony's favorite meal: French fries dipped in a chocolate egg cream. Sounds terrible, I know, but believe me, it's good.

So, as it turned out, Anthony and I were enrolled in the same poetry program, taught by none other than the great Allen Ginsberg himself. We got an apartment together and fixed it up as best we could, which wasn't very, as both of us were broke (this poetry program wasn't exactly cheap). After we both got beds and dressers for our bedrooms we had no money left for kitchen or living room furniture. Oh, well. One day we found one of those huge old wooden spools from the phone company, rolled it home and—voilà!—a kitchen table. No chairs though, so we mostly ate on the floor. Depending on who was cooking we'd either have *matzo* ball soup or spaghetti and meatballs, always the same argument accompanying the meal: Were Italians dumb Jews or were Jews nerdy Italians? Obviously this was long before I worried about being politically correct, or come to think of it, ever heard the term. Like I said, Anthony and I were thinking about poetry and furniture, which he combined in an ingenious manner: One day he came home with a Styrofoam head he found on the street outside a wig shop and placed it over the mantle of our fake fireplace. Two days later, complete with straw hat and wire-rimmed glasses, the head was a dead ringer for William Carlos Williams, the poet we happened to be studying. Our decor was complete when I brought home a child's little red wagon from the Salvation Army and poured a pan of water into it. For those of you who don't know much about poetry, I'll let you in on the joke: William Carlos Williams's most famous poem, which Allen Ginsberg (or Ginzy, as we called him) drummed into our head all summer, was called "The Red Wheelbarrow." I can't quote it exactly, since I never did pay that much attention in class, but it was something about how everything depended on this red wheelbarrow that was full of water and parked near a bunch of chickens. The brilliance of this particular poem completely escaped me, but Anthony was quite taken with it and recited it at least a dozen times a day. In fact, whenever anyone visited our little house for the first time, Anthony would run over to the little red wagon and begin flapping his bent arms up and down and squawking like a chicken in order to see how literary-minded our newest visitor was. No one but Ben ever passed the red wheelbarrow test, but Ben comes later on in the story.

So much for our literary careers. Anthony was quite talented, actually; I wasn't. I only remember one poem I wrote that summer, and now that I think about it, it's kind of spooky. One day I came home and Anthony was hysterical, which was nothing unusual. "Jo, my gay nerves are shot. Go into my room. Hurry."

"What is it, a spider?" I grabbed a shoe, being the butch of the family even back then when I didn't know the word. A minute later I came shrieking back into the living room. "Oh, my God, Anthony, where did they come from?" The "they" I was referring to was hundreds, maybe even thousands of horseflies all swarming at Anthony's bedroom window, trying to get out.

"What do I know? Something must have hatched." He ran to the store and came back with two huge cans of Raid. "The hell with karma," he yelled and charged into his bedroom spraying away. Now by this time Anthony had become a quasi-Buddhist and believed in not killing any sentient beings, lest God knows what would happen to him the next life around. So who got stuck holding the bag full of flies? None other than yours truly. At least I got a fairly decent poem out of it, called "Flies":

> Anthony and I discover hundreds
> of Woody Allen–size flies
> clumped together like quivering blackheads
> on the white walls of his bedroom.
> "The hell with karma," he yells,
> running out to buy a can of Super Raid,
> which we spray on the walls,
> windows, ceiling, and carpet.
> "Raid kills bugs dead," I say,
> quoting the commercial and wondering
> what kind of Brownie points we're scoring
> with whoever's in charge of our next life.
> Anthony refuses to meet my eye
> as I stand holding a brown bag full
> of half-dead sentient beings,
> their legs sticky and still kicking
> in the dying afternoon.

Not bad, huh? Maybe I could have been a poet. Anyway, isn't that weird? The only poem I remember writing that summer is about death and karma and all that stuff, and had Anthony in it to boot.

Anyway, who knew what the future held that summer? We were young, we were good-looking...well, at least one of us was. Anthony's attributes certainly didn't go unnoticed. He had a string of admirers, though none of them were as ardent as himself. It was not unusual for me to stumble out of bed in the morning and find him gazing at his reflection in the bathroom mirror wearing nothing but a shower cap perched upon his head at a jaunty, beret-like angle. Anthony wouldn't leave the house until he looked absolutely perfect, and he actually thought unattractiveness was a crime that should be punishable by law. "Will you look at that?" He'd grab my arm and point to some poor unfortunate who not only wasn't blessed with good looks like Anthony but was all decked out in lime-green polyester besides. "Five years in the slammer, no parole," he'd bark over his shoulder. I'm sure now that Anthony's dead, people will talk about him like he was a saint, but believe me, he wasn't. He never got on my case about how I presented myself to the world though, and back in those days I was not a pretty picture. I had long stringy hair that hung in my face, and I wore the same thing every day: baggy jeans with a shapeless, faded T-shirt. I didn't really pay any attention to my appearance and neither did Anthony, which only further reinforced my suspicions: My body was of little consequence, something I was just forced to lug around.

Anyway, if anyone should have been arrested that summer, it was Anthony, who roamed the streets in flimsy red silk running shorts or skintight jeans with holes in strategic places. Either outfit left little to the imagination. It was always amusing to watch Anthony on the prowl. He'd see someone he liked, sidle up to him, stick his thumb in his mouth, and pull it out real s-l-o-w-l-y. It worked every time, and I spent many, many afternoons waiting for Anthony to give me the high sign (a pink- and black-striped necktie hanging from our front doorknob) so I knew it was safe to come home.

Everything changed when Mark entered the picture. When Anthony and Mark first laid eyes on each other at the New York

Deli, it was like time stood still. Anthony didn't even finish his egg cream before he made his move. And before I knew it, Mark had moved in with us (at least he had some furniture). This was definitely serious: Before Mark, Anthony had never even let any of his boy toys spend the night. He didn't want any of them to see him first thing in the morning before his face woke up and took its beautiful shape.

Mark and I became fast friends too. After all, we had a lot in common: We both loved Anthony. Still, I was beginning to feel like a third wheel, so luckily Ben came upon the scene at just about this time.

What can I say about Ben? He had eyes that could rival Liz Taylor's, dimples Shirley Temple would have died for, and extraordinary black hair that fell in ringlets past his waist. "My Aunt Ethel always said it was a shame such hair was wasted on a boy," he told me, "so I grew my hair long to make her happy."

"And did it?"

"Don't ask," Ben said, rolling his eyes just like a member of my very own family, proving you don't have to be from New York to be a New Yorker, as long as you're Jewish. Ben became a regular at our house, especially on the nights I cooked my famous *matzo* ball soup.

Ben had entered the poetry program late—he was always late for everything—so he hung out with Anthony and me to catch up on assignments. Anthony suspected he was hanging around for other reasons too.

"He likes you," Anthony whispered. "Go on, fuck him. I can't. Mark would kill me, so it's up to you. For God's sake, somebody has to do it."

"We're just friends," I whispered back, even though I wasn't really sure about that. Ben unnerved me. I knew he was attracted to me, and I was sort of attracted to him, but something held me back. Now when I think about it, I know it was his gender, but back then all I knew was that he confused me. He was very feminine-looking, and very gentle besides, which is what drew me to him. But whenever our bodies made contact, even casually, I immediately pulled away.

Once we were actually mistaken for a couple, in a funny way. The four of us were walking home from an open poetry reading, the kind that drags on and on and makes you swear you're never going to read let alone write another poem in your life. Anthony and Mark were up ahead, as Anthony was constantly trying to give Ben and me the opportunity to be alone together. Out of nowhere, a car pulled up and heads yelled out the window: "Hey, faggots! Blow me, you dykes!" Then they roared away. Anthony's response was to shriek, "We're homos! We're healthy as the milk you drink," and plant a nice, wet kiss on Mark's lips. Ben and I just looked at each other, speechless. Finally I broke the ice. "It must be your hair," I said, and just for the hell of it, took one of his ringlets and twirled it around my finger. I felt nothing, but later that night I did have a classic erotic dream of Ben and me wrapped together in his hair, except Ben had breasts and all the other female trappings, becoming, as my grandmother would say, the "*shayneh maidel* of my dreams." But shortly after that night, Ben cut his hair and moved in with a poet named Christine, who I'm sure knew next to nothing about homemade *matzo* ball soup.

At the end of that summer, Ben moved on to California, and Anthony moved back to New York, with Mark in tow. I stayed put, due mostly to inertia, working odd jobs and trying to sort out my life. Finally I decided to move back to New York too, where at least I could get a decent egg cream. Anthony was delighted. "It's not for nothing I work out at the gym five days a week," he said as we lugged cinder blocks up six flights of steps to build bookshelves in my new railroad apartment. Anthony thrived on city life, but I did not. The noise and the dirt and the crime got to me. "You need to meditate." Anthony had obviously kept up with his Buddhism. "You need to tame your mind." I actually allowed him to convince me to fork over a hundred bucks to attend a weekend meditation retreat on Lexington and twenty-third. There we sat on little cushions in a room full of other *meshugenehs,* listening to our teacher, who said her name was Dharma or Karma but who looked very much like a woman I went to high school with named Debbie Finkelstein. She gave a short *spiel* on the Buddha and then said we were to sit absolutely still with our backs straight for forty-five minutes, just following our breath. That was it? I looked at Anthony, thinking, *Here I am in the most exciting city in the world paying someone a hundred bucks so I can sit and do nothing?* I don't know if he read my mind, but all of a sudden he smiled and then I smiled and then he started to laugh and then I started to laugh and we just couldn't stop. I'd get it together and settle down and then he would too, and a minute later I'd start to giggle again and so would Anthony. Soon our laughter traveled around the entire meditation hall interrupting everyone's concentration and the teacher asked us to leave and that was that.

So I left New York and moved up to a small New England town where there was not an egg cream to be found, even though at least half the population was made up of transplanted New York Jews like myself. And then one day I was sitting at Friendly's when the waitress took my order along with my heart, and I realized that lo and behold, I was as bent as Anthony himself. Of course I wanted him to be one of the first to know. "It's not for nothing you lived with me that whole year," which was a nice way of saying, *I told you so.* "When do I get to meet the little woman?"

"Soon," I said, but soon never came. Lisa and I were completely wrapped up in each other—I finally learned bodies did have a purpose after all—and by the time our relationship ended three years later, I was a new woman. Not only was I a lesbian, but I was a feminist, and an angry one at that. I thought men were useless—straight, gay, and otherwise. So gradually Anthony and I lost touch, except for the occasional birthday, Christmas or *Chanukah* card.

Years passed, how many I'm ashamed to say. I was in and out of several relationships, searching for Ms. Right, and I'd become an English teacher at a very hip alternative high school where I could be out. I had long ago realized I wasn't really a poet, but teaching English suited me and allowed me to indulge my love of literature. One day, while thumbing through yet another obscure literary magazine that crossed my desk, I came upon a poem written by none other than Anthony Scarnici. Without a moment's hesitation I picked up the phone and dialed Anthony's number, which miraculously still resided in my brain. Of course he wasn't there. Nor was he at the number the person who was there gave me. It took some doing, but finally I tracked him down.

"Hi, Anthony, it's Jo from Brooklyn. Remember me?"

"Of course I remember you," Anthony said in a strange voice. It was like he was talking in extra slow motion. I rolled my eyes. Was he sleeping at four o'clock in the afternoon? Or maybe on quaaludes? (We had done our share of recreational drugs). Anyway, it was clear now was not a good time to talk. "I'll call you back and we'll make a date," I said. "I'd love to see you. "How's Mark? How's your writing? Never mind, I'll call you tomorrow."

"Okay," Anthony said, and then added, "Mobility's a problem right now, but you can come visit me. Just call first to make sure I'm up for having visitors. I have days and I have days."

And that's how I found out Anthony had AIDS. He'd been sick for over a year, so I guess he just assumed that I knew. He'd found out unexpectedly too. He went to give blood to get some extra cash and they ran a blood test on him. When he came back for the results, they told him he was positive. Without any warning or anything. Just like that.

Of course I went to see him right away. Mark opened the door and we fell into each other's arms and cried. Then I composed myself and walked into Anthony's bedroom. There he was, the boy whose theme song was "You're So Vain," looking like hell with yellowish skin, thinning hair, and little red spots all over his face, which was incredibly gaunt. He motioned for me to sit on the bed. "I still do all my entertaining horizontally," he said with a wry smile. I had to move his legs to make room for me to sit down. "Nice hat," he said. "Let me see." I gave him my purple softball cap and not only did he try it on, he picked up a hand mirror from his nightstand and admired himself.

I didn't stay long since it was clear he was very tired. "Next time you come, we'll go to the bookstore on St. Mark's Place," he said, and I said sure, even though I knew there wouldn't be a next time. A month after I saw Anthony he lost his eyesight and caught pneumonia. He went into the hospital and never came out. I meant to go see him, but I just couldn't face it. Dealing with difficult things, like my feelings, for example, is not exactly my strong point.

So like I said, I didn't especially want to go to the funeral. But I had to. Because there was no one in my life I could talk to about Anthony. There was no one who would laugh when I said, "Remember the time Anthony got mad at Mark for taking a bite of his quiche and stormed out of the restaurant and made us search the entire city for him because he had the only house key?" If you didn't know Anthony, it just wouldn't strike you as funny. And I needed to be with people who knew Anthony. So I went. I kind of wanted someone to come with me, but I didn't know who to ask. I didn't have a girlfriend at the time, which is why what happened happened.

The service was in a classroom of some community college where Anthony had taught a poetry class years ago. There were lots of people there, but no one I knew. Friends of Anthony's and a few relatives, including his sister, who was a year older and looked exactly like him, and his mother and father standing on either side of her. Mark finally arrived, but I couldn't get near him as everyone swarmed to pay their respects. Finally some music began, and then Anthony's sister said a few words. Then one by one, various people stepped up to the front of the room. Someone sang a song, someone played a message Anthony had left on her answering machine, someone just hung on to the podium and cried.

And then I heard my name. "Joanne?" I turned around and there was Ben, who I hadn't seen since I left Colorado all those years ago. I had the same feeling I'd had a decade earlier when I saw Anthony standing in Boulder's New York Deli among all those strangers: a *landsman*. Someone from home.

"Hi," I whispered. "Late as usual." He grinned that dimpled grin and we grabbed each other in a bear hug and cried. After a minute he squeezed me extra hard, and then we let go of each other. Or almost let go. We sat there holding hands, and it felt strange. Very strange and scary and wonderful. I felt a warm flush spread across my face and neck and down to various other parts of my body. I couldn't look at Ben. *Stop it,* I whispered to myself. *Are you crazy? You're at a funeral. What kind of pervert are you? And besides, you're a dyke.*

d Ben's hand, and he squeezed mine back. No doubt
was thinking what I was thinking. My body was
tiny on me and there wasn't a damn thing I could do
hout a word, Ben and I rose and walked out, hand in
l me to an empty classroom and kicked the door shut.
stopped as he lifted me by the waist onto a desk and
ard, for all he was worth. I dove into that kiss, and
w what was happening we were moaning and groan-
bing at each other's clothes as frantically as two
the back of a '57 Chevy. Of course neither of us was
ndom, so we didn't go all the way, but pretty damn
enough to make us both come, which started us both
ich other's arms again.

y we composed ourselves, and Ben shyly turned
ne to tuck in his various body parts while I did the
t on the windowsill and Ben took a crushed pack of
ut of his shirt pocket.

believe we just did that," he said, offering me a cancer
n I actually took, even though I don't smoke—I figured
ell.

v," I said. "I can just hear Anthony saying, 'I can't believe
finally did it at my fucking funeral.'" I shook my head.

" Ben smiled and straightened my shirt. "Oh, God,
What did we just do?"

ing my legs back and forth. "I'll tell you what we didn't
aid softly. "We didn't bring Anthony back."

," Ben sighed. "We didn't." He looked out the window for a
, and then he looked back at me. "So anyway," he said, trying
nd casual, "what have you been up to for the last decade?"

Well, I've been a lesbian for seven years," I said, and that,
bined with the look of shock on his face, struck me as hys-
ally funny. I started to laugh and just couldn't stop and Ben
ked up too. What a day. Finally we calmed down, though Ben
med somewhat concerned about the whole thing, even more
ncerned that I was.

"Did I ruin it for you? I mean, being a lesbian and everything..." he fumbled for words.

"Well, the lesbian thought police will probably arrest me ar
minute now, but what the hell. I don't know what came over me

"Me either," Ben said. "I mean, I have a wife and a kid ar
everything up in Vermont."

"You do?" For some reason, now I didn't feel so bad. I guess
evened the score a little. "So now what?" I asked. "We certain
can't go back in there." I motioned with my head.

"No," he said. "Want to get something to eat?"

"I don't think so." I looked at him. "That would be too in
mate."

He smiled. "Are you sure? I could really go for some Frenc
fries and a chocolate egg cream."

"Maybe some other time." I pitched my cigarette stub out t
window. "See ya," I said, rising to go.

"See ya," Ben said, giving a little wave.

I turned and left the room and the building without looki
back. With Anthony gone there was no one I really wanted to ta
to. There was no one to share the great irony of the moment wit
and that was a real pity, let me tell you. With Anthony gone, the
was nothing to do but head up the street, even though I ha
absolutely no idea where in the world I was going.

Comfort

You had been on your way to do an errand, though you can't remember what it was you'd needed. A box of envelopes perhaps, or a roll of tape. But you'd turned the corner and there *she* was, the woman you'd had a crush on for over a year. She was staring into the window of a café, trying to decide whether to go in maybe, but no, actually she was studying her own reflection, you realized, for she reached up and tucked one stubborn piece of hair under her beret. You loved her for that. Then she opened the door and went into the café and you sighed and walked on, knowing you probably wouldn't catch sight of her for another three months, probably not until spring.

So you walked on and got your stamps or your menstrual pads or whatever it was, and on the way back you found yourself entering the very same café, which was odd, because you are not a café sort of person. You much prefer a twenty-four-hour diner with coffee and homemade apple pie to cappuccino and Black Forest cake. But there you were, holding a cup of Mocha Java of all things, looking around for a place to sit. There were no empty tables, and as you pondered your situation, *she* looked up and smiled. Was that an invitation? Later you'd say it was and she would say it wasn't, but nevertheless you found yourself floating toward the empty chair opposite her. *Floating,* I say, because your feet were not touching the ground.

"Do you mind if I sit down?" you asked.

She shook her head, and the silver earrings she wore rang like little bells. She was reading a thick book you couldn't see the title of, but you thought she was probably an English major, with her earrings and beret and all. She didn't return to her book, but put a feather in the page to mark her place and then slapped it shut as though she'd been waiting for you to arrive and was even a little annoyed that you were late.

"I'm Alexandria," she said, extending a delicate hand. You took it, wondering what to do with it, tempted to bring her hand up to your lips and kiss it, but you just held it gently.

"I'm Tammy," you said, amazed that you remembered your own name, amazed that it hadn't changed as you felt the rest of you had. Somehow you knew your whole life would be different from this moment on. Her hand was soft, her fingers slim, and she wore one silver ring with a blue stone in it. She took her hand back and smiled and you stared at her mouth as if you had never seen one before, as if you'd never noticed how wonderful it was the way lips curve over teeth, the red against the white, the sweet tip of the tongue. Suddenly you realized you were staring, so you looked down at your own hands, which seemed big and clumsy by comparison, and you didn't look up again until you felt your blush subside.

She asked you questions and you answered them. You told her about your life, you suppose, about growing up in a small town and always feeling different; about running away to a big city and your first awful year when you lived in that rooming house with no kitchen and the bathroom down the hall and the man next door who hung his bananas on a rope strung from one end of the room to the other so the roaches wouldn't get them. All the while you were talking you were thinking, *I sound so dumb, I'm talking too much, she must be bored by all this,* but still you went on. You told her about hanging out in bars and how you didn't do that anymore and how you left the city and moved to this town five years ago with nothing in your pocket but the name and phone number of a high school friend who was rumored to be "different" as well.

So here you were, working as the maintenance person of your apartment building for free rent, and working part-time at a print shop three days a week for spending money. Left you lots of time to think, you said. You were thinking of taking a computer course; you'd heard that's where the money was, the way of the future and all that.

She said she had a computer and did you want to see it? You blinked, not sure you heard right. Was she inviting you back to her room? Was this the modern-day equivalent of *Would you like to come up and see my etchings?* Maybe you were misinterpreting her, but you knew she was a lesbian by the labyris around her neck and you sure hoped she didn't smile at everyone the way she was smiling at you.

She stood, and you did too, though your knees were quite rubbery. You followed her out the door and up the street, out of the downtown area, heading for the college. She talked about her computer some, how her father bought it for her, how easy it was for her to write papers now, and you realized she was probably nervous too. You wondered if she did this all the time, though you still weren't sure if she was thinking along the same lines as you. She was so pretty, even in that ridiculous hat and black sweater and purple boots. You thought she was nineteen, twenty at the most, but later she told you she was twenty-five, just a year younger than you. Her life hadn't been easy either, though she'd never had to worry about money the way you did. Her parents had found her in bed with her best friend her senior year of high school, and the day after she graduated they kicked her out. Her father had been against it, but her mother stood firm. So her father kept in touch with her over the years, sending her money every month, trying to make up for her mother's disowning her. He was footing the bill for her tuition, even though this was her third try at college. And yes, she was an English major.

She led you to an old Victorian house. She had the attic apartment: two rooms and a bath. One room was the kitchen and one room was everything else: living room, study, and bedroom combined. In one corner was a stereo and a stack of records, across from that a desk with the now-famous computer, and of course what your eyes were very busily avoiding: the bed. She closed the door behind you and kicked off her little purple boots, motioning for you to do the same. It felt like it took you hours to unlace your sneakers. Everything seemed to be moving in slow motion: the hands of the clock on the wall, Alexandria as she moved toward you and took your hand, the sun as it crept across the bed, first warming her belly, then her breasts, then her beautiful face as she lay next to you afterward, half asleep, content as a cat that had just licked up a bowl of cream.

You had never been more wide awake in your life. You had never done such a thing before: made love to a woman you hardly knew in the middle of the afternoon. You had only had two lovers: one in the city, an older woman who was married, and one who had broken your heart two years ago by leaving you to go back to her ex. You didn't think sex was all that important anyway. You were a loner.

But she, well, you certainly never met anyone like her before. She was good at sex, the way one is good at cards or playing the piano. You could tell it was something she did often. You didn't want her to do it with anyone but you. She laughed when you told her that. She put her arms around you and said she always wanted someone to love her enough to be jealous. You were surprised, for as she said the words you realized you did love her, even though you didn't believe in love at first sight. You believed you got to know a person slowly and you learned to love them day by day.

Which is exactly what happened. You saw each other every day, and you slept together every night. Sometimes you made love, and sometimes you didn't. Sometimes you just held her and stroked her hair away from her beautiful face and kissed her forehead. She said she felt safe with you. She said she trusted you because you had honest hands. Honest hands. You liked that.

You learned things about her. You learned she liked breakfast in bed on a wooden tray with a pink rose in a glass vase. You learned that she hated to cook and if left to her own devices would have popcorn for supper. You learned that she could wiggle her ears and raise one eyebrow at a time, that her favorite color was purple, and that she didn't wear underwear in the summer under her long cotton dresses.

You taught her things too. You taught her how to blink across the room at a cat and sit very still until it blinked back. You taught her how to seal up her windows for winter and how to plant morning glories along a fence for spring. You taught her how to find the constellations up in the night sky—the Big Dipper, Cassiopeia's Throne, Orion's Belt—and how to wish upon a star. In the summer a tenant moved out of your building, and she moved in. A year after that you rented an apartment together. By now you were working full-time at the print shop and she had dropped out of school again. She got a job working in a day care center and you were afraid she'd want her own child, but she said no, you and the dog were quite enough, thank you, for you had gotten her a puppy for her birthday that year.

And so the days passed and the years passed and you were quite happy. You became a partner at the print shop and she opened her own child care center, after finally finishing her degree. You both worked hard, though you made sure you took plenty of vacations too. One day you noticed some gray in her hair. One day she noticed your body had thickened, like the strong trunk of a tree. How had it happened? All of a sudden the puppy was an old dog with a white muzzle. And you were still happy.

You had managed to stay together all those years as you had watched other couples break up. You friends split over monogamy and nonmonogamy, wanting to parent and not wanting to parent, staying put or moving to California. And of course the big three: money, space, and sex. You didn't fight about money because you kept yours separate; and you didn't fight about needing space because you wanted to spend all your time together. Sometimes you did quibble about sex, especially in the beginning, for she was much freer than you. But that had shifted, and as a matter of fact over the years you'd even managed to surprise her with a trick or two.

Sometimes lying in bed at night you'd wonder what your life would have been like if you hadn't wandered back to the café that day. What if she'd been sitting with someone else? What if she hadn't smiled? What if... But she would just shush you by putting her fingers against your lips. *It was meant to be,* she'd say. *Why question it?* You weren't questioning the rightness of it; you were sure about that. It was just that to you it was a miracle that all these years later she was still beside you at the supper table, she was still beside you in bed at night, her face was still the very first thing you saw every blessed morning. And she, not that she took you for granted, but she accepted it more easily, as though she always knew this would happen to her, that one day the woman of her dreams would walk into her life and sweep her off her feet and they would live together happily ever after. And so you grew older and happier still, for every day with her added to your happiness. Even though you loved her with all your heart and soul and you couldn't imagine loving her any more than you already did, your love grew and grew.

And then all of a sudden it was time to retire, and there you were, two old ladies in flannel pajamas, laughing because you didn't know if these were your reading glasses or hers, and she couldn't remember whose teeth were in the pink glass on the bathroom sink. And then it wasn't funny anymore because you knew you would have to lose each other and you couldn't tell if it was better for you to die first, for how could you stand living without her; but then again, perhaps she should go first, because you couldn't bear the thought of her being so sad without you.

You knew you would always be together no matter what, so when the end came you were sad, terribly sad, but you did manage alone, just as you had done before her. You kept most of her things, including the beret she had worn that very first day. Sometimes you held it on your lap and stroked it like a cat. Other days you spread the big picture album across your lap and there she was again, smiling into the camera or shaking a finger at you pretending to be cross, or arching her back with her hands on her hips in a Marilyn Monroe pose. Some days you did nothing but cry, and you would hear her voice out of nowhere scolding you gently. *Now, now,* she would say, and then you would smile and cry even harder.

Many of your friends were gone too, and those that weren't offered what comfort they could, but it wasn't much. You hadn't been big socializers, but instead had hoarded your precious free time to yourselves. Maybe you should have gone out with other people more, but no, you didn't regret one single second you had spent with her, and if you had to do it all over again you wouldn't change a thing.

And that was your comfort.

FROM

Out of the Closet and Nothing to Wear

(1997)

A Femme Shops Till Her Butch Drops

To shop or not to shop? That is the question one lazy Sunday morning when Flash, the cats, and I are lounging around the breakfast table drinking various forms of cream (straight up or with coffee).

"I can't believe you want to go shopping today," Flash says.

I can't believe she can't believe it. Flash knows my fantasy vacation is a week at Mall of America. Flash knows my all-time favorite movie is *Scenes From a Mall.* Flash knows I always want to go shopping.

"But it's a beautiful day." Flash points out the window.

I agree. "It's a beautiful day for shopping."

"But you don't need anything." Flash tries a rational approach.

"Yes, I do. I need to shop."

Flash doesn't get it. Butch that she is, Flash doesn't understand a femme's need to run her hands through racks of leather, wool, and silk. Flash gets no thrill from trying on trendy, overpriced, poorly made, age-inappropriate garments she has no intention of buying. Flash finds no joy in smoothing different colors of eye shadow along the back of her hand with a tiny brush, looking for just the right shade. But I do.

"I'll make you pancakes," I bargain. "I'll do the dishes after." She's not impressed. "I'll let you have supper in front of the TV tonight."

"It's a deal."

An hour later we arrive at the mall, pull into a space and I am off, racing through the parking lot with Flash in hot pursuit. "Slow down," she pants, grabbing onto the shoulder strap of my purse like it's a horse's rein. "We've got all day."

"No, we don't." I keep up my pace. "The mall closes at five."

"But it's noon."

"My point exactly." I yank open the door to Filene's Basement and rush inside.

Our first stop is the shoe department. "Ooh, look at these." I pick up a pump as Flash groans.

"More black shoes? Don't you have like seven pairs?"

"No," I say, indignant. I have like twenty-seven pairs. I have one-inch heels, two-inch heels, three-inch heels, Cuban heels, platform heels, mules, slingbacks, and slides. I have black heels with ankle straps, black heels with cut-out toes, black heels with ankle straps *and* cut-out toes. I have black heels of velvet, suede, crushed leather, patent leather, and, though I hate to admit it, manmade materials. Not to mention black clogs, flats, sandals, loafers, moccasins, ballerina slippers, jellies, and cowgirl boots. Flash is right. I guess I don't really *need* another pair of black shoes.

But these are so cute. They're soft leather miniboots with two-inch heels and a heart-shaped zipper on the side. It's love at first sight, and they fit perfectly. "Are you getting them?" Flash asks.

"I'll have her hold them." I nod toward the salesclerk, and Flash shakes her head. I have been known to have dozens of salesclerks in different shops hold things for me for hours. Why? It leaves my hands free, which makes it easier to shop.

We leave the shoe department and pass a rack of pants, where Flash picks up a pair of tan chinos identical to the ones she's wearing. "Should I try these on?" she asks.

"Sure," I say, glad she's getting into the swing of things. We head toward the ladies' fitting room but get stuck in a huge traffic jam at the Clinique counter.

"What's going on?" Flash asks.

"They're giving out free gift packages. You get a sample lipstick, eye shadow, comb, body gel, and a cute little carrying case." My voice rises in ecstacy. "Look, all you have to do is buy thirteen dollars worth of cosmetics."

"How is that free?" Flash wonders out loud.

I know it is useless to explain. "C'mon," I say, elbowing my way up to the counter. I buy a lip pencil and mascara, which I receive along with my free bonus gift in a huge shopping bag.

"Isn't this great?" I am flushed with the excitement of the first purchase. Now the pressure is off; I know I won't go home empty-handed. "Let's go try on your pants."

"Never mind," Flash puts the pants down on a nearby rack. The poor girl is exhausted, but I have just begun to shop.

I drag her across the mall to Steigers, which is about to go out of business. Everything is at least forty percent off. I can barely contain myself. My fingers fly through racks of blouses and blazers at breakneck speed. And then I see something across the room that makes me tremble.

A black sweater. Not just any old black sweater. A beaded black sweater. Made of cashmere. With shoulder pads. A sweater's sweater. A dream of a sweater.

Flash states the obvious. "You have a black sweater."

Now of course I don't have *a* black sweater. I have dozens of black sweaters. I have a scoop neck, a V-neck, a cowl neck, a boat neck, a turtleneck, a crewneck, and an off-the-shoulder. I have a button-down, a backless one that comes down to my knees, and another that's cropped to show off my navel. I have black sweaters with long sleeves, short sleeves, three-quarter sleeves, and dolman sleeves. I have black sweaters of wool, cotton, cashmere, mohair, velour, ramie, and acrylic. I even have a beaded black sweater. But not like this one.

"Hold, please." I give Flash my Clinique bag. "This too." She slips my pocketbook onto her shoulder and groans under its weight as I take off for the dressing room. Once inside, I fling off my blouse and throw it to the floor like some sex-starved maniac. Then I gently ease the sweater off its hanger, slide it onto my body, and turn around to admire my reflection in the mirror. The third button from the top is missing, but that's a minor detail. I am gorgeous.

I leave the dressing room in search of Flash. "What do you think?"

"It's you."

"Really?"

"Of course. Why is one sleeve rolled up?" Flash points to my right arm. I roll down the cuff and hear a tiny ping as something hits the ground. "Oh, my God," I gasp. "The missing button." Tears fill my eyes. I am unspeakably moved by the kindness of some stranger, no doubt a tried-and-true shopper like myself, who cared enough to keep sweater and button united so that someone other than herself could completely enjoy the garment. Such an act of selfless goodness, especially in this day and age, momentarily stuns me and convinces me that all is right with the world. So much so that I shush the voice in my head that's telling me to pocket the button, show the sweater's tragic flaw to the salesclerk and demand another ten percent off.

"Are we done for the day?" Flash asks, unable to hide the hope in her voice.

"Let me just get those shoes." We head back toward Filene's. "They're perfect for this sweater. All I need is a black skirt."

"Don't you have a black skirt?"

I shake my head because of course I don't have *a* black skirt. I have many black skirts. A mini, a maxi, a midi, and a midcalf that's slit halfway up my thigh. A velvet, a rayon, a leather, a suede, and one with three gold buttons going up the side. I also have a black pleated skirt, a skintight skirt, a linen skirt, an A-line skirt, and an itchy wool skirt that my grandmother bought me in 1979.

Of course when we get home I must try on my new sweater and shoes with all these skirts and various black stockings (opaque, mesh, fishnet, sheer, back-seam, seamless, lace) while Flash watches a *Laverne & Shirley* rerun on TV. During a commercial I pirouette in front of her. "What do you think?"

"Your seams are crooked."

"Fix them." I hike up my skirt and Flash drops to her knees to check my seams. All of them. Very, very slowly. And carefully. Lucky for us, it's an extremely long commercial.

Hours later Flash and I change into our pajamas and crawl into bed, exhausted but content. Just like any other typical American family after a day at the mall.

PMS: Please Menstruate Soon!

Of all the joys of lesbian life, which are much too numerous to mention, there is one I would just as soon live without: the pleasure of two women living together, loving each other, and having PMS at the same time. It is not a pretty picture, believe me. Luckily I no longer have to worry about this less than fabulous situation, because my beloved Flash has tapped into her ancient female wisdom and figured out how to never have her period again. Yes, Flash is the envy of all our baby boomer and Generation X friends: She has worked hard and achieved menopause. And it's a good thing too, as I have enough premenstrual tension for both of us. And this is the beauty of being a lesbian: My lover has been through it all before. Only someone who has walked a mile in my mules (in swollen feet, no less) could possibly understand and put up with the monster I become for seven days out of every month.

Sunday (Day One): It is three o'clock in the morning. Flash stumbles into the bathroom to find me squatting in the tub, stark naked, scrubbing the hem of the shower curtain with a Brillo pad. "Why are you doing that now?" Flash asks, genuinely curious.

"Because I can't stand the *shmutz* in this house for one more minute," I say, applying all the elbow grease I can muster.

"Why don't you come to bed?" Flash holds out her hand. "The dirt will still be there in the morning."

"Over my dead body," I say, doubling my efforts.

"Somebody's PMS," Flash singsongs.

"I am not PMS!" I shriek, throwing the Brillo pad at Flash's head. She ducks and goes back to bed, hoping she can get some sleep. She'll need her strength: The fun has just begun.

Monday (Day Two): I am standing at the oven, poking freshly baked oat bran muffins with a toothpick to see if they're done. Now that the house is cleaner than when my parents came to visit, my nesting instincts have shifted into the realm of nourishment. Flash and I have terrible eating habits, and I am determined to change them. These muffins are a good way to start; supposedly they have more fiber than our socks. I set the table with soy butter, organic jam, the muffins, and coffee. Flash comes into the kitchen, slumps into a chair, and sips her morning caffeine.

"Have a muffin, dear," I say in my best Donna Reed voice.

"No, thanks," Flash says.

"But breakfast is the most important meal of the day," I remind her.

"I haven't eaten breakfast since 1969," Flash reminds me, as if I haven't noticed that for the past six years the only thing Flash has ingested before noon is coffee and an occasional Flintstone vitamin.

"But I made them for you," I wail, tears gushing from my eyes.

"I'll take one to work and have it for lunch," Flash promises.

"But I want you to eat it NOW!" I shriek, suddenly enraged.

I snatch a muffin and hurl it across the room. Flash grabs her car keys, ducks out the door, and calls, "Have a nice day."

Tuesday (Day Three): Flash comes out of the shower and finds me sitting in my bathrobe on the edge of the bed, the picture of despair. "What's the matter?" she asks cautiously.

"I have nothing to wear," I say.

"Oh, is that all?" Flash is hardly concerned, as she hears this from me at least once a day. "C'mon, I'll help you pick something out."

She opens my closet door and does a double take. Hangers, hangers everywhere, as far as the eye can see. With nothing on them.

"Honey," Flash says slowly, "what happened to your clothes?"

"They're gone," I say miserably.

"Gone where?"

"To the Salvation Army. I got sick of them."

Flash stares at me in amazement. "All of them?" she asks.

"Yes, all of them. Oh, except this."

I walk over to my dresser and pull out a skintight black velvet catsuit I bought on a whim and have never dared wear in public. Flash makes me put it on and drives us to the Salvation Army. I buy back my entire wardrobe, which much to my delight is participating in a two-for-one, half-price special. "Look at all these fabulous clothes," I exclaim, "and they're going for a song."

Wednesday (Day Four): The alarm goes off, and Flash opens her eyes to find me sprawled on top of the blankets covered in nothing but Saran Wrap, with a red rose between my teeth. "In the mood?" she asks.

I bat my eyelashes in reply.

"Honey, you know I have to get to work." I pout as she ponders. "Tell you what. I'll come home for lunch," she says, "I promise."

But when Flash bounds up the back steps at exactly one minute after twelve, she finds me weeping in front of the bathroom mirror. "What's the matter now?" she asks.

"My eyebrows are uneven," I sob, pointing at my reflection. "My forehead is slanted. My nose is off-center. My whole face is crooked."

"Don't be ridiculous," Flash says. "You're beautiful." She reaches to take me in her arms.

"Don't touch me," I scream, running from the room. Flash runs after me, waving a white tissue as an offering and a sign of surrender.

Thursday (Day Five): Flash comes home from work to find a stranger sitting on the couch. "Hello," she says. "Have you seen my wife?"

"I am your wife," I say. "How do you like it?" The *it* I am referring to is my hair. Yesterday it was brown and curly and hanging in ringlets to my elbows as usual. Today it is blond, spiked, and half an inch long, sticking up from my head like the crew cut my brother suffered all through junior high.

"It's a wig, right?" Flash, always the optimist, runs her fingers over my buzz cut.

"You don't like it," I say, the tears, which are never far off, starting to form.

"No, it's cute." Flash tries to muster up some enthusiasm.

"I've always wanted to do it with a bleached blond." As soon as the words are out of her mouth, Flash regrets them. I go right for her jugular.

Hours later, after Flash has said 4,357 "Hail Lesléa's," I forgive her and allow her to take me to the mall, where I discover a whole new world of accessories: hats.

Later that night the full impact of what I've done hits me. I can't buy my hair back from the salon at half price.

Flash tries to comfort me. "It'll grow back." she assures me. "Just promise you won't pierce or tattoo anything."

I promise, but just to be sure, Flash makes me hand over my cash and credit cards until the week is over.

Friday (Day Six): Things are coming to a head. I've been crying over long-distance commercials and eating chocolate-covered potato chips all morning. There is a blemish on my chin the size and shape of Canada. My breasts are so huge, I've taken to calling them Norm and Gus (short for enormous and humongous). I paint my nails Deep Slut Red. Suddenly I have an urge to wear white pants, even though Memorial Day is months away. I go to my closet, but Flash has put a padlock on it. I try to call her at work, but I can't remember the number. I hang up the phone and drop the receiver on my foot. The only thing left to do is take a nap. I dream I am drowning in a jar of Paul Newman's extra-chunky spaghetti sauce.

Saturday (Day Seven): My friend arrives (according to my mother, that's what nice girls say). Flash and I are jubilant. We toast my success as if I just landed a six-figure advance. Now that I am back to being my old lovable self, I apologize to Flash for my behavior. "I'll be better next month," I vow, but she doesn't believe me.

"We've been through this seventy-two times," she reminds me. "Oh, c'mon," I say. "I'm not always this bad." "That's true," Flash says. "Sometimes you're a lot worse." I remind Flash that it's really all her fault. If she would only teach me the secret of menopause we wouldn't have to go through this every month. But she refuses. "When you're older," she promises. "You've still got a decade to go." I hope we both live through it.

Butch in Training

"Package for you." Flash huffs and puffs and deposits an enormous carton onto the kitchen table with a groan.

"Who's it from?"

"Your editor."

"My editor? What could she be sending me?" I watch curiously as Flash slices the box open with her pocketknife and dumps the contents onto the table. Envelopes, envelopes everywhere, as far as the eye can see. "Fan mail!" I shriek, tossing a fistful into the air. I grab one as it falls from the sky and open it with glee. But there's no letter inside. Just a photo. And not just any photo. It's a portrait of a femme wearing nothing except butt floss.

"What is this?" I pick up the envelope for a clue and notice it's addressed to my beloved. "Flash, this is for you."

"Let me see it."

"Not on your life."

"Hey, this one's for me too." Flash opens an envelope that smells like Poison clear across the room. "Dear Flash," she reads out loud. "I am a twenty-two-year-old blond, buxom, blue-eyed femme, looking for a butch…"

"Give me that." I snatch the letter away as Flash opens yet another.

"Dear Flash, if you ever come to your senses and leave that woman…"

"Are they all for you?" I can't help but whine.

"No." Flash fishes an envelope from the pile. "This one's for your mother."

"Oh, for God's sake." I continue the search and finally find an envelope with my name on it. "Dear Lesléa," I read. "I've been reading your column for years and I've just got to know: Is Flash really as wonderful as you make her out to be? If so, do you share?"

Now listen up, ladies: Of course Flash is not as wonderful as I make her out to be. She is a thousand times more wonderful than mere words on paper could possibly convey. And no, I do not share. Even as a child I never let anyone near my favorite toy, so get over it, girlfriend. But I will let you in on a little secret: When I first met Flash, she was a tiny bit rough around the edges. I wasn't worried, though. Most butches can and must be trained. You too can turn your butch into a dream butch and have her eating out of your hand (or any other body part you desire) in the wink of a false eyelash. But you must begin immediately.

Unbeknownst to Flash, I started training her on our very first date. I have to give her credit: She knew enough to ask me out for Saturday night, and she knew enough to pick me up at eight. (If your butch says, "Let's get together Tuesday night. Do you want to drive or should I?" forget it.) Flash knew enough to arrive in a fresh-pressed shirt, creased pants, and snappy shoes, and she knew enough not to be late.

Flash even knew enough to bring me a flower. A rose, in fact. Which I'm sure would have pleased the average femme. But I am not the average femme. I am what some call a high femme. I prefer to be known as a high-maintenance femme. While Flash meant well, it was clear to me she needed to learn some basic math: Diamonds come one by one. Shoes come in pairs. Roses come by the dozen. Since butches tend to be so sensitive, I approached the subject with my usual tact. I took the rose and said, "Thank you," like a lady. Then I got out a huge vase and ran enough water in it to fill the Atlantic. "Don't you have anything smaller?" Flash asked. "No," I said, setting the lonely rose on the table, making a visual point.

A minute later, Flash made mistake number two. "You look nice," she said. The average femme would have taken that to be a compliment. But this high-maintenance femme hadn't spent the last two weeks shopping for the perfect outfit and the last seven hours bathing, shaving, bleaching, filing, polishing, combing, brushing, drying, moussing, spritzing, spraying, and applying five pounds of makeup to have all her efforts summed up in one little four-letter word. I started at the bottom and worked my way up: "Do you like these shoes?" I asked Flash, pirouetting on my three-inch heels. "They're fabulous," she answered. "And do you think I look okay in such a short skirt?" I ran my hands along the fabric. "You look really good in it." "What about my perfume—is it too sweet?" I waved my wrist in front of her nose. "You smell wonderful." "Do you think my hair looks good like this?" I fussed in front of the mirror. "Your hair looks great."

When I felt sufficiently admired, I announced I was ready to go and glanced at my wrap, which was draped over a chair. Flash didn't move, so I picked up my coat, handed it to her, and turned around. Then I backed up and slid my arms into the sleeves. "Thanks," I said, with a sweet smile. When we got down to her car, Flash made another faux pas by walking around to the driver's side and starting to get in. I stood on the sidewalk by the passenger door, waiting. When she yelled, "It's open," I yelled back, "It doesn't look open to me."

Soon we were both in the car, heading for a cozy little restaurant on the outskirts of Lesbianville. After Flash parked the car and got out, I watched her walk halfway across the parking lot before she realized that she was alone and unless she wanted to eat her dinner that way she had better turn around, come back, and open the car door for me. I took her arm as if it already belonged to me (the better to steer you with, my dear) and maneuvered her across the pavement, letting go just as she opened the restaurant's door, so I could enter first.

Once at our table, I decided to simply sit down, rather than instruct Flash on the fine art of pulling out a lady's chair for her. I saved that lesson for our second date, so as not to overwhelm her. However, when our waiter asked us what we wanted to drink and Flash said without hesitation, "I'll have a..." I simply had to knock my knife clear across the room and ask her to retrieve it, so I could order my glass of white wine before she asked for her Budweiser.

During dinner, I schooled Flash in the fine art of paying complete attention to a femme. When she started concentrating on something else, like her food for example, I shrugged my shoulder just so, causing the spaghetti strap of my bustier to slide down my arm in a slow, mesmerizing manner. At dessert time, I ordered chocolate mousse and used my tongue to maximum effect. Assuming that Flash, like most butches, was completely fascinated by all the feminine accoutrements that totally baffle them, I searched through my purse frequently ("What in the world does she have in there?" I could practically hear Flash wondering). Of course I touched up my lipstick at the table ("How does she do that without a mirror?" Flash silently marveled). Before the meal was through, I had done my job and convinced her that I was, without a doubt, the femme of her dreams and the woman she could simply not live without.

At the end of the night when Flash took me home, I could tell she was nervous. She pulled into my driveway and kept the motor running. I gave her an insulted look that asked, *Don't you think I'm attractive enough to see the evening through?* Immediately she shut the engine, which prompted another indignant look: *How dare you presume I want you to come in?* The poor girl didn't know whether she was coming or going, which is just the way I wanted her. "May I have the honor of coming inside?" Flash finally asked, and in fact still asks every time we come home from a date, even though we've been living together for over six years. Once inside, I set the mood with candles, music, and wine. I motioned for Flash to sit down on the couch and then I sat on her lap, closed my eyes, and puckered my lips. When she finally kissed me, I acted surprised, as if it were all her idea. Then I let her take the lead, and she proved to be my dream butch by making all my dreams come true.

But who knew I was creating a monster? Here we are, years later, with Flash up to her elbows in fan mail from femmes fatales, and I don't like it one bit.

"Listen to this one," Flash says. "Dear Flash, I am writing a book called *Butches Are From Mars, Femmes Are From Venus,* and I have a feeling you would be the perfect research assistant...."

"Dream on, sister," I say, plucking the letter out of Flash's hand. "You are not to answer any of these letters," I tell her in a stern voice. "I'll answer them."

"Don't tell me you're jealous," Flash says.

"Jealous? I'm not jealous," I say, picking up a pen. "I'm just going to thank all your fans for writing and let them know that if they even think about sending any more letters..."

"Watch what you write," Flash says nervously. "I don't want them all to think I'm henpecked."

"You're not henpecked, Flash," I tell her.

"I'm not?" She sounds surprised.

"Of course not," I remind her. "You're pussywhipped."

"Pussywhipped? I'll show you who's pussywhipped." Flash shoves all the envelopes to the floor, picks me up, and slings me over her shoulder like a mail sack. She carries me off to the bedroom, where she proves yet again just who wears the pants in this family. And if she wants to think that was all her idea, who am I not to let her?

The Butch That I Marry

"Hey, Flash," I whisper to the prone body lying beside me in the dark. "Flash. Flashy. Flash-Flash. Flasheroo. Flashkins. Flashmeister." But it's no use. It's one minute past midnight, and my beloved is fast asleep. I haven't the heart to wake her, even to wish her happy anniversary. Yes, it's been six blissful years since Flash and I became wife and wife, but I remember our wedding as though it were yesterday.

Before the wedding came the proposal, of course. We'd only been going out for two months when Flash got down on one knee and asked, "Will you marry me?" I got up on two elbows, peered over the side of the bed, and asked, "Where's the ring?" Flash, having none, quickly looked around her bedroom and offered instead a good-luck onyx stone that she'd had for years. Not the kind of rock I'd hoped for, but I accepted nevertheless and immediately started making lists: people to invite, people not to invite, the menu, the music… Flash wanted to celebrate our engagement in a different, more traditional manner, but I pushed her aside. "There's no time for that now," I said, reaching over her back for a pen and pad from the nightstand. "We've got a wedding to plan."

In the weeks to come, I kept waiting for Flash to surprise me with an engagement ring. When none appeared, I started dropping hints. I sang "Diamonds Are a Girl's Best Friend" when we showered together. I said "Give me a ring sometime" instead of "Call me later" when Flash left my house for work. When Flash asked if I had plans for Saturday night, I said, "As a matter of fact, I have a previous engagement." All to no avail.

Finally Flash and I took a trip to our local lesbian jeweler to choose our wedding rings. In all the excitement of choosing matching bands, the matter of an engagement ring was simply forgotten. Flash wanted us to start wearing our rings right away, but I was stern. "Nothing doing. We can't wear them until we're actually married."

"Can we at least try them on?" Flash asked. We did, and they looked gorgeous. "Let's just wear them out to the car," Flash said, and I relented. "Let's just wear them out to brunch," she said. "Let's just wear them until I take you home." "Let's just wear them while we're doing the nasty." Needless to say, from that day forth we never took off our rings. Not even when I brought Flash home to meet the folks. You would think that my mother, who notices everything, including the one gray hair in my left eyebrow ("You really should touch that up"), would notice a gold band on the fourth finger of her only daughter's left hand and say something about it. Especially since said daughter's new "friend" was wearing an identical ring on the fourth finger of her left hand as well. But you see, my family actually invented the "don't ask, don't tell" policy, and has been practicing it for years. Flash was amazed. "You mean you're not even going to tell them about the wedding?"

"Of course not," I said. "Then I'd have to invite them."

"You're not inviting your parents?" Flash was aghast.

"You're not inviting yours," I reminded her.

"My parents are dead," Flash pointed out, as if that was any kind of excuse. Then her face took on a look of concern. "Who's going to give you away?" she asked.

I didn't hesitate. "My therapist."

"But," Flash was visibly pale, "I thought it was traditional for the femme's family to pay for the wedding."

I kissed her cheek. "You're my family now," I said, throwing my arms around her. Flash was so moved, she didn't know whether to laugh or cry.

In the months to come, Flash and I met with a printer, a florist, a photographer, a caterer, a bartender, a DJ, a band, a rabbi, a hairdresser, a dressmaker, a shoemaker, and a tailor. We compiled a huge guest list, since after all, our wedding was going to be *the* social event of the season. But when our caterer informed us that her sliding scale started at twenty-three dollars a plate, we quickly realized who our seventy-five closest friends really were. Not that any of them bothered to return the little reply card enclosed in their invitation complete with envelope and LOVE stamp. A week before the wedding, our caterer was tearing out her hair. "You've got to tell me how many guests are coming," she cried. I tried to explain that lesbians think RSVP stands for "Respond Slowly Versus Promptly," but she was not amused.

On the morning of the wedding, I went off to have my hair done and my nails polished. At ten o'clock I returned home and began to dress. I had just fastened one stocking to my garter belt when the phone rang. Mitzi, who had come over to help, answered. "It's your mother," she whispered, covering the mouthpiece with one hand. I grabbed the receiver, frantically. My mother never calls me on Sunday mornings. "Who died?" I asked.

"No one," she answered. "I just woke up thinking about you, so I decided to call. So, what's new?"

"Nothing."

"So, what are you doing today?"

My mind raced. What could I tell her? I remembered that old fiction writing adage: *I lie in order to tell the truth.* I decided to try the opposite and tell the truth in order to lie: "Getting married."

"Very funny."

Phew. I knew she wouldn't believe me. "Listen, Ma, I have some people here. I gotta go," I said, hanging up the phone. I fastened my other stocking and continued getting dressed. Soon I was covered from head to toe in silk and rhinestones, complete with something old (my grandmother's brooch); something new (my dress); something borrowed (a tampon from Mitzi); and something blue (the string on the tampon). Flash, who looked stunning in her cream-colored satin shirt and black tuxedo pants, also had her period. We'd never bled together before, and we promptly decided that the simultaneous shedding of our uterine walls was a sign from the goddess that our union was meant to be.

Then before we knew it, *the* moment had arrived. Flash and I stood under the *chuppah,* her Best Butch to our right, my Dyke of Honor to our left. We were surrounded by our loved ones, who all wore their finest: everything from combat boots, cutoff shorts, and nose rings to high heels, velvet gowns, and diamonds. And those were just the boys. The girls wore their best Birkenstocks, drawstring pants, and T-shirts with slogans on them like BUT MA, SHE *IS* MR. RIGHT or MONOGAMY EQUALS MONOTONY, depending on their point of view. Flash and I faced the rabbi, who started the ceremony by saying that the two of us looked beautiful and very much in love. Of course I started to cry. Then the rabbi started to cry. Then Flash, who is too butch to cry in front of me, never mind before seventy-five of our nearest and dearest, proceeded to have an allergy attack.

When things calmed down, the rabbi continued. Flash and I said our vows, exchanged rings, sipped wine, and kissed. Then the rabbi emptied the wine glass, and with great ceremony, wrapped it in a napkin and placed it on the floor for Flash to crush. I caught Mitzi laughing out of the corner of my eye. Later I asked her just what was so funny. "You left the price tag on the bottom of the wine glass," she said, still giggling. "Even from across the room I could see that it was fifty percent off."

"So what?" I asked, indignant. "You think I would let Flash break crystal I paid retail for?"

After we were pronounced Butch and Bride, the party really went wild. Flash and I were hoisted up on chairs and paraded around for all to see. Our friends toasted us and danced circles around us. The food was so fabulous, even the vegetarians couldn't resist diving into the swan-shaped chopped liver centerpiece. Both wedding cakes (one traditional, the other sugar-, wheat-, and dairy-free) were divine. I tossed my bouquet and Flash threw my garter. We smiled so much our faces hurt. At the end of the day, we drove off to a nearby hotel. I didn't want to take off my wedding dress yet, so Flash worked around it. We fell asleep in each other's arms, and we've slept that way ever since.

I sigh with contentment and look at the clock on the night table. It is now half past twelve, and Flash is still deep in dreamland. I decide to let her sleep. There'll be plenty of time to celebrate tomorrow. Maybe I'll even surprise my beloved with breakfast in bed. But the surprise is on me. When I open my eyes I see a vision of loveliness: Flash, handsome in her silk bathrobe, stands before me holding a breakfast tray. "Happy anniversary," she says, setting the tray down on the bed. I *ooh* and *aah* over the fresh coffee, the bagel and lox, the red rose. "What's this?" I ask, holding up a small gift box.

"Remember the night I proposed to you?" Flash asks. I nod my head, dreamily. "I never forgot what you said."

"I said yes."

"No, you didn't." Flash says. "You said, 'Where's the…' "

"Ring! Oh, my God!" I tear open the box and gasp at the sweetest, most stunning, most beautiful diamond ring I have ever seen. At last, the rock I have always wanted. "Is it too late to get engaged?" Flash asks. I grab her by the neck and kiss her in reply. My butch. I think I'll keep her.

FROM

Girls Will Be Girls

(2000)

The Babka Sisters

Sit down, *shah,* you ready? You got your tin can going there, you want to make a test, make sure my voice is good, everything is working all right? Okay, so now I'm gonna tell you a story, a story I never told nobody. Why I'm telling you, a stranger, I don't even know, but all right, *eppes,* it's time.

Once upon a time, a long, long time ago, around the Stone Age it was, *takeh,* I was a young *maidl,* and quite a looker I was too. I know what you're thinking, you look at me now and what do you see? A fat old lady wrinkled like a prune danish with hair like cotton candy. But *nu,* I had quite a shape in those days. My hair I wore in a braid down my back thick as a man's arm, my skin was smooth as a baby's *tuchus.* You don't believe me but you wait, *mameleh.* Gravity ain't got no favorites; it catches up to everyone, *eppes,* someday even you.

So my childhood ain't nothing to talk about. An ordinary girl I was, I went to school, I came home, I helped my mother with the housework. Sure, five children she had, four boys and me, so who else is gonna help her? I had friends too, boys and girls, no one special, there was a group of us that stuck together, to the movies we went, and to get a *nosh* at the diner, dancing once in a while, you know, we did all the things young people do.

And then, when I was sixteen, a new girl moved into the neighborhood, and that girl I had such a feeling for, I just couldn't take my eyes from her. You know the expression "love at first sight," sure, who doesn't, well, of course that's what it was. But what did I know, we was two girls; girls don't fall in love with girls, who ever heard of such a thing? I just knew I wanted to be her friend, help her out, you know, show her around. It could be overwhelming, such a place, to a person who first walks in and don't know from it, *eppes,* it takes a while to get used to, it was a very big school.

Look, here's a picture of her, my Evie. You see, here we are, both in the last row. That's our class picture from eleventh grade, we was both tall girls; now I'm all stooped over like an old turtle, but back then my back was straight as a *Shabbos* candle, from my posture my mother was always proud. Ain't she gorgeous, my Evie? Look at that dark curly hair, black as midnight it was. Medusa I used to call her, *eppes,* it was that hair that started the whole thing. Dark curly hair and blue eyes, very unusual for a Jew, but I'm telling you, her eyes were as blue as mine are brown, you can see, under the cataracts my eyes are dark like coffee you drink when there's no milk in the house. And could she fill out a gym suit, my Evie! Listen, years ago, no girl wanted to be skinny. Like sticks all you girls are now. What do they call them, the supermodels there, *feh,* one puff of wind could knock them right down. We used to laugh at girls like that, girls with no hips, no *tuchus.* We used to feel sorry for them, the poor things.

So where was I? Oh, Evie, of course, Evie. The first day I saw her, she was in the lunchroom sitting all by herself, *takeh,* and I was ashamed, a whole school, maybe five hundred boys and girls, maybe a thousand, and not one person held out a hand. Nobody said, you must be lonely, here, I'll sit with you, I'll talk to you, I'll show you where to take your tray. And blind they all was, they couldn't see this was no ordinary girl, this girl was something special, a gift from God she was, and nobody could see what was sitting there right before their very eyes?

So I got my sandwich, egg salad I got, and a carton of milk, and I took my *tuchus* over and put it down on the seat right next to her. "How do you do? I'm Ruthie," I said, and that's when I knew I was lost, when I looked for the first time into those eyes. Like diamonds they twinkled, like stars, like the sun dancing on the ocean in a million pieces, all that and more was shining in my Evie's eyes.

"I'm Evie," she said. "How do you do?" I couldn't even answer her, my voice was gone, on a trip it went, a vacation all of a sudden it took, I couldn't find it, so I went to take a drink of milk, but I was so nervous, can you believe it, I started to choke. And to make things worse, Evie clapped me on the back, and when I felt her hand touch me, even through my sweater and my blouse, I felt a charge, like a jolt, like I just put instead of the plug my finger in the socket, God forbid, but I swear, sure as I'm sitting here, it's true. And Evie was so concerned, she looked at me, so serious. "Are you all right?" she asked, and all I could see was those two eyes above me, blue as the sky, like God finished making the heavens and he had a little fabric left over and decided the only thing left to do was make those little bits of heaven into Evie's eyes. Finally I got hold of myself, and we ate our lunch and had a conversation, about what I couldn't tell you, whatever young girls talk about, school and families, this and that. Whatever she said, I don't think I heard a word. I was too busy drowning in those blue, blue eyes.

Evie and I became fast friends after that. Every day we ate lunch together, every day together we walked home from school. Evie lived around the corner from me, how lucky could I get? I began to think maybe I did shine a little bit in God's eyes. Sometimes we'd study at Evie's house, sometimes we'd study at mine. We became like part of each other's families; I would eat supper by her, she would eat supper by me. The *Babka* Sisters my mother used to call us, you know what *babka* is, darling? A dessert so sweet, with cinnamon they make it sometimes, sometimes with chocolate. Evie and I loved it, we ate it all the time, so my mother gave us like a nickname, you know like a joke. "Look who's here, the *Babka* Sisters," she'd say after school when we rang the bell.

Sometimes we'd have sleepover dates too. It was nothing unusual, all the girls did in those days. Evie would sleep over my house, I had my own room, not that we was so rich, but because it ain't nice: A girl can't sleep with her brothers, so what could my mother do? Evie had a sister—Shirley her name was—and they shared one room, two beds they had, two dressers, two desks, everything matching, you know, except the two girls, they didn't match so good. They was different as day and night, they used to fight like cats and dogs, so over to our house Evie came, every chance she could.

So where was the boys, I bet you're thinking. Two teenage girls, gorgeous like we was, and neither of us had a fella? Me, the boys was never interested in, I was too much of a tomboy for them. My mother used to wring her hands, "Ruthie, take little steps, why do you have to walk like a truck?" And Evie, I think the boys were afraid of her, so beautiful she was, and so smart, she beat them by a mile, and then they'd have to get past me of course to get near her, we was always together, and I wouldn't let them so easily by.

Sometimes when Evie and I were up in my room studying, I'd watch her out of the corner of my eye. So gorgeous she looked, studying or writing or just chewing her pencil. If she glanced up, I'd look away quickly, but once in a while, I'd meet her gaze. And sometimes I caught her staring at me too. "What?" I'd say, feeling kind of nervous, though I didn't know why. "Nothing," Evie would answer with a shrug and a smile.

One night Evie was sleeping over—it was *Shabbos,* I remember—my mother had made such a beautiful supper: her *matzo* ball soup that she was famous for all up and down the avenue, and fresh *challah* from the bakery, and a roasted chicken, we was so full we was busting after, such a feast it was. Evie and I helped my mother with the supper dishes, and then we first had coffee and *babka*—no matter how stuffed we was we always had room for *babka*—and then we went up to my room. Evie had been a little quiet that night, and a few times I caught her staring at me across the supper table, but I didn't ask no questions. I figured if she had something to tell me, she'd tell. She looked a little moony that night, and I was only afraid she shouldn't tell me she had a crush on a fella, she couldn't spend so much time with me now, on dates she was gonna go, and believe me if that's what Evie was going to say, I wasn't in a big hurry to find out.

Evie went into the bathroom to get undressed like she always did, and I got undressed as well. We both wore long, white nightgowns, cotton they were, everybody did back then. I turned off the light, lifted back the covers, and got into bed. It was dark, but not so you couldn't see; the moon shone right in my window, I still remember, it was full that night. Like a spotlight it was, shining down on Evie when she came back to my room. Like a movie star she looked, I remember, there was something different about her, and then I realized what it was: Instead of in a braid, all her hair, all those thick black waves were loose and hanging down.

"Ruthie, will you brush my hair?" Evie asked, her voice slow and thick and dreamy, and when I climbed out of bed and went to her, my movements were slow and dreamy too. I took the brush from Evie's hand and stood behind her in the moonlight, brushing her hair from the crown of her head all the way down to her tiny, tiny waist. Up and down my hands went, brushing her hair for hours it seemed, days maybe, long after the last knot was untangled, long after her hair shone like a wet, black stone. Hypnotized I was, like a spell I was under, I couldn't move a muscle except for my arms that couldn't stop brushing, brushing. I only wanted that moment to never end: me, Evie, the hairbrush, the moonlight. If I died right then and there I wouldn't be sorry, because I had already tasted a bit of heaven. But thank God my time wasn't up, for what happened after that I wouldn't have missed for anything: Evie turned around, the hairbrush clattered down from my hand, and before I even knew what was happening, there she was, my girl in my arms.

"Ruth," she whispered, and her mouth was so close to mine I could feel her sweet breath on my skin, and I breathed it in, wanting every part of her. "Ruth," she said again, not Ruthie, but Ruth, like my name was holy, a prayer that could only be answered with her name, "Evelyn," like the song of the nightingale it was, so sweet on my lips. "Evelyn," I said again, "Evelyn." "Ruth," she answered, and then she put her mouth on top of mine, and then we didn't say no more.

Her lips, how can I describe her lips? Sweeter than *challah* they were, sweeter than *babka,* and soft, so soft, I was almost afraid if I licked them they would dissolve on my tongue, they would melt away like water. When Evie kissed me, the world as I had always known it came forever to an end, and a new world, a world so sweet, so fine, so holy and precious took its place instead.

It was Evie who broke that kiss and led me to the bed, the same bed we had slept in together for so many nights, but like *Pesach,* I knew this night would be different than all other nights, I knew there would be no nightgowns that evening to separate flesh from flesh. Evie was so confident, so unashamed, so proud, *takeh,* of her feelings for me, that I wasn't even afraid. She took my hands and put them on her breasts, and I gasped at their softness, their firmness, their ripeness, so smooth and white her breasts were, her nipples so hard and rubbery and sweet I swooned to take them under my tongue.

What, so surprised you are that an old woman like me should talk so? All you young girls with your blue hair and pierced eyebrows, up there at the university in your women's history class, you think there was no such girls in my time, you think you're the first, you think maybe you invented it? Well, I've got news for you: there's more to tell, so either turn your tin can off, and I'll keep quiet, or put your eyes back in your head, sit still, and listen.

Now then, I'll never forget that night as long as I live. So gentle Evie was, but so fierce, too, like a *vildeh chayah,* you know what that means, like a little wild beast. "Here," she said, putting my hand where it never went before. "Harder," she said, "lower. Like this," and she'd put her hand on top of mine and show me what to do. Where she learned such things I didn't know, I didn't want to know. What did I care? All I wanted was to hear her breath coming hard and fast against my ear, her little cries of *"Oy, oy, oy,"* and then "Ruthie, my Ruthie," and then just "yes, yes, yes." Oh, how she crooned as my hands went up and down, in and out, all over her, my Evie who trembled, and shook, and yelped so loud I was only afraid my mother shouldn't come in, and then finally fell back against the pillow and was still.

And if that wasn't enough, *dayenu,* then Evie decided it was my turn. And when she put her hands on me, when she put her mouth on me, when she set my body on fire, I melted into the bed, *takeh,* like a puddle of *shmaltz* I was, all ooze and no bone. And then hours later, when the moon had moved halfway across the sky and the stars were almost gone, we fell asleep, close, Evie's sweet little hand in mine.

The next morning we got up late, so quiet the house was, I knew it was empty except for that devilish look in Evie's eye. We picked up where we left off the night before, and so caught up in each other we was, we didn't hear my mother's foot on the step, we didn't hear her hand on the knob, my poor mother, so innocent she was, what did she know, she threw open the door, and said, "So, *nu, Babka* Sisters, it's almost noon, ain't you getting up?" But of course we was up already, Evie was up on top of me in fact, stark naked she was, her hips going up and down like a horse on a merry-go-round, her arms reaching for the sky.

"Gottinyu, vey iss mir, my God." My mother shrieked, Evie rushed to cover herself, the door slammed, I started to cry.

"Don't," Evie whispered, licking my tears like a puppy. "It's all my fault. I couldn't stop myself."

"What'll we do?" I wailed, but before Evie could answer, my mother came upstairs again. This time she knew enough to knock. "Ruthie, I think your friend better go home now," she said—"my friend," she couldn't even say her name—and then one-two-three, Evie was gone.

Oy, was I in trouble, was my goose cooked, I'm telling you. My mother wouldn't even look on me, so ashamed she was. And my father didn't know what to do, he knew something was wrong but he didn't know what. My mother wouldn't speak of such things to him, but with one look she told him and my brothers I was in trouble but good. So no one talked to me at home, but never mind, I had bigger problems to worry about. On Monday when I went back to school, Evie was absent. I couldn't remember her ever being absent before, and I was worried sick. What happened to her? Did she hurt herself, did her parents know? Were they punishing her, did she maybe run away? I only wanted to run to her house, but I didn't dare, so much trouble I was in already, if I didn't come straight home from school, my mother would kill me for sure. And I wanted to be right by the phone when Evie called—surely she would at least call? But call she didn't; instead a letter came. All typed up it was, all formal, like a business letter it was, *eppes,* and this is what it said:

Dear Ruthie:

I don't want to see you anymore. What we did was wrong, we should be ashamed of ourselves. It's a blessing your mother came in when she did; we're still young, we still have a chance to live the life God wants us to, with a husband and children and grandchildren, God willing. I am getting help from the rabbi, and I hope you will do the same.

And she signed it "Evie," and that was all.

Turn off the tape recorder, will you, darling, I need a minute to catch my breath here, maybe a drink of water you could get me, there's a cup there, over by the sink. It still feels like a punch in the stomach. I remember reading that letter over and over, a thousand times I read it, and all the while I could barely breathe. I called her of course, right away I called her, but her mother wouldn't let her come to the phone. She never even came back to school again, *eppes*, a few months later the whole family moved away, and Evie, my sweet, sweet Evie was gone.

So what can I tell you? The years went by, life goes on, it don't wait for nobody, *eppes*, I graduated from school, I got married, two children I had, a boy and a girl. I never really had feelings for my husband, but he was a good man, kind, a good provider. And my children, may they live and be well and call me once in a while, my children I loved, of course, after all they are my own flesh and blood. With my husband, I did my duty. When he wanted me to come to him, I came. He deserved that much, after all, and I tried not to let him know for me it was nothing, a waste of my time, but *eppes*, such a thing is hard to hide, I think, *takeh*, he knew. I tried not to think about Evie, too painful it was, like a thousand knives going right through my heart, but every once in a while I couldn't help myself. I'd see someone who looked like her on the street, and I'd wonder, where is she now, is she married, is she happy, is she all right, but of course I never knew.

And then one day, years later it was, the children were already married, I think my little granddaughter was already born, my little Madeline, ooh, you should see her, darling, so smart, so cute, just like a little pumpernickel she is. Anyway, one day out of nowhere, Evie's face came to me like a dream, like a vision, I just couldn't get her out of my mind. By this time my husband was gone already, he died young, a heart attack it was. Did he love to eat, my husband. I always told him to lighten up on the butter, go easy on the eggs, but did he listen to me? No, so, *nu*, here I was, a widow at fifty-three. That ain't so old, but already I was going a little crazy, every time I turned around, Evie's face I saw, on the bus, on the TV, late at night when I closed my eyes. Five days it's like this, and then all of a sudden, as suddenly as she came, just as suddenly, she's gone. And then four days after that, a letter I got, it fell into my hands from nowhere, straight out of the sky:

Dear Ruthie:

Maybe you don't remember me, so many years it's been, and who knows, maybe it's best to let sleeping dogs lie. But I was in the hospital last week, five days I was there, a stroke they thought I had, an aneurysm maybe. They're still not sure, but I'm telling you, I almost died. A person changes from an experience like that, you know, I got home, everything looked different. I started thinking long and hard about my life—such a close call it was—but God in His wisdom took pity on me and gave me a second chance. So, nu, *I started thinking about you, Ruthie. I know you never wanted to see me again, you said so in the letter, I still have it, after all these years I could never throw it away, and maybe you still don't want to know from me, but I thought what could it hurt, so much time has passed, I'm going to write to you, and maybe you could write back to me and let me know you're still alive. Are you okay, Ruthie? Are you happy? Have you had a good life? If you don't want to answer, I'll understand, but I want you to know I never forgot you, and I ain't mad on you for what happened.*

Your old friend,
Evie

My heart started pounding so, I was only afraid I shouldn't have a heart attack. I sat down on the kitchen chair and read the letter again, once I read it, twice, a thousand times. I couldn't believe Evie had found me again after all these years. *Nu,* I'm still in the old neighborhood, I only moved a few blocks away, *eppes,* but still, I had a different last name. Maybe she hired a detective, I didn't know, I was too excited. I only found out later she knew someone who knew someone who knew someone... You know, it was a miracle from God that brought us back together, plain and simple, that's what it was. And finally after all these years, I knew what had happened, I put two and two together. I realized my mother wrote Evie a letter, the same letter Evie's mother wrote to me, and neither one could be further from the truth. I told Evie so, I sat down right then and there and wrote her a letter, my hand trembling so, I didn't know if she would be able to make out the words, so shaky they were on the page. I told her I loved her then and I loved her now. I told her how I couldn't stop thinking about her the five days she was in the hospital, like a vision she was, her face pale as a ghost. Two days later I picked up the phone and heard her voice, three days after that I picked her up at the airport and held her in my arms.

This time there was no one to hide from, no one to come up the stairs and disturb us. Now we had all the time in the world to frolic in each other's arms. For days we stayed in bed, days and days and days, until I said, "Evie, *mameleh,* we have to eat, *eppes,"* and we stopped what we was doing to order in Chinese food and then got back in bed to feed each other with chopsticks, with our fingers, licking chow mein off each other, laughing all the while. At first I was shy with Evie, a blushing bride I wasn't no more, the flesh and the ground was having a meeting, you know what I'm saying, I wasn't no spring chicken, but Evie told me, *shah,* "You're beautiful, Ruthie, just like I remembered." And I remembered too. My hand remembered her breast, my mouth remembered her thigh. Two widows we were, two grown-up ladies with grown-up children yet, it's hard for you to imagine, but oh, such a time we had, Evie and me, such noises that came out from our throats, our bodies bucking up and down so, I was only afraid we wouldn't break the bed, and they'd find us there all in a tangle, two old ladies who couldn't *utz* themselves up from the floor. You, you're young yet, you think you know from sex, but just wait, and boy did I wait, for over thirty years I waited to put my hands on her, my Evie, to lick her breasts, her belly, to drown once more in her smile, her eyes. Did we rock, did we roll, did we shriek, I'm surprised the house didn't burn down, so hot for each other we was. It's a well-kept secret, darling, but you should know, old ladies do know from such pleasures, believe me, you'll see. You think you got it good now, just you wait. You know, like they say, the best is yet to come.

I don't even regret the years we spent apart, Evie and I. God has His reasons after all, and I'm not even mad no more on my mother, may she rest in peace. She only did what she thought was best, she and Evie's mother too. Evie and I had fourteen good years together until God looked down one day and said why should Ruthie Epstein have it so good, such a gorgeous *maideleh* she has, it's enough already, and God put up His hand and said to Evie, come, and so she did, so sweet she was, so good, God took a look and decided He wanted her all for Himself. All right, Evie and me, we've been separated before, God wants me down here and her up there, *eppes,* who am I to complain? Fourteen years we had, and boy did we make up for lost time, believe me, I'm telling you.

So that's all there is, there ain't no more. You can turn off your robot there, I told you enough, a secret I keep close to my heart that I never told nobody before. Even my own children didn't know, why should I tell them? They thought it was so nice, a roommate I had, I shouldn't be lonely, and when they came to visit, Evie slept somewhere else, the house was big, we had plenty room. I'll tell you something, even when the children wasn't visiting, sometimes she slept in another room. When you're old sometimes you want to spread out, you got a little gas maybe, you need a night to yourself.

All right, I'm tired now, so much talking, talking, talking, but I hope you got what you wanted. I hope you get an A in your women's history class. All right, history, herstory, whatever, this is my story, it's a mystery, *eppes,* why I was so lucky, so blessed, you should only be so lucky, may God shine such good fortune down on you. Believe me, God has His ways, *eppes,* you think it's a coincidence that out of all the old ladies in this nursing home here, you picked me to interview, into my room you came waltzing in? You and me, we've got something in common. We're cut from the same cloth, darling, *nu,* I can tell. And listen, *mameleh,* it's nothing to be ashamed of. Maybe your mother don't like it, your father, whoever, give them time. It's a different world today, they'll come around. You're young, you're a beautiful girl even with the purple eyebrows, *eppes,* you should only live and be well and find your own Evie, God willing, and may she live and be well and have a long happy life together with you.

What Ever Happened to Baby Fane?

Times are getting tough for a loud, proud Jewish fag hag like *moi.* My friends are dropping like fruit flies, as Fane used to say. Yes, used to say, for my beloved Fane has left us all in the dust for that Great Back Room in the sky.

Fane. I first met him a year before his untimely demise at an open poetry reading held at Queers-R-Us, our local coffee shop/hangout/pickup joint. Ours is a small community where everyone knows everyone (and more than likely has slept with everyone), so I noticed him right away. His hair fell to his shoulders in thick black ringlets not unlike my own (later we found out we'd both gone through a "Jewfro" stage at the exact same time). He was wearing perfectly pressed black jeans (which he admitted, when asked, were dry-cleaned), cowboy boots, and a black T-shirt that said I SURVIVED THE BRONX. Being a born and bred Brooklyn girl who has never been short on *chutzpah,* I promptly introduced myself.

"I'm Missy," I said, extending my hand.

"Fane," he replied, shaking it, which inspired me to slide the top of my jersey off my shoulder in a *Flashdance* sort of way and burst into song: "Fane! You're gonna live forever. You're gonna learn how to fly." Fane laughed, a deep, scratchy, throaty, big-enough-to-live-in laugh, and I was, as they say, smitten from day one.

"Sit, sit, *tateleh.* I'll buy you a cawfee," I said in my best Brooklynese, but Fane had other plans. One of the poets, a tall, dark handsome lad built like Michaelangelo's David, was the sole reason Fane had just sat through three hours of Allen Ginsberg wanna-bes, so if anyone was going to have the pleasure of his company for the rest of the evening, it certainly wasn't going to be me.

"I'll cawl you," Fane promised, matching my New Yawk accent

vowel for vowel. He wrote my number on a napkin, stuffed it into his back pocket, and went off to pursue the stud of his dreams. I didn't really mind, though. I was sure Fane would call, and he did, the very next day. "I'll take that cup of coffee now," he said in a weary voice that let me know he'd been up the better part of the night and could really use it.

"C'mon over," I said, putting some water up to boil. Fane arrived in a T-shirt that said START YOUR DAY WITH ME and asked for a grand tour of the house. I showed him my meager digs: a small living room, kitchen, and tiny bedroom.

"Is this the closet?" he asked, opening the door without waiting for my reply. He took a step inside and started moving my clothes down their rack like a housewife at Macy's Close-Out, looking for the ultimate sale. "Nope, nope, unh-unh, no…" He moved my blouses, pants, and the occasional skirt aside until his eyes lit up. "Now, this is perfect," he said, lifting up a silver lamé minidress I bought on a whim and hardly ever wore.

"Wait, it has matching mules." I dug through my Imelda Marcos–size shoe collection until I found the three-inch heels.

"Excellent." Fane oohed and aahed over the shoes, holding them up to the light for closer inspection. "Are they comfortable?"

"I've never worn them…" I paused dramatically, "…standing up, anyway."

Fane took a step back as his hand flew up to his heart. "My dear," he said in a false British accent, "you absolutely shock me."

I rolled my eyes. "Oh, c'mon, Fane. You know how those butches are."

"I know no such thing. Anyway, I didn't peg you for such a femme."

"I didn't say I was a femme."

Fane studied me. "Well, you're certainly not what I'd call a butch."

"I'm what's known as a hardtop convertible," I said, which made Fane laugh out loud. He balanced one silver shoe on the flat of his hand and asked, "Can you walk in these?"

"Sure, why? You want to borrow them?"

Again Fane feigned shock. "*I* don't want to wear them, Missy.

I want *you* to wear them..." this time Fane paused dramatically, "...to my funeral." And that's how I found out Fane had AIDS. He had left New York City for our small seaside town because he was looking for a quiet place to live. And a quiet place to die.

Fane and I became fast friends, or—you should pardon the expression—buddies. It was one of those friendships where you meet someone and immediately feel you've known them forever. Or maybe our friendship fast-forwarded so quickly and so deeply because Fane knew he didn't have a lot of time left (hence his favorite T-shirt, I'M LOOKING FOR MR. RIGHT AWAY). In any event, Fane and I started hanging out on a daily basis. I had recently joined the ranks of the gainfully unemployed, and Fane had taken early retirement. So what do two queers do with so much time on their hands? They rent movies, of course. Fane and I were both total film buffs; in fact, when asked, I told people I was using my unemployment to write a screenplay, thus our daily screenings could be written off as "research."

Perhaps Fane and I bonded so well because we had each spent most of our respective childhoods in darkened movie theaters eating stale popcorn and lusting after the stars we saw in front of us on the silver screen. We both agreed *Dr. Zhivago* was our all-time favorite movie; Fane had a major crush on Omar Sharif while I had it bad for Julie Christie. We'd both had our first sexual encounters while watching a movie: Fane got beat off by someone his father's age while watching *The Man Who Knew Too Much,* and I, believe it or not, had actually fallen for the popcorn trick while watching *Love Story.* For those of you who don't know about the popcorn trick (Fane didn't), it's when a guy cuts a hole in the bottom of his popcorn bucket and sticks his penis inside. Then when his date reaches in for a handful of corn, she comes up instead with a handful of dick.

"I'll have to try it sometime," Fane said after I explained it to him.

"Just don't try it with me," I said, like Fane ever would. We were sitting on his leather couch as we did every morning, having already downed an entire pot of coffee Fane had brewed with cinnamon sprinkled over the grounds. Today's film was *Hush...Hush, Sweet Charlotte.* Fane opened the bag of chocolates that lay between us—and was usually devoured before the opening credits stopped rolling—and started happily munching away. Fane made no apologies for his bad habits: He smoked like a chimney, ate chocolate by the pound ("I like it like I like my men: dark, hard, and bittersweet"), and drank Jack Daniel's with dinner every night, not enough to get drunk, just enough to take the edge off and help him fall asleep.

After the movie, we took our usual walk into town for a leisurely lunch and stroll by the water. Fane led the way to the breakwater and climbed carefully over the rocks. "Have I told you this is where I want my ashes scattered?" he asked, one hand held up to shield his eyes from the sun glinting off the sea.

"Only a million times, Fane."

"And have I told you I want you to sing, 'Where Have All the Faggots Gone?' at my memorial?"

"Yes, dear."

"And have I told you—"

"What a control queen I am?" I cut in to finish his sentence.

"And damn proud of it." Fane chuckled until his laugh turned into a cough, which turned into a wheeze, which turned into a gasp, which finally, after a scary moment, turned into steady, shallow breathing once again. After Fane caught his breath, we slowly made our way back to his place so he could nap and I could read a book or just watch him sleep. I loved being in Fane's house; he was an art collector, and the walls of his apartment were covered with paintings and drawings, all beautifully framed. My favorite piece of his didn't hang on the wall, though. It sat on Fane's mantle: a shiny green ceramic high-heeled shoe that had once belonged to his grandmother and was now used as a candy dish. "It's so I always remember the little Jewish princess inside me," Fane said, waiting to see if I'd take offense.

"It takes one to know one" was my politically incorrect reply.

I asked Fane about his grandmother, and he told me she was the only one in his family who had truly loved him, but she was long gone, as was his mother, both victims of breast cancer. And his father? "The old geezer isn't exactly proud of his *faygeleh* son," Fane said, lighting up a cigarette. "I haven't even seen him since my mother's funeral, and that was over fifteen years ago. My father's new wife, the Wicked Bitch of the Bronx," Fane exhaled with a vengeance, "is much younger than my old man, and she doesn't want her two sons to know about their fairy stepbrother. And my father, the world's most henpecked husband, can't stand up to her. *Ach,* the hell with them. It's their loss, right?" Fane stabbed his cigarette out in a Mr. Peanut ashtray, even though he hadn't even smoked half of it.

Clearly Fane was done with the conversation, but I wasn't. "Does your father know you're sick?" I asked.

"He doesn't even know I'm alive." Fane snorted, and then started choking on some phlegm. I didn't want to upset him further, so I dropped the subject and didn't bring it up again.

Besides being tired and having that awful cough, for a long time Fane showed no overt signs of having AIDS. We didn't talk about his illness much, but it was always with us. I remember one day in particular when we were having Sunday brunch with a trick of his named James and a friend of mine named Hal. James was all stuffed up with allergies, Hal had a splitting headache, and I was doubled over with menstrual cramps.

"And how are you?" someone finally thought to ask Fane.

He waved his hand as if to brush away the question. "Besides having a fatal disease," he shrugged, "I'm fine."

"AIDS is not a fatal disease," James reminded Fane between sneezes.

"Tell it to my T cells," Fane said. "All three of them."

"What about the new cocktails?" Hal asked.

"Cocktails, *shmocktails.* I tried them, remember?" We all did remember, because it would be hard to forget how sick Fane had gotten on the new drugs, which seemed to work for every other person on the planet except him. Almost every day as we sauntered through town, Fane and I would see someone who had been at death's door the month, the week, the day before, and now not only were they fine, they looked better than they had even before they'd gotten sick. Fane, on the other hand, was the exception who proved the rule. He had been much, much sicker on the drugs than off them, with stomachaches, cramps, and worst of all, nonstop diarrhea. His doctors made him try several different combinations, but nothing worked except going off meds completely. As soon as the drugs were out of Fane's system, he felt one hundred percent better—but only for a little while. Then his downhill slide began.

A few months before he died, Fane started giving away his clothes. Always on the thin side, he now made Kate Moss look fat as Divine. "Here, take this." He handed me a gorgeous cashmere cardigan the color of cranberry juice right after we'd finished watching Susan Hayward in (and I kid you not) *I Want to Live!*

"Too big?" I asked, holding the sweater up to my shoulders.

"No," Fane answered. "It clashes with my lesions."

And so it began. First Fane went blind (very *Wait Until Dark*), and then he went bald (very *King and I*). Despite all the outward signs, I was taking a Scarlett O'Hara approach to the whole thing. "I'll think about it tomorrow," I told my reflection in the bathroom mirror every morning before I went off to Fane's. I was still holding on to my denial, even when Fane's ex-lover Rudy moved from New Jersey to live with him so he wouldn't have to go to a hospice. I was hurt that Fane hadn't asked me to be his roommate, and when I told him so he just smiled and started singing that old Dinah Shore hit, "It's So Nice to Have a Man Around the House."

"But Fane," I broke in mid chorus. "I'm unemployed. How can Rudy take that much time off work?"

Fane's reply shocked me. "Missy, dear," he said, "It's not going to be that much time."

Still, I ignored the writing on the wall and held my chins and my hopes up, but both were dashed one afternoon when out of the blue Fane uttered three little words: "Call my father."

"Your father?" I couldn't have been more surprised if Fane had asked me to call the man on the moon.

"I want to see him—well, not *see* him," he said, reminding us both he was blind. "It would be nice if he came before I died."

"Okay." I picked up the receiver and dialed. Fane immediately closed his eyes and fell asleep, or pretended to. Either way, I was on my own.

"Mr. Oppenheimer?" I asked, even though I knew it was

Fane's father. It had to be; his voice sounded just like his son's. "I'm a friend of Fane's, and I'm calling because..."

"Who is it, Stanley?" I could hear Mr. Oppenheimer's wife yelling in the background. "Just hang up if it's a solicitor. Don't tell them anything..."

"Who is this?" Fane's father asked.

"My name is Missy, and Fane asked me to call you because he's sick."

"How sick?" Mr. Oppenheimer's voice dropped to a whisper, like a kid who didn't want his mother to know he was on the phone.

"Sick enough for him to ask me to call you," I said, not knowing any other way to make my point. "He'd like you to come."

"When?"

"As soon as you can."

"I'm really busy at the office right now," Mr. Oppenheimer said a little too quickly. "Maybe I'll make it out there in a few weeks."

"He may not have a few weeks," I said, choking on the words I had resisted saying for so long. "Look, here's the number: 555-0542. Why don't you call when you can fit your only offspring into your busy schedule." Without waiting for an answer, I hung up.

Fane immediately opened his eyes. "Is he coming?"

I relayed our conversation.

"Pussywhipped prick," he muttered before closing his eyes again.

Mr. Oppenheimer didn't call back that week, and I was afraid we were running out of time. Everyone else came to visit: Fane's friends from New York, the dean of the college where he had taught, even his ex-wife, Prudence. Rudy and I didn't let anyone stay too long, as even a half-hour visit tired Fane out. Ever the gracious host, he would never admit his guests were a drain. He just held court from the hospital bed we had dragged into the living room, barking orders to whomever was closest at hand. "Get Martin a pillow for his chair; he has a bad back. Bring Bethany a Pepsi; she likes it straight up, no ice." Fane needed to show all of us he was still in command, and I, for one, needed to believe it was so. For as long as I possibly could.

Fane was getting weaker by the day, so I called his father again. "Look, he's your son," I said to Mr. Oppenheimer, as if I were telling him something he didn't already know. "Can't you honor your own son's dying wish by coming to see him?" I even played the Jewish trump card: guilt. "Mr. Oppenheimer," I said, "how are you going to feel if you never see Fane again? Are you really going to be able to live with that?"

"He's the one who should have thought of that a long time ago," Fane's father said, "before he started living a ho-mo-sex-u-al lifestyle." Mr. Oppenheimer stretched out the word to make sure I knew what it meant. "This is all Fane's fault. He made his bed, and now he's lying in it."

No, Daddy Dearest, I wanted to say. *I made his bed, and now he's dying in it.* But I doubted Mr. Oppenheimer would appreciate gallows humor at this point, so I just hung up and went in to tell Fane what had happened. But when I saw, despite everything, the look of hope on his face, I just couldn't do it. "I got a busy signal," I lied, not having the heart, or perhaps the guts, to tell Fane what his father had said. "I'll try again later," I added, but I doubt Fane believed my ruse.

It didn't much matter anyway, because the next day Fane took a turn for the worse, and the end really began. First he stopped eating, except for the bits of chocolate I'd hold up to his mouth for him to lick like a lollipop. Then he stopped smoking, which was really distressing to me. Fane and I had fought bitterly about his cigarettes; I never let him smoke in my house, so even when he was well enough to go out, he hardly ever came over. When he first became bedridden, I had to hide his matches so he wouldn't fall asleep with a lit cigarette and burn down the house. Now he was too weak to smoke, yet his lips pursed and his cheeks sucked in as if he were inhaling, even in his sleep. And half the time it was hard to tell whether Fane was asleep or awake, because mostly what he did was lie motionless in bed with his eyes closed. Once, when I was sitting by his side, he asked me if I was waiting for the D train, and I knew he wasn't asleep or awake: He was in another world, waiting for the subway in the Bronx. I tried not to show him how panicked I was. "Fane," I said calmly. "You're not in New York.

You're on the Cape in your apartment." But he didn't believe me, and besides, I realized that wherever he thought he was had to be a whole lot better than where he actually was, so I joined him there. "God, Fane," I said, "do you think this train will ever come?"

"Whenever it'll come, it'll come. I'm not in such a big hurry to get where I'm going," was his somber, startling reply.

Sometimes, just for old times' sake, I'd put a movie into the VCR so Fane could at least listen to the soundtrack, but he wasn't really interested anymore. Nor was he much for conversation, so mostly I just sat with him and massaged his dry skin with almond-scented moisture cream. "You have such soft hands," I said to Fane after rubbing them a while.

"You have such a soft heart," he replied. It was the last thing he ever said to me, because the next morning he lost the ability to speak.

Rudy and I became very protective of Fane after that. We decided his days of entertaining were over. People still dropped by constantly, bringing bags of food Fane could no longer eat, and though they would never admit it, some of Fane's friends seemed relieved when I told them he no longer had the strength for company. They stayed around anyway, and soon Fane's kitchen became the hottest new hangout in town.

"Did Fane ever tell you about the time he baked a batch of pot brownies for the faculty Christmas party?" one of his colleagues asked the crowd sitting around Fane's kitchen table.

"I think that was the year he dressed up as a nun," a former boyfriend added.

"What was his name, Our Mother of the Perpetual Hard-on?" a recent trick asked.

"He was always the life of the party," another colleague remarked.

"Was?" I hissed through clenched teeth. "*Was?* He isn't dead yet, you know."

"Sheesh, what's with her?" Everybody looked at me as if I had gone mad, which I had.

"I think all of you better clear out," I said, and I sure didn't have to ask them twice. And if they thought I was nothing but a big party pooper, who cared? I just couldn't stand sitting around Fane's kitchen table, telling stories about him and laughing, when he lay upstairs in the living room dying, so near, and yet so very far.

The last night of Fane's life, Rudy and I were downstairs in the kitchen eating a late supper of cold Kentucky Fried Chicken someone had dropped off earlier. It was a crisp August night, with just the right amount of chill in the air, and the sky was covered with stars.

"Listen to the wind." Rudy looked up from the drumstick he was gnawing on and cocked his head to the side. "It just came up out of nowhere. Weird. It sounds like a ghost."

"It's spooky," I agreed, mid chomp. Then we looked at each other in horror, realizing at the same time it wasn't the wind at all. It was Fane. We dashed up to the living room and there was Fane, sitting up in bed for the first time in over a month. His eyes were wide with terror, and sounds were coming out of his mouth I had never heard from a human being before.

"Fane, it's Rudy. I'm here, baby. Lie down." Rudy tried to lower Fane back onto the bed, but he was too agitated to relax.

"I'll call the nurse." I ran for the phone and speed-dialed hospice. After I explained to the nurse what was going on, she explained to me what was going on: "Fane's body and spirit are battling it out now," she said in a voice filled with kindness. "There's nothing you can do but witness his struggle."

"Isn't there anything to make him more comfortable?" I asked.

"You have morphine there, right? Give him eight drops under the tongue now, and eight more in half an hour. That should calm him down."

I told Rudy what to do, and together we got the drugs into Fane, but they didn't do any good. He continued to moan and groan and pant and sweat like he was about to give birth or come or both. *Well, what did you expect?* I asked myself as I ran to get a cold washcloth to soothe his sweaty head. *Did you really think Fane would look at you, take one last breath, and fade away like Margaret O'Brien playing Beth in* Little Women? Fane was not ready to die and did not want to die. And though we didn't want him to go either, we made ourselves tell him it was time to let go.

"C'mon, Fane," Rudy said. "You don't have to put up a fight anymore. We know how brave you are. You can go."

"It's okay, Fane," I tried to sound like I believed it. "We'll be all right without you. Just relax and give in to it. Let go."

"No!" Fane roared once, between gasps for breath. Rudy and I could barely look at each other; we were so ashamed of betraying Fane like that. But what else could we do? Nothing except wait for Rudy's watch to beep, telling us it was time to give Fane morphine again. I filled the eyedropper, and Rudy brought it up to Fane's mouth. Another fifteen minutes went by before Fane's breathing slowed and he lay back down. I thought he had stopped breathing altogether, but after about half a minute he drew in another raspy breath: the death rattle. Rudy and I kept talking to Fane, since we had both been told that hearing was the last sense to go. Another twenty minutes went by, and then Fane took in one final breath, exhaled noisily through his open mouth, and was still.

"He's gone," Rudy said. "Bye, Fane."

"Bye, Fane," I echoed, and then out of nowhere I began to chant ancient Hebrew words I thought I had forgotten long ago. *"Sh'ma, Yisroel. Adonoy Elohanu. Adonoy Echad."* Rudy looked at me, surprised: We both knew Fane hadn't set foot inside a synagogue in over thirty years, since his *bar mitzvah*. I shrugged. "Just in case," I said. "And besides, it couldn't hurt."

The next day there was lots to do. We dressed Fane in his NOBODY KNOWS I'M A FAIRY T-shirt so the undertaker could take him away. We filled out endless forms, got rid of tons of meds, and called hundreds of people, including Fane's father. "Don't you think he'd want to know?" I asked Rudy.

"Whatever," he said with a shrug. And I suppose he was right: Fane's father didn't want to know from his son when he was alive; why should he care he was dead? But I knew Fane would want me to make the call, so I picked up the phone. This time a female voice answered.

"Is Mr. Oppenheimer there?" I asked.

"Who's calling please?"

"It's Missy. I'm a friend of Fane's."

"Yes?"

"He's dead."

"Oh, my God! Stanley! Stanley!" Fane's stepmother was immediately hysterical. "Stanley, come to the phone right now! Stanley!"

"What's the matter, Phyllis?" I heard Mr. Oppenheimer say as he picked up the phone. "Who is this?"

"It's Missy. Fane's dead." I have to admit, I did get a little perverse sense of satisfaction at being the one to deliver the news.

"Fane? *Vey iss mir, Gottinyu,* my boy. My son."

Sure, I thought. Now that Fane's dead, Mr. Oppenheimer could once more claim him as his own. "When did he die? Last night? Why did you wait so long to call us? Why didn't you tell me he was so sick?"

Take three guesses, I wanted to say, but even I could not be that cruel. "It happened very fast," I said, even though last night had been the longest twelve hours of my life. "I'll let you know about the funeral."

We didn't really have a funeral for Fane. Rudy waited around until his ashes arrived, and then we walked out to the breakwater and scattered them over the sea. Two weeks later we did have a memorial, and, as Fane had hoped, it was *the* social event of the season. The place was packed to the gills with boys: boys in dog collars and leather chaps; boys in tight muscle tees with tattoos strewn across their forearms; boys in faded jeans and baseball caps, dark sunglasses hiding their red-rimmed eyes. It was Fag Hag Heaven, and I played it to the hilt in my silver lamé.

"Did Fane pick out your outfit?" more than one boy asked.

"But of course." I pivoted on my stilettos and walked away so they could admire the way the shoes hit my heels with sensational slaps. The overall mood was strangely festive, like it was all one big party, which it would have been if the guest of honor had graced us with his presence. But he did not, despite his ex-wife's insistence that she could feel his spirit hovering by her side.

When everyone was done shmoozing and cruising, the formalities began. Rudy, back from New Jersey for the occasion, played Master of Ceremonies. He started things off by reading us a letter he had written to Fane, telling him how much he loved him, and by the time he was done there wasn't a dry eye in the house. Then James, who had shaved his head in mourning, took the stage and told us we must not remain silent; rather it was our responsibility, whenever a gay man died, to make a really loud noise. Then he took a deep breath and let out a wail that made my blood run cold. Fane's ex-wife was next. Though they married as teenagers and were only together for a few years, she said Fane was the only man she had ever really loved.

"Oh, get a life," Rudy murmured. I poked him in the ribs and told him to keep quiet. Then it was open season on Fane. His students told us what a wonderful teacher he had been, his colleagues told us what a wonderful scholar he had been, his boyfriends told us what a wonderful lover he had been. Then I stepped up to the podium.

"I have a letter to read," I unfolded a piece of paper, "from Fane's father." There was an audible, collective gasp from Fane's mourners, and then a loud shushing as everyone told everyone else to keep still.

"Dear Missy," I began. "Thank you for telling me about Fane's death and for inviting me to his memorial. Fane and I did not have an easy relationship, as you know; we disagreed about many, many things. Still, he was my son, and I did love him in my own way. I am not a bad man, despite what you may think. Perhaps, if anything, I was a bad father. In any event, I want to thank you and all the people who took care of Fane for me. I'm sure it wasn't easy. Fane was not an easy person. But I'm grateful he did not die alone. Sincerely, Mr. Stanley E. Oppenheimer (Fane's father)."

"Heavy," someone muttered from the front row.

"What an asshole," someone else mumbled. Then everyone was talking at once, and Rudy had to scream into the microphone that we were serving light refreshments back at Fane's apartment and everyone was invited.

It was strange being back at Fane's house; I hadn't been there since the day after he died. The hospital bed was gone, and Rudy had tagged all the artwork according to the will Fane had left behind. People tried not to seem too excited as they scanned Fane's paintings to see which ones they had inherited, but every once in a while I'd hear an enthusiastic "All right!" burst through the air. There was nothing on the wall with my name on it, but then I had a hunch, and sure enough, there on the mantle was the green ceramic shoe Fane's grandmother had given him, which, according to the pink Post-it on its heel, now belonged to me. I took it home, filled it with candy, and placed it on my kitchen table. Every day I take a few minutes to look at it and remember the good news: Fane no longer has AIDS. And then I pop a piece of chocolate into my mouth: so dark, so hard, so bittersweet.

(for Victor Fane D'Lugin, 1945–1996)

Homo Alone

The phone rang just as Deborah deposited a half-dollar–size plop of creme rinse on top of her head. "Oh, shit." She stepped out of the shower without bothering to turn off the water and padded into the kitchen on sopping wet feet. "Hello?"

"Is Emily Tannenbaum there?"

"No, she isn't."

"Is Mr. Tannenbaum there?"

"There is no Mr. Tannenbaum," Deborah snapped. "Who is this?"

"This is Gretchen, calling from Sears about the vacuum cleaner."

"You can talk to me about the vacuum cleaner."

"Oh, are you Emily's mother?"

Deborah snorted. "No, I'm her lover."

The woman from Sears paused. "Excuse me?"

"I said I'm her lover. I know all about the vacuum cleaner."

The woman paused again. "I'm afraid I don't understand. Is Emily Tannenbaum a man or a woman?"

This time Deborah let a few seconds go by before she responded. "*Emily* Tannenbaum? Lady, what do you think?"

"I think I'll call back another time."

"Fine." Deborah slammed down the phone and returned to the shower. *Stupid bitch,* she thought as she worked the creme rinse through her hair. The last person she wanted to think about this morning was Emily—Emily, who was her lover, the key word here being *was.* Was, as in past tense. As in was not any longer. As in what was wrong with Emily anyway? Deborah couldn't believe that one day out of nowhere, two weeks before graduation, Emily had decided she was bisexual and needed to "explore her options." *Give me a break,* Deborah thought, scrubbing her scalp a little more vigorously than necessary. "That's what you get for dating a Smithie," she chastised herself out loud. When she had started going out with Emily, Deborah had never even heard the term LUG: Lesbian Until Graduation. And she wished she had never heard of it now. *Christ, instead of diplomas, Smith College should just give out diaphragms,* she thought, bowing her head to give her hair one last good rinse. And of all people, Emily, the Big Dyke on Campus. If a solicitor called and asked Emily if Mr. Tannenbaum was home, she would say, "Sure, but you can't speak to him."

"Why not?" Gretchen from Sears would ask.

"Because we chopped him up into teeny tiny pieces and put him in the freezer," Emily would answer before hanging up the phone.

Those were exactly the kind of girls you had to watch out for, Deborah reminded herself. The ones that went from one extreme to the other. First they shaved their heads, pierced their nipples, and changed their names to Glenda Goddess-Worshiper or Diana Diesel-Dyke. Then they turned around and married a nice Jewish doctor, had two-point-five kids, and bought a station wagon. Which was exactly what Emily was doing. Deborah had been absolutely furious when she found out. *She* had proposed to Emily long before Allen was even in the picture. "That's very sweet," Emily had said when Deborah got down on one knee. "But I'm way too young to make a commitment." *Emily must have aged very quickly in the last six months,* Deborah thought as she slipped on her robe and went back into the kitchen for a second cup of coffee. Either that or she'd gotten herself knocked up, a possibility Deborah didn't even want to consider, as that would prove beyond a shadow of a doubt that the woman who wouldn't let Deborah penetrate her with fingers, tongue, or sex toy ("That's so patriarchal") had let Allen Plotnick pulverize her pussy with his penis. And chances were high that Emily was preggo, because Deborah's ex didn't even know Allen for three months before a big old schlocky-looking diamond ring appeared on her finger. She and Deborah, on the other hand, had gone out for over two years. "Two years I wasted on that has-bian," Deborah told the Xena poster on the wall. "And she wouldn't even move in with me."

Deborah had begged Emily to give up her tiny dorm room and move into her two-bedroom apartment, but Emily wouldn't budge, afraid her parents would find out. "You know what Daddy says," Emily told Deborah. "No permission, no tuition." And she had giggled, even though Deborah didn't find it the least bit funny.

The closest Emily had come to making a commitment was buying Deborah the vacuum cleaner. "If we're still together when I graduate, I'll move in," she'd said. "Meanwhile, you'll have Esther to keep you company." Yes, Emily had named the vacuum cleaner Esther and bought Deborah one of those stupid coverings to go over the vacuum that made it look like a three-foot doll standing in the corner. Deborah thought it was the ugliest thing she had ever seen. It had a mop of orange yarn hair tied in two pigtails, buttons for eyes, a red stitched smile, and a blue gingham dress. Of course Emily had doctored Esther up a little by draping a T-shirt over her that said I'D RATHER BE MUFF DIVING and hanging a three-inch labyris around her neck, the same labyris Emily had worn, once upon a time when she was busy smashing the patriarchy instead of fucking it. Deborah stared at Esther ruefully, wondering what Gretchen the Sears lady would think about that.

Deborah put half an English muffin in the toaster oven and sighed. She knew it was going to be a bad day: She hadn't even been awake for an hour and already she had spent way too much time thinking about Emily. But Deborah didn't know just how bad the day was going to be until the phone rang again and she picked it up.

"Hi, Debbie."

There were only a handful of people on the planet who still insisted upon calling her that, none of whom she wanted to speak to at the moment.

"Hi, Ma. How are you?"

"Fine, fine. Listen, Debbie, I need to know if you're coming for Thanksgiving or not."

Oh, God, Thanksgiving. Deborah had forgotten all about it. "Can I let you know next week?"

"No, I need to know now so I can plan."

"What's there to plan?" Deborah was stalling for time. "It's not like I eat a lot, and I can bring my own folding chair."

"Debbie." Deborah could practically hear her mother frown. "Do you have other plans?"

"No, but..."

"Great, we'll see you around four o'clock. Come earlier if you want, and be careful how you drive. There'll be lots of traffic."

"I know how to drive, Ma." Deborah tried to remind her mother that, believe it or not, she actually was an adult, as opposed to a four-year-old who had somehow managed to get her driver's license. But Mrs. Lewis had already hung up.

"Oh, great." Deborah heard the bell on the toaster oven ring, but she had completely lost her appetite. "I don't want to go home for the holidays, Lucy." Again Deborah addressed the poster on the wall. Deborah had been doing a lot of mother work in therapy lately, and when her therapist asked her who her ideal mother would be, she hadn't hesitated. "Lucy Lawless."

"As Xena or herself?" her therapist had asked.

"Both," Deborah had answered. And after the session she had run out and bought herself the poster, which she talked to more frequently than she thought healthy, but what the hell. "So, what do you think, Xena, should I go home for the holidays or what?"

Xena, of course, didn't reply, but Deborah remembered what Emily had to say when she asked her the same question last spring after Mrs. Lewis invited Deborah home for Passover. Emily stood up from the table, her mouth full of French toast, and put her hands on the back of Deborah's shoulders. "March," she said, steering her across the apartment.

"What do you see in here?" she asked, making Deborah halt in the bedroom.

Deborah looked around. "My bed, my dresser, a picture of you and me at Gay Pride, my laundry basket..."

"And what do you see in here?" Emily turned Deborah around so she was facing the living room.

"My TV, my couch, your leather jacket, your Birkenstocks, your book bag..."

"And what about in here?" Emily dragged Deborah back into the kitchen. "The point is," Emily said, after they had toured the entire apartment, "*this* is your home. I just can't stand it when dykes start in with this 'home for the holidays' crap, like the homes we've created for ourselves don't really count. Now, if you want to talk about going to your *parents' house* for the holidays, I'd be happy to discuss it with you."

"What about going homo for the holidays?" Deborah suggested.

"What about going homo right now?" Emily asked, then answered her own question by giving Deborah a kiss that tasted of maple syrup and lasted the rest of the afternoon.

They had gone to Deborah's parents' house for Passover, and it had been quite the experience. Deborah's brother David had been there with his wife and two children. He had also brought along their nanny, and Deborah could tell her parents were very proud of themselves for being liberal enough to actually allow a person of color to sit beside them in their own dining room. Deborah's father had made a great show of introducing her to everybody: "This is Vonda," he said, putting his hand on her shoulder and leading her around. During the *seder,* he had addressed all his explanations to her. "We call this *matzo,* Vonda," he said, breaking a piece in two and offering her the bigger half. "When we had to flee the evil pharaoh in Egypt, there wasn't time to wait for the bread to rise." Mr. Lewis spoke as if he had actually been there. "So we baked the dough....

"Daniel." Vonda spoke sharply. "Leave your brother alone."

"He started it." The two little boys were wrestling over a Game Boy, which wasn't supposed to be at the table.

"Michael, give me that." Vonda held out her hand, and Michael pushed his chair back. But before he could climb down from it, Daniel shoved him, and he lost his balance, hitting his head on a corner of the table.

"Ow! Ow!" Michael wailed into Vonda's arms.

"It's okay, Michael," David soothed him from across the table. "You're okay. Nothing happened, big boy. You're fine. That didn't hurt."

"Sure," Deborah whispered to Emily. "Tell the kid how he

feels. Deny his reality. Teach him big boys don't cry. Way to go, brother."

When everything had calmed down, they continued the *seder*, reading responsively from the ancient Maxwell House *Haggadah* Deborah's father still insisted upon using. Deborah wasn't sure if she believed in God or not, but if She did exist, She sure had an ironic sense of humor, because who got to read aloud the part about slavery? Why, Vonda, of course.

"Once we were slaves," Vonda looked around the room, fixing each family member with her eyes, "but now we are free." Deborah didn't dare look at Emily, who was kicking her under the table, afraid she would burst out laughing, which would not have gone over well at all. Since Emily was sitting next to Vonda, she read next, and when she changed the word "Forefathers" to "Ancestors," all hell broke loose.

No wonder Deborah's mother hadn't asked if Emily was coming to this year's *seder* or not, even though Deborah had yet to tell her Emily was no longer part of her life. Oh, Mrs. Lewis would have tried to sound sympathetic upon hearing the news, all right. Deborah could just hear her mother say, "Oh, honey, I'm so sorry," in a tone of voice that made it clear she wasn't sorry at all. Then she'd add something philosophical, like, "Don't worry, Debbie. There are plenty of fish in the sea." And again Deborah would know her mother meant she hoped Deborah would try some fish of the male persuasion. Going home alone while being homo alone was not a great idea, but what could Deborah do, dial Rent-a-Dyke? *Maybe I'll fall in love between now and November 24th,* Deborah thought, finally retrieving her ice-cold breakfast from the toaster oven. *Yeah, right. And maybe Esther the vacuum cleaner will get up and dance.*

✤

Thanksgiving Day was bright and sunny, one of those cold, crisp, snappy days that makes you glad to be alive. Deborah—who had been hoping for a tornado, hurricane, freak snowstorm, or any kind of disaster that would make driving impossible—was out of luck. She alternated blasting the Spice Girls and the Rude Girls on her tape deck as she drove two hours west to the Boston suburb her parents called home. *C'mon now,* she said to herself as she turned the corner of her old block. *It won't be so bad. They're your parents. They love you. It might even be kind of fun.* "Oh, sure, easy for you to say," Deborah had barked at her therapist, who had uttered those same words to her a few weeks ago. Her therapist had tried to get her to think positively, but she had reminded the woman that her name was Deborah, not Pollyanna. Then her therapist changed tactics and asked her what she could bring along with her so she would be able to hold on to herself and not feel so invisible out there all alone in Heterosexual Land. Did she have a something special she could keep in her pocket, like a crystal, a gemstone, a rock?

"How about my Xena poster?" Deborah mused aloud. "With a six-foot Amazon plastered on my mother's kitchen wall, I'd feel a hundred times better." Her therapist hadn't said anything, but bless her heart, she had found Deborah a miniature chakram, the embroidery hoop–shaped weapon Xena used to fight the enemy wherever she encountered it. Deborah had been very moved by this present and attached it to her key ring, which she now attached to her belt loop as she got out of the car.

"Well, here goes nothing." Deborah started up the driveway, but before she could take a deep breath to steady herself, the front door flew open.

"Debbie's here," her mother called into the bowels of the house. "Come in, sweetheart, I was getting worried about you. I bet there was lots of traffic."

"Ma, it's only ten after four."

"Maybe you should stay over, Debbie. Why should you drive home in the dark? Give me your coat. What did you do to your hair? I thought you said you were growing it out. You came by yourself this year?" Mrs. Lewis wasn't even remotely successful at hiding the delight in her voice. "Everyone, Debbie's here," Mrs. Lewis announced again as Deborah unsnapped her leather jacket.

She drifted into the kitchen behind her mother, ambivalent as always about the strict gender division of the party: girls in the kitchen preparing the food, boys in the living room watching the game. On the one hand, she could almost get into bonding with the female contingent of her family; on the other hand, she hated that the women had no qualms about serving their menfolk hand and foot. In fact, right on cue, Mrs. Lewis handed Deborah a tray of Ritz crackers covered with Velveeta cheese. "Why don't you take these inside, dear, and say hello to your father?"

"Debbie!" Mr. Lewis half rose out of his chair to greet his daughter but then got distracted by some movement on the wide-screen TV. "C'mon, you idiot, run with the ball. Run! *Ach,* bunch of losers." He took the tray from Deborah and set it down on the coffee table. "How are you, sweetheart? Wait a minute, he dropped the ball? He *dropped* it?" Deborah's father dropped himself back down into his seat, shaking his head in disbelief.

"I'm fine, Dad," Deborah answered her father, even though she knew he couldn't hear her. No one in the room acknowledged her presence: not her brother David, not her nephews Michael and Daniel, not her uncle Marvin, and not her cousin Peter. Deborah went back into the kitchen, because she didn't know what else to do. Her mother handed her a potato peeler and a bag of lettuce to wash.

"Debbie will make the salad. She always makes such good salads. She has a knack for it." Mrs. Lewis started emptying the contents of the refrigerator's vegetable bin onto the kitchen counter. "Aren't these tomatoes gorgeous? And look at the size of this green pepper—isn't that something? Don't forget to peel the cucumbers, Debbie. You know your father hates the rind."

"How are you, darling?" Deborah's Aunt Rona looked up from the Stove Top stuffing mix she was pouring into a microwavable casserole dish. "What are you doing with yourself these days?"

"Well, I just started a new project at work that's really interesting. I'm in charge of..."

"Oh, my God, the rolls!" Aunt Rona grabbed a pair of pot holders and yanked open the oven door. A dark cloud of smoke billowed out. "Quick, quick, get me something to put these on. And somebody open the door before the smoke alarm goes off."

"I'll do it." Sharon, Deborah's sister-in-law, opened the back door and started fanning the smoke in her direction.

"Where's Vonda?" Deborah asked her, instead of saying hello.

"Vonda? Oh, we got rid of her months ago. I never liked that girl's attitude. We've had the worst luck finding someone who isn't afraid of a little hard work. Can you believe we've been through three or four since the summer, and a new one starts Monday? I hope to God she works out. I can't take this anymore. Can I close the door yet?" Sharon yelled into the room.

"Close it, close it. I'm freezing already." Deborah's mother spooned some lumpy gravy over the turkey, which was sitting in a bathtub-size aluminum foil roasting pan on top of the stove. "Debbie, I'll finish the salad. Why don't you go inside and set the table? Everything's over there." She pointed with her chin just in case Deborah happened to miss the piles of plates, cups, saucers, and salad bowls stacked two feet high on the kitchen table. Deborah grabbed some dishes, glad for the chance to escape into the dining room and have a minute or two alone. But to her amazement, when she stepped into the dining room, she found she wasn't alone at all.

"Aunt Sadie?" Deborah gasped. She dropped the plates on the table and went over to a woman sitting by the window in a wheelchair. "Aunt Sadie, how are you?" Deborah knelt down and stared into Aunt Sadie's eyes, which were as empty as the brand new gravy boat Sharon had just placed on the dining room table. Deborah stayed where she was for a minute before she straightened up and went back into the kitchen. "Ma," she tried to keep her voice steady. "Why is Aunt Sadie sitting in the dining room all by herself?"

"Why? You want to know why?" Mrs. Lewis sighed. "The nursing home called and begged me to take her, so what could I do? She was the only one on her floor who had no place to go, and the nurses there, they deserve a day off once in a while—they have families too."

"Why is she sitting all by herself in the dining room?" Deborah repeated her question, then moved out of the way so Aunt Rona could get a stick of butter out of the refrigerator. "Why don't you bring her in here with us?"

"Debbie, it's too crowded in here, she'd only be in the way; we're tripping over each other as it is. Besides, she likes sitting by the window. She always has, ever since I was a little girl."

"But Ma—"

"Debbie, please, we'll all be in there before you know it, as soon as the game is over." Mrs. Lewis looked toward the living room, and, as if on cue, a rousing cheer erupted from that direction. "Sharon, honey, can you taste this and tell me if it needs more salt?"

Deborah knew she had been dismissed, so she returned to the dining room, but instead of setting the table, she knelt down in front of her Great Aunt Sadie again and took her hand.

"I'm really, really happy to see you, Aunt Sadie. I'm sorry it's been such a long time." How long had it been? Deborah couldn't remember the last time she had visited the nursing home. *Oh, great,* she thought. *Not only am I lousy daughter, I'm a lousy great niece too.* "I had no idea your health had gotten so bad," she said in a shaky voice. Out of nowhere tears filled her eyes. "You must be really lonely. Does my mother or Aunt Rona ever come visit you?" Aunt Sadie continued to stare out the window with dull, lifeless eyes.

"Listen, Aunt Sadie, everyone's going to be in here soon, and it's going to be a total zoo. So do you mind if I just sit a minute with you?" Deborah straightened up and pulled a dining room chair next to her great aunt. They sat in silence for a few minutes, and Deborah felt a tentative peacefulness, tinged with unbearable sadness. "You know, we never really got a chance to know each other," Deborah said to her great aunt. "I wish you could tell me what your childhood was like, what my grandparents were like, what my mother and Aunt Rona were like when they were little girls." Aunt Sadie didn't move or even blink. "Well, I can tell you about me, Aunt Sadie, even if you can't tell me about you. Okay?" Since Aunt Sadie didn't nod, Deborah nodded for her and began.

"First of all," Deborah gripped the chakram hanging from her belt loop and took the plunge. "First of all, I'm a lesbian, Aunt Sadie. Did anyone ever tell you that? Your very own great niece is a big old boot-stomping, lavender-wearing, rainbow flag–carrying diesel dyke." Just saying the words out loud in her parents' house was terrifying, yet having said them, Deborah found herself sitting up straighter in her chair. "See these hands, Aunt Sadie?" She lifted her palms and flexed her fingers. "These hands have given *mucho* pleasure to a lot of women. Don't be shocked. I don't mean hundreds or anything. Let's just say more than a few." She lowered her hands and placed them on Aunt Sadie's arm. Her great aunt didn't flinch or pull away. "I was really in love with this one woman, Aunt Sadie. Her name is Emily. I'm sorry you never got to meet her. We're not together anymore. She's getting married, to a man, and I think she's even having a baby. Can you believe it? I can't believe it. I really, really miss her." The tears that had been simmering in Deborah's eyes spilled onto her cheeks. She brushed them away with the back of her hand, sighed, and sat back in her chair.

"Debbie, is the table done? We're almost ready." Mrs. Lewis came into the dining room and started dispensing plates and glasses to each place setting. "Turn her around, would you?" She opened the top drawer of the sideboard with a yank and started counting out silverware. "You'll sit over there next to her, okay, Debbie? She needs help cutting her food."

"They lost, the bums." Mr. Lewis came into the dining room the minute the table was set. "Need any help in here, Sylvia?"

"Your father." Deborah's mother shook her head, smiling. "His timing has always been perfect."

"Like everything else about me, right, baby?" He put his arm around his wife's ample waist. "When do we eat?"

Soon they were all sitting around the table: David and Sharon at one end, with Michael and Daniel between them; Cousin Peter across from David, flanked by his parents, Aunt Rona and Uncle Marvin; Deborah with Aunt Sadie on one side of her and her mother across from her; and of course the head of the table was claimed by Mr. Lewis, who stood over the turkey, a huge carving knife in his hand.

"All righty," Mr. Lewis sang out, lifting the knife like he was a conductor and it was a baton. "Who wants what?"

"I'll take a wing," David spoke first.

"Dark meat for me," said Peter.

"We want light meat, right, Debbie?" Mrs. Lewis winked at her daughter. "We don't want to lose our girlish figures."

"What about giving thanks?" Deborah tried to inject the original meaning of the feast into the holiday. "Shouldn't we say grace?"

"Oh, right, Grace. Hey, Grace," Mr. Lewis called over his shoulder. "Let's eat."

Soon the conversation consisted entirely of *Please pass the this* and *I'd like some more of that,* punctuated by the clanking of serving spoons against platters. "Everything is so delicious," Aunt Rona mumbled with her mouth full, "if I do say so myself."

"Michael, watch it," Sharon pointed to her son's soda glass. "Daniel, move that away from the edge of the table, please."

"I'll do it," Michael shouted, knocking the glass over in his enthusiasm.

"I didn't do it," Daniel announced, reaching over the spill for more mashed potatoes.

"Finish what's on your plate first. I told you he wasn't big enough for a glass," David scowled at Sharon. "Where's his plastic cup?"

"I am so big enough," Michael yelled.

"You are not," Daniel yelled back.

"Boys." Sharon got up from the table to get some paper towels.

"Sit, sit. I'll take care of it." Mrs. Lewis sprang up, as did Aunt Rona. "Sylvia," she said, "you sit, you've been working like a dog all day. Debbie, darling, get up and get your mother some paper towels. They're in the kitchen."

Why can't David go? Deborah wanted to whine. *It was his kid who spilled the soda, not mine.* But she knew if she said the words out loud, she'd sound as immature as Michael and Daniel, who were only three and four years old.

Soon everyone was stuffed, and a lull descended upon the room. The men sat back and loosened their belts while the women bustled about, clearing off the table. All the women except Aunt Sadie, who sat with a gob of yam on her chin, and

Deborah, who refused to lift another finger until one of her male relatives got up to help.

"Who wants coffee?" Mrs. Lewis asked, her index finger poised to count.

"How about some pumpkin pie?" Aunt Rona placed a pie on the table and started cutting slices.

"Small ones for the boys," Sharon said, setting out a pitcher of milk and a box of Sweet'N Low.

"I want a big piece, Aunt Rona," Michael yelled.

"Me too." Daniel chimed in. "Make mine bigger than Michael's."

"Boys." Deborah could see Sharon was ready to crack. "Let's take your pie inside. I'll put Raffi on the stereo for you."

"Yay!" Michael and Daniel raced out after their mother. Soon the sounds of "The Wheels on the Bus" and "Baa Baa Black Sheep" could be heard faintly over the rumbling dishwasher.

"Ah, peace and quiet," David sighed.

"They're such good boys," Mrs. Lewis said.

"Angels, absolute angels," Aunt Rona threw her own son a look. "What I wouldn't give to have two gorgeous grandsons like that." She cut a sliver of pie and popped it into her mouth. "If you eat it with your fingers, it doesn't count, right, Debbie?" Deborah didn't bother to reply.

Despite the coffee, everyone sank into the traditional post-turkey stupor. Even Deborah's mother and aunt let the dessert dishes linger on the table as the men talked about cars and computers and the women picked at the food. Sharon came back in and snuck a bite of pie from David's plate before sinking into her chair. No sooner had she sat down than the boys came tearing into the room again.

"Daddy, can I sit on your lap?" Michael started to climb up David's legs without waiting for an answer.

"No, I want to sit on your lap." Daniel tried to push him off.

"What happened to Raffi?" David asked. "Don't you want to listen anymore?"

"We can hear it from here," Daniel said, as the dishwasher switched to a quieter cycle and the words to "Row, Row, Row Your Boat" filled the room.

Aunt Rona clapped her hands and started singing along. "C'mon, boys. Row, row, row your boat..."

Deborah rolled her eyes, wondering if it was too early to excuse herself and head home. Just as she was about to rise, something off to the left caught her eye. It was Aunt Sadie, who had suddenly come to life, clapping her hands, bobbing her head, and bouncing her body to the music.

"Aunt Sadie?" Deborah was mesmerized, watching her great aunt sway to the song. Her movements started out small, but then grew larger and larger until she was half out of her chair.

"Aunt Sadie, calm down. What are you doing? You're going to hurt yourself." Mrs. Lewis was at Aunt Sadie's side in an instant, her hand steadying the back of her wheelchair. "Rona, give me a hand here. Is it time for her medicine? She's not supposed to get excited."

"You're the one who's getting excited, Ma," Deborah pointed out. "Leave Aunt Sadie alone. She's not hurting anybody. If she wants to dance, let her dance." Of course no one listened to Deborah.

"Aunt Sadie, sit down." Rona joined Mrs. Lewis and together they tried to subdue their aunt, but it was no use. Deborah could tell Aunt Sadie was very strong. Finally they gave up, and then, as if it were all her idea, Deborah's mother gave a wave of her hand. "*Nu,* so dance, Aunt Sadie. C'mon, we'll all dance. What are you doing, the samba, the rumba, the lindy hop?" She tried to make a joke.

Aunt Sadie, who hadn't uttered a word in years, at least not that anyone present could remember, opened her mouth and spoke loud and clear. "I'm doing the lesbian, Sylvia. You know the lesbian. Deborah taught me. Anyone can do it."

Deborah couldn't believe her ears. She didn't know which was more amusing, what Aunt Sadie had just said or the expression of sheer horror that had come over her mother's face. Time stood still as Deborah glanced about the room, noticing the same shocked look had etched itself onto the face of everyone else as well. Even Michael and Daniel, sensing something important was happening, kept absolutely still. In fact, everyone stayed frozen as they watched Aunt Sadie shaking her booty to the beat, a huge smile plastered across her face, as Raffi sang, "This old man, he played one, he played knick knack on my thumb…" Deborah didn't know whether to laugh or cry until Aunt Sadie raised both her arms and turned in Deborah's direction. Then Deborah knew there was absolutely nothing she could do. Nothing except scrape back her chair, stand up, go to her great aunt, and dance.

Eggs McMenopause

Insomnia equals insanity. And believe me, I should know. I haven't slept in two years. *Two years.* Ever since September 10, 1996, when my period stopped on a dime. Damn. Who knew I was out of eggs? Not me. It's not like I got any kind of warning or anything. One month there I was, bleeding away like a stuck pig, and the next month—*bam!*—dry as a bone.

So the question is, would I have done anything differently had I known? Thrown myself a party? Saved my last bit of menstrual blood in a jar like Paul Newman's spaghetti sauce? Found some guy to fuck at the Last Chance Motel so I could finally be a mother once and for all? Not that I ever wanted to be a mother, you understand. It's just that once I knew I couldn't be, all of a sudden that's exactly what I wanted to do. Grow big as a house. Give birth. Breastfeed. The whole nine yards. It was ridiculous. Sort of like pining away for a lover after you've broken up with her. You know how it is—you don't want to be with her anymore, *you're* the one who called it quits, you can't even stand the fucking sight of her—but as soon as she has her arm around somebody else's waist, you want her as much as you've ever wanted anyone your whole life. More. And if you make the mistake of telling her that, and if she makes the mistake of running back to you, then—poof!—your desire disappears as finally and completely as my last egg. That's human nature for ya. Go figure. We all want what we don't have, until we get it, and then we don't want it anymore.

Like my period. God, when I was a teenager, I was dying to get my period. I was the last kid in my class to get it. All the other girls wore their sanitary napkins like badges. "I can't have gym today, Miss Allbright. I have *my friend,*" they'd say in a stage whisper loud enough for all the other girls to hear. They carried their bodies differently too. Like they had some holy wisdom between their legs that I was just dying to get my hands on. *Please,* I'd pray every night before bed. *Please, I'll do anything. Just let me get my period. Please.* I'd rush to the bathroom every morning, shut my eyes, and listen to the sweet music of my pee hitting the toilet water. Then I'd take a deep breath, wipe, and open my eyes. But every day that pink toilet paper came up with *nada.*

Then one morning I pulled down my pajamas, and before I even sat down on the pot I saw they were stained with thick, brown blood. I was so surprised—I didn't even know what it was. I thought I was dying. I had no idea how I cut myself down there, as I didn't spend any time down there at all, much less with a sharp instrument. I told my mother, and she slapped me. Twice. Slap-slap, once on each cheek. It's a Jewish custom, though it's also a custom not to tell you it's a custom, so of course I thought I had just done one more thing to make my mother mad. After the slaps, she gave me a belt and a sanitary napkin and told me to be careful, I was a woman now, and I'd bleed once a month until I was at least fifty, so I better watch myself, soon all the boys would be after me.

Well, she was partly right, my mother. I did bleed until I was fifty, but the boys were never after me. The girls were after me, or to be more precise, I was after the girls. Girls with their periods, girls without their periods, tall girls, short girls, fat girls, thin girls, I didn't care. I wasn't fussy. I just wasn't happy unless I had some sweet, warm female thing in my arms. Which I haven't, in case you're wondering, for a long, long time.

It's not that I'm a dog or anything, you understand. It's just that menopause, in case you haven't gone through it yet, doesn't make you feel like the most attractive woman in the world. First of all, you bloat. I looked in the mirror one day and thought, *Damn, who the hell snuck in here when I wasn't looking and injected helium under my skin?* I looked like a balloon from the goddamn Macy's Thanksgiving Day Parade. Second of all, you sweat. Night sweats, day sweats, morning, afternoon, evening sweats. God, I grew hotter than hell and didn't wear a winter coat for two whole years, and New York City in fucking

February isn't exactly Miami in July. I couldn't bear the thought of anyone coming near me; in fact, I could hardly stand to be near myself. And on top of all this, I got pimples—pimples!—at my age. I looked like a walking, talking case of Acne Anonymous. And then of course I was so sleep-deprived, I could have walked right past Miss America (who happens to be just my type) and I wouldn't have even noticed.

So one night when I couldn't sleep, I started doing the math. I got my period when I was sixteen, and it stopped when I was fifty. That's thirty-four years, times twelve months a year, equals four hundred and eight periods. Four hundred and eight eggs. Could make the world's biggest omelet. Or something.

Call me crazy, but I got obsessed with the number. Four hundred and eight. They say your ovaries are the size of two tiny almonds, so how could they hold two hundred and four eggs apiece? That's a lotta eggs. Being a visual gal, I wanted to see them. I wanted to feel them. So I bought them. Went down to the corner store and bought thirty-four dozen eggs. A few dozen at a time. I might be crazy all right, but I don't want the whole neighborhood knowing just how loony I am. Luckily, I live in New York, where there's a corner store on every corner. I just worked the neighborhood and bought a few dozen here…a few dozen there…

At first I just stacked the cartons one on top of the other in the living room. Four stacks in the corner: two stacks of eight dozen, two stacks of nine. To tell you the truth, I was a little afraid of them. I had to live with them for a while, you know, get used to them. I mean, to my mind, they represented my unborn children, in a twisted sort of way. I even started naming them. Went right through the alphabet: Annie, Bonnie, Carol, Deliah, Ellen, Francis, Grace. You get the picture. Then I started in with boys' names: Adam, Barry, Carlos, David, Eddie, Frankie, Greg. I had to do it fifteen fucking times. Abigail, Betty, Claire, Deborah…Allen, Burt, Craig, Daniel…Amy, Barbara…Angel, Bernie… Pretty sick, huh? That's nothing compared to what I did next.

Next, I unpacked them and started placing them around the apartment. Now, if you've never been up here, let me tell you, this place ain't exactly the Plaza. It's pretty tiny, just three small rooms, and I haven't redecorated in a while. Since the Ice Age, as a matter of fact. But I'm not complaining. My hovel is perfect for one person. One crazy person and her four hundred and eight eggs.

The first place I put them was on the couch. Eight dozen fit there, and another eight fit on the bed. Three dozen covered my kitchen table, and two dozen filled the shower. A dozen fit in the bathroom sink, and another dozen filled the sink in the kitchen. Twenty-three down and eleven to go. I had no choice then but to lay them out on the floor. It looked kind of like an inside-out Yellow Brick Road. The floor was covered with eggs except for a twisted, windy path that led from the bedroom through the living room, through the kitchen, and out the front door.

When I was finally finished, I have to say it—I felt pretty damn proud. Sure, I had used up my eggs—nothing much to it; women do that all the time—but how many women have actually replaced them? I stood in the narrow path in my apartment, looked around, and felt smug. For about two seconds. And then I started feeling incredibly horny. All those eggs! I mean, have you ever felt an egg, I mean really felt an egg? They're very sensual, you know. They've got a little weight to them; they're heavy and smooth, not unlike a woman's breast that fits just right in the palm of your hand. I took two eggs off the floor and held one in each paw for a minute, closing my eyes and just bouncing them up and down a little. God, I felt like a cat in heat. No, not a cat, a pussy. I wanted some, and I wanted it *now.*

So what could I do? *Go out, you old fool,* I said to myself. I hadn't been out for about a million years, and the thought of it was more than a little daunting. Had I lost my charm? (Had I ever had it?) There was only one way to find out. Go out. So I did. I got all dressed up in a jacket and tie, did something with my hair, put on my motorcycle boots, and hit the street. I didn't even know if the bar I used to haunt was still there—part of me prayed it wasn't, and part of me prayed it was. I heard the disco beat half a block a way, and it pulled me inside like a magnet. God, it felt good to be out with the girls.

Now before you jump all over me and tell me I should be calling them women, let me tell you, these were girls. To my mind, anyway. I wasn't old enough to be their mother, you understand. I was old enough to be their grandmother. Sure, you do the math. Eighteen and eighteen is thirty-six, plus eighteen more is fifty-four. Which is just a year and a half shy of how old I was. And how shy. I almost turned around and marched out the door the second after I marched in, but traffic was going against me, so I went with the flow and headed straight (so to speak) inside. I mean, what the hell? I had dragged myself out of the house, and there was no one back there waiting for me but the ingredients for about two hundred Egg McMuffins. I might as well pretend to enjoy myself.

I headed for the bar and parked myself on an empty stool. Asked the bartender for whatever was on tap, leaned back on my elbows, and looked around. Luckily, I didn't have to look far. There were two gals to my right, one more gorgeous than the other. Were they together? It was hard to tell. Both of them were dressed in black from head to toe: black sweaters, black stockings, black skirts, black shoes. I doubted they were lovers, because after all, what can two femmes do together? But then again, this is a new generation. Femmes go with femmes, butches go with butches—hell, I've even heard that the newest happening thing is for girls to go with boys. Though what's so new and radical about that is way beyond me.

I pretended I didn't notice the two babes, of course, but I kept my eye on them and tried to eavesdrop on their conversation. Easier said than done, as the music was really pumping, and though I hate to admit it, my hearing isn't what it used to be. I can't believe I'm turning into one of those old broads who walk into a bar and whine, "Why does the music have to be so loud? Can't they turn it dow-ow-own?" But like I've already told you, age does strange things to a person. So I couldn't really hear, but I could see all right, and let me tell you, both these dames were drop-dead gorgeous. One of them had that short, bleached-out blond, rhinestone glasses, dog-collar-around-the-neck look. Very East Village, not exactly my type. The other one, though, I'd lick her boots any day. She had long black hair down to her waist, and she was at least six feet tall, even without the five-inch platform shoes. God, her legs went on forever, and I couldn't stand that they weren't wrapped around my waist that very minute. But before I could even ask the bartender what she was drinking so I could send one over with my compliments (a move that makes them swoon, or at least did in the old days), she turned from her gal pal, tossed all that glorious hair over her shoulder in a huff, and flounced into the crowd.

Now let me tell you, if there's one thing I love even more than dykes, it's dyke drama. I sidled up to Miss St. Mark's Place and asked, "Is she your girlfriend?"

"Why don't you ask her?" She pointed to the object of my affection, who had obviously changed her mind and returned to the scene of the crime.

Well, I always was one to follow orders. Pointing to the blond, I asked the goddess standing before me, "Is she your girlfriend?"

"What did she say when you asked *her*?" Mademoiselle thrust her fists onto her hips and looked at me with blazing eyes.

This was beginning to feel like therapy; every question I asked was being answered with another question. "She said to ask you." I looked the towering Glamazon in the eye and held her gaze as she snorted and shook her head. "C'mon." She held out her hand, to my delight and amazement. "Let's dance."

Well, she sure didn't have to ask me twice. I slid off that bar stool like a greased pig and let her lead me to the dance floor, where I attempted to move these old bones to the music, if you could call it that. All I could hear was some kind of throbbing, pumping techno beat. Perfect for humping, I thought, and as if my girl had a Ph.D. in mind-reading, she pulled me into her and started working away. I hate to admit it, but my knees actually buckled, and I had to hold on for dear life. Luckily there was a lot to hold on to. Like I told you, this girl was beyond tall. Her crotch came up to my hipbone, and her breasts were at eye level. I smelled her sweat and her juice and her perfume, and just kept my hip jutted out so she could go to town. "Ooh, baby, you are something else," I murmured, and somehow found her nipple in my mouth. Cashmere never tasted so good, let me tell you. A few times I tried to look up at my dancing damsel, but either her eyes were closed or they were focused in the direction of the bar. Was she using me to make her girlfriend jealous? Did I care? Hey, a revenge fuck was better than a mercy fuck, though to tell you the truth, from this babe-and-a-half I'd have taken either.

When the music changed, we headed back toward the bar, and much to my relief the Blond Bombshell was gone. I couldn't tell if Mandy was pissed, relieved, or disappointed. (Once her come was all over my jeans, I figured I had the right to ask her name.) Without a word, she hopped up on that still-warm bar stool, drained what was left of her gal pal's drink, and drew me toward her by wrapping those mile-long legs around the base of my butt. I felt her muscles clench as she held me tightly, and I realized I couldn't get away even if I wanted to. Which I didn't, in case you're wondering. I may have gone bananas in other departments, but I wasn't so far gone that I'd look this gift horse in the mouth.

"You live around here, baby?" Mandy whispered, letting her tongue roam the highways and byways of my grateful left ear.

"Just a few blocks away," I panted, and let me tell you, it was a good thing she had me by the butt because my legs were beyond Jell-O.

"Let's go." She released me, and I commanded my skeletal system to get a grip as we made our way out the door. Once outside, I tried to lean her against a lamppost and kiss her a bit, but it was embarrassing for her to have to bend down an entire foot just to get her mouth anywhere near mine. Clearly I had to get this girl on her back as quickly as possible, so we hustled down the street and up the steps to my apartment. I thought about carrying her over the threshold, but when I opened the door, I couldn't believe my eyes. The eggs! I had forgotten all about them. Would she notice? I decided to play it cool, since after all, what choice did I have?

"Walk this way," I said, bending over like Groucho Marx and waddling down the narrow path to my bed, which was of course completely covered with eggs. I considered whipping away the bedspread, like a magician who pulls a tablecloth out from under plates, glasses, and silverware without disturbing them, but that would have been too dramatic. Besides, it wouldn't have worked.

But Mandy, bless her heart, was foolish with youth, liquid courage, or just a wacky sense of humor. "The yolk's on you," she said, reaching for an egg which, she cracked with one hand on the bed frame like a young, beautiful Julia Child. Then she deposited the contents of the shell expertly and neatly on top of my head.

"Allow me," I said, and with cool yolk dripping down the side of my face and neck I sent all eight dozen of those babies flying with one grand, gallant sweep of my arm. As they rolled, cracked, and crashed to the ground, I prayed Mandy wouldn't forsake me and run screaming out the door. But not to worry. I sure know how to pick 'em, if I do say so myself. Mandy just flopped down on the now-clear bed and rolled onto her back, with her hands behind her head and a look that said loud and clear, *Okay, I've done my job; now it's up to you.* God, I love those femmes.

"Over easy," I remarked as I bent down to unbutton her sweater. She wore no bra, and damn if her breasts didn't remind me of two eggs sunny side up. I cracked an egg onto her chest and licked her nipples through the yellow goo. She laughed and opened her legs which, had somehow worked their way out of her skirt. Crotchless panty hose—what will they think of next? Clearly Mandy had been expecting to get some action that night, but being fucked with an organic egg by a butch three times her age probably wasn't exactly what she had in mind.

I moved the lucky egg slowly up one magnificent thigh until it was right up against the path to glory. I pressed it against her and rolled it around and around until the shell was slippery and slick. "You move, it breaks," I said, teasing her with the tip of it.

"It breaks, you eat it," she replied, squeezing her legs together and cracking that ova in two.

Well, suffice to say, my cholesterol level skyrocketed that night, clear through the fucking roof. I had egg on my face, and I didn't mind one bit. We crunched our way through my entire apartment, and that Mandy wasn't squeamish in the least. I licked egg off her toes, off her nose... We fucked in every room, and by morning there wasn't an egg left to scramble. Four hundred and eight eggs smashed to smithereens. That's gotta be worthy of the *Guinness Book of World Records,* don't you think? I tell you, I was so spent by the time the sun came up, I didn't know if I was wide awake or dreaming. I shut my baby blues and didn't open them again until that afternoon, when I woke up alone in my bed, fresh and clean as a newborn chick. Mandy and the eggs were gone, and so were the bags under my eyes. I blinked a few times, wondering if I had imagined the whole thing. Had it all been just part of some deranged menopausal fantasy? I stumbled into the kitchen, where my question was answered by a note I found on the table: Thanks for an eggs-citing evening. Love, Mandy. The note was anchored by one perfectly round, white egg, upon which Mandy had drawn a goofy smiley face with a blue magic marker. And even though an egg was the last thing I wanted, I'd worked up such an appetite from last night's activities, I cracked that sucker in tow and fried it up on the spot. And I tell you, it was the most delicious thing I'd eaten in my entire life.

FROM

She Loves Me, She Loves Me Not

(2002)

Stranger Than Fiction

L.B. runs into the house breathlessly, her wavy red hair flying every which way as she flings her books, papers, scarf, and hat across the kitchen table. Harriet looks up over the top of her black-framed reading glasses with a bemused smile. *I married a hurricane,* she thinks, not for the first time.

"I had the most *amazing* class," L.B. pants, still all in motion. She yanks open the refrigerator door, pulls and pushes things around until she finds what she's looking for—the orange-peach-pineapple juice marked with her initials so Harriet won't gripe when she drinks straight out of the carton. Which she does right now.

"Your fiction workshop?" Harriet asks, putting down her crossword puzzle.

"No, my advanced journalism class? God, I love my professor. She is so smart and so *cool.*" When L.B. gets excited she talks like the undergrad she was not so long ago, all question marks and italics. Harriet is sometimes charmed by this and sometimes annoyed, depending on her mood. "She was teaching us about interviewing? And she said a teacher of *hers* once said that you know your subjects are really speaking from the heart when they stop talking in complete sentences? *And,*" L.B. interrupts herself to swipe the back of her mouth with her sleeve, "she told us two questions that are guaranteed to make that happen."

"And those two questions are?" Harriet asks.

"Thank you for coming in for your interview today, Ms. Jacobs." L.B. sits at the table, takes Harriet's hand, and kisses the inside of her palm. Then she picks up the pen Harriet has just put down—Harriet always does the crossword in purple ink to give her confidence—and speaks into it as though it were a microphone.

"The first question is—wait a minute, you don't mind if I tape this, do you?" L.B. pretends the cordless phone lying on the table is a tape recorder and mimics switches it on. "Testing, testing. All right. You have to tell the person you're interviewing that you're taping them and record their consent for your own protection."

"I know," Harriet says. L.B. has told her this before.

"So is it okay to tape you?"

"Yes, yes, tape away." Harriet plays along, waving at the phone.

"So," L.B. continues speaking into the pen, "the first question is, 'Can you please tell me what you know about the circumstances of your birth?' "

"My birth?" Harriet raises an eyebrow.

"Yes, your birth. You were there, weren't you?"

"Of course I was there," Harriet leans back in her chair, pulls off her glasses, and shuts her eyes as if she could see the scene that occurred fifty years ago. "It was August 17th—you know that. My mother was cranky because I was late."

"As usual," L.B. points out.

"As usual," Harriet agrees. "One of my many bad habits that started in the womb. Anyway, it was hotter than hell that summer, one of the hottest Augusts on record according to my mother, and living in a fifth-floor Manhattan walk-up probably didn't help. I'm sure the window fans my parents had did nothing but blow the hot air around." Harriet waves her hand in front of her face as though it were August instead of December. "So there she was," she continues, "bigger than a barn with this baby who refused to come out. On top of that, she had my two-year-old brother to take care of. And my father, who never lifted a finger around the house—but that's another story."

"Go on." L.B. tilts her head and gazes at Harriet with those big emerald eyes that still startle with their splendor.

"So," Harriet clears her throat, coming back to herself. "Since I was obviously in no hurry to make my grand entrance, they decided to do a cesarean. And it's a good thing they did, because when they slit my mother open," Harriet pulls her fist across her midsection in an exaggerated motion, "there I was with the umbilical cord wrapped around my neck." Harriet's right hand flies up to her throat, and she gasps and bulges out her eyes, replaying the scene. "As a child, I never could stand to have anything pulled over my head. To this day, I can't wear a turtleneck." Harriet's hand strokes the underside of her chin, which is only slightly less taut than it used to be. "I can't even stand to wear a necklace or a scarf, though I probably should do something to cover up this turkey wattle I've got going here."

L.B. frowns. "Harriet, you do not have a turkey wattle."

"You're too kind, my love." Harriet smiles in spite of herself and tries to think of more dramatic elements to add to the story. "When my mother saw I was a girl, she cried. She said it was because she was so happy, she always wanted a girl, but I think it was because she knew how much heartache I would cause her. Which I guess I did." Harriet lifts her shoulders in an "oh, well" shrug. "Oh, and I almost forgot this part: When I was born I had long black hair that all the nurses took turns combing—they said they'd never seen so much hair—so thick and dark and long—on a newborn before. I left the hospital with a ponytail—or maybe two pigtails—no, a ponytail I think—anyway, what difference does it make? The point is they gave me a poufy little hairdo and put ribbons—and not just any ribbons—pink ribbons, pink *satin* ribbons—in my hair, can you imagine? You know how I feel about pink. I looked like one of those, you know, those stupid whaddya-call-its you win at the fair, you know—those stupid, goddamn kewpie dolls."

"Aha!" L.B. sticks one finger straight up in the air.

"Aha, what?"

"Right there at the end you started speaking in incomplete sentences. Just like my professor said you would when you felt passionately about what you were saying."

"Of course I feel passionately about someone tying pink satin ribbons in my hair." Harriet is indignant. L.B. knows she'd rather stick needles in her eyes than ribbons of any color in her short-cropped hair, which over the years has turned from black to salt-and-pepper to a handsome silvery gray. "From the day I was born, people were trying to make me into someone I had no interest in being." Harriet lets out a disgruntled sigh. "So, Ms. Reporter, what's your second question?"

"My second question, Ms. Jacobs, is, 'Have you ever had a near-death experience?' "

"Yes, on the day I was born."

"On the day you were born?" L.B. stares at Harriet blankly.

"Remember? The umbilical cord?" Harriet repeats her birthing reenactment.

"Oh, right. That's interesting, don't you think? Both experiences on the same day?" L.B. pretends to write something down, then looks up at Harriet. "Okay," she says brightly. "Your turn."

"My turn for what?" Harriet asks.

"Your turn to interview me. Here, take the microphone." L.B. holds out the pen. "Ask me about the circumstances of my birth."

"I don't have to, darling," Harriet takes the pen out of L.B.'s fingers and grasps her lover's freckled hand with both her own. "Didn't your mother ever tell you?" she asks softly. "I was there."

✤

"Harriet, put your hand here. No, lower. And press harder. Even harder. Yeah, yeah, that's it."

Harriet exhaled deeply and licked her upper lip, which was salty with sweat. She hoped Celia didn't know how badly she was shaking inside. Harriet had waited so long—her whole lifetime maybe—to hear Celia say those very words. She'd dreamed about touching her, skin-to-skin, for more nights than she dared to admit, not to mention the hours she spent wide awake, fantasizing about what it would be like to put her hands all over Celia's soft, freckled flesh. And now the moment had finally come, but not in the way Harriet had ever expected.

"Can you feel it? Wait a second." Celia pushed a few strands of coppery red hair behind her ears and shifted her massive weight around on the worn plaid couch before putting her hand on top of Harriet's and pressing her palm even farther into her hard, round belly. "There! He just kicked. Did you feel that?"

"You're supposed to say 'he or she,' remember?" Harriet reminded Celia what they'd learned in the consciousness-raising group they attended in Cambridge once a week.

"Oh, right. He or she. So did you feel him—I mean him or her—or it, kick?"

Harriet pressed her hand into Celia's belly again. "Wow." She looked up at Celia, who was grinning madly, already proud of her genius of an offspring. "You've got a soccer player growing in there."

Celia laughed. "Do I ever! Or maybe he or she's just inherited my big, ugly feet. Which I used to be able to see." Celia spread her bare toes wide and tried to catch sight of them over her bulging stomach, but it was an impossible task.

"They're not ugly," Harriet said for the millionth time. She didn't understand what the big deal was with Celia's feet. Sure, they weren't the prettiest things in the world—whose were?—but they weren't uglier than most people's. True, they were flat as tires with all the air let out, and she had practically no nail on the littlest toes, but so what? Who noticed feet anyway? And besides, weren't they supposed to love and accept all parts of their bodies unconditionally and not buy into the patriarchy's impossible standard of beauty, since less than two percent of the population looked like that anyway? At least that's what the leader of their consciousness-raising group had told them. Easy for her to say, Harriet often thought, since the tall, thin woman looked like a fashion model and fit into that two percent herself.

"They're probably uglier than ever, all swollen up from being pregnant." Celia curled her bottom lip under and made a face. "Thanks a lot, babycakes." She cupped both hands together in front of her mouth and bent her head, directing her words to the child she had growing inside.

"Let me massage them," Harriet said, sliding off the couch onto the shag carpet and pulling one of Celia's feet into her lap.

"Heaven," Celia leaned her head back and shut her eyes.

"We're supposed to do one nice thing every day for the part of our bodies we hate the most," Harriet said, reciting the homework from their group. The group leader was trying to get them to love and accept every part of themselves unconditionally. Especially Celia, who seemed to be her pet project. "How are you going to love the little boy or girl growing inside you if you can't love yourself?" the leader asked her over and over.

"Umm," Celia relaxed into Harriet's hands as they kneaded the flesh between her heel and her instep. Harriet tried not to let Celia's moan of pleasure go straight to her groin, but it did anyway. She closed her eyes, resisting the urge to pick up Celia's foot and kiss the sweet center of her fallen arch. Harriet had recently realized that she was in love with Celia and probably had been ever since the day they first met. And she didn't know what in the world she was going to do about it. Telling the women in her CR group that the part of her body she hated the most was the fourteen coarse hairs that grew around her right nipple was a piece of cake compared to admitting that she was in love with Celia.

They'd met a few years earlier, on a Sunday at the Laundromat. Celia was putting up a sign advertising for a roommate, and Harriet was scanning the bulletin board looking for a place to live. They'd gone out for coffee and found they had a lot in common: They were both recent graduates with useless liberal arts degrees, Harriet's in English Lit and Celia's in Theater; and both of them worked jobs they considered temporary, while they tried to figure out what to do with the rest of their lives: Celia was waiting tables and Harriet was driving a taxi. Celia had just rented a two-bedroom apartment in Somerville and needed someone to share the rent. They shook hands on the deal, and Harriet brought over her meager belongings that very afternoon.

Though they had a lot in common, there were differences too. Celia liked folk music—Joni Mitchell, Joan Baez, Buffy Sainte-Marie—while Harriet preferred wilder women: Janis Joplin and Grace Slick. Celia decorated her room with Indian-print bedspreads and beaded curtains, while Harriet kept her room as sparse as a Buddhist's cell (in fact she was deep into Jack Kerouac and all the Beat poets, though Celia thought they were a sorry, drunken lot). The biggest difference between them, however, was that Celia, though she was only twenty-two, was in a big rush to find Mr. Right, settle down, and have a family. Harriet was in no hurry to do the same. In fact, Harriet wasn't even sure she ever wanted to get married and have a baby.

"It's the seventies, Celia," Harriet said one night when they were baking a batch of chocolate chip cookies, having enjoyed a little "herbal refreshment" after dinner. Harriet perched herself on the kitchen counter, banging her bare feet against the cabinets while she wove her long black hair into an uneven braid and tried not to stare too hard at Celia's denim-covered behind as she bent over to open the oven. Even if she weren't stoned out of her mind, it would still be the most delicious-looking thing she'd ever seen. "Women have a lot more options now." Harriet tried to concentrate on what she was saying. "We don't have to get married and have children. We can do anything. Even run for president."

"But President Jacobs, what if some of us just want to stay home and take care of babies?" Celia shut the squeaky oven door and handed Harriet a rubber spatula covered with cookie dough to lick.

Harriet pondered this as she ran her tongue up and down the spatula, shutting her eyes and giving in to the sensual experience of sucking the sweet batter off the pliant rubber. She almost swooned as she felt Celia's hand on her arm.

"President Jacobs? I asked you a question. And are you finished with that?"

"Oh, yeah." Harriet slapped the now-spotless utensil into Celia's upturned hand and picked up a half-empty bag of bittersweet chocolate chips, which she poured directly into her mouth. "I suppose if taking care of babies is what you really want to do," she said, and it was obvious by her tone of voice—even with her mouth full—that she couldn't imagine choosing this option. "But Celia, why settle for a life like our mothers'? We don't have to be tied to some guy, picking his socks off the floor, cooking his meals, washing his clothes...we can do something meaningful with our lives."

"I think raising a child would be meaningful." Celia ran a finger around the rim of the mixing bowl to collect a clump of batter, which she scraped against her teeth. "And besides," she pulled her finger out of her mouth with a loud, wet smack, "my husband is going to do fifty percent of the housework. At least."

Yeah, right, Harriet thought. Most of the guys Celia brought home—and there were many—wouldn't know what to do with a broom or mop if they tripped over one. Especially the last guy, whom Celia really seemed to be gaga over. Until Harriet told her that after he and Celia had made love (she'd heard them through the paper-thin walls) and Celia had fallen asleep, her date had come into Harriet's bedroom and asked her if *she* wanted some. And the way he'd said it, it was clear he thought he was doing Harriet an enormous favor.

"Get the hell out of here," Harriet had hissed, and he did, much to her relief. She hadn't been scared; grossed out was more like it. But the worst part was, a few minutes after he'd left her room, Harriet could hear him and Celia going at it again. And it made Harriet crazy to know that some jerk who clearly didn't give a flying fuck about Celia got to put his hands all over her, while Harriet, who would lay down her life for the woman, had to lie in bed all alone, so close yet so far away.

The next morning, after Celia kissed her beau goodbye, she came into the kitchen, where Harriet was making a breakfast of scrambled tofu and whole-wheat toast. "Can I have some?" Celia asked, her green eyes wide and dreamy. "I'm starving." Celia stretched her arms lazily overhead and let out a deep, contented sigh. "Oh, my God, what a night I had. You know, Harriet, he could really be *the one.* I know you think I'm like the boy who cried wolf, but seriously, this one's really different than all the others. He's—"

"Celia." Harriet hated to burst her bubble, but knew she had to. "He came into my room last night."

"What? What do you mean?" Celia asked, and Harriet told her. And it turned out he was *the one* all right—the one who had fathered her child. Not that she ever saw him again. As soon as Celia told him over the phone that he was going to be a father, Mr. Wonderful was history.

"Don't worry, Celia," Harriet said one morning after Celia had thrown up for the third time. "I'll take care of you." Harriet liked playing nursemaid to Celia, holding a cold washcloth to her forehead when she didn't feel well, accompanying her to the doctor's office, making sure she ate healthy meals and didn't lift heavy things. And Celia seemed to have had enough of men for the moment. She was done with cruising the bars and picking up guys for one-night stands she always hoped would last longer. She had to be responsible. She was going to be a mother, for God's sake. She even let Harriet drag her off to her women's liberation group, though that was more Harriet's thing than hers. But as Celia often told Harriet, she hated being alone in the evenings, when she felt scared and overwhelmed by what was happening inside her body. And the group did turn out to be pretty interesting. They adopted her, in their own way, buying her bottles of organic prenatal vitamins, loaning her books about natural childbirth, and offering to go to the doctor with her when Harriet had to work. Since Celia's parents were staunch Catholics, mortified that their only daughter was having a child out of wedlock, they offered no help at all. The women in the group were Celia's family now.

After the group had run its ten-week course, the women met one last time to throw Celia a surprise baby shower. Celia laughed with delight over all her presents: tiny T-shirts and booties in every color of the rainbow except blue and pink; a non-sexist toy chest that included both dolls and trucks; and storybooks that defied stereotypes: *William's Doll* by Charlotte Zolotow and *Girls Can Be Anything* by Norma Klein.

"You guys," Celia beamed at her friends, and for once their facilitator didn't go on a diatribe about the use of the word "guys" to describe a group of women. "If it's a girl, I'm naming her Libby, for women's liberation."

"Hear, hear!"

"And if it's a boy, she's naming him Liberace," Harriet joked, and everybody laughed.

Two weeks later Celia went into labor. Harriet had gone to the store to get them a late-night snack: hot fudge sundaes from the ice cream shop around the corner. "And don't forget, I want marshmallow topping *and* whipped cream on mine," Celia reminded Harriet, who thought that combination was totally disgusting. She chalked it up to the strange cravings expectant mothers were supposed to have and did as she was told.

"I'm back with the goods," Harriet called as she let herself into the apartment. Celia, who had been sprawled on the couch when Harriet left, didn't reply. "I'll be right there," Harriet called again, heading into the kitchen for two big spoons. Utensils in hand, she brought their booty into the living room. "Here you go." Harriet held out the treat, but Celia hardly moved.

"Harriet," her voice was barely a whisper, "I think it's time."

"Time?" Harriet put Celia's ice cream down on the old camping trunk they used as a coffee table, pried open the lid of her own container, and dug in.

"Harriet, I think I'm in labor."

"Oh, my God." Harriet dropped her spoon. "Okay, okay, don't panic. Everything's under control. Did your water break? Are you having contractions?"

"I...ooh..." Celia doubled over and clutched her belly.

"I'll take that as a yes. Okay, okay, don't panic," Harriet said again.

"I think you're the one who's panicking." Celia sat up slowly as the contraction subsided. "Just call a taxi and get my suitcase, okay?"

"Okay, okay. Taxi, suitcase, taxi, suitcase."

"Harriet, relax. You're a total wreck."

"Of course I'm a wreck. You're having a baby."

Harriet completed her tasks and helped Celia get to her feet. They walked down the hallway and waited outside until the taxi came. Celia remained strangely calm.

"Aren't you nervous?" Harriet paced up and down, pausing to lift one hand over her eyes as she scanned the street. "Where the hell's that goddamn taxi? I knew I should have taken my cab home so I could drive you myself."

"It'll get here," Celia said, and just as the words left her mouth, it did.

When they arrived at the hospital, Celia and Harriet were whisked into the softly lit birthing room. Celia's midwife arrived, and Harriet took her place at Celia's head, coaching her to breathe as they had practiced during their Lamaze class. Celia clutched Harriet's hand and panted rapidly. It was a fast labor and an easy delivery; Celia had often joked about her "childbearing hips" and how she was built for breeding. The midwife caught the baby and laid the newborn on top of Celia's stomach.

"Hello, you precious perfect gift from God, my child who I love more than anyone else in the world." Celia whispered the words she had practiced over and over, wanting the first sentence her baby heard to be full of nothing but love. *Whom*, Harriet grimaced, having corrected Celia a dozen times to no avail. "You don't want to start the kid off illiterate," she'd said, bad grammar being one of her obsessions. But it would be cruel to point that out now to Celia, who looked exhausted but exhilarated as she stared at her bundle of joy.

"Look at that tiny tuft of red hair," Harriet marveled. "And all those freckles."

"Isn't he or she beautiful?" Celia whispered.

"Oh, my God, we haven't even looked," Harriet said, and Celia gently turned the baby.

"It's a girl," she said. "Oh, my precious, precious girl. My sweet daughter. My Libby," Celia crooned as tears rolled down her cheeks. "Oh, Harriet, I'm so happy. This is so perfect." She let out a little sigh. "Except…except…"

"Except what?" Harriet asked, not taking her eyes from Libby.

"Except," Celia sniffed, "I just wish my mother was here."

"Your mother?" Harriet was astonished. "After all the awful things she said about having a child out of wedlock?" Harriet couldn't bear to utter the word "illegitimate," the term Celia's mother had used, in front of Libby.

"I know." Celia wiped at her eyes with the back of her hand. "But you'll see when you're a mother." Celia drew Libby close. "Whatever you do, Libby, you can always come to Mama and tell me all about it. Whatever it is. I'll always be here for you, sweetheart. No matter what. Always."

"Me too," Harriet whispered, though she didn't know whether she was talking to Libby or Celia. Or both.

And they were a family, in an odd sort of way. Celia took care of the shopping, cooking, and cleaning, and Harriet doubled up on her taxi shifts so she could support them both. Celia had no interest in going back to work as she was adamant about not putting Libby in day care.

"But you worked in a day care center," Harriet pointed out one day when she came home early in the morning exhausted from driving most of the night.

"I know, that's why I'll never put Libby in one," Celia said, dipping a tiny spoon into a jar of organic baby food. "Children should be with their mothers the first few years of their lives. I mean, I saw some of those kids take their first steps, Harriet. That shouldn't have been me, that should have been their mothers. You want some more carrots, honey?" She turned her attention back to Libby, who was opening and closing her hands rapidly like she always did when she got excited. The first time Harriet saw her do that, she'd laughed. "Wow, how does she move her hands so fast?" she'd wondered aloud. "What'd you put in the kid's bottle, speed?" Celia had laughed too and told Harriet she called it "Libby's hands of delight."

"Of course we never told any of the parents that we saw their kid's first step," Celia went on. "We were instructed to say, 'She *almost* walked today, Mrs. Parker. You'd better keep a close eye on her. It could be any minute now.' I mean, I would just *die* if I missed Libby's first step."

"But Celia," Harriet couldn't bring herself to say what was on her mind. Some mothers *had* to work. As Celia would have to if she didn't have Harriet's help. Harriet supposed Celia could live on welfare and food stamps, but she would never let that happen. And didn't Harriet have what she wanted? For the most part, yes. But the part that was missing—the part about Harriet being in love with Celia but still afraid to say so—was getting to be more and more of a problem. Harriet knew she needed to tell Celia, but she just couldn't push out the words. And besides, Celia was changing. First it was not believing in day care, and then it was deciding to go to church. Harriet had been shocked to see Celia and Libby in matching flowered dresses early one Sunday morning.

"Where are you going?" Harriet had asked, stumbling into the kitchen in an oversize tie-dyed T-shirt, her hair held back with a rubber band she'd pulled off the rolled-up newspaper on the front porch. "I was going to make whole wheat waffles."

"We're going to church," Celia said, straightening one of Libby's sleeves.

"You're going where?" Harriet wasn't sure if she was wide-awake or dreaming.

"We're going to church," Celia repeated. "I want Libby to grow up with some kind of spiritual background."

"Not *Catholic* church?" Harriet groaned, but she was afraid she knew the answer.

"See you later," Celia called, and she and Libby were out the door.

It just got worse and worse. Soon Libby's wardrobe consisted solely of pink outfits, and the toy trucks and airplanes Celia had gotten at the baby shower vanished into thin air. And then to top it all off, Celia started dating an older man she had met at Mass one Sunday, a man whom Harriet disliked upon sight.

"I'm here to pick up my girls," he said the first time he came over and Harriet answered the bell.

"First of all, they're not yours," Harriet said, her arms folded like a sentry guarding her castle. "And second of all, one of them is a girl and the other one is a woman."

"Is that Phil?" Celia called from the kitchen. "I'll be right there." And when Celia caught sight of Phil, a light shone in her eyes that Harriet had never seen before. Even Libby's hands of delight started going a mile a minute when Phil smiled at her, much to Harriet's dismay.

"Phil, this is my roommate, Harriet."

"Charmed," Phil said, never taking his eyes from Celia and Libby.

"Can you hold her while I get my coat?" Celia asked.

"Of course," Harriet and Phil said at the same time. They both reached out, their hands colliding in midair. It would have been almost funny, Harriet thought bitterly, except of course it wasn't.

Celia started spending a lot of time with Phil, and Harriet saw less and less of her. She knew it was only a question of time before she lost Celia for good, but still, she wasn't about to go down without a fight. And as far as Harriet could tell, they hadn't slept together yet. At least Phil had never stayed over at their apartment, and Celia hadn't stayed out all night. So there was still hope, as far as Harriet was concerned.

One night when Harriet was playing peek-a-boo with Libby in the living room, Celia came out of her bedroom in a new pink dress. Her shoes were the exact same color, and she clutched a matching pink purse as well. *You look like an overgrown Easter egg,* Harriet wanted to say. "Going somewhere special?" she asked.

"Phil's taking me to a fancy restaurant, and I think," Celia paused to study herself in the mirror over the fake fireplace and smooth a strand of hair, "I think he's going to propose."

"What?" Harriet had been staring at Celia, thinking redheads really shouldn't wear pink—she'd read that in a women's magazine years ago—and though she hated that this fashion tip was stuck in her long-term memory, she had to admit it was true. Celia, with her freckles and ironed-out hair that was sure to frizz by the end of the evening, looked awful. But Harriet wasn't going to be the one to tell her that. "Celia, you can't possibly be thinking of marrying Phil."

"Why not?" Celia, evidently satisfied with her appearance, turned from the mirror. "He treats me so well, Harriet. Not like all those other guys, who only wanted to sleep with me. Phil doesn't believe in sleeping together before marriage."

"Since when did you get to be so old-fashioned?" Harriet covered her eyes, then pulled her hands away and smiled at Libby. "Peek-a-boo! I see you." She wanted to cover her ears as well.

"And besides, Libby needs a father." At the sound of her name, Libby turned toward her mother and smiled.

"Why?" Harriet asked. "I can take care of you. Haven't I been doing a good job?"

"Oh, Harriet," Celia shook her head. "You've been great, but did you think this could last forever?"

Yes, Harriet thought.

"I mean, sooner or later we're both going to get married and you're going to have kids of your own..."

"Celia," Harriet's heart was beating in her throat like a small, trapped bird. "Celia, I love you."

"I love you too, Harriet," Celia said automatically. "Now, make sure you wind up Libby's mobile when you put her down.

You know, the one that plays 'Jack and Jill.' She can't fall asleep without…"

"No, I mean I *love* you, Celia. I mean the way Phil does." There. She said it. Harriet looked down at her hands, and then, being a glutton for punishment, raised her head and stared with morbid fascination at Celia's face as her words registered. Shock, fear, disbelief, and finally what appeared to be disgust rearranged her features.

"That isn't funny, Harriet," she finally said.

"It wasn't meant to be," Harriet said quietly.

"You mean you're like that woman Orca?" Celia's voice rose in horror. Orca, whose name had been Cynthia until she came out and reinvented herself by shaving her head, letting her enormous breasts swing free, and tattooing a double women's symbol on her upper arm.

"Well, not exactly," Harriet said, and then instantly felt awful for betraying a sister. "I mean, yes. Yes, I am like Orca. I'm a woman-loving woman too."

"Oh, my God." Before Celia could say anything else the doorbell rang. "I have to go." She glanced from Harriet to Libby and back again, and for a minute Harriet was afraid Celia wasn't going to leave her daughter with a baby-sitter who also happened to be a pervert. But Celia just said "Be good," blew Libby a kiss, and was gone.

Harriet tried to stay up until Celia got home, but sleepiness got the better of her. When she stumbled into the kitchen the next morning, the diamond ring on Celia's finger woke her up with a start, like bright sunlight cutting into her eyes.

"Isn't it stunning?" Celia said, extending her hand. "We're moving in with Phil at the end of the month, Harriet. I can't wait to tell my mother."

Harriet blinked a few times, trying to absorb this information. Being not quite awake, it took her a minute to realize that "we" didn't mean her and Celia, it meant Libby and Celia. "Your mother?" Harriet asked.

"She's going to be so thrilled that I'm finally getting married and Libby is going to have a father." Celia spilled some Cheerios onto the tray attached to Libby's high chair. "Of course she would have been a lot happier if I'd done things in the correct order, but that can't be helped now."

"I thought Phil didn't believe in sex before marriage," Harriet said, moving toward the coffeemaker in slow motion. Maybe if she didn't allow herself to fully wake up, she could convince herself this was a dream.

"Who said anything about sex?" Celia asked. "Phil just thinks—and I agree—that, that, umm…under these circumstances, it would be best if I moved in with him as soon as possible."

Under these circumstances… Harriet knew what that meant. But what was the point of saying anything?

There were only two weeks left in the month, and Harriet dragged herself through them. She hated being away from home, as she knew her time with Celia and Libby was drawing to a close, but she hated being in the apartment too. More often than not Phil was there, making Harriet feel like a third wheel. A fourth wheel, really. Phil, Celia, and Libby made the perfect little family. And where did that leave Harriet? Nowhere.

On moving day, Celia let Harriet hold Libby as she and Phil loaded the last of Celia's boxes into the van Phil had rented. "Aren't you going to give me your new address?" Harriet asked when it was time to say goodbye.

"Look, here's some cash to cover her share of the bills." Phil slapped a pile of money into Harriet's hand. She wanted to throw it at him, but the truth was, she needed it too badly to make such a dramatic gesture.

"But how will I get in touch with you?" Harriet asked Celia, staring into Libby's clear green eyes.

"I'll call you," Celia said.

But of course she never did. She didn't even invite Harriet to the wedding. Not that Harriet would have even thought about going. Once Celia and Libby were no longer part of her life, Harriet became a militant feminist lesbian and swore off anything to do with heterosexuality and the patriarchy. She made herself as unfeminine as possible by growing out the hair on her legs and under her arms and cutting the hair on her head as short as possible. She started volunteering at a newly formed rape crisis center, joined a food collective, and moved into an all-lesbian household. Later Harriet grew less extreme; she grew out her buzz cut, put on a bra, and went back to school for the advanced degree she needed to open her own therapy practice (solely for women and girls of course). She spent most Friday and Saturday nights in gay bars, and over the years took many women home with her. Some stayed for a night and some stayed for a year or even longer, but ultimately Harriet found herself alone. She tried monogamy, nonmonogamy, and serial monogamy, all of which worked for a while...until they didn't.

When she turned forty, Harriet decided to try two things she'd never tried before: sobriety and celibacy. It was time to do a little internal work, take some breathing space, fall in love with her new, middle-aged self. Harriet needed to find out who she was, where she was going, what she wanted. Somehow the time had flown and one day Harriet realized with a start that she'd been celibate for five years. Whoa. She looked into the mirror, stared long and hard into her deep-brown eyes, and uttered something she remembered her mother was always fond of saying: "Enough is enough." Harriet was ready to settle down, to be half of a couple, to have that part of her life settled once and for all. "Some smart, funny, sexy, fabulous woman is out there just waiting for you," she told her reflection. "And boy, is she lucky."

But where to find such a creature? It was the mid 1990s; no one went to the bars anymore. Harriet thought of all the advice her happily and not-so-happily married friends had given her over the years: Take a class, read the personals, let us fix you up. And she thought of the advice she often gave her single clients: Just live your life fully. You'll meet someone when you least expect it. Above all, don't look desperate.

Harriet decided to take her own advice. She didn't really have time to take a class and couldn't very well answer a personal ad—what if it turned out to be one of her clients? And forget blind dates. The few she had gone on had all been disasters. Harriet had learned that someone could look awfully good on paper—be just the right height (ridiculous as it sounded, Harriet didn't want a girlfriend taller than she was), have the right interests, believe in the right causes—and still be an utter bore. Or worse, have no sense of humor. Or even worse, be lousy in bed.

One afternoon Harriet had a few hours to kill between clients and decided to while away the time in a café that had just opened up a few blocks from her office. The place was rather pretentious: dark and crowded with little round tables, each one occupied with someone nursing a cappuccino and trying to look as cool as possible, either by wearing sunglasses or reading a book of poems by the likes of Allen Ginsberg, Sylvia Plath, or Ranier Maria Rilke. The upstairs was standing room only, so Harriet went down to the lower level and parked herself at a corner table. She switched on a little lamp, opened up a very uncool psychology journal, and promptly shut it in favor of looking around. *My shoes are probably older than half the kids in this joint,* she thought just as a server came to take her order.

"Coffee, tea, or me?" the young woman asked. Harriet chuckled as she looked up.

You, Harriet thought as she stared into the most incredible green eyes she had ever seen. Even in the semidarkness, the woman took her breath away. She had wonderfully thick red hair and a million freckles that Harriet wanted to count with her tongue. But it wasn't just her features. There was a daring and an openness about her face that Harriet found enormously appealing.

"What's your name?" Harriet asked, startling herself.

The woman was unfazed by the question. "My friends call me L.B."

"And what do your lovers call you?" Harriet couldn't believe the words that were flying out of her mouth.

L.B. grinned. "Wouldn't you like to know?" she asked.

"Yes, I would. Very much." Harriet didn't know what had come over her.

L.B. wrote something down on her order pad and ripped off

the top page. "Call me sometime," she said, handing Harriet her phone number.

Harriet resisted the urge to bring the scrap of paper up to her lips and kiss it. She felt dazed, drugged, in a time warp. "L.B.," she said, "I think I'm old enough to be your mother."

"Cool. I don't have a mother." L.B. looked over her shoulder. Customers were waiting. "So what'll you have?"

"An iced coffee, please."

"Coming right up." L.B. flounced off, and Harriet sat back and enjoyed watching her in action for a good forty-five minutes. L.B. flitted from table to table, leaving, it seemed to Harriet, a string of admirers both male and female in her wake. Did L.B. give her phone number to anyone who asked? Was Harriet just one of many hopefuls?

At quarter to four, Harriet rose from her table. L.B. was immediately at her side. "On the house," she said as Harriet opened her wallet.

"Thanks."

"I have a thing for older women," L.B. said, moistening her lips with the tip of her tongue.

"I'll call you." Harriet could barely get the words out. She felt herself flush and prayed she wasn't having a hot flash.

"I'll be waiting." L.B. cleared Harriet's empty glass and used napkin with one sweep of her hand.

Harriet climbed the stairs and made her way to the front of the café, shaking her head in disbelief. What in the world had come over her? She had never acted so outrageously in her life. She squeezed past a folksinger who sat near the door wailing, his guitar case propped open with a sign that said IF YOU'RE AFRAID OF CHANGE, DROP IT IN HERE. Again Harriet chuckled and tossed in a few coins. Wasn't she always telling her clients the only constant thing is change? And hadn't she sworn to herself she would take her own advice?

Before she could lose her nerve or talk some sense into herself, Harriet pulled her cell phone out of her shoulder bag and dialed L.B.'s number.

"Hey, you've reached the redhead. Lucky you. Leave your number and I'll call you back. *If* I feel like it."

"It's Harriet. From the café. The woman you treated to an iced coffee." Harriet felt all of twelve years old. "Listen, you are clearly someone I need to get to know. What are you doing tomorrow night?" Harriet left her number and shut off her phone. *I did it,* she thought, feeling more proud of herself than the deed warranted. Would L.B. call back? It was more important to Harriet than she'd care to admit. She tried to tell herself it was just five years of horniness suddenly catching up to her, but she knew it was more than that. L.B. had gotten under her skin. Harriet hoped she was older than she looked, which was about twenty-five. It turned out she wasn't.

Over dinner at an Italian restaurant the following night, they exchanged life stories. L.B. had grown up in Pennsylvania but no longer had anything to do with what she called her "family of origin." She was taking some time off from school before going back for a master's degree in writing. "I'm majoring in life right now," she said as she tore a hunk of bread in half and used a piece to mop up a puddle of olive oil.

Harriet gave L.B. the nutshell version of her own life: her traditional, conservative, stifling childhood; how she had burst out of the closet in the seventies after college and became an ardent feminist; the political movements she'd been a part of; her recent success with becoming sober. L.B. listened intently and at some point in the evening started holding Harriet's hand. *I'm a goner,* Harriet thought, feeling her legs turn mushy as the tiramisu she and L.B. were now sharing. It wasn't exactly robbing the cradle—L.B., it turned out, had been on the planet for a quarter of a century—but still, she was a good twenty years Harriet's junior.

When it was clear which way the night was going, Harriet felt she had to ask. "Doesn't our age difference bother you?" She looked into her coffee cup rather than meet L.B.'s eyes. And then, being a therapist, she couldn't help but wonder if L.B. was just looking for a maternal figure. "What did you mean yesterday when you said you didn't have a mother?"

Now it was L.B.'s turn to look down into her cup. "My parents disowned me when I came out. Both my mother and my father—well, he's not my real father, but he's the only father I know—anyway, both of them are very strict Catholics. I knew I probably shouldn't tell them I was a dyke, but I couldn't help it. I felt so hypocritical, taking their money to pay for college when I knew I was doing something they'd totally disapprove of. I guess I do have some Catholic guilt in me after all." L.B. smiled sheepishly. "Anyway, I haven't talked to them since I was a junior. I got financial aid and put myself through school. Been on my own for a long time. So I may be only twenty-five, but I'm kind of an old soul. And I've learned that superficial differences like age, race, whatever, really don't matter. Since I know what it's like not to be loved," she raised her eyes to Harriet's, "I know how to love very well. Very, very well." L.B. enunciated each word carefully. "I know it involves taking risks. Not being politically correct. Letting your head go and following your heart."

"Let's get out of here," Harriet said, waving for the check.

The next twelve hours were everything Harriet could have hoped for and more. L.B. was an absolute goddess, with her eager young body that curved in and filled out in all the right places. She was open and willing, creative and energetic, and extremely attentive. Harriet felt good in places she hadn't been aware of in years, if ever. The hard knobs of her elbows, which until now had never been kissed. The backs of her knees. The ladder of her spine. L.B. told Harriet she was perfect and interrupted any self-deprecating and what she called ageist remarks Harriet made by putting her hand over Harriet's mouth. Harriet swallowed her words and kissed L.B.'s palm as her hands wandered up and down her magnificent, responsive body.

In the morning, after they made love again, Harriet grabbed the bathrobe hanging from the bedpost and rose to put on the coffee. She hunted around for the breakfast tray she hadn't used in forever and popped two English muffins into the toaster oven too. *Breakfast in bed, why not?* Harriet thought, getting out her best cloth napkins. When she came back into the bedroom, a naked L.B. sat up and smiled.

"Umm, coffee," she said, reaching out with both arms, her

hands opening and closing rapidly, like high-speed lobster claws. Harriet raised an eyebrow and L.B. laughed.

"This?" she asked, looking down at her hands, which were still going strong. "I always do this when I see something I want. I've done it ever since I was a baby. My mother used to call it my hands of delight."

Harriet felt all the blood in her body rush to her feet as she gripped the handles of the breakfast tray tight. "What does L.B. stand for?" she asked, her voice a shaky whisper.

"Libby Bernadette. Why?"

"Oh. My. God."

✣

Harriet closes the newspaper and puts it on the kitchen counter. She'll finish the crossword later while L.B. does the dishes. It's Harriet's night to cook, and she outdoes herself with a vegetable lasagna that "rocks my world," as L.B. puts it. L.B. asks Harriet to rub her feet after dinner; the new inserts the doctor gave her to lift her arches are killing her. Later, after watching the ten o'clock news, they have dessert: Harriet nibbles a small, plain dish of vanilla frozen yogurt, and L.B. devours two scoops of fudge ripple ice cream drenched with marshmallow topping and whipped cream. L.B. seems to take the news that Harriet attended her birth in stride, as she does most things.

"It's not like I didn't know you and my mother were roommates," L.B. says, as Harriet had told her that long ago, the first morning after the first night they had spent together. Their first night together had almost been their only night together, since Harriet was extremely upset about the whole thing. But L.B., whom Harriet referred to as "younger and wiser," convinced her to give their relationship a try. "What if I'm the one true love of your life?" L.B. had asked, looking directly into Harriet's dark eyes. "How could you risk not giving me a chance? Besides," she'd said, "this feels so good. Even though it's only been a night and a morning, I feel like I've known you forever."

Harriet winced. "I have known you forever," she said, wondering how something so unbelievable could feel so right.

And five and a half years later, it seems that L.B. is "Ms Right," since Harriet has never been happier. Still, she worries how this new bit of information will affect L.B.

"I think it's cool," L.B. says later when they are lying in bed, side by side. "Besides my mother, you're the first person I ever saw. Maybe I should write a short story about it. Nah," L.B. shakes her head. "No one would ever believe it."

"Truth *is* stranger than fiction," Harriet says, gathering L.B. into her arms. They lie there holding each other for a few minutes, and L.B. is so quiet, Harriet thinks she may have fallen asleep.

"L.B.?" Harriet strokes the side of her cheek.

"Hmm?"

"I know the circumstances of your birth, love, but you never told me if you've ever had a near-death experience."

"Oh, yeah," L.B. nestles into Harriet's shoulder. "I have one every night."

"Every night?" Harriet pushes back a little so she can look into L.B.'s eyes. "What are you talking about? Do you have sleep apnea or something?"

"No, baby." L.B. is smiling. "Don't you know I almost die of happiness every night lying here next to you?"

"You're too much." Harriet shuts her eyes and leans down to give L.B. a kiss. L.B. kisses her back, her front, and both her sides, tracing every inch of Harriet's body with her two greedy hands of delight.

Keeping a Breast

You are lying on your back, in bed, your hands behind your head, your lover moving over you softly like a summer breeze. She plants tiny kisses along your jaw, under your chin, in the carved-out hollow between your shoulder and your neck. You sigh, shift, watch her out of half-closed eyes, think, not for the first time, how lucky you are. Your lover moves to your breasts with her hands and her mouth. Your nipples stand at attention, eager for her to begin. You have been together long enough for her to know just how to please you, but not so long that the thrill has disappeared. Your lover knows every inch of your body, every hair, every wrinkle, practically every pore. You sigh again, your whole being reduced to a puddle of pleasure. You could do this forever, and you know she could too. So when your lover stops what she is doing, you think she is teasing and play along. "Don't. Stop. Don't. Stop. Don't stop." But your lover has stopped. She studies you, her forehead furrowed in three crooked horizontal lines. You want to write *I love you* on those three little lines, and you lift a finger to start tracing the letters, but then your lover speaks, and you stop before you begin. "What's this?" she asks, her voice not curious but concerned. You are not worried. What can it be, a beauty mark, a pimple, a mole? Your lover takes your hand and moves it to the outside of your right breast, which has fallen back into your armpit as it always does when you lie on your back. "Feel that?" she asks. You shake your head, and she presses your hand harder until you can no longer deny what she has found: a lump. A lump that presses against the flesh of your fingers like a small, irritating pebble in the bottom of your shoe.

Talk about killing the moment.

You have always had breasts. Of course you know that isn't true, but you can't remember life without them. There must have been a time, though, when all you had were two tiny nipples small as snaps sewn onto your chest. Then breast buds, though you don't think they called them that when you were growing up. You remember a lot of talk about "developing" when you were a teenager—as if you are film in an instant camera. You hate your plump, less-than-perfect body and despise having your picture taken, but your father tells you to stop being silly and snaps you out in the backyard in your bathing suit working on your tan, or coming down the living room steps on the first day of school in a brand-new skirt and sweater. His camera spits out the photo, and you watch in dread and fascination as the image on the shiny paper slowly takes shape. You develop right in front of your own and your father's eyes. And there isn't a damn thing you can do about it.

✤

"It's nothing," you tell your lover. "It's just my lumpy mashed-potato breasts." That's what the doctor calls them every year during your physical exam as her fingers ply your flesh. "Do you do a self breast exam?" she always asks. Some years you lie and say yes. Other years you fess up and tell her the truth. You can't tell the lumps from the bumps, you say. It feels like one big mass of stuff. "If you do it regularly," your doctor tells you, "you'll get to know your breasts. Then you'll be able to tell if anything changes." She uses the flats of her fingers to press your breasts around and around. You do not think of your lover. You think of your cat, who kneads you with his paws every morning using this same amount of pressure. "Your breasts feel perfectly normal," the doctor finishes up. "Like lumpy mashed potatoes. What you're looking for is a hard lump. Like a pea, bean, or marble." You nod, vowing to turn over a new leaf. You'll do a breast exam every month, eat more vegetables, drink more water, take up jogging. Of course you do none of these things.

"It's nothing," you tell your lover again, hoping she'll go back to what she was doing. But your lover has a built-in bullshit detector. She hears the fear in your voice. She sees through you so easily, you might as well be Saran Wrap. It is one of the things you love and hate about her.

✤

Your breasts arrive the summer between fifth and sixth grade. You spend all of July and August at sleep-away camp. You laugh at the girls who are so homesick they live for the mail and cry themselves to sleep. You love being away from your parents. You feel incredibly free. You even have a boyfriend. His name is Jed, and he is the first person (besides your father) to call you beautiful. He loves it when you gather up all your long, thick black hair, hold it aloft for a split second, and then let it tumble over your shoulders and neck. Jed is a good five inches shorter than you, but you don't care. It only matters when you slow-dance, and instead of putting your head on his shoulder, he puts his head on yours. He also puts his hand on your breast one night down by the lake when you sneak out to meet him. You are lying on the ground; he is lying on top of you, and before you know it he has snaked his hand between your bodies. Your breath slows and quickens at the same time. So does your heartbeat. You wonder now which breast it was, the right one with the I'm-sure-it's-nothing-lump, or the left one which will be the one that's left if the right one is taken away.

When your parents pick you up from camp, you stop at a Howard Johnson's on the way home to get something to eat. You wait for a table with your mother, while your father goes "to use the john." As soon as he is gone, your mother grabs you by the arm, digs her fingers into your skin, and whispers loud enough to make your cheeks burn with shame, "I don't care what you did in the woods down there, but now you're back in civilization, and the first thing we're going to do when we get home, young lady, is buy you a brassiere." You don't know how she knows, but she does, and you blame her for the fact that even though Jed promised he'd write, call, and visit, you never hear from him again.

✤

"Do you think it's cancer?" you ask your lover when it's clear she isn't going to pick up where she left off. She shakes her head. You know what she is thinking, but you can't help it: You're a pessimist, you always assume the worst. When you lost your job last year, you immediately feared becoming a bag lady; when the cat didn't eat or use his litter box for three days last month, you thought the end was near (it wasn't).

"It's probably just a cyst," your lover says, but you know her as well as she knows you, and her voice is less confident than you'd like it to be. "Call the doctor tomorrow and have her take a look at it."

"Okay." You give in and lie quietly in your lover's arms for a few minutes, letting her stroke your back and smooth your hair. You feel safe in her arms; nothing bad can happen as long as you are wrapped up like this. You wish you were your cat so you could purr. Your lover kisses your forehead, your nose, your cheek, your chin, and soon she resumes what she was doing before, much to your relief. You come fast and hard, your orgasm over almost as soon as it begins. Afterward, you cry.

Your best friend reads about the pencil test in *Seventeen* magazine and wants you both to try it. You climb the steps to her bedroom, and she closes the door behind you. Without a word, you turn back to back and take off your shirts. You wait for her to go first. She puts a pencil under her breast and you hear it clatter to the hardwood floor. You wait as she tries again. Once more the sound of wood against wood. Now it's your turn. You lift your flesh and slide the pencil under your breast. It stays put. You try your other breast. The pencil is cold against your skin, where it seems to have found a home for all time. You even jump up and down a little, as a joke, sort of, but it isn't funny and the pencil doesn't move. You both get dressed and accept your fate: Your best friend is too small to wear a bra; you are too big to go without. The pencil test is over and both of you have failed.

✤

The next morning you call your doctor's office. Of course you are put on hold. You listen to the Muzak, one hand holding the receiver, the other wandering over your breast. Maybe it's gone, you think. Maybe you imagined it. After all, no one in your family has ever had cancer. Not even your mother, who smokes two packs a day. What are the other high-risk factors? You can't remember. But it doesn't matter. The lump is still there, hard, stubborn, undeniable. You quickly take away your hand, afraid that you'll irritate the lump, afraid that worrying it will make it grow. But like a child who can't help wiggling a loose tooth with her tongue, your hand finds its way back to the upper, outer quarter of your right breast, where trouble has been brewing—for how long?—without your knowledge. Don't they say that by the time you can feel a lump it's been growing inside you for two years? Or is it ten? Again you can't remember.

Finally the nurse comes on the line and sets up an appointment for next week. Next week? But what about the lump? She assures you one week won't make any difference one way or the other. You don't know whether to feel panic or relief.

✤

The lady in the lingerie department at Macy's has glasses perched on the tip of her nose and a measuring tape looped around her neck like a snake. She measures your bust size by pulling the tape tight around your back and bringing the two ends around in front. You almost die as the back of her hand accidentally brushes one of your nipples. "Thirty-four," she reads aloud to your mother, "and I think she's a B cup already."

"Thirty-four B?" Your mother's voice is full of shock and disdain, as though you've done something wrong, as though you grew your breasts on purpose, all by yourself. You tell her to wait outside the dressing room while you walk through the curtain and pull it closed tightly behind you. You take off your shirt and put your arms through the straps of one of the lacy white bras the saleswoman handed you. Now what? You reach behind your back, your bent arms flapping up and down like useless wings as you try to match hook and eye, but it's impossible. Just when you think you're going to need your mother's help after all, you figure out how to put on the bra by fastening the hooks around the front of your waist and then swiveling them around to the back and pulling the bra straps up over your arms. There.

You suck in your stomach and study yourself in the mirror. You look like what your older sister would look like if you had one. You gather up all your hair, hoist it above your head, and let it rain down around your shoulders. You arch your back and put your hands on your hips like a girl modeling a bikini in *Seventeen* magazine. You purse your lips at your own reflection, and just as you are about to blow yourself a kiss, your mother's arm appears through the slit in the curtain. The rest of her follows. "How are you making out?" she asks, the saleswoman standing behind her like a shadow.

"Mom!" you shriek, rushing to cover yourself. Your mother backs out, stepping on the saleswoman's foot. This would all be funny, you think, if it was happening in a movie instead of to you.

✤

The week before your doctor's appointment, your lover can't keep her hands off you. You tease her about a second honeymoon as she leaves the dishes after supper to carry you into the bedroom. You grab and claw and clutch at each other, yet you are soft and tender too. The last time you were like this was when your grandmother died. You drove down to New York, checked into your hotel room, and, as you and your lover undressed to change into good clothes for the funeral, something came over the two of you. You don't know who started it, but in an instant you were thrashing around on one of the double beds in the room, rolling from side to side, first you on top of her, then she on top of you. You were the last ones to arrive at the funeral parlor, and though your mother couldn't possibly have known what you'd been up to, you could hardly look at her. You were sure everyone in the room could smell your lover on your hands.

Your lover's hands are on your breasts now. She asks if it's all right, and you nod. You want her to touch them and only them. You leave your jeans on so that you are topless and barefoot. Your breasts are very sensitive; you are one of those women who can come just from having your lover touch your breasts. You are proud of this, as if it's some kind of talent, like wiggling your ears or curling your tongue. As you begin to melt under your lover's mouth, you think, *Please, God, don't take this away from me.*

✤

You sit on the exam table, your clothes folded on a chair, replaced by a white johnny dotted with small blue flowers that ties in the back. Paper crinkles under your legs and your butt; you have been waiting for a good twenty minutes, after sitting in the lobby for just as long. Not only that, you had arrived early for your appointment. Your lover wanted to come with you, but you nixed the idea and sent her off to work. There are only a certain number of days she's allowed to take off from her job and you want her to save them, just in case, though of course you didn't tell her that. She would have only teased you again for thinking the worst. You sigh, shut your eyes, let your left hand find its way to your right breast one last time. It's still there. The lump. Your mind whirls: one lump or two? Is that a lump in your breast or are you just happy to see me? Don't just sit there like a lump on a log. "Stop it," you say out loud just as your doctor enters the room.

"How are you?" she asks, and you don't know why, but tears well up in your eyes. She studies your chart, giving you a minute to get hold of yourself. Then she sighs too, as if you are both resigned to something. "Let's have a look," she says, coming over to the table and motioning for you to lie down.

You let her slide the johnny to your waist as you lift your arms over your head. She feels your right breast, starting in the center near your nipple and working her way out in a clockwise spiral. You know when she has come to the lump, not because you can feel her feel it but because her expression changes and she utters a little "hmm," something she has never done before. Usually she makes idle chatter when she examines your breasts: the weather, an upcoming holiday, whatever. You are both lesbians, and though you do not travel in the same social circles, it's still a bit awkward. You and your lover have joked about the good old doc and how many pies she's put her fingers in. Professionally, of course.

But this is nothing to joke about. You'd been counting on her to dismiss your concerns with a little chuckle and maybe even chastise you for being a hypochondriac, but she does no such thing. She feels your other breast, and you remember her telling you that if you feel something suspicious on your right breast, feel your left breast to see if there is something similar there. Clearly there isn't; now the doctor is feeling your right breast again, and again she mutters, "hmm." Then she tells you to get dressed.

"I am concerned about this," your doctor says when she comes back into the room. "When was your last period?" She looks at the chart again. "Three weeks ago." She answers her own question. "So you're due next week. Why don't you come back in three weeks, after your period, and we'll see if anything changes. In the meantime, I want you to cut out coffee, take four hundred units of vitamin E per day, and have a mammogram." You nod as she fills out a slip of paper. "Do you have any questions?"

Only one: When will this all be over?

✤

Breasts, bosoms, bazooms, bazookas, boobs, boobies, boobalas, teats, tits, titties, titskis, titskilehs, nipples, nippies, gazungas, headlights, hooters, hangers, jugs, knockers, maracas, milk duds, mams, mammies, mammos, mondo busto, eggplants, pamplemousse, melons, boulders, pimples, udders. Flat as a pancake, flat as a board. Hey, want a bust in the mouth? She's like a third world country: undeveloped. Buxom, busty, built, stacked, ripe for the pickin', well-endowed. Do your boobs hang low, do they wobble to and fro? Victoria's Secret. Frederick's of Hollywood. Tit-slinger, harness, over-the-shoulder-boulder-holder. Ze-bra. Bra Mitzvoh. Two men were walking abreast. Keeping abreast of the situation. Breast friends. Bosom buddies. It was the breast of times, it was the worst of times. Breast Area: Enter Here.

✤

You haven't had a mammogram for five years, since you were thirty-seven. Your doctor told you it was silly to have one then; you were too young, your breast tissue too thick, but you had insisted because your friend Viv had found a lump in her breast that turned out to be malignant and it freaked you out. Viv was a health food nut, she'd had a child before the age of thirty, there was no cancer in her family, she exercised regularly, ate no chocolate, drank no coffee or soda; in other words, she did everything she was supposed to do and still her body betrayed her. After her diagnosis, Viv became a breast cancer activist. She let everyone feel her lump before she had it and her breast removed; she didn't wear a hat, scarf, or wig to cover her bald, shiny head; she organized a group of survivors who held potluck dinners once a month and made special visits to women who needed to have mastectomies.

"Every time we visit a woman who's about to have surgery, the same thing happens," Viv tells you one day at lunch. Viv eats an enormous seaweed and sprouts salad and sips bancha tea; you gulp coffee with your gooey grilled cheese sandwich. "The woman looks around," Viv says, "and slowly it dawns on her: She's the only person with two breasts in the entire room. Then—you can almost see it on her face—she realizes she will survive, that a breast is only a breast, it isn't your life. And then she cries with relief."

You don't tell Viv what you suspect: that the tears she witnesses over and over again might not be tears of joy, and that you hope and pray she belongs to a club that would never have you as a member.

✤

You arrive early for your mammogram and are shown into a dressing room with lockers, almost like a gym. But instead of a swimming pool or Nautilus equipment waiting to welcome your body, there is only a cold, hard mammogram machine. The technician is very nice; she apologizes for what she has to do. She places your left breast onto a smooth, ice-cold plate, then lowers another plate and tells you to take a deep breath as she squeezes the plates together. You hold on tightly to a metal railing beside you and try to keep breathing. Was it this bad the last time? You can't remember. The technician leaves, then comes back to release you and change the plates. She positions your right breast, and as she leaves the room you begin to feel dizzy. The room is growing dark, your head is spinning; all of a sudden you're nauseous, you actually see spots before your eyes. Your hand begins to lose its grip and the next thing you know you are sitting in a chair with your head between your knees, the technician's hand rubbing your back.

"Are you all right?" she asks.

You are so embarrassed you want to die, you think, then you hasten to correct yourself in case anyone, like God, is privy to your thoughts. You don't want to die; that's why you're here, isn't it? Slowly you sit up and face the technician. "Did you eat anything this morning?" she asks. You shake your head. You never eat breakfast. Then you remember the time you gave blood a few years ago—you'd fainted then too. They pumped you up with orange juice and doughnuts afterward, and that's what the technician offers you now. You eat, drink, sit in the waiting area for a while, watching other women go in, come out, get dressed, and leave with their prize: a pink carnation for a job well done. After half an hour, the technician asks if you think you're up for trying again. You nod and follow her in. This time you complete the procedure without incident. Later you will joke about the whole thing and tell your lover how you were hanging there by your tit, the technician all aflutter. Again your lover will see right through you. She will zing your favorite movie line right at you, the one spoken by a distraught Katharine Hepburn in *The Lion in Winter* that you yourself are fond of quoting: "Laughter is how I show my despair."

✤

What do they say, one in every ten women gets breast cancer? No, they say one in every ten women is a lesbian. Is it one in nine? One in eight? How do they come up with those numbers anyway? You find yourself studying women on the street. Every one you see has breasts. Round, floppy breasts. Small, perky breasts. Whatever the shape, they definitely come in twos. Maybe all the cancer survivors have had reconstructive surgery. Or maybe they're wearing falsies. You're sure they don't call them that anymore. Prosthesis. Breasts. Such hard words to say. They don't exactly roll off the tongue. Prosthessssisssss. Breast-st-st-st-stssss. You have to hiss the words out, like a snake.

You remember a poster from your early feminist days. It showed a photo of a woman who'd had one breast removed. She'd covered the scar across her flattened chest with a flowery tattoo, and under the photo was a poem she had written. You can't remember much of it, something about a tree. That poster hung on the walls of every women's bookstore you'd ever been to. Viv had one over her bed. You remember lesbians talking about Amazons who had chosen to remove one breast so they could be better archers. Now women are having their breasts taken off and calling themselves FTMs or tranny boys. You once saw a news story about a woman whose mother, grandmother, aunt, sister, and cousin all died of breast cancer. The woman had a double mastectomy even though she had no signs of cancer. If all these women could go through it, so can you. You still don't know what *it* is. It could be nothing. It could be everything.

✤

Your lover brings in the mail and hands you your stack. Phone bill, credit card statement, *People* magazine, letter from the health center. You wait until your lover goes into the other room to listen to her phone messages before you tear open the envelope. You unfold the single sheet of paper and see immediately that it is a form letter, telling you that your mammogram showed "no definite signs of cancer at this time." Does that mean it showed indefinite signs of cancer at this time? You study the letter intently, but it offers you no further information than the standard advice you already know: Do monthly self breast exams and have a mammogram every year.

Your lover comes back into the room talking about dinner. You show her the letter. "That's good, isn't it?" she asks, her voice cautious. You suppose so, yet you still feel glum. Your period has come and gone, but the lump has not gone with it, as you had hoped. You'd been counting on it dissolving like a lump of sugar in a cup of tea, and you'd spent more time than you'd care to admit fantasizing about canceling your next doctor's appointment. You imagined yourself telling her over the phone that the lump was gone, vanished into thin air, hocus-pocus, abracadabra, now you see it, now you don't. But as your lover, who is in one of those relentless twelve-step programs, is fond of saying, "Denial is not a river in Egypt."

✤

The morning of your doctor's appointment, you spend a long time in the bathroom. You wash, scrub, rinse, shave, moisturize, powder, and puff. You baby your breasts. You talk to them. You coo, cajole, tell them not to worry, whisper that everything will be okay. Still, your mind gets the better of you. You force yourself to imagine the worst: what it would be like to lose your breast. It's hard to go there. You are extremely squeamish about blood. You remember taking a friend with stomach cramps to the emergency room a few years ago. The friend insisted you stay with her, and for some reason the doctor let you. As soon as the nurse put the IV into your friend's arm, you hit the floor. When you came to, you saw the nurse was not amused. "That's why we ask friends to stay in the waiting room," she scolded, showing you the door.

How would you handle an operation? And how would you handle being lopsided? You know many women decide to have reconstructive surgery, and you imagine that you would too. A former lover of yours had breast reduction surgery a year ago. She told you more than you wanted to know: how the doctor had taken off her nipples, made her breasts smaller, and then reattached them. You imagine your ex-lover's luscious brown nipples on a cold metal tray, like two Hershey's Kisses, waiting to be returned to her body. She wanted to show you her new and improved breasts, but you declined the offer.

You get dressed and convince yourself to eat something before you leave for the doctor's office. There's not much in the refrigerator, just a few Tupperware containers with leftovers in various edible and inedible states. You put a glop of mashed potatoes in the microwave before the irony of the situation hits you and you hear your doctor's voice in your head, talking about your "lumpy mashed-potato breasts." Some comfort food, you think, as you shovel in bite after bite after bite.

✣

You know the routine by now—fill in the form: name, address, date of birth, date of last period, method of birth control, why you are here today. Under birth control you put your usual flip answer: *lesbianism—one hundred percent foolproof!* You ponder the next question, biting the tip of your pen. I'm here because I'm queer because I'm here because I'm queer. The little chant spins round and round your brain. You shake your head to clear away the noise. I'm here because my lover made me come. I'm here because I always do what's on my calendar. I'm here because I ate too much fatty food when I was growing up. I'm here because I did something in a past life that screwed up my karma. I'm here because what goes around comes around. I'm here because I don't know what else to do.

Finally you fill in the line next to "Why are you here today?" with four little words, "Because of my breast," but you accidentally omit the "r" and the word "breast" reads "beast." Because of my beast. Is that a sign? Of what? You really should start meditating again, you tell yourself. You need to quiet your mind.

As soon as you hand the receptionist your form, your name is called and you are ushered into an exam room. This time your doctor does not keep you waiting long. She glances at your chart, then tells you to lie down. She is all business today as she explores your body. She asks if you would mind if she brought an intern in to feel your breast, and you are so detached from your body, you say you wouldn't mind at all.

She goes out and returns a minute later with the intern, who looks about seventeen and is a man besides. You can't believe the possibility the intern would be male never even occurred to you. Your doctor is a lesbian, just like you: Doesn't she know most lesbians don't like men touching their bodies? But you aren't really angry at her—you're angry at yourself. How could you be so stupid? But it's too late. Your doctor is already showing him where to feel, and suddenly you are no longer in the room. You are at college twenty years ago. You see a sign posted in the student center: FEMALE STUDENTS: MAKE $50 IN TWO HOURS. CALL NOW: 555-0978. You call and are told to come to the science building the next day. You lie splayed across a table, topless, while half a dozen young men in lab coats—the future doctors of America—file by, each of them examining your breasts. One boy—you can still see his bespeckled, pimply face—gets very excited. "I think I found something!" he exclaims, and everyone rushes over. The professor, a tall, middle-aged man with wavy salt-and-pepper hair who reminds you of your father, pushes him gently aside and uses his expert hands. "That's nothing," he tells his students. "These breasts are perfectly normal." You get dressed, receive your fifty dollars in cash, go home, and crawl into bed even though it's the middle of the day. You still don't know why you did it. Sure, fifty dollars went a long way back then, but still, your parents had set you up with a bank account. You didn't need the cash.

You felt proud of your breasts twenty years ago. Had you hoped they would all be bowled over by your beauty? Were you looking for love, admiration, acceptance? A week later you see one of the students on the street and your eyes meet. "Do I know you?" he asks, and you think it's a pickup line, except he does look familiar.

"Are you a student?" you ask.

He nods. "Premed," he says proudly, and then it hits you both at the same time. Even though you can't see your own face, you're sure it's as red as his is, as he mumbles something and rushes away. As red as you're sure your face is now as the intern thanks you and backs out of the room.

After you get dressed, your doctor comes back to give you the news. "It doesn't feel really suspicious to me, but it doesn't feel unsuspicious either. Since we can't be sure, let's just go ahead and remove it."

"My breast?" you shriek, your hands automatically flying up to protect it.

"No, no, no. The lump."

"Oh." You are so relieved you don't ask about other options. It's like that old coming-out strategy—call your parents and say you have something very important to tell them: You only have six months to live. After they get completely hysterical, say you were only kidding. The news is: You're gay. No big deal. Right? Right? Right?

✤

Your lover takes the day off and drives you to the hospital. You are glad she'll be there in the waiting room, though you feel guilty for making her miss a day of work. She tells you to stop being ridiculous, but you feel still feel this is all your fault. There must have been something you could have done to prevent it. Been nicer to your mother? Given more to charity? My karma ran over my dogma, you think as you hug your lover goodbye and let them take you away.

You don't look as they put the IV into your arm. As you begin to feel nauseous, they tell you to count backward from one hundred and you get to ninety-seven. The next thing you know you are in the recovery room, and the first thing you see is your lover's face. "Your sister's here," the nurse says, all smiles.

"I don't have a sister," you say before you recede into a drugged-out fog again.

When you take the bandage off the next day, your breast is black and blue. You are not really in pain, but still you take the Tylenol they sent you home with, just in case. You have to wear a bra day and night, and you are squeamish about having anyone hug you. Friends come and go, send cards, flowers. You are the hostess-with-the-mostest, making sure everyone has what they want to drink, entertaining everyone with your war stories. Some women from Viv's group show up, even though Viv has moved out of state. Somehow they always know where to find you. They tell you about their latest achievements and defeats: They've convinced several local lingerie stores to have plastic breasts imbedded with cancer-like lumps in their dressing rooms so women can feel them and know what they're looking for; they've haven't yet been able to convince Mattel to put out a Breast Cancer Barbie. They tell you when their next meeting is and invite you to join them. But you are not ready for your membership card, a voice inside your head gloats. Until another voice pushes that one aside and reminds you: not yet.

Your doctor gives you the good news: Your tumor is benign. The news startles you; it is the first time she's used the word "tumor." You thought you had a lump, but no, you had a tumor. A benign tumor. It's called a fibroadenoma—such a big word for such a little lump. But it's gone and you're out of the woods. For now. Yes, your doctor tells you, it can come back. No, there's no way of telling whether it will or won't. You should do breast exams every month and have a complete physical once a year, including a mammogram. Cut down on caffeine. Eat five servings of fruits and vegetables a day. Exercise regularly. Be grateful.

That night you feel euphoric, giddy, goofy. When your lover gets home, you seat her at the kitchen table. "What's this?" she asks, motioning to the cardboard square and plastic chips you've put at her place.

"We're playing bingo," you tell her, and though she looks puzzled—what in the world?—she goes along, to humor you.

"A, one," you call out. Your lover puts a chip in the corresponding space on her card.

"B, nine," you say, watching her face. She puts down a chip with no response.

"B, nine," you call again.

"You already said that," says your lover.

"B, nine," you repeat, ignoring her. "B, nine," you say even louder. "B, nine. B, *nine. BEEE*, NINE." You say it again and again, until your lover finally gets it.

"Benign?" she asks.

"Bingo!" you yell as your lover leaps up, knocking over her chair in her haste to embrace you.

"Benign! Benign!" You both scream the word over and over as you jump up and down all across the kitchen floor with your arms linked around each other's waist, laughing like maniacs.

✤

You didn't know you would have a bright red scar that would, over time, fade to pink, but never completely heal. You didn't know the area around the scar would remain angry-looking and hard. You didn't know it would be a long, long time before you could look down at your right breast and not think about dying. You didn't know your lover would become less spontaneous and somewhat hesitant, more likely to ask rather than grab like she used to. You didn't know that she, the strong, silent one, had been scared out of her wits too.

You didn't know you would never be the same but that some parts of you would actually be better. You're more aware now. You don't take things for granted. You have been given a second chance and you embrace it eagerly, your face lifted toward the sun, your arms flung to the skies, your mouth open wide to greedily gulp great fistfuls of air, like life.

Bashert

"These are amazing."

"Incredible."

"I've never seen such fabulous paintings."

"I've never seen such a fabulous model."

Susan just smiled and tried not to spill the glass of white wine she was holding as an eager patron of the arts jostled her silk-clad arm in his haste to get a closer look at her work. And instead of sipping her wine, she drank in the moment many were calling her overnight success, though she knew it had begun with another moment more than twenty years ago…

✤

"You're going to Israel for a year, to work on a *kibbutz,*" Susan's parents said to her in 1977, the summer after she graduated from the State University of New York. "No need to thank us for this wonderful opportunity we're giving you. Just go, see, enjoy, and maybe you'll even learn something about yourself."

What Susan's parents didn't tell her was this: *Over a million Jewish men in this country and you couldn't find one to marry? What's wrong with you? Twenty-one years old you are, with no boyfriend, no career—a B.S. in art history—that and a token will get you a ride on the subway—what else can we do but ship you off to the land of milk and honey and see what God has in mind for you to make of yourself?*

And so Susan packed a few articles of clothing along with her charcoals, drawing pencils, and sketch pads, kissed her parents goodbye, and boarded an El Al jet filled with *sabres,* or native Israelis who spoke the language of her people, though Susan hardly understood a word. She knew, from reading a travel brochure, that a *sabre* was literally a fruit that was tough on the outside and sweet and tender on the inside, and she could understand why her fellow travelers were so dubbed—at least because of the outside part. They didn't talk as much as bark at one another, their words filled with the language's trademark guttural utterings, each one sounding like the beginning of a spit.

Susan leaned back in her seat and closed her eyes as the plane lifted into takeoff. She liked being surrounded by people she looked like—people with olive skin, dark hair and eyes, noses that hardly looked like ski slopes, and full lips—and she didn't mind being unable to communicate with them. On the contrary, she found it strangely comforting. Susan often thought of her life as a movie, a black-and-white foreign film with distorted sound and a grainy picture, shown at an art house with uncomfortable creaky seats. Going to the Jewish homeland was just the next scene in the film of her life that someone else was forever directing. Susan didn't try to protest, didn't try to rewrite the script, didn't ask for a different part. She didn't board the plane willingly or unwillingly; she took her seat and buckled up automatically, just as she had gone off to college, putting one foot in front of the other with a sigh, hoping for the best.

The flight, which lasted an entire day, was completely uneventful until the wheels of the plane touched ground. Then, as if on cue, the *sabres* burst into song: "Hatikva," the Israeli national anthem, whose title, Susan knew, meant "The Hope." Even though she could have joined in—she knew the words and the melody from singing it in temple during the High Holy Days—she remained silent and let the fervor and passion with which the Israelis sang envelop her. By the time the plane got to the gate, Susan's eyes were brimming with tears. The song ended just as the FASTEN SEAT BELT sign was turned off. Then the moment was broken and chaos ensued, with everyone jumping up to grab their carry-on luggage and dash off the plane.

Susan made her way over to a man standing at the gate flashing a hand-lettered sign that read KIBBUTZ VOLUNTEERS. She showed him the letter she'd received assigning her to a medium-size agricultural *kibbutz* in the northern part of the tiny country, near a city called Haifa. Other people brandishing letters approached as well, and when a dozen of them had gathered, the man herded them out to a van and whisked them off into the night. Susan slept through most of the bumpy ride, until she was handed off, like a baton in a relay race, to a volunteer waiting for her at the *kibbutz* entrance. She was driven by Jeep to a dorm and then led, stumbling, to the room she would call home for the next twelve months. She tried to be quiet, as three other girls were already sleeping in the small, crowded cubicle, but she couldn't help turning on the light for just a minute, and she was forever glad that she did, for there on her mattress lay a spider, a huge brown bristly-hairy spider that she was in no hurry to share her sleeping quarters with.

"Oh, my God," Susan gasped in a stage whisper loud enough to wake the girl in the next bed.

"What is it?" the girl whispered back, her voice sleepy and annoyed.

"A spider. It's bigger than my fist. I've never seen—"

Susan's words were interrupted by a *thwack!* as the girl threw a shoe onto her bed, sending the spider scurrying away. "You'll get used to them," she murmured, rolling over and going back to sleep.

Susan didn't have much time to get used to anything, since she was woken up the next morning at five o'clock to get ready for work. She'd been assigned the orange fields, which the *kibbutzniks* called *Pardis,* meaning Paradise. Susan introduced herself to her new roommates: Rona, who hogged the bathroom, blow-drying her hair for a good half-hour even though it frizzed up the minute she stepped outside; Yael, neé Janet, who though born and bred in Hoboken, N.J., now spoke English in short, broken sentences with a pseudo-Israeli accent; and Madeleine, who hailed from England and didn't understand why they had to wake up so early—it wasn't like the "bloody oranges" were going anywhere.

At six o'clock sharp a small truck arrived to pick up Susan and company. All the volunteers were dressed alike, in regulation *kibbutz* clothing: white T-shirts, khaki shorts, canvas work boots, and cotton hats. Susan, always sensitive to color—or lack of it—thought they looked like a studio full of blank canvases waiting to be painted. But as soon as they were dropped off in the orange grove, sleepy as she was, Susan saw the beauty of the contrast between the volunteers' drab clothing and their colorful surroundings. No wonder it was called Paradise: The trees were lush with emerald leaves that shone in the sun; the sky was a perfect cornflower-blue, the likes of which Susan had never seen; and to top it all off, the sweet, intoxicating smell of oranges wafted through the air like the perfume of an elegant woman who had just left the room. Susan felt a bit lightheaded from the aroma, the early hour, and undoubtedly a severe case of jet lag. She took a swig of water from the canteen hitched to her belt and tried to get hold of herself as she listened to the instructions a man named Shlomo was yelling in her direction. But it was useless to pay attention. She couldn't even figure out what language Shlomo was screaming in, let alone understand what he was talking about.

Each volunteer was given a rickety wooden ladder, a white canvas bag, and a row of trees. Somehow Susan figured out that her mission was to drag the ladder to the start of her row, lean it up against the first tree, climb to the top rung despite her fear of heights, drop oranges into the canvas bag slung across her shoulder, climb down the ladder, walk to the end of her row, and dump the fruit into a crate the size of her new living quarters, all without injuring herself. This, she found out, was easier said than done—in Hebrew or any other language—since the more oranges she dropped into her bag, the heavier it grew and the shakier her balance became. As Susan tried to shift her weight, the ladder beneath her shifted its weight as well. Several times she held on for dear life as the ladder threatened to topple; twice she even found herself praying to a God she didn't believe in—but, she reasoned once her safety was secured, if God wasn't here in Paradise, where else would He be?

To her surprise, the skin of the oranges, even when they were ripe, was not orange in color, but rather a dark forest-green. When she saw the other volunteers up in their treetops were snacking, she followed suit, digging her thumbnail into the thick rind of an orange and pulling it back to expose the pale orange pulp inside.

Susan tore into a section with her teeth, and as juice dripped down her chin she marveled at how sweet the fruit tasted, much, much sweeter than any orange she had ever eaten at home. There were two ways to tell if these green oranges were ripe: if they came off the tree easily (they had to be twisted by the stem, not yanked) and by their size. Shlomo—who Susan learned from Madeleine was from Argentina and therefore spoke Hebrew with a thick Spanish accent—handed Susan a measuring tool made of wire, shaped into a circle, like a child's oversize bubble wand. She was instructed to hold the tool up to orange after orange to see if the fruit was big enough to pluck. Of course it didn't take long for one of the male volunteers to hold up his wand to a girl's bosom, first one breast and then the other, to see if either one was ripe. The girl merely giggled, as did several other volunteers; some of them even called for the boy to bring his wand over to see if they measured up. Susan just ignored him.

By eight o'clock the sun was hot and bright orange in the sky and a whistle was blown, signaling breakfast. All the volunteers clamored down from their ladders and made their way to a cluster of picnic tables set up outside a cabin-like structure where Shlomo had prepared a feast Susan couldn't believe: fluffy omelets made with avocados grown on the *kibbutz;* huge bowls of creamy white yogurt topped with swirls of amber-colored honey; sandwiches made of *challah* and Nutella; and for dessert, *halvah,* a sticky sweet brick made of honey and ground sesame seeds. Susan, whose father was a dentist, wondered if she'd have any teeth left by the end of this "life experience" her parents had given her. Still, she chowed down with the best of them, passing the salt and pepper when motioned to but mostly remaining silent as conversation and jokes in Hebrew, Spanish, Danish, Russian, and English swirled around her. Susan sat with the English and American girls, whom she could at least understand, but she felt distant from them, and distant from herself. Of course she was awfully far from home—halfway around the world!—but that really didn't matter. Susan always felt removed from whatever situation she found herself in, like she was underwater or behind a window made of thick, smoky glass.

After breakfast it was back to work until noon, and then it was quitting time. The intense heat of the sun forced everyone down from their ladders and back into the truck to be driven from the fields to the main dining hall in the center of the *kibbutz*. Lunch was served at exactly one o'clock, and Susan, who barely ate breakfast at home—a cup of coffee and maybe half a buttered bagel—was surprised that despite her Paul Bunyan–size breakfast, she was ravenous. The *kibbutzniks* ate their main meal of the day in the afternoon—vegetable soup, broiled chicken, baked potatoes, cooked carrots, and of course dessert, a sheet cake with chocolate frosting that set Susan's teeth on edge. Still, she filled her belly then retired to her room for a much-needed nap.

Less than an hour after her curly head hit the pillow, there was a knock on the door. "*Ulpan!* Fifteen minutes," someone called. *Ulpan* meant Hebrew school. Susan dragged herself out of a deep sleep and rapped on the bathroom door.

"Just a minute," called a disembodied voice Susan recognized as Rona's.

"She lives in there, love." Madeleine gestured with an open compact, then began powdering her nose. Madeleine was one of those women who tried her best to turn any getup—even a bland *kibbutz* outfit—into a fashion statement. A great deal of cleavage showed above the neckline of her white cotton T-shirt, and she'd tied the bottom of it up in a knot so that her belly button peeked out over the khaki shorts that tightly hugged her abundant thighs.

"Rona. Hair." Yael pointed to her own scalp and shook her head in disapproval. The curls of her short "Jewfro" bounced up and down with the motion.

Finally Rona emerged and Susan entered the bathroom, which contained a sink with a mirror hanging over it, a toilet, and, instead of a shower stall, a spigot with two faucets underneath mounted right into the wall. When Susan showered, the toilet and sink got soaked, as did her clothing and towel. Not only that, a good two inches of water remained on the floor, until she figured out she had to push it all toward a drain in the corner with a rubber squeegee. The water moved slowly until Susan removed a glob of Rona's hair from the drain. "Dorm life, *kibbutz* style," she sighed as she hurried to get dressed and catch up with her roommates who were also headed out to *ulpan.*

"Shalom, shalom." Ze'ev, the Hebrew teacher, greeted his students with great enthusiasm and motioned for them to sit down at the large circular table in the middle of the room. Ze'ev's classroom was outfitted with a desk and a blackboard, above which hung green sheets of paper with the Hebrew alphabet printed in large white letters. Susan, who had dropped out of Hebrew school after only a year and never had a *bat mitzvah,* stared up at the letters, but try as she might she couldn't drag their sounds up from the dredges of her long-term memory bank.

"Ze'ev." Ze'ev pointed to himself then pointed to Susan.

"Um…"

"He wants to know your name, love," Madeleine whispered.

"Susan."

"Shoshana." Ze'ev bestowed upon Susan the same Hebrew name she'd been given long ago by her childhood Hebrew schoolteacher. *"Ahnee Ze'ev. Aht Shoshana."* He pointed to Madeleine. *"He Malka."* Then Ze'ev turned to the class and asked *"Me Malka?"* They answered in response, pointing to Madeleine, *"He Malka."* Susan was utterly confused until Madeleine explained in a whisper that *he* meant "she," *me* meant "who," and *who* meant "he." Other than Madeleine's explanatory whisperings, not a word of English was spoken during the entire lesson, and by the time the hour and a half was over, Susan's head was spinning.

From four-thirty to six-thirty, the volunteers had free time. Not knowing what else to do, Susan went back to her room and unpacked her things. There were no dressers or bureaus for the volunteers; instead each room had four metal, high school–like lockers along one wall. Susan opened the door of the only locker without a lock on it (she'd have to ask someone where to get one) and was touched to see a "welcome" packet inside. The packet consisted of a brochure explaining the history of the *kibbutz,* a chocolate bar, a package of cookies, and a pair of socks with the *kibbutz* logo on it.

After Susan unpacked, she grabbed her sketch pad and went outside to sit on the grass near the volunteers' residence hall.

She'd promised herself she'd draw every day, even if only for ten or fifteen minutes. *A real artist has to be disciplined,* she reminded herself, though she knew she wasn't a real artist. Real artists were passionate. Real artists were creative. Real artists were driven. Susan knew she wasn't any of these things. Oh, she could render a passable likeness of a flower, a table, a rock, or anything else that was placed smack-dab in front of her. But her drawings were wooden; they lacked any kind of feeling or emotion. They didn't really *express* anything. That's what her college professors said anyway. They kept telling her to loosen up. "Your still lifes have no life in them," one of them had said. "Just let your fingers go," said another, taking her wrist in his big, hairy hand and shaking it up and down until her arm flopped like a rag doll's. "That's it," he nodded in approval. "Now try and draw." She didn't think it made a bit of difference, and even though the teacher had said "That's better," she could tell he didn't mean it.

Susan squinted her eyes against the bright sun and decided to draw some of the low, flat buildings around her. She needed to work on her perspective anyway. But as soon as she put charcoal to paper, she was interrupted.

"Drawing, eh? I'm Jeremy, from Canada. You're new here, eh?" Jeremy flopped down right next to her, crossed his long, skinny legs, and pushed his glasses up his nose.

"Yes," Susan said, reluctant to introduce herself.

"Susan, right? I sat across from you at *ulpan*. Which do you prefer, Susan or Shoshana? They call me Jacob, but I can't get used to it." Susan continued to draw without answering Jeremy, but that didn't stop him from keeping up a running conversation.

"I've been here about a month. It's all right, don't know how long I'll stay. They've already asked me about making *aliyah,* but I don't think I'll go that far, what about you, eh?"

"What's *aliyah*?" Susan asked as she shaded in the side of a building.

"Oh, you know, moving here. Permanently. Becoming an Israeli citizen. You've heard of the Law of Return, haven't you?" Susan tucked a lock of dark hair behind her ear and shook her head, so Jeremy explained. "It means every Jew can become a citizen, no questions asked. They'll be bothering you about it before long, so you'd better start thinking it over. Hey, want to take a walk after dinner?" Jeremy abruptly changed the subject. "The nights here are very romantic."

Was he asking her out on a date? "Thanks, but I'm really tired. Still jet-lagged. Sorry."

"All right. Maybe another time, eh?" Jeremy scrambled to his feet and stood over Susan for a moment with his arms folded, casting a long shadow over her work-in-progress. "I don't think you've got it quite right," he finally pronounced before turning on his heel and walking away.

"I think Jeremy fancies you," Madeleine said later as she and Susan walked to the dining hall for dinner. "He's cute. Do you fancy him as well?"

"Oh, I don't know. He was just being friendly," Susan said.

"Since when have you met a bloke who's just being friendly?" Madeleine shook her head and stuck her fists on her hips. "Watch out for the *kibbutzniks,* love, especially the married ones. They've heard you American girls are easy." She winked as she handed Susan a tray.

Dinner was a light meal, much to Susan's relief: plain yogurt with tomato and cucumber salad, *matzo* and *challah* with several types of mild cheeses, and fresh fruit for dessert. After dinner, Madeleine, who'd appointed herself Susan's personal welcome wagon, escorted her into the canteen, where the volunteers, as well as some of the young Israelis, gathered to drink coffee, eat sweets, and—as Madeleine informed Susan in case she couldn't see for herself—pair off to take a walk in the woods and smooch.

"You see him over there?" Madeleine pointed with her cup as she and Susan waited in the coffee line. "That's Mike. He's lovely, isn't he? But he knows it, thinks he's God's gift to women. He's from California, a real playboy type; he's been here about two months, and he's already been with several girls. Last week he was with her." Madeleine indicated one of the volunteers from Holland, who was tall and slim and had blond wavy hair down to her waist. "And now he's with her." She nodded toward a woman who could have been a carbon copy of the first one she'd pointed out, only her hair was flaming red. "Now, Jeremy, he was with Yael for a while, but she dumped him for that handsome *sabre*." Madeleine pointed across the room. "I fancy Stuart." Madeleine, who had been whispering all this time, dropped her voice even further. "But he won't give me the time of day. Maybe you could talk to him for me, love, what do you say?"

"Oh, I don't know." Susan and Madeleine reached the front of the line, and Madeleine showed Susan how to make coffee the Israeli way: Drop a spoonful of instant espresso into your cup, add five packets of sugar and about a tablespoon of hot water. Mix that up into a gooey paste, add another half a cup of boiling water, then top it all off with half a cup of milk. Susan's lips curled as she drank her concoction, but she forced herself to swallow, reminding herself *When in Rome...*

"Here comes Jeremy," Madeleine raised her cup to him in greeting then started to sidle off but Susan grabbed her arm.

"Hello, ladies," Jeremy said, though it was clear he was speaking to Susan. "*Mah-nish ma?*"

"*B'seder.*" Madeleine answered.

"How's everything? Fine." Jeremy translated for Susan. "Maybe I could be your tutor."

"Ooh, I bet he could teach you a thing or two," Madeleine nudged Susan's arm. "Go on, you two. *Lila tov.*"

"*Lila tov*." Jeremy replied. "Good night."

"I'm really tired. I'm going to bed. Excuse me." Susan hurried out of the canteen and headed to her dorm room. She wasn't interested in Jeremy, and she hoped he'd get the message soon. As she walked down the path lit only by moonlight, she caught sight of several couples strolling arm in arm, and several others standing perfectly still, not strolling at all.

Susan hurried along, trying to make herself invisible and not disturb anyone. She wasn't particularly interested in romance, and she hoped the *kibbutz* wasn't going to be a repeat of college, which had basically been a repeat of high school. Girls getting all giggly and googly-eyed over boys who thought they were good for one thing and one thing only: Wham, bam, thank you ma'am.

Not that Susan was a prude or anything. She'd had her share

of sexual experiences; after all, it was the seventies, the height of the sexual revolution, and everyone was screwing around. But for some reason the boys who "scored" with a different girl every night were revered as studs and the girls who brought home a different guy every night were degraded as sluts. And what, Susan wondered, was so revolutionary about that? She didn't think romance was all that important, anyway. Her art was what was important, and of the few boyfriends she'd had, none of them had taken her work seriously. Carl, a tall, athletic-looking boy whom she saw on and off during her sophomore year, had shown interest at first, but as time went on Susan saw the real reason for his curiosity: He was hoping she would draw him. Even though, as Susan pointed out, she didn't do portraits, she did still lifes and landscapes. She tried explaining to Carl that portraits were tricky, and most of the time the subject was disappointed with the finished product, even when the artist was a pro, which Susan was not. She'd only taken one figure drawing class, which was required for her major, and then went back to inanimate objects, which were much safer—they didn't argue with you about what they looked like. A portrait artist needed to have that special something to capture a person's essence on canvas, and whatever that special something was, Susan knew she didn't have it.

"Just try," Carl kept insisting despite Susan's protests, and so one day she did, mostly to shut him up. They'd just had an afternoon quickie; Susan had jumped up as soon as it was over and was already dressed, but Carl was still lounging on the single bed in her dorm room, naked, his leather belt looped around the doorknob as a KEEP OUT sign for her roommate, who was due back from her chemistry class any minute. Susan took out her art supplies and tried her best, but even Carl had to admit her sketches weren't very good. When he actually said, "Oh, well, back to the drawing board," Susan knew their affair was over.

There had been a few other boys on and off throughout the rest of her college years, but none of her affairs (calling them relationships would be stretching it) lasted more than three or four months. Susan never had trouble attracting boyfriends—she was of average height and weight, with dark brown hair and eyes, someone a boy wouldn't necessarily notice in a crowd, but someone he wouldn't be ashamed to show off to his buddies either. She was the kind of girl a guy would ask out when he didn't have the nerve to approach the girl he really wanted to be with: the curvy blond bombshell who wouldn't give him the time of day unless he was the school's star football player. Susan didn't mind, though. She only dated because she thought it was expected of her. And she didn't want her friends to think there was something wrong with her.

And she liked sex. She liked the things her body did, the way it seemed to rise and expand like a loaf of *challah* baking in the oven before her orgasm exploded, sending little zings of energy everywhere: to her hands, her feet, the nape of her neck, the small of her back, the insides of her thighs. Afterward Susan felt like she sparkled, and she loved to look at herself in the mirror then, to see the red flush spread across her chest and neck all the way up to her cheeks. It was the only time she ever felt truly beautiful. But the truth was, she didn't always come when she was with a boy, though she never had any trouble by herself. By herself it was more intense. She could take her time and not have to worry about what someone else was thinking or what someone else wanted. And best of all, afterward she could just lie in bed naked with the covers pulled up to her chin and smile. She didn't have to wrap her arms around some sweaty, smelly boy and tell him what a wonderful lover he was. She didn't have to dodge the wet spot. She didn't have to wonder when whoever was sharing her bed would leave already so she could get back to her latest painting, waiting patiently for her over in the art building, propped up on its wobbly easel.

Susan got undressed and crawled into her tiny bed, first making sure there were no spiders under the thin cotton blanket. She slept well, not even hearing her roommates come in, until the five o'clock alarm woke her to get ready for work again.

And so the weeks went on: *Pardis* in the morning, *ulpan* in the afternoon, socializing in the evenings. Susan found she enjoyed working in the orange groves. She liked the color her skin was turning: a golden brown similar to the blond oak table in her parents' dining room. She liked the muscles that formed in her upper arms and the backs of her calves. She liked the feeling of accomplishment that came when she got to the end of her row and started up the other side. And she was making slow but steady progress with her Hebrew. She could actually hold a simple conversation about the weather or the time, though she still had trouble reading and writing. She managed to draw a little every day too, though more often than not some boy, either a volunteer or *kibbutznik,* interrupted her, wanting to take her for a walk, or better yet back to his room. Susan was continually shocked at the bluntness of these offers and always declined politely, as she did in the evenings at the canteen with Madeleine at her side wistfully staring at the "blokes" she fancied, most of whom ignored her.

Summer melded seamlessly into autumn. The days were still hot, but not as fiercely so; some nights Susan even had to wear a light sweater to walk back to her room from the canteen. *Rosh Hashanah* came and went, as did *Yom Kippur.* Susan was shocked to see that the *kibbutzniks* celebrated the Day of Atonement by having a picnic instead of fasting, and no one even mentioned going to synagogue. There were also field trips for the volunteers on *Shabbos,* the only day of the week they didn't have to work. Once they went to the Dead Sea, and Susan saw what she'd always heard was true: You could float on your back and read the newspaper; there was so much salt in the water it was impossible to sink. Another time they went to Jerusalem to shop at the *shuk* and visit the Wailing Wall. Susan bought some earrings made of silver and turquoise-colored Elat stones from an Arab who cut the price in half "for your eyes," he said, "your pretty, pretty eyes." She stood at a distance from the Wailing Wall for a long time, watching men and women approach the ancient structure, pushing tiny pieces of paper between its cracks, before she knew what she wanted her "letter to God" to say: *Please keep my parents safe, well, and happy.* Susan, though not exactly happy herself, was not exactly unhappy either. She had grown used to life on the *kibbutz;* she was in a holding pattern, but just as she began to relax into her days, everything changed.

It began with the weather. The rainy season arrived, and the words "soaked to the skin" took on a whole new meaning for Susan, who had never experienced such torrential downpours before. The rain came down in absolute sheets, and even when it wasn't raining the air was cold and clammy. The first day the rains began, Susan ran out to the porch to take in a few pieces of laundry she had hung over the railing to dry. When she lifted a navy blue pullover, a dozen buttons clattered to the porch's wooden floor, making a small, tinny racket. Susan was puzzled: How did all those buttons come loose at once? She knelt to scoop them up and then realized to her horror that they weren't buttons at all, they were hard-shelled black beetles that had holed up for shelter. Susan dropped the sweater with a shriek; it slid over the railing into the mud, where it stayed for several months before someone picked it up and took it away.

Working in *Pardis* was out of the question now. First Susan was reassigned to the laundry, which she hated, then she worked briefly in the *kibbutz*'s equivalent of a day care center, but she didn't fare well there either. Susan was intrigued with the way children were raised on the *kibbutz*: From the time they were six months old until they turned eighteen and went into the army, they lived away from their parents in a large building called the children's house. Each section of the children's house had about six kids in it, who grew as close as siblings to each other. Children saw their parents for three hours a day during the week and all day on *Shabbos*. Susan tried her best, but it was difficult for her to work in the children's house because even though her language skills were slowly improving, she still spoke less Hebrew than a typical four-year-old, making it impossible for her to have any control over her pint-size charges.

That left the kitchen. Madeleine cringed visibly when Susan told her of her new work assignment.

"What's so bad about the kitchen?" Susan asked as she enjoyed what the volunteers considered a special treat: pieces of bread toasted on the metal safety grates of the small kerosene heater that tried in vain to take the dampness and chill out of their room.

"Norit," chorused Madeleine, Yael, and Rona together, pretending to shiver in fright.

"Who's Norit?" Susan asked.

"I'm sure you've seen her, love, sitting by herself in the back of the dining room in khaki trousers and a big white hat?" Madeleine licked butter from the tips of her fingers.

"Tall. Grand. *Gadol,*" Yael said, holding up her arms in a wide circle indicating girth.

"She eats girls like you for breakfast," Rona warned as she knelt in front of the heater to turn her toast with one hand, the other keeping her long, straightened hair out of danger.

"It's because she never married," Madeleine explained. "And she has to be, what? Thirty, thirty-five? She's probably never even had a chap."

"Old maid. No good." Yael tsk-tsked.

"This one girl, Andrea, from Massachusetts?" Rona said. "She told me Norit goes into the chicken house, picks out a bird, cuts its head off with a cleaver, and laughs as the poor headless body runs around the coop."

"Ewww!" Madeleine pretended to gag on her toast.

"Cannot be true," said Yael. She crossed both her hands around her own throat in protection, and then looked at Susan with sympathy. "*Mazel tov,* Shoshana. Good luck."

Susan wasn't too worried about working with "Norit the Nazi," as some of the volunteers called her behind her back (though not within hearing range of the *kibbutzniks,* many of whom were Holocaust survivors). Surely the stories about her were exaggerations, and if Susan just stayed out of her way and did as told, she'd be fine. But it was impossible to stay out of Norit's way. The woman was enormous, and her bulk took up most of the narrow, crowded kitchen where Susan worked, peeling cucumbers, slicing tomatoes, and digging the eyes out of potato after potato. Try as she might, Susan couldn't work fast enough for Norit, who didn't say much, but she didn't have to: A silent scowl was enough to inspire Susan to double her efforts and pick up her pace, even though her arms ached from scraping pounds of carrots against a grater that was in dire need of sharpening.

Norit flew about her domain, barking orders, brandishing knives, reaching for oversize pots and pans that hung on huge hooks above her head and banging them down onto the stove with a clatter. Her hair was a mass of sandy curls; try as she might, they would not stay contained beneath the white chef's hat that stood upright upon her head, adding to her already impressive height and stature. Susan guessed Norit was more than six feet tall and weighed at least two hundred and fifty pounds. Yet she was all speed and muscle, lifting enormous vats of soup off the stove, pummeling mountains of *challah* dough into submission with her enormous bare hands, hauling in yet another fifty-pound bag of carrots for Susan to peel and grate. Susan was a bit afraid of her, like everyone else—but she was fascinated too, and she couldn't help staring at Norit, though she quickly averted her eyes and went back to work whenever the woman so much as glanced her way. Norit was a mad, whirling dervish of energy. Unlike the other Israeli women, she didn't turn all coy and giggly when a man entered the room. She had no patience with anyone—man, woman, or child—who got in her way or prevented her from completing the job currently at hand. Norit meant business, and Susan admired that. Still, did she have to be such a stern taskmaster? By the time they broke for breakfast, Susan was in a sweat; by the time lunch came around, she was beyond exhausted. She noticed no one sat with Norit at either meal. The *kibbutzniks* ate on one side of the dining hall, the volunteers on the other, and Norit just sat in the back at a little folding table, sipping a cup of tea and munching a dry piece of *matzo*.

Each day after work, Susan went back to her room and drew whatever she found there: Yael's tired, muddy, Van Gogh–like boots slouched against each other in the corner; Rona's ragged, stuffed teddy bear lying sideways on her pillow; a still life of Madeleine's lipstick, compact, and black lace bra. But one day, weeks into the rainy season, Susan was seized with cabin fever. There was an hour or so before *ulpan,* and she decided to take a walk. There was actually a break in the rain, though it was far from sunny—it was foggy and misty, almost like Susan was walking through a cloud. She donned a yellow slicker, jammed a pencil and a small sketch pad into her pocket, and started on her way.

She walked down the path to the canteen, around the dining hall, and past the small, square homes of the *kibbutzniks,* each one built exactly alike. Susan didn't have a particular destination in mind; she just wanted to go somewhere she hadn't been before, so she walked wherever her feet decided to take her. After a while, though, she realized she was headed toward something:a sound that was very faint at first but grew louder and stronger with every step. Someone was singing. She couldn't make out the words, as they weren't in English, but the melody was lively; Susan could imagine it being sung by a barful of men clinking beer steins and chugging their brew down in one long, uninterrupted swallow—except the person singing the song was a woman, her voice round, lusty, and full. Her song put a bounce in Susan's step and a smile on her face, though she didn't know why. Maybe because Susan herself would never sing a song like that, so lively and full of joie de vivre. Susan was curious to see who was singing, even though she imagined the woman wouldn't want to be disturbed, in the same way Susan hated to be bothered when she was sketching. Still, she put one foot in front of the other until she turned a corner and stopped dead in her tracks, unable to believe what she saw.

It was Norit. Enormous, intimidating, gruff, no-nonsense Norit singing at the top of her lungs. And not only that. She was stark naked, standing underneath an outdoor shower rigged to the side of what must have been her living quarters. Susan knew a decent person would turn and walk away immediately, but she just couldn't move; the sight before her was too mesmerizing. It was as if someone put a spell on Susan, changing her legs into two slim tree trunks rooted into the ground.

Norit, underneath her dirty white uniform smeared with butter, flour, and cooking grease, was magnificent. More than magnificent. Stunning. Ravishing. Gorgeous. Her body was massive, full of curves and crevices, simultaneously hard and soft, sturdy and delicate, completely unlike Susan's body, which had always seemed fine before but now seemed wholly inadequate compared to the work of art that was Norit. As she turned this way and that, soaping herself up, rinsing herself off, and singing all the while, Susan continued to stare at Norit's flesh-covered form, a feast for the eyes, a true masterpiece. How her plump arms shimmered, how her rounded belly curved, how alluring were the two sweet folds of flesh above her waist, how dainty were her tiny feet, how abundant her dimpled thighs! And as if all this weren't enough—(*dayenu,* as the Passover song goes)—when Norit finally spotted Susan, she didn't shriek and rush to cover herself or yell at Susan to run away. Instead she opened her arms wide and smiled, as if to say, *Look at me. Aren't I fabulous?* and then motioned impatiently for Susan to come join her, as if she'd been waiting for this moment all her life, and what in the world was taking her so long?

And Susan, who had been surprised at everything that had happened to her thus far in this strange yet familiar land, wasn't surprised at all. Finally she was wide awake, no longer sleep-walking through what she knew hadn't been much of a life. Finally, the movie of her existence was reaching its climax; at last the director who lived rent-free in her brain was calling for action. And Susan complied: She took off her raincoat, her rain hat, her rubber boots, all the clothing she'd been wearing for weeks in order to stay dry, and dashed into the water. She wanted to be like Norit, drenched, soaked, saturated. The wetter the better. Norit soaped her up, scrubbed her down, singing all the while. Susan felt renewed, rejuvenated, reborn. And for the rest of that afternoon, and many days that followed, Susan at long last learned the subtle nuances of Norit's foreign tongue and discovered just how sweet and tender on the inside a tough, gruff *sabre* could be.

Of course Susan and Norit didn't live happily ever after, though they did live quite happily for the rest of the year, until Susan's time in the Holy Land drew to a close. Of course there were many tears shed and many promises made, all of which were eventually broken. Susan never did go back to Israel, and Norit never did come to the States for a visit. Their tearful, once-a-month phone calls dribbled to an end, and their letters dwindled down to birthday and *Chanukah* cards. One day a letter Susan had sent to Norit came back stamped "No longer at this address," and that, she concluded, was the end of that.

Until the year that Susan turned forty and, right on schedule, had her midlife crisis. After Susan had returned from Israel (with no boyfriend in tow, much to her parents' dismay) she'd gone back to school for her teaching certificate and made peace with the fact that while she would never be a great artist, she could still have art at the center of her life. She taught drawing and painting at a community college in upstate New York, where she had settled down; she also volunteered her time at a nursing home, helping the residents work with modeling clay, which was good for their gnarled, arthritic hands. She'd had a serious relationship that had lasted the better part of a decade, and though it hadn't worked out in the end, Susan and her ex-lover remained the best of friends. And now she had a brand-new lover, a round, ripe, luscious woman named Beverly who made the short hairs at the back of her neck stand on end every time she walked into the room. Life was good—better than good—but still there was something missing. Susan, on the brink of turning forty, was feeling nostalgic, but nostalgic for what? She didn't have a clue.

As part of entering a new decade of life, she decided to clean out the large shed she had built behind the house to use as a studio. She'd recently read a book on the ancient art of feng shui and was intrigued by the notion of creating beauty and peace in one's life by making one's living space and work space as soothing and peaceful as possible. In order to do this, Susan learned, she needed to hold up every object she owned and put it to the test: Did she feel good about the object? Did it reflect who she was today? Did it add to her feeling of well-being or detract from it? Susan was sitting on the floor in the middle of her studio surrounded by piles: things to keep, things to box up and store, things to give away, things she wasn't sure about. She had just come to her old sketch pads from her trip to Israel and was flipping through the pages when there was a knock at the door.

"It's open," Susan called, knowing who it was.

"Want some company?" Beverly poked one foot cautiously into the room. She knew Susan's studio was sacred space and never entered before permission was granted.

Susan looked up and smiled. "C'mon in."

"What are you doing?" Beverly stepped carefully around the piles, knelt beside Susan, and kissed her on the cheek.

"Just sorting through my things. In with the old, out with the new, you know, trying to deal with turning forty."

"The best is yet to come, honey. You'll see." Beverly, having crossed the great divide into middle age several years ago, spoke with authority. "Hey," she looked down at the sketch pad Susan was holding. "I thought you didn't do portraits."

"I don't," Susan said, despite the hard and fast evidence to the contrary spread across her lap. "I just did these as a favor for someone."

"Who's the model?" Beverly squinted her eyes for a better look.

Susan felt her face grow red. "Norit," she whispered softly.

"Wow, she's a looker. Should I be jealous?" Beverly teased.

"No," Susan wasn't in a teasing mood, "you should be grateful. If it wasn't for her, I wouldn't be with you."

"Is that so?" Beverly looked from the drawing to Susan.

"She changed my life," Susan said, and then told Beverly the story of Norit, hunting up the one photo she had of her.

"Wow," Beverly said when Susan was done. "What a risky thing to do, to seduce you like that. And how brave of you to just dive in."

"Norit said it was *bashert,*" Susan said with a faraway look in her eye.

"What does *bashert* mean?" Beverly asked.

"It's hard to translate, but it means fate, kismet, something like that." Susan grew silent for a minute, not telling Beverly that *bashert* had another meaning: Norit had called Susan "bashert" as an endearment, meaning "my destiny," and Susan had called Norit "bashert" as well.

"Wow," Beverly said again, still studying the sketches. "I guess I owe her big-time."

"So do I," Susan said, closing the sketch pad and putting it on top of the "I don't know" pile.

"Were the drawings for her?" Beverly asked, studying the photo of Norit.

Susan nodded. "She liked them a lot, but I don't know. I never did anything with them." Susan shut her eyes for a minute, remembering the endless arguments she'd had with Norit, who, like Carl, had longed to pose for her. First she'd teased her: "Am I not attractive enough for you?" she asked, putting one hand on her hip, the other behind her neck, and then throwing her head back in a fashion model's pose. Susan laughed and tried to explain that it wasn't Norit's lack of beauty; it was her own lack of talent. But Norit didn't buy that. "*Lama lo? Lama lo?* Why not? Why not?" she kept asking, her impatient voice growing louder and louder until one day Susan shrieked, "Because I'm no damn good!" and then, to her horror, burst into tears. Norit had held her and stroked her and then abruptly pushed her away. She disappeared into the bathroom for a moment and then returned without a stitch of clothing on. Susan reached up to undo the top button of her own blouse, but Norit didn't want to make love. She wanted Susan to draw her and demanded she do so in a voice that would not take no for an answer. Susan dried her eyes, glared at Norit, and drew.

"*Tov. Yoffi.* Good. Pretty." Norit had been pleased, but Susan, always the perfectionist, saw only the flaws in her sketches. She put them away and, though Norit continued to ask, plead, and demand, never drew her again.

"I know how you can pay her back." Beverly's words cut through Susan's thoughts. "May I?" She reached for the pad after Susan nodded. "You can work on these."

"What do you mean?"

"I mean, these are stunning. Look at the lines, the shapes, the shadows. These drawings have something those don't." Beverly waved a plump arm at the studies of fruit and furniture hanging on the wall. "I may be going out on a limb here, Susan, but these drawings have...I don't know...heart. They have your heart. And soul. They're alive. Your other paintings…I mean they're good and everything, but they don't…they don't move me like these do. Even unfinished, these sketches have a life to them your other work doesn't have. Oh, God." Beverly looked down at her hands. "Me and my big mouth. Did I go too far? Are you going to break up with me?"

"No," Susan said slowly, looking from the sketch pad to the wall and back again. "Only because I know you're right. But I don't know if I can do it."

"Why not?"

"I don't know." Susan flipped through the sketches. "They're so…so out there. I'm afraid of exposing Norit like that."

"I think," Beverly stayed Susan's hand with her own, "you're afraid of exposing yourself like that."

"But all I have are these sketches and this one photo," Susan whined. Knowing she'd been found out, she looked for any excuse. "You know I need to have something in front of me in order to draw it."

Beverly threw Susan a look that said *I'll love you whether you rise to the occasion or not, but both of us know what's really going on here,* and then got to her feet. "I'll come by later, okay?" she said. Then she tiptoed out of the studio, shutting the door behind her.

For the rest of that afternoon Susan drew. She drew from memory, she drew from experience, she drew from deep inside her. And when Beverly came back later that evening with take-out Chinese food to share, she didn't have to say what Susan already knew: That afternoon's work was the best she'd ever done.

Susan hadn't submitted her work to galleries for years, but with Beverly's coaxing, which grew into insistence ("It's not for nothing you're dating a pushy broad") she took slides of her work and sent them out. First she was accepted to group exhibits, then she sold a painting or two, and at last a New York gallery offered her a one-woman show. When the letter came, Beverly grabbed Susan's hands and whirled her around the room. "You did it!" she shrieked, engulfing her lover in a big bear hug.

"You mean *we* did it. I never would've done those paintings if it weren't for you," Susan pointed out, eager to share the glory.

"I didn't do anything," Beverly shot back. "It was *bashert.* Meant to be."

✣

Susan looked up at her paintings, framed so elegantly and hung so expertly on the gallery's walls. She'd obscured Norit's face for the most part, with a raised arm or a turn of the head, just to be on the safe side, even though twenty years had passed and she was sure that Norit, like herself, had changed over time. Still, Susan wanted to be sure that Norit remained unrecognizable. It was a small world, and one never knew—perhaps somehow, someday Norit would stumble across her paintings. Susan wondered what Norit would think of them. The woman had no shame when it came to her body, and Susan imagined she'd be flattered, proud, pleased. At least she hoped so. She closed her eyes for a moment and whispered to Norit, *toda raba,* thank you so much. For everything. For teaching me to love you and therefore love myself. For holding me tight and letting me go. For inspiring me and believing in me. For this moment that I've waited for all my life. And even though the room was noisy with the *oohs* and *aahs* of the crowd, Susan could swear she heard Norit's voice close to her ear, whispering *Bashert, vah-kah-sha.* My destiny, you're welcome.

Mothers of Invention

"Hi honey, I'm homo." I flung open the back door and tossed my usual and, in my opinion, extremely clever greeting into the empty kitchen, where it was met with an unusual and not nearly as clever silence.

"Phoebe?" I called again. It wasn't like her not to answer. I threw my keys down on the mail-strewn table and poked around the living room, dining room, and bedroom, but there was no Phoebe to be found. Where was she? There weren't that many hiding places in the tiny ranch we had somehow managed to buy a little over two years ago. Maybe she was waiting for me in her walk-in closet wearing nothing but a few feet of Saran Wrap and her favorite red fuck-me pumps. That would be just like Phoebe, who liked to start the weekend off with a bang. Last Friday I dragged my weary ass home from another day at the salt mines only to find my beloved standing at the stove calmly stirring a stainless steel pot of homemade tomato sauce with a long wooden spoon, adorned in nothing but a yellow-and-white checkered apron tied loosely at the waist, her luscious butt bared for all the world to see. That's my Phoebe. She sure likes to keep me guessing. And God bless her, she makes it a point to keep our sex life hopping. Phoebe sets the rules around here, and luckily they're pretty simple: She insists we do the hokey-pokey at least twice a week "whether we want to or not."

I cracked open a beer, plopped myself down on the couch, and called halfheartedly, "Come out, come out, wherever you are," knowing my plea was useless. Phoebe would come out when she was good and ready. But when I finished my brew and there was still no sign of her, I began to worry. I knew she was home—her maroon Saturn was hogging the driveway—so where was she? I was just about to get up and conduct a more thorough search of the premises when I heard the bathroom door open. Quick as a wink I wiped my mouth with the back of my hand and rose to give my girl a proper greeting.

"Hi, baby," I said, but to my surprise Phoebe didn't head right into my open arms and nestle her head against my waiting chest. Instead she pushed me away and burst into tears.

"Baby, what's wrong?"

""Don't call me baby," she wailed, sobbing in earnest with her shoulders shuddering and snot running from her nose like, well, like a baby. And then, idiot that I am, I remembered.

"Oh, no. Did you get your period?"

"Yes." Phoebe's voice broke into a sad little gulp of a hiccup as she finally melted against me and let me hold her.

I stroked her auburn curls and offered inadequate words of comfort. "Poor you," I murmured. "Poor Phoebe. Poor baby."

And by the time I realized what I'd said, Phoebe had run back into the bathroom, slamming the door behind her.

When Phoebe's upset she likes to be alone, so I grabbed another beer and headed out the way I came. There was a rickety lounge chair on our back porch with my name on it, so I parked myself, took a swig, and swallowed. The summer sun wouldn't be setting for at least an hour, so that gave me plenty of time to think. Of course my thoughts turned to Phoebe. And while my heart ached for her, my sympathy was tinged with a good, healthy dose of relief too. It was no secret I felt ambivalent about having a baby. I've never really wanted one, though I've never really not wanted one either. I simply didn't think about it. It's not like I was ever going to fall into bed with someone and wake up the next morning big with child. I knew I liked girls from the time I was a young pup—maybe fifteen or so—and I've never even kissed a guy, let alone done something that would result in me winding up a mother-to-be. I suppose I always knew there was the possibility I'd fall in love with a "late bloomer" who hadn't realized she was a lesbo until after she'd married some guy and had a couple of kids. But that never happened, even though it easily could have. I've always been a sucker for older women.

So I thought all that was settled, and then along came the

"gayby boom." It seemed like a million dykes woke up one morning and heard the same sound: the nearly deafening roar of their collective biological clocks tick-tocking away. Overnight support groups were formed, hotlines for sperm-runners were set up, and before you could even say "turkey baster," gay pride was overrun with dyke-style nuclear families: two women pushing a baby carriage, a dog on a lavender leash trailing behind them.

Now, the dog part I can understand. I've always wanted a dog. And not some wimpy, yappy little thing like a poodle or a Chihuahua either. I want a dog's dog. A chocolate lab, a blue-eyed husky. A dog you don't have to bend over to pet. A dog that can rest its mighty head against your thigh. But our house remains a pooch-free palace because Phoebe, who is perfect in nearly every other way, is just not an animal person. She doesn't want some big galoot of a mutt tracking mud all over our nice, clean floors and shedding its smelly wet fur on our nice, clean (secondhand) furniture. Come to think of it, I haven't brought up the canine question in quite a while. Now I kind of wish I'd gotten a puppy before I met Phoebe. Then she wouldn't have had a choice—we would have been a package deal. But I didn't think it was fair to have a dog when I was living solo. The poor thing would have been all by its little lonesome from nine to five and sometimes longer, since there was many a night when, Don Juan that I used to be, I never made it back to my apartment. Then when I moved into Phoebe's place, between all my stuff and all her stuff, things were so cramped there was hardly room to add a hamster, let alone fifty pounds of bark and fur.

I thought when we finally bought our house the time would be right. But I found out that buying a house—especially a fixer-upper like ours—is like getting a full-time job. Which would have been fine except I already had a full-time job. Now instead of coming home and putting my feet up (and maybe convincing Phoebe to give them a little massage), I need to get busy and do something useful like tear up the kitchen floor, mend the back steps, or rescreen a window on the front porch—there's always something that needs to be done. And Phoebe's been pretty busy too, planting the garden, sewing curtains for the windows, buying little rugs for the hallway—you know, adding a woman's touch to the place so it feels all warm and cozy. Like a love nest. I should've known it was only a question of time before Phoebe started talking about a baby. After all, what's the use of a nest without any eggs in it?

Way back when we first started dating, Phoebe told me that someday she wanted to have a baby, but I didn't pay too much attention to what she was saying. First of all, she said she wasn't planning on getting pregnant for a "really, really, really long time," and second of all, I was so knocked out by her she could have said, "Someday I'm going to be a cloistered nun," and I would've paid her no mind. Neither of us paid the other much mind, come to think of it. It was all just pillow talk. We'd live happily ever after someday with her baby and my dog, and we'd take a year off and sail around the world, maybe live in Alaska for a while (something I've always wanted to do) or gay Paris (something she's always wanted to do). You know how lovers talk.

And besides, smitten as I was, I had no idea we'd actually stay together this long (six years and counting). It's not like either of us had a stellar reputation in the longevity department. And we didn't plan any of this. It all just sort of happened, in typical lesbo fashion. After we'd gone out for a while and Phoebe finally let me into her pants, I began spending every night at her apartment. After a few months of that, I realized how stupid it was to be paying all that extra rent just for a place to hang my clothes, so I moved in with her. Then, after we'd lived together a while, both of us decided it made no sense for us to be shelling out so much dough to a landlord when, for just a little more money, we could be investing in a place of our very own. So, with the money Phoebe's mom left her after she died, we bought the house.

Not that I'm complaining about any of this. There's no one I'd rather be with than Phoebe, and I should know since I've been with plenty. It's not like I was the playgirl of the Western world or anything. I was the playgirl of the Western, Eastern, Northern and Southern world. Think I'm exaggerating? Entire softball teams could be formed by my ex-lovers. Entire softball *leagues*. What can I say? I've been with tall amazons and short goddesses. Plump beauties and hipless cuties. Femme tops, femme bots, lipstick lesbians, and glamazons. Androgens, kikis, jocks, and, though I hate to admit it, in moments of sheer desperation, even a butch or two. Lesbians, has-bians, bisexuals, bi-lesbians. Girls who were straight but not narrow, girls who were narrow but not straight. Rude girls, crude girls, shrewd girls, and lewd girls. Shy girls, sly girls, dry girls, and fly girls. I've had lovers, fuck buddies, sweethearts, and pains in the butt (sometimes all at the same time). I've had a main squeeze, a honey, a girlfriend, and a partner. I'd thought I'd been with just about every type of woman under the sun.

And then I met Phoebe.

Phoebe is all of the above and none of the above. Phoebe is adamant about not calling herself a lesbian, but as I pointed out one lazy Sunday afternoon when I had four fingers deep inside her, she isn't exactly straight either. Phoebe replied, between grunts and groans, that the only labels she wore were on the inside of her size-twelve jeans, a pair of which, at that moment, were balled up in a heap on my living room floor. Phoebe has told me over and over that she thinks labels are limiting, and she likes to be open to all possibilities. From the start she was an enigma to me, the original die-hard dyke. She once told me her name literally means "personification of the moon." And what could be more mysterious than the moon? One night it's so high and brilliant in the sky you feel a sudden kinship with your pagan ancestors and find yourself howling with awe and delight. Another night it's a snippet, no bigger or more significant than the white part of your little left pinkie nail. Then it's gone altogether, and then it reappears more magnificent and luminous than ever. And that just about describes my Phoebe.

We met on a warm summer night, not all that different than this one, at a mutual friend's graduation party. I was on the prowl, as usual, and she was on the rebound, though she wouldn't tell me if her last lover was a guy or a gal. I'd had a few drinks and made some comment about her being a Phoebe and me being a Robin and us being birds of a feather or something like that. I think I might have said I wanted to tweak her beak too.

"Another time, birdbrain."

"Sorry I ruffled your feathers," I slung at her back as she turned to walk away in a huff. But even half-looped as I was, I couldn't help noticing her ass. Phoebe's ass happens to be the eighth wonder of the world. And she knows it. And works it too, in those so-tight-they-look-like-she's-been-sewn-into-them size-twelve jeans of hers. That night her jeans were white, and I could have howled at her caboose, round and full and mesmerizing as a full moon. But, thank God, I did no such thing. I merely muttered, "Wish I had a swing like that in my backyard," just loud enough for her to hear.

"You should be so lucky," she shot back over her shoulder before disappearing into the crowd.

Flighty bitch, I thought, but of course I knew a challenge when I heard one. And Phoebe knew I knew. Knew I'd call, even though she didn't say another word to me all evening, let alone give me her phone number. Knew I'd get it from our host, along with a warning: "Now, Robin, Phoebe's not like other girls. Don't fuck with her." Whatever that meant. Knew enough to be busy the first *and* second Saturday night I called to see if I could take her to dinner. Knew unavailability is the most potent aphrodisiac known to womankind. And knew, I'm proud to say, though she sure didn't act it, that she wanted me *bad,* from the moment she first laid eyes on me. And, thank God, Phoebe knew just how to clip my wings too.

She wouldn't sleep with me for months after we started dating. Wanted me to court her. Wanted me to woo her. Said she needed me to prove I was worthy of getting the goods before she handed them over. You'd think I'd just tell a snotty bitch like that to stick it where the sun don't shine, but Phoebe's attitude had the opposite effect on me. I wanted to win her over. I wanted to clean up my act. I stopped flirting, cut down on my drinking, and even learned how to shine my shoes and iron my pants. I felt like a teenage boy—with blue balls and a perpetual hard-on. Which isn't a bad way to feel. I was in a constant state of expectant ecstasy: Would tonight be the night? Phoebe gave me just enough—plenty of kisses and a little tit now and then—to keep me coming around. "Less is more" is her philosophy. And it worked like a charm.

Phoebe's no dummy. She knew I'd been around the block and then some. Knew I was the love 'em and leave 'em type, and she wasn't having any of *that*. No, Phoebe had turned a corner in her own life, unbeknownst to me, and decided it was time to settle down. At least for a while. And so she cast a spell on me, stealing my heart before I even knew it was missing, like a magician who shows you your wedding ring in the palm of his hand before you realize it's gone from your finger. I was caught hook, line, and sinker. Before I had a chance to bid my bachelor days adieu, they were gone.

No one believed that two wild things like us had a chance in hell of making it, but we figured we'd show them. This was different. I didn't know Phoebe before I met her (obviously), but I knew myself and I sure felt different. Me, the butch who'd rather be committed than make a commitment, now actually liked calling Phoebe every day from work to see if I was going over to her house or she was coming over to mine. I liked moving in together, lining up my loafers, sneakers, and work boots with her flats, slingbacks, and slides. And even though it was scary as hell, the day we signed the mortgage papers was the happiest day of my life.

Phoebe likes to say she tamed me. According to her, before we started dating I probably thought she was "just a girl. A pretty girl maybe, a curvy girl definitely, but still, just a girl like any other girl." The difference is, now that we've been together all this time, Phoebe is *my* girl. Now I could walk into a room of a hundred girls just her height, weight, and coloring, and I'd pick her out in a heartbeat. Even if I just saw her from behind, because I've memorized the shape of her behind. Even if I was blind, because I know her smell by heart. Even if I couldn't see her or smell her or hear her voice, I'd know her by the touch of her hand. It's amazing; I don't even look at other women anymore. Who could compare to my Phoebe, whose blue eyes I've looked into a thousand times (the right one is slightly larger than the left); whose breasts I've fondled a million times (the left one is slightly higher than the right); who sometimes whistles through her nose when she sleeps, who has a birthmark shaped like the Statue of Liberty on her belly, whose lovely face is even more familiar to me than my own.

I was amazed at how well married life agreed with me. Well, not married life in the legal sense of the word, of course. And even if we could get married, I wouldn't want some flimsy little certificate holding us together anyway. That's the beauty of being a lesbian: We don't have to fill out the paperwork. I can hoof it any time I want to. But I don't want to. Imagine that. I'm like a feral cat who finally allowed herself to be coaxed in out of the cold and the rain to sit on a nice comfy couch in front of a warm, cozy fire. *What did I think would be so bad about all this?* I wondered night after night as Phoebe and I snuggled under the blankets together, hugging and kissing and going to town. I kept waiting for the shoe to drop, the bickering to start, the lesbian bed death to set in. I knew it was inevitable. Every couple has problems, right? No relationship is perfect. It took a long time, but finally the shoe did drop. Only it wasn't a shoe. It was a tiny yellow bootie.

Phoebe, who gets up with the birds—with the phoebes in fact, who call her name over and over right outside our bedroom window starting at five in the morning—had gone off in search of tag sales, a Saturday morning ritual I never did understand. As far as I'm concerned, Saturday mornings are for sleeping in, making love, and falling back to sleep again. But according to Phoebe, the early bird catches the worm, so off she went, leaving me deep in dreamland. But it's a funny thing: Our bed just isn't a fun place to be when Phoebe's not in it. So after a while I got up, helped myself to the coffee that Phoebe had left in the pot on the stove, and decided to do something industrious. Phoebe had been bugging me to paint the bathroom, so I decided to get to work. I was up to my eyeballs in peach-colored paint when she came flouncing into the tiny room.

"Robin and Phoebe sitting in a tree. K-I-S-S-I-N-G." She laid a nice, fat, wet one on my lips before I could even put my paint roller down.

"You're in a frisky mood," I said when she finally let me up for air.

"First comes love, then comes marriage, then comes Phoebe with the baby carriage." She finished her little ditty and held up two tiny yellow booties, waving them around like flags.

I guess I'm pretty thick, because I still didn't see what she was getting at. Or maybe I didn't want to see. "Earrings?" I asked.

"Robin!" Phoebe lifted her foot to stamp it in exasperation, but then changed her mind and her tune. "Aren't they adorable?" she crooned, holding them closer for me to inspect. "I got a matching hat too. This woman over on Union Street is some knitter. She had all these cute little sweaters too. Maybe after breakfast we can go back and look at them."

"Wait a minute." I left my roller in its paint-filled aluminum tray and led Phoebe out of the bathroom into the kitchen. The little yellow hat she had bought to match the booties was spilled across the table. "Are we having a baby now?" I asked Phoebe. "What's going on?"

"Robin, you know I want a baby. And I'm thirty-seven. And a half. The time is now."

For some reason that reminded me of this art installation an old lover of mine had dragged me to once, full of this avant-garde garbage I didn't understand. One thing kind of tickled me, though: Someone had hung up a clock but removed the hour hand and the minute hand, leaving only the second hand sweeping around the clock face. The artist had called it "The Clock of Eternity." She could just as well have called it, "The Time Is Now." Or "The Jig Is Up."

Still, I thought I'd try the rational approach. "Phoebe," I said, "you haven't talked about having a baby for a long time. Why are you bringing it up today? Babies are expensive, and we're still catching our breath from becoming homeowners. Can't this wait a year?" *Or a lifetime,* I wanted to add. But I knew that would be futile. Once Phoebe makes up her mind about something, it's no use arguing with her.

"It's not like this is a surprise, Robin. I told you from the start I wanted a baby."

And I told you from the start I wanted a dog shot through my mind, but I knew this wasn't the moment to bring that topic up.

Instead I said, "And I told you from the start I didn't know if I wanted to be a parent."

"And I told you from the start I really didn't care."

Which was true. Phoebe had made it clear that my feelings didn't much matter one way or the other. She got all high and mighty about it, launching into a speech about how each woman's body was her own to do with as she pleased, and every woman has the right to reproduce or not, no matter what anyone else feels or says about it. In other words, she was going to have a baby. With me or without me. Whether I wanted to participate or not.

Phoebe didn't say anything more about the baby for a few months, but she didn't have to. As they say, actions speak louder than words. Like take the morning when, after a particularly acrobatic and mutually satisfying horizontal tango, I got up, pulled on some boxer shorts, and made us a big breakfast of bacon, eggs, and home fries. Phoebe entered the kitchen wearing a short red nightie I bought her one year for Valentine's Day and sat at the table waiting to be served. I set her plate down, but before she had taken her first bite of breakfast she jumped up to turn the frying pan so its handle wasn't pointing outward, reminding me, without a word, not to endanger the life of our future child, who could have grabbed the tempting handle, pulled down the hot, grease-filled pan, and done permanent damage too scary to even think about. Another day I came home and found that she had moved our potentially poisonous cleaning supplies—the Windex, bleach, Mop & Glo, etc.—from under the sink, where they were within easy grasp, to a cabinet above the refrigerator, where even I, never mind a child, couldn't reach them without a stepladder.

And then came the toilet bowl clamp. Phoebe had read some tear-jerking article in one of those parenting magazines she kept bringing home about a poor woman whose toddler had fallen headfirst into the toilet bowl and drowned. Phoebe had gone out that day to buy the clamp, ensuring that we would never have a chance to be visited by that particular heartbreaking tragedy.

"Phoebe, get real," I said, studying the white plastic thingamajig she was trying to fasten around the toilet seat cover.

"Robin, I am getting real," she said. "This is it. Next month I'm going to inseminate."

Call me the world's biggest sucker, but given the options— life without Phoebe or life with Phoebe and a miniature Phoebe— what choice did I have? I couldn't figure out how it happened, but somehow, over the years, life sans Phoebe had become unimaginable. Me, the lesbian formally known as Bachelor #1, had finally met her match, and I wasn't going to do something as stupid as lose the girl of my dreams over something as tiny as a newborn. A little angel with clear blue eyes like my Phoebe's and a mop of curls the color of an Irish setter. At least that's how I pictured the kid: an exact replica of Phoebe, complete with a smattering of freckles across her nose, a dimple in her left cheek, and a beauty mark on her right. I never even considered that the little she might be a little he, or might look like our donor—not that we'd ever know, since he was to remain forever anonymous. At least Phoebe and I agreed on that, once I reluctantly copped to the fact that this was actually happening. Neither of us wanted some dewy-eyed dad knocking on our door six days, months, or years down the road, wanting to claim the carrier of his gene pool. And since money was an issue, we decided to do things the old-fashioned dyke way, outside the system.

Leave it to the girls. We had it all figured out. One dyke would get the sperm from any number of guys, whose only requirements were they could prove they tested negative for AIDS and had no interest whatsoever in what happened to their precious goo once it was deposited in a clean baby food jar. Dyke A would collect the sperm and hand the jar to Dyke B, not telling her from whom it had come. Dyke B would give the jar to us, but not tell Dyke A which one of her potential breeders was receiving the goods. Anonymity assured, and all for a fraction of what the clinic route would cost. (Believe it or not, sperm can cost as much three hundred bucks a pop.)

It all seemed easy as pie. Phoebe started trying to pin down her ovulation by charting her periods, which were pretty regular. She took her temperature first thing every morning—she wouldn't even talk to me before she read her thermometer. And she spent hours in the bathroom inspecting her mucus like it was the most fascinating thing in the world. When Phoebe thought she was in the time zone when she could become pregnant—a couple of days before ovulation through the day after—she'd call our faithful sperm runner, who, after getting some guy to whack off for us (an image I tried not to think about) would show up at our door, baby food jar in hand. My job was to help Phoebe insert the sperm—which smelled to high heaven, thank you very much—then sit with her while she lay on our bed with her feet propped up on the wall and her legs sticking up straight, the better to let gravity help nature take its course.

"Robin, you're being really good about all this," Phoebe said, her face radiant at the mere thought of being pregnant.

I shrugged off the undeserved compliment. "Hey, if Mama ain't happy, ain't nobody happy," I told her, quoting a T-shirt I'd seen in one of the millions of maternity catalogs that were clogging up our mailbox on a daily basis.

But Mama wasn't happy, because Mama was having a hard time becoming a mama. The sperm didn't take the first time, the second time, the seventh time, the twelfth time. Phoebe got very discouraged. Every month she'd get all hopeful, lying there with her legs up in the air and me sitting beside her reading aloud a kids' book she was especially fond of, like *Winnie the Pooh* or *The Cat in the Hat*. Then after an hour or two, I'd take her out for ice cream. Phoebe figured it was never too early to start eating for two, but I think that was just an excuse for her to indulge in her favorite treat: a gooey banana split made with chocolate chip, pistachio, and strawberry ice cream. Phoebe would try not to think about it, but each and every month she was sure the insemination was successful, and each and every month it got harder and harder for her when reality arrived in the form of blood stains on her pink satin underwear. I tried to convince her not to take it so hard every time, but she waved away my attempts to console her.

"You don't understand, Robin. You've never wanted anything this badly," she said, her words hurting my feelings for reasons I didn't fully understand. Probably because they were right.

Finally Phoebe went to the doctor and had a million tests

done, but they couldn't find anything wrong with her. Except maybe that her eggs were getting old. So she convinced herself that there was a problem with our donor, but our sperm-runner told us that for the past several months she had been using a few different guys who had each successfully sired a child. That really got Phoebe down. The next thing to discuss was fertility drugs, but my girl won't even take aspirin. She was scared to put all those chemicals in her body, and I didn't blame her. Besides, neither of us was crazy about the idea of twins or triplets, which was a good possibility if she went on the drugs. The idea of adding just one human being to our family was overwhelming enough. The day we had that discussion was the day I found out something I didn't know about Phoebe: My "feminism is not a dirty word" girlfriend didn't believe in abortion.

"What happened to 'each woman's body is her own'?" I couldn't help asking as we sat in Friendly's, Phoebe having one of her post-insemination banana splits and me sipping a mug of lukewarm coffee.

"I didn't say I didn't believe in it for other women," Phoebe defended herself. "I just know *I* couldn't do it. Like, remember that woman who had a litter of seven kids because she couldn't tell her doctor to abort some of the fetuses even though that would give the ones that remained a better chance of survival?" I nodded; the woman had been all over the news. "I'd be the same way." Phoebe paused to think while she licked some green ice cream off her spoon. "I don't get it. I'm not even forty yet, my periods are regular...why am I having so much trouble?"

"Maybe you're too tense about it," I said, as if I really knew anything. "Didn't the doctor say it was important to relax?"

"Yeah, but that's so much easier for straight people. They just throw out their condoms and birth control pills, go at it like bunnies, and don't even think about it. So even if nothing happens, at least they have a good time."

I don't think Phoebe meant to take my heart out of my chest, put it on the table, and smash it to bits with the side of her fist, but that's the effect her words had on me. "Phoebe," I said after a few minutes, when I could find my voice. "The door's open.

You're not a lesbian, as you've so often informed me. You can walk out the door and do this the good old-fashioned way anytime."

"Oh, my God. Robin, I didn't mean it like that." Phoebe got up and came around to sit next to me in the booth. I couldn't look at her. "Robin." She tried to turn my face toward her, but I wouldn't give an inch. She sighed and took my hand, which flopped in her palm like a dead fish. "Robin," Phoebe said, "if this is meant to happen, it will. And if it's not meant to happen, it won't. That's all there is to it. And besides, I've made a decision."

"What?" I asked, finally turning to her.

"If I'm not pregnant this time, I'm going to take a break. I can't take it anymore," she said, and then she started to cry.

"Hey, hey, wait a minute, Phoebe." I put my arm around her and kissed her forehead. "No use crying until you know for sure. For all you know, you could be pregnant this very minute. C'mon, now. Don't throw out the baby with the bathwater." She didn't even smile.

Well, Phoebe wasn't pregnant, and true to her word, she did take a break from inseminating. And little by little, our lives got back to normal. I could roll over and give my girl a kiss in the morning without almost putting my eye out with the thermometer that was stuck in her mouth. We could have wine with dinner again. We could even go to the mall and walk by Gap Kids without her having a meltdown. As the months went by, I, being the Queen of Denial, thought the issue was closed and Phoebe had made peace with her non-mommyhood status. But I was wrong. A few weeks ago, out of the blue, Phoebe announced she was ready to try again.

Which brings us to today.

I sighed, raised my carcass off the chair, and headed inside, my empty beer bottle in hand. To my surprise, Phoebe was in the kitchen, mixing up the ingredients for one of my favorite dinners, macaroni and cheese with her special killer crust. Ani DiFranco was singing on the stereo, and Phoebe had put on lipstick and some kind of makeup that tried but failed to hide the puffiness around her eyes. She greeted me with a smile I hardly deserved. *My brave little soldier,* I thought, but I didn't say anything. It was hard to read her, and I knew enough to wait for her to make the first move.

"You hungry?" she asked, like nothing had happened. I nodded and made myself busy tossing a salad together and pouring our drinks. We sat and ate, mostly in silence, but not that easy, comfortable silence we often share, when both of us have had a hard day at work and neither of us feels much like talking. No, this silence, full of so much that's unsaid, felt like the quiet that has settled over two people on a first date, when they both know there's no chemistry between them but neither of them knows how to get out of an awkward-as-hell situation. Phoebe's macaroni and cheese stuck in my throat and tasted like wallpaper paste.

Finally I couldn't stand it anymore. "Phoebe," I started, but she cut me right off.

"I don't want to talk about it," she said, jumping up to clear our plates. "It's over. I'm done."

"But—"

"No buts." Phoebe was at the sink with her back to me, but I'd have bet the rest of our mortgage she'd begun to cry.

Over the next couple of weeks, Phoebe pulled herself together and acted like there was nothing on her mind. Well, maybe that's that, I thought, cautiously. Phoebe never was one to hold a grudge. Maybe she wasn't one to hang on to a plan gone awry either. She put away all the baby things she had collected, the clothes, the books, the toys, hoping maybe the old "out of sight, out of mind" thing really did work. And maybe it did, because weeks went by and she never brought up the topic again.

But the funny thing was, now *I* was thinking about it. Constantly. I even tiptoed toward bringing the subject up with her, but each time I came close, I wound up chickening out. I wondered why Phoebe had never mentioned adoption. I knew it would be an expensive way to go, but money would never have stopped Phoebe. The only conclusion I could come to was my beloved wasn't ready to open herself up to the possibility of more heartache. Which certainly was possible if you went the adoption route. We knew one lesbian couple who went through the whole process—the application, interviews, home visits—but in the end they weren't approved. Another couple Phoebe knew had been approved, but they'd had to wait more than two years to get a child. No, maybe, as Phoebe had said and now obviously believed, it just wasn't meant to be.

You'd think this turn of events would make me happy, and while part of me felt an enormous sense of relief, part of me felt something else too, something that kept me from turning cartwheels and jumping for joy. I couldn't put my finger on it at first. I just felt empty. Like there was a hole inside. Kind of how you feel when you miss someone. This really puzzled me: How could I miss a baby who never existed, a baby I never even wanted in the first place? Then one night at dinner, I realized I didn't miss the baby. I missed Phoebe.

It was an unusually warm mid-September evening, and we were sitting at the picnic table in the backyard eating a simple supper of hamburgers I had cooked up on the grill. The sun was setting, and the whole sky looked like a lovely watercolor painting of yellows, golds, and oranges, the same colors as the late blooms in Phoebe's flower garden.

"Look, Phoebe," I said, pointing to the sky with my forkful of potato salad. "You and God must be in cahoots." I nodded my chin toward her chrysanthemums.

"Yeah, right," she muttered—so unlike my Phoebe—and then she turned away so I wouldn't see the tears in her eyes. A minute later she recovered. "Red sky at night, sailor's delight," she said brightly. "If the weather holds, maybe we could go for a hike tomorrow."

"Okay," I said, pretending not to hear the false cheer in her voice. And then all at once it hit me—Phoebe's voice had been full of that phony, rah-rah, "everything's okay" tone for the past several weeks. And I hadn't been with it enough to notice. Or to see that the light that usually glittered in her eyes was gone. As was she. Oh, she was there all right, pouring me a cup of coffee, then sitting beside me, leaning her head on my shoulder and stroking my hand. But her core was gone. Her essence. The

Phoebeness of her had taken flight. And for the first time in my life, I wanted something as much as Phoebe had wanted to have that baby. I wanted my baby back.

Like I said, I'm a go-with-the-flow kind of gal, and I don't really plan things. What I've learned is, when you don't plan things, life plans things for you. Without you even knowing. One fall weekend, when Phoebe was away visiting a friend, I found myself alone and totally bored. I picked up a lesbian and gay magazine we'd gotten as a free promo in the mail, and I happened upon an article about a dyke whose girlfriend was deathly ill. She'd had diabetes since early childhood, and her time was running out. She needed a kidney transplant, and she needed it fast. And the dyke, without a moment's hesitation, had volunteered to donate her flesh and blood. Furthermore, she didn't even see what the big deal was. "I love her," she said in a boxed quote. "I never even thought about not doing it. What's mine is hers, and what's hers is mine."

Now, I don't usually read these kind of articles—they're more Phoebe's cup of tea than mine—but for some reason I read the whole story from beginning to end, and by the time I was finished I had more than a glimmer of tears in my eyes. I put the magazine down, wiped my soggy cheeks, and suddenly, just as I blew my nose, a lightbulb appeared above my head, shining as brightly as the light that used to shine in Phoebe's eyes.

What's mine is hers and what's hers is mine, I thought as I ran up to the attic. It didn't take long to find what I was looking for: the box full of how-to-get-pregnant books and pamphlets Phoebe had collected during Operation Baby. I read everything I could that night and picked up where I left off the following morning. It all seemed easy enough. My periods were totally regular—you could set your clock by them. They arrived every twenty-eight days at exactly ten minutes after ten in the morning. Really. It was some sort of phenomenon, I guess, though I'd never really thought about it much. Until now.

The trick was, according to what I'd read, you don't ovulate fourteen days after you get your period; you ovulate fourteen days before you get your next period. Which makes it harder to pin down. But since I'm so regular, I just calculated when my next period was supposed to start and counted back fourteen days. Then I looked up our trusty sperm-runner, who seemed surprised to hear from me, since Phoebe was always the one who had called. I told her Phoebe had gotten too emotional about the whole thing, and I would be the one to handle all the details from now on. And I would be the one to meet her at the door.

On D-Day, which fell during the week, thank God, I took the day off from work so Phoebe wouldn't know what was happening. I locked the door after the sperm-runner left and snuck the jar she'd handed me down the hallway into our bedroom like it was full of drugs or stolen goods. Then I stripped off my jeans and BVD's and thought, *Well, here goes nothing,* as I inserted the sperm with a syringe. That done, I lay on my back and walked my feet up the wall until my body was shaped like a giant L. How long did it take to get pregnant? A second, a minute, an hour? I wished I hadn't slept through high school biology, but it was a little late for that. And it was a little late to wonder about what I had just done to myself. As Phoebe said during one of those rough periods she hit when she was still trying to become preggo: *If this is meant to happen, it will. And if it's not meant to happen, it won't.* Only time would tell.

I figured I had a good half-hour to kill, so I set the timer and shut my eyes to catch forty winks, but my position wasn't exactly conducive to slumber. And even if it was, my brain was spinning like a merry-go-round. My mother's voice, of all things, echoed loud and clear in the memory chambers of my mind: "Every woman in our family has a back-tipped uterus," she'd told me long ago during our one and only mother-daughter talk. "That means you can get pregnant just by having a boy look at you." She'd laughed at the expression on my face, realizing I was so young and naive there was actually a chance I was taking her words literally. "What I mean is," she explained, "you come from a long line of fertile women. Both your grandmother and I got pregnant the very first time. So be careful." And that was the end of our discussion.

I guess it made sense for me to think about my own mother at a time like this, but that didn't mean I had to be happy about it. If I did get pregnant, giving birth would be just about the only thing I'd have in common with the woman who spread her legs and released me to the world. Weird to think at one time we were so close we took up the exact same space, and now we were so far apart we probably wouldn't recognize each other if we passed on the street. No, in fact the last time I saw my mother, she didn't know me at all. But in some ways that turned out to be a good thing.

My mother has Alzheimer's. She resides in a nursing home but lives in a fantasy world. I fly across the country to see her only every other year or so, and I'm not sure why I even do that. Out of guilt, I suppose, but what should I feel guilty for? Sure, I'm a lousy daughter, but she's a lousier mother. She's the one who abandoned me, not the other way around, which is what she thinks, since I stopped visiting her long before she lost her mind. We were never very close, but through most of my childhood we at least pretended to have something of a relationship. Until the day I sent my parents a coming-out letter. My mother, who never even showed the letter to my father, sent me a letter back in which she called me "sick, perverted, and disgusting," among other things. At least she didn't disown me, but what she did was in some ways worse—she acted like I'd never even told her.

"How's Jonathan?" she asked whenever we spoke on the phone. Jonathan was the boy I hung out with in high school, who my mother hoped I would marry, and who of course turned out to be as queer as yours truly.

"He's fine, Ma. Hey, listen, did you read the article I sent you about the gay youth center I'm volunteering at?"

"No, dear."

"Why not?"

"Robin, I don't know. I just haven't had time. So how's that boy Douglas? It's so nice you two wound up at the same school. Do you see him anymore?"

"No, Ma." Douglas was an asshole who tried to feel me up once during a high school field trip, but my mother knew his mother from around the neighborhood, so of course she thought he was nice. "Did you get the PFLAG pamphlets I sent you?"

"I don't know, Robin. Maybe they're around here somewhere."

"Well, will you look at them?"

"I can't promise. Your father and I are very busy. How's the weather up there? Cold?"

And it was just as bad in person. Whenever I tried to talk about my life, she would change the subject. And my father wasn't much better. He was hardly ever home; since we always needed money, he worked extra shifts whenever he could. When he did remember he had a family and actually spent some time in the house, he didn't bother with us much; he always headed straight for the living room before the rest of us were done eating supper, to turn on the TV and watch a baseball game, a boxing match, or whatever sports event happened to be on.

The only reason I did bother coming home from school was to see Max, the dog I grew up with. That cocker spaniel was my only friend from the time I was twelve until the day I left for college. He died when I was twenty-four—I still can't look at his picture without bawling—and after that it was just too unbearable to set foot in my parents' house anymore. So I stopped visiting, and my calls home dwindled down to once a month, once every other month, and then not even that. It got to the point where I spoke to my parents two or three times a year, which seemed to be just fine with both of them and me.

The last time I went to see my mother, I tried, I really did. There wasn't much I could do about the crew cut I was sporting, and I sure wasn't going to put on a dress, but I cleaned up the best I could. Phoebe offered to come with me, but some things you just have to do alone. And besides, why waste money on an extra plane ticket unless we were going somewhere fun? Phoebe thought we could make a vacation out of it, but when I go to see my mother I don't like to stick around. I'm in, I'm out. Hello, goodbye.

At least that's the way it usually is. But this time my mother jumped to her feet and lit up like the sun when I strolled into her room at the nursing home. "Hel-*lo,*" she said, as though she'd been waiting for me, her voice full of joy and her arms open wide.

I took a few more cautious steps into the room and dropped

the box of chocolates I had brought onto the bed. "Hi," I said, stopping a few feet from her. I hadn't physically touched my mother in a long time. "How are you?"

"Fine, fine," she said, dismissing my question. "Aren't you going to give your own mother a hug?"

"Sure," I said, hoping my tone wasn't giving away my surprise. I took the tentative final steps that closed the gap between us and let her embrace me. She's a big-boned woman, and tall besides, and her arms, though doughy, were strong. I didn't dare breathe, because I knew if I did I would break down and cry, and I sure didn't want that to happen. Why ruin our one good moment in fifteen years? But not to worry—I didn't ruin it. My mother ruined it.

"Let me look at you." She finally released me and took a step back to eye me up and down, with a mixture of shyness and pride. "You look good," she said, finally passing judgment. "The girls must be climbing all over themselves just to get a glimpse of you."

This was too much. This couldn't be my mother. "Ma?" I asked, puzzled. Was she on some new medication with an anti-homophobic serum built right into it?

"Sure." She plopped herself down on the only chair in the room and motioned for me to sit on the bed. "So tell me, is there someone special in your life?"

"As a matter of fact, there is," I said, thinking, *If some queer-friendly alien has taken over my mother's body, I might as well enjoy myself.* "Her name's Phoebe. You'd like her, Ma. She's really pretty and she's really—"

"Phoebe?" My mother cut me off. "What happened to Gloria?"

"Gloria?" I'd never dated anyone named Gloria. At least that I could remember.

"Yeah, you know. Gloria. You brought her to the house just the other night. Remember, she loved that strawberry rhubarb pie I picked up at the bakery, had two big helpings, a skinny girl like that, wonder where she puts it. She's a nice girl, that Gloria, you should hold on to a girl like that..."

Oh, my God. Gloria. Gloria was my older brother's girlfriend. *When he was in high school.* The night my mother was reminiscing about took place over twenty years ago. And she hadn't seen my brother in almost just as long, except for the day of my father's funeral. No, I was the one who made sure, despite everything, that she was taken care of when my aunt, the only one who'd kept in sporadic touch with me, called to tell me my mother was wearing her nightgown with nothing underneath it to the grocery store. My mother was putting on water for tea and forgetting about it until she almost burned down the house. My mother was wandering around strange neighborhoods at night, ringing doorbells and asking for a cup of hot chocolate. My mother needed to be taken care of, and I took care of her. No, I didn't have her move in with me, but still, I did the best I could.

And for that, this was the thanks I got. Her look of delight wasn't for me, her darling, dutiful daughter. No, with my short hair, pullover sweater, and pressed jeans, she thought I was Kevin, her firstborn, her son, the child who could do no wrong even though he'd deserted the family long ago, first to become a Hare Krishna, then a Jehovah's Witness, and last I heard some kind of Jesus freak. The only one who ever heard from Kevin was my aunt, and that was only when he needed money, which of course he never bothered to pay back. But still, my aunt would send him a blank check without a moment's hesitation, just as I'm sure, as my mother so clearly proved, that Kevin could walk in here, even after all these years, and be clasped to her heaving bosom, no questions asked.

I realized by the silence in the room that my mother had just asked me a question and was waiting for an answer, but I had none to give. I'd already gotten more than I'd bargained for: a hug—meant for my brother, but a hug nevertheless—so I bade her a fond farewell and headed out the door, straight for the airport.

When the timer rang, I shook my head like a wet puppy hoping to clear my mind and swung my legs down from the wall before my brain decided to take any more trips down memory lane. I figured the half-hour I'd spent flat on my back was enough time to seal my fate, so I pulled on my clothes and headed into the kitchen for what could turn out to be my last beer for a very long time. I wondered if I'd follow in my mother's and grandmother's footsteps and become pregnant on the first try. First and *last* try, as I seriously doubted I'd ever do this again. I was already half-regretting my noble deed and fully hoping it would all come to naught. That way, I could tell Phoebe what I'd done (I had the empty jar for proof), score some big Brownie points, and have our lives continue just as they had before.

But just my luck; for once in her life my mother was right. That night, at exactly seven minutes after four, with Phoebe slumbering and unsuspecting beside me, I woke up in a total sweat, my tits all swollen, tender, and hard. And I mean *hard*. Like steel or granite. Clearly this was no ordinary case of PMS. Unless PMS now stood for Pre-Mommy Syndrome.

Still, it was no use telling Phoebe until I was absolutely sure, so I kept my little secret a few more weeks, just in case it was a false alarm. Old Faithful (Phoebe's nickname for my period) didn't arrive the day it was supposed to, but still I kept mum, waiting for just the right time to tell her, whenever that would be. I tried to act normal, despite feeling completely nauseous every morning after about the first week and a half. I found if I just lay in bed completely still for a while, it would pass, but of course Phoebe knew something weird was going on.

"Are you all right?" One Tuesday when I was still under the covers even though the snooze button had gone off three times, Phoebe, who'd been up for hours, came around to my side of the bed and perched on the edge of the mattress. "What's up?" she asked, stroking my damp forehead. "You're all sweaty. Are you sick? Do you think you have a fever?"

"No, I'm fine," I said, thinking, *If she keeps rocking the bed like that, I'm going to puke all over her for sure.*

"Want pancakes for breakfast?"

"Okay," I mumbled, knowing she'd really be suspicious if I refused such a generous offer. I waited until she was busy in the kitchen, and then I dashed into the bathroom, ran the water hard, and barfed my brains out. Afterward, I felt better and came to sit at the table.

"You don't look so good," Phoebe remarked as she put a plate in front of me. Just the sight of those steaming hot cakes was enough to make me upchuck all over again. "In fact, you haven't looked good in over a week."

"Thanks a lot," I said, picking up my fork. "Am I losing my good looks? Is it all over for me at thirty-three?"

Phoebe wasn't in a joking mood. "Can I ask you something?" She sat down across from me.

"Sure," I said casually, trying not to panic. Could she possibly know? How? For some reason, I still wasn't ready to tell her. Maybe because that would make it real, and I wasn't sure I was ready to face that yet.

"Robin, there's no easy way to ask this, so I'll just say it." Phoebe kept her eyes down, studying her place mat, and my heart started banging around in my chest. "Robin, are you having an affair?"

"What?" I burst out laughing, which I'm sure was not the reaction Phoebe had expected. Maybe my hormones were already going to my head, because I laughed and laughed until the tears ran down my face. Phoebe just looked at me like I was someone she had never seen before. I kept trying to calm down and speak, but every time I started talking my words grew all shaky and I broke out laughing again.

"Shall I take that as a no?" Phoebe couldn't help smiling after a while, probably at how ridiculous I was acting. "It's just that you've been awfully quiet lately, and we haven't, you know, in kind of a while."

"It hasn't been that long, Phoebe," I said, though the truth was I couldn't remember the last time we had done the nasty. For reasons unknown to Phoebe, I hadn't been feeling as ardent as usual lately. "Hey," I tried to catch her eye, "I thought we were non-monogamous anyway."

"In theory," Phoebe the label-avoider reminded me, finally looking up. "Not in practice." She studied me closely. "So answer me. Are you having an affair? Or just losing interest in me?"

"None of the above." I reached across the table for her hand. "But I have been keeping a secret from you." *The time is now,* I thought as Phoebe's face changed. *The jig is up.*

"Is it a surprise?" she asked. Phoebe loves surprises.

"Yes."

"Let's see. Is it bigger than a bread box?"

"Not yet."

"Not yet?" Phoebe's brow furrowed. "So it's something that grows. A plant?"

"No."

"Hmm. Is it in the house?"

"Yep."

"Is it in this room?"

"Yep again."

Phoebe got up and looked around the kitchen. She opened cupboards and poked around, but didn't find a thing. She ransacked the oven, the broom closet, and the silverware drawer. Finally she searched my face but couldn't read it.

"I give up," she said, sitting down again.

"Phoebe." This time I kept my gaze down and studied my place mat. "There's no easy way to tell you this, so I'll just say it." I looked up into my girlfriend's eyes, hoping my words would bring their spark back. "I'm pregnant."

"What?" Phoebe's features scrambled all over her face trying to settle into one emotion, but shock, disbelief, joy, and grief were all vying for attention. "Robin?" She said my name like a question, and so I answered it. I showed her the article about the dyke with the diabetic girlfriend and told her what I'd been up to the past few weeks. Phoebe just stared at me as I spoke, shaking her head and making these sounds that were somewhere between a laugh and a cry. When I was through with my story, she got up, and without saying a word, hugged me so hard I thought she'd break my bones. And that night we had the best sex we'd ever had (and we've had some absolutely transformational episodes, let me tell you). So, if nothing else, at least we're back to making whoopee, I thought the next morning as I bent over the toilet bowl and gagged up my breakfast.

Phoebe was all sympathy. She fed me soda crackers, made me tea, insisted I put my feet up and not lift a thing. I thought maybe she'd be resentful that I was the one who was pregnant, and got to experience all the joys (ha!) of the condition. Believe me, with the way I was feeling I'd have traded places with her in a heartbeat. But Phoebe bore me no grudge. If anything, she felt bad that I was feeling so awful and there was nothing she could do about it. She even offered to throw up every time I did—she'd been bulimic all through college, so she was a pro—but I declined her generous offer. She kept asking what she could do for me, as she was so knocked out over what I was doing for her (as frankly, so was I). If she had any feelings of envy, she kept them to herself. And then, not to be outdone, my Phoebe came home one day with a little secret of her own.

"I've got a surprise for you, Robin," she said, a smile playing around her lips.

I'm not big on surprises, but I humored her. "Is it bigger than a bread box?"

"Not yet."

"Not yet? Oh, my God, *you're* pregnant."

"Don't be silly." Phoebe put her hands on her belly, which was as flat as mine was round. "Guess again."

"Umm, I don't know. Is it in the house?"

"No."

"No? Is it out in your car?"

"Nope. It's on the front porch."

"Why, is it too heavy for you to carry upstairs?"

"Just go get it," Phoebe said, steering me by the shoulders. I opened the front door, and there on the porch sat the cutest, sweetest, tiniest, most adorable black-and-white, blue-eyed puppy you ever saw. I scooped him up and actually started bawling, which I immediately blamed on my hormones, but I don't think I fooled Phoebe one bit.

"He's a Harlequin Great Dane," Phoebe told me once I'd managed to calm down long enough to carry the puppy upstairs, where she promptly peed on the living room floor.

"A Great Dane?" I was shocked all over again. "Phoebe, he's going to weigh over a hundred pounds."

"I know," Phoebe said, grinning like this was the best news she'd ever heard. "I figured the bigger the dog, the more you'd know how much I love you."

So there we were, two girls, a kid, and a dog. Well, the kid wasn't there yet, but he or she soon would be. Phoebe cleared out all the junk that was collecting dust in our second bedroom, painted it yellow, and filled it with all kinds of baby stuff: a crib with an animal mobile hanging over it, a changing table with a poster of a lamb on the wall next to it, a trunk of toys, a shelf of books, a bureau filled with miniature clothes. I didn't help much; I was too busy training Spot, our overgrown puppy, to sit, stay, come, and most important, not crap on the carpet. And besides, I thought Phoebe would feel more a part of things if she was in charge of getting the house ready for little Miracle Growth, as she had dubbed our offspring. We still hadn't decided on a name (and since I was the one to pick out our dog's less-than-original moniker, Phoebe was a little worried), so Phoebe called the baby all sorts of things. Tiny Dancer, Small Potatoes, Buried Treasure, Tweetie Pie. I didn't call the kid much of anything; despite the hard and fast evidence of my growing abdomen, I was still in semi-denial that something alive and soon-to-be kicking was growing inside me.

One night when I was just starting my second trimester, Phoebe came home with several books of baby names. I moved over to make room for her next to me on the couch and wrestled with Spot over his chew toy while Phoebe studied page after page. Phoebe had let out a long sigh of relief when I got to my fourth month, since, according to the endless books she read on the subject, the first trimester is an absolute minefield of dangers. In fact, many mothers-to-be don't even tell anyone they're pregnant until they've made it to their twelfth week. But now that I was safely out of the woods, we were free to spread the word. We were also free to bond with the kid, though Phoebe had wasted no time on that, becoming completely attached the second I'd told her. As for me, well, that was another story. The little monster, which is how I thought of the creature inside me, was nothing but trouble, causing me heartburn, indigestion, exhaustion, headaches, and a set of extremely ugly varicose veins behind my left knee. Who could bond with such a bad seed? I tried to keep my complaints to myself, but I was hardly successful. Phoebe thought if the beast had a name, I'd soften up a bit.

"I think we should pick a name that'll work for a boy or a girl," Phoebe said, looking up from her reading, "so we can start using it right away." (Phoebe was adamant about not knowing the child's sex until the day I gave birth.) "And besides," Phoebe, ever the progressive, added, "what if our kid grows up to be transgendered?"

I had to say, I'd never thought of that, but since Phoebe brought it up, I let her run some names by me: Pat. Chris. Dana. I wasn't crazy about any of them.

"Too bad Robin's already taken," I said as Phoebe pored over the books in her lap.

"Robin…" Phoebe repeated, thumbing through the R's. "Hey, did you know your name, in addition to being a bird, means 'shining fame?' "

"Oh, so this isn't a pregnant glow?" I pointed to my face and sat up clumsily, trying to negotiate my blooming belly. "Drop it," I said to Spot, who had just brought me his favorite toy. "Hey, I've got it." I tossed the slimy tennis ball across the carpet and turned back to Phoebe. "Let's give the kid a bird name too. Like Phoebe. Or Robin."

"Okay," Phoebe laughed. "How about red-winged blackbird? Or yellow-bellied sapsucker?"

"No, Phoebe, I'm serious." I don't know why I suddenly cared so much all of a sudden, but I did. "Let's see." I stroked Spot's head absently and stared out the window, as if some feathered friend would fly by with the answer in its beak. "Let's go through the alphabet. Albatross. Bluebird. Cardinal…"

"Dodo…"

I ignored her. "What about Dove? Or Finch? Grackle?" Phoebe rolled her eyes, but I continued. "Heron, Ibis, Jay…Hey, Jay's not bad. What do you think?"

"Eh."

"Okay, let's see. I can't think of anything that starts with 'K,' can you?" Phoebe shook her head. "All right, let's skip it for now. Lark, Magpie…"

"Lark. I kind of like that," Phoebe said, surprising me. "You know, happy as a lark." She looked it up in her baby books, but not finding it, got up to get a dictionary. Spot leapt onto the now-vacant left side of the couch and snuggled beside me.

"Listen to this, Robin." Phoebe was so excited she didn't even yell at Spot to get off the sofa. "Lark," she read out loud. "One: a merry, carefree adventure. Two: innocent or good-natured mischief. Three: to have fun, frolic, romp. I think it's perfect."

"I don't know," I pretended to frown. "I was starting to like Dodo."

"You dodo." Phoebe grabbed a pillow off the couch and bonked me over the head with it. I retaliated, and a rousing pillow fight ensued, followed by a rousing fun-filled frolicking romp. Phoebe was definitely happy as a lark that day and for many days afterward. I, on the other hand, was up, down, and sideways. My moods, like most pregnant women's, were all over the map, but for the most part I guess I could say I was content. Phoebe was happy, and that's why I was doing this, right? In a few months it would be over, my baby would have her baby, and I'd have my life back. At least that was the plan. And then, right when I was hitting the home stretch, the trouble began.

It was early evening, and I was home alone—Phoebe was working extra hours, figuring we'd need the dough—and I had just come in from taking Spot for his walk. Or rather, I had just come in from having Spot, who could easily be mistaken for a Holstein cow at this point, take me for a walk. It was pretty hard to tell just who the alpha dog was between the two of us. Phoebe had insisted, after talking to someone who knew someone who knew someone whose shoulder had been dislocated when her dog pulled too hard on its leash, that I take Spot to dog obedience school. And my big kahuna of a puppy (eighty-five pounds and counting) had done me proud. But sometimes lessons were tossed out the window, when, for example a squirrel crossed our path, like one had done right at the end of the street. Spot had given me a run for my money, but with my extra weight behind me, I'd managed to rein him back.

Spot was panting on the cool kitchen floor, and I was sprawled on the living room couch. Though spring had barely ended a few weeks ago, the temperature was already inching its way toward the ninety-degree mark. I sure wasn't looking forward to spending my last month big as a house during the—excuse me, Spot—dog days of summer. Especially since my furnace had gone haywire over the past few weeks and my temperature was usually somewhere between roasting and boiling. It was especially hard for me at night when I couldn't get comfortable anyway, having always slept on my stomach, which was impossible now. So between having to sleep on my side and sweating like a pig even with just a sheet covering Phoebe and me, I was one unhappy camper. Add to that my perpetual backache, frequent farting, and urge to pee every two seconds, and it was no wonder I was getting grumpier by the minute.

The previous night I had just about had it, because on top of all the lovely symptoms I've already described, I was hit with some wicked stomach cramps accompanied by a stinking bout of diarrhea that just about killed me. After I dragged my blimp of a body off the toilet and managed to clean myself up, I went to find Phoebe, who was in the baby's room sitting in our brand-new rocker, content as can be.

"Listen," I snarled at her, "when Lark finally does arrive, you can have him."

"Or her." Phoebe got up and offered me the rocker.

"Whatever." I wasn't in a politically correct mood. "Listen, when all this is over, I'll have carried Lark around for nine whole months, so I say you carry Lark around for the next nine."

"Fine by me," Phoebe said, opening her arms. "I'd take him now if I could."

"Or her," I said, and Phoebe smiled.

I wished I could give Lark to Phoebe this very minute, but Phoebe was still at work and Lark was still tucked in tight. Or so I thought. As I lay there, too lazy to get up and pour myself some iced tea, I felt some fluid leak down my thigh. *Oh, shit,* I thought, *did I pee on the couch? What kind of role-modeling is this for Spot?* I got up to head into the bathroom yet again, but the fluid stopped. So I lay back down, but it started up again.

"I'm fucking leaking," I said aloud, and then, since I was so befuddled with hormones, my next thought was, *Phoebe's going to kill me if I ruin these pants.* If you think you have a hard time buying clothes, try being a pregnant butch. Luckily, Phoebe is a whiz with a needle and thread and made me a closetful of drawstring trousers. It took me a full five minutes to stop worrying about my pants and start worrying about the baby. Had my water broken? It couldn't have; it was at least a month too early. I got up slowly and went into the bedroom, where Phoebe had about a million books on pregnancy. Shit, there it was. Signs of premature labor: cramps, with or without diarrhea—check. Lower back pain—check. Rupture of membranes—check, check, check. Every time I stood up, the fluid stopped pouring out of me, but when I lay down again, the floodgates opened. Was I in labor or wasn't I? Only my doctor would know for sure.

Before I phoned the doctor, I called Phoebe at work. "But it's too early," she said, like she was telling me something I didn't already know.

"Just come home," I told her, keeping my voice as neutral as possible. Then I called my doctor, who said: Go directly to the hospital. Do not pass go. Do not collect two hundred dollars. *C'mon, Phoebe, move it,* I prayed silently as I waited for her to pull into the driveway. Spot, sensing something was up, came into the bedroom and rested his great head on the mattress beside me.

"Spot, I think I'm going to have a baby," I said, stroking him. "The real thing. Not like Dodo." My sweet puppy's ears tilted forward at the name of the doll Phoebe had brought home for us to cuddle with in order for Spot to get used to the idea of having an infant in the house. "This is the real thing, Spot. Lark is going to laugh and cry and walk and talk...I hope." Suddenly the thought that it was too late to turn back, coupled with the terror that there might be something wrong with the baby, hit me like a sucker punch. What if Lark wasn't all right? But how could that be? My doctor said I was healthy as a horse. I'd done everything by the book: completely stopped drinking, eaten the so-healthy-they-made-me-even-more-nauseous meals Phoebe had cooked for me, even taken a pregnant women's exercise class. I didn't smoke (Phoebe wouldn't even let me enter a room in which someone was puffing away), I left the kitchen when the microwave was on, and the biggest problem I'd had besides the nausea, headaches, varicose veins, and deadly gas was constant and wicked heartburn. I'd gotten regular checkups, and the amniocentesis had come out perfectly normal. *If I fuck this up, Phoebe will kill me* ran through my mind as the other mother of my child finally ran through the door.

"Robin, what's going on?" she asked, but there was no time to explain. The backache I'd had all morning was getting worse, and spreading to my abdomen. I felt like I was going to either lay the biggest fart of the century or soil myself with diarrhea just like a baby—just like our baby—surely would do time and time again, as soon as said bambino was safely in our arms. Right? Right? I kept begging Phoebe for reassurance as we sped toward the hospital.

"Of course everything's fine," Phoebe said, not daring to take her eyes off the road as she pushed the pedal to the medal. "Just relax, Robin." *Yeah, right.*

If you're like me, you can't stand the sight of blood, so I'll spare you the gory details and give you just the facts: I was in premature labor, and our daughter, Lark, was born premature. Turned out I had an "incompetent cervix," which is not a harsh judgment on my inept plumbing but an actual medical term. My doctor didn't pick up on it because it's hard to diagnose until after a woman has already had a miscarriage or gone through premature labor. In other words, hindsight is twenty-twenty. What happens, basically, is that your cervix opens before it's supposed to and your fluid leaks out. But if you stand up, the baby's head moves down to cover the opening and stop the fluid. Like a little plug.

Phoebe said Lark was just in a big old hurry to come out into the world and meet us. And of course our child would be precocious and do everything ahead of schedule. Including race out into the world. I thought Lark was probably just sick and tired of being inside her bumpy, grumpy, nonlovey-dovey blob of a birth mother. If only I had been kinder to her, I thought, as I lay there in bed, trying to gather my strength (I'd been in labor for sixteen hours). Would it have killed me to sing to her, talk to her, or at least stop complaining every time she gave me a good swift kick in the ribs? Lark wasn't an idiot. She wanted to make her great escape and meet the mommy who crooned to her night after night, holding one fist up to her ear and speaking into my protruding belly button like it was the mouthpiece of an old-fashioned telephone. "Hello, little Lark," Phoebe would say in a voice chock-full of love. "How's my sweet baby today?" she'd ask, turning her head so her ear lay flat against my belly, listening for a reply. Who wouldn't be in a rush to lay eyes on the woman who belonged to that sweet, gentle voice?

The nurse had whisked Lark out of the delivery room right away and brought her to wherever they bring preemies, barely pausing long enough to tell us she was a girl. They had to do all kinds of things to her: make sure her temperature and her glucose were stable, check for respiratory distress, anemia, infection, things like that. Frankly, I only half-listened to what Phoebe was telling me. All I wanted to do was sleep.

After I rested for a few…minutes? hours?—hospital time has a mind of its own—the nurse came in and said we could go and see Lark, but I told Phoebe to go ahead. I was too tired. Which wasn't entirely true, but I wanted to give the two of them a chance to bond. After all, I still wasn't sure I wanted to be a parent. That hadn't changed, despite everything I'd gone through. I thought of myself as Lark's birth mother, but instead of giving her up for adoption, I was giving her up to Phoebe, who decided that if I was Lark's birth mother, she was Lark's "earth mother."

I must have drifted back to sleep because the next thing I knew Phoebe was shaking me awake, her mouth curved into a huge smile, though tears were raining down her face. "Robin, she's so amazing," Phoebe said, taking both my hands and squeezing them. *Who?* I thought for a groggy moment, but then I remembered where I was. "She's really, really tiny, but she has all her fingers and toes, and the nurse says she thinks she's going to be fine."

"But there's a chance she won't be," I said, in an odd, flat tone.

"Only a *slight* chance, Robin. She's pretty strong, small as she is, and I'm sure she's stubborn too, especially if she takes after you. She just has to gain some weight," Phoebe said, laughing, "just like this roommate I had when I was at the eating disorder clinic—Belinda, her name was—she probably didn't weigh much more than little Lark weighs right now, but she pulled out of it—"

"Phoebe, you're babbling." I held my hand up to stop the words that were pouring out of her mouth.

"Oh. Sorry." Phoebe stopped abruptly but then started up again. "I'm just so happy, Robin. Aren't you happy? Happy as a lark. Happy as a clam. Happy as a pig in shit. Happy as a—"

"Phoebe," I cut her off again.

"What's the matter?"

"I'm tired. I didn't get any sleep last night, remember?"

"I know. I didn't either."

"Hey." Suddenly I had a brilliant idea. "Can you get me something to drink?"

"Sure. How about some apple juice?"

"Whatever."

"I'll be right back. Don't go anywhere." Phoebe dashed out, and by the time she got back I had closed my eyes again. I wasn't really asleep, and I felt bad, but the truth was, her giddy euphoria was getting on my nerves. Maybe I had an instant case of postpartum depression, or maybe I'm just a callous son of a bitch, but I was feeling about as maternal as Spot's soggy, chewed-up tennis ball. Call me a cad, but at the moment I had no desire to see Lark at all. What I really wanted to do was get up, get dressed, go home, and take Spot for a walk around the block. I had given Phoebe what she wanted, hadn't I? Now it was time for what I wanted: I wanted my life back.

What's so special about a baby anyway? I wondered as I lay there pretending to doze. Every baby just grew up to become a person, and tell me the truth, how many people do you know who are really and truly special? Every asshole that cuts you off in traffic, every rude bastard who bumps into you on the street and doesn't say excuse me, every bored-stiff, gum-snapping, don't-do-me-any-favors teenage salesclerk who ignores you at the mall, all of them started out being somebody's baby. So what's the big deal?

Phoebe should have known to leave well enough alone, but she was too excited. "Wake up, Mommy," she whispered, poking my arm with a cold bottle of juice.

"Don't call me Mommy," I said with as much emotion as the day so long ago when Phoebe scolded me for calling her "baby." I still didn't know what Lark was going to call me, but it sure wasn't going to be Mommy. A mommy with a buzz cut? Give me a break.

"The doctor says you can go home tomorrow, but Lark has to stay here until she gains weight." Phoebe's chin trembled, but she held on and didn't cry. "But we can see her every day and talk to her, sing to her..."

"How's Spot?" By the clock on the opposite wall, I saw that it was way past my boy's suppertime.

"Spot?" Phoebe said his name like a foreign word she couldn't quite wrap her mouth around. "Fine, I guess."

"What do you mean, you guess?"

"Robin, you just had a baby, for God's sake. Spot is a dog. An animal. I'm sure he's fine."

"He'd better be," I growled. All of a sudden it was too much of an effort to hide my grouchiness.

"C'mon, Robin. Let's go up and see Lark." Phoebe pulled back the sheet covering me, but I pulled it back.

"Leave me alone," I snapped, turning over on my side.

"What's the matter with you?" Phoebe asked, but as I didn't know, I couldn't answer her. I just wanted her and Lark and everyone else in the world to go away.

But Phoebe, of course, wasn't going anywhere. "What's the matter with you?" she asked again. "Don't you even want to see your own child?"

"Phoebe, what's the big rush? We'll be seeing her every day for the rest of our lives."

"Oh, my God." Her voice dropped to a whisper. "You are acting really weird, Robin. You don't even want to see her? What kind of mother are you?"

"First of all, I'm not a mother, I'm a parent," I reminded her of what we had agreed upon. "And second of all, lots of mothers aren't interested in their babies. Some give them up for adoption. Some leave them in bus stations. Some flush them down the toilet. Some..."

Phoebe stared at me, shocked. "I don't even know you anymore," she said, leaving my room to go back to the nursery again.

"...abandon their daughter and don't speak to her again unless they mistake her for her brother," I said to myself. Christ, did I have to be thinking about my mother now on top of everything else I was going through?

I was sitting up, staring glumly out the darkened window when Phoebe came back. "The doctor said it's normal for some new mothers—parents—to respond with distance to a baby in distress." She sounded like a textbook.

"So I'm normal." I crossed my arms and glared at her. "Don't try to change me."

"I'm going home." Phoebe bent down to kiss my stubborn mouth. "I'll be back first thing in the morning. Do you want me to bring you anything?"

Spot, I thought, but even I couldn't be cruel enough to say that. So I stayed mum, and Phoebe left me alone.

But wouldn't you know it, the night nurse didn't. "Nurse Nellie here," announced a big teddy bear of a man who looked forty (and I'm sure he'd say fabulous) as he breezed into the room. "And how's Mommy doing?" he asked, grabbing the chart at the foot of my bed.

"Christ, we *are* everywhere." I shook my head. "I'm not Mommy," I informed my new lady in waiting, whose name tag read "Lee."

"Well, you sure ain't Daddy." Lee pointed to the front of my hospital gown, which I saw had two round, wet stains on it.

"What the hell?"

"You're leaking, Elsie. We're going to have to get you a breast pump."

"A what? Christ," I said again. "I thought my job was over."

"Your job is just beginning, honey." Lee shook down a thermometer and motioned for me to sit up. "You've signed on for the rest of your life, missy. No weekends off. No holidays. No paid vacations. You're in it for the long haul, pal. Especially with a girl. So, who does she look like, you or Papa?"

"There is no Papa," I told him. "My girlfriend and I used 'man in a can.'" When Lee just looked at me blankly, I explained, "You know. A sperm donor."

"Eek!" Lee put his hand over his heart and then tsk-tsked. "What a waste. Oh, well. So, does the baby look like you?"

"I don't know."

"I guess it's too early to tell, huh? Especially with a preemie."

"No, it's not that. I haven't seen her yet."

"What?" Lee gasped and put his hand over his heart again. "Are you crazy, girlfriend? Get out of that bed. C'mon, now, you're getting up."

"But it's nighttime," I whimpered, like a sleepy little girl. "And don't you have to take my temperature?"

Lee stuck his thermometer in my mouth and pulled it out two seconds later. "Perfectly normal," he pronounced, without even glancing at it. "And it doesn't matter if it's day or night. Babies don't know the difference. All they know is asleep and awake. So c'mon."

"All right. I might as well get it over with."

"What?" This time Lee clasped both hands up to his chest. "Are you trying to give me a heart attack? What kind of mother are you?"

For the third time that day I said, loudly and clearly, "I am not a mother. I am a parent."

But that only made Lee laugh. "Hey, you know what they say: If it looks like a duck and walks like a duck and quacks like a duck..." When I didn't respond, Lee enlightened me. "Listen, you can call yourself Old Father Time for all I care, and it still won't matter—the baby's going to treat you like her mother. Especially when you give her some of that." He nodded to the front of my soggy gown.

"The baby has a mother," I told Lee, who handed me some terry cloth slippers. "Her name is Phoebe."

"Auburn hair, blue eyes, hubba-hubba-hubba?" Lee moved his hands through the air outlining the shape of an exaggerated hourglass figure.

"Yep."

"Ooh, Mama. Oops, sorry," Lee cringed as I glared at him. "I saw her when I first started my shift. Wow. That's some chick you got there."

"Don't I know it," I mumbled. "If it wasn't for that chick, I wouldn't be here in the first place."

"Okay, okay. Time for a chat." Now that he had finally gotten me sitting up, Lee pushed me back down against my pillow. "I was the star pupil in my psych class, and you are one classic case, baby. Now, tell me what's going on for real. I won't even charge you my usual eighty-five bucks an hour."

I sighed and told Lee everything. Took it from the top and went right down the line: how Phoebe and I met and fell in love, her insemination trials and tribulations, the article I'd read that changed our lives, Spot, my mother... I'm sure it was way more than he wanted to know, but Lee was great. He spent so much time with me, I'm sure he could have lost his job, but as he said, "If we don't take care of the family, who the hell will?" I'm sure Lee had some sad tale of his own to tell—I could see it in his eyes—but for now I was center stage. Until I was done. Then he stepped into the spotlight.

"Okay, Robin Redbreast, listen up. This is a multiple-choice test. Are you: (a) feeling guilty you disappointed Phoebe by delivering an underweight baby ahead of schedule who might have some problems; (b) afraid Lark isn't going to make it, so you don't want to get too attached until you know for sure; (c) afraid Phoebe will love Lark more than she loves you; (d) afraid Lark will love Phoebe more than she'll love you; (e) afraid Spot will love Lark more than he loves you; (f) you can stop me any time here—afraid that..."

"Okay, stop." My head was spinning as Lee's words whirled through my mind.

"Seriously," Lee nodded encouragement, "which one is it?"

"None of the above," I said, then told him the truth. "I'm afraid Lark is going to grow up to hate me."

Lee leaned against the bed and folded his arms. "Why?"

"Because the apple does not fall far from the tree," I said. "Why wouldn't she hate me? I hate *my* mother." To my horror, as the soon as the words were out my eyes filled and I began to cry.

"I don't think you hate your mother," Lee said gently. He turned away for a minute, giving me time to compose myself. I was grateful he understood us butches and our pride.

"From everything you've told me," Lee continued, "I think you love your mother. That's the bitch of it, isn't it? If we could only hate them—"

"I knew it." I interrupted him. "Tell."

"Yeah, yeah, so what else is new?" Lee shrugged his shoulders like he really didn't care, but I knew he did. "Another queer kicked out by his immoral majority parents. Blah, blah, blah. Big deal."

"Damn right. Big fucking deal."

"Yeah, whatever. Anyway, as I was saying, it would be so easy if we could hate them. But we don't. We fucking love them. Despite everything. Don't we?"

It was hard to admit it, but I had to. "Yes. We do."

"Well, then, if we love our parents after all they've done to us, how can you think Lark will hate you when you haven't even had a chance to fuck her up yet?"

"Even though I really didn't want her and only did it for Phoebe?" My voice caught around Phoebe's name and cracked as though it would break.

"First of all, Lark doesn't know that." Lee handed me a tissue. "And second of all, you didn't not want *her,* personally. She wasn't real to you. She was just an idea, a concept. But as soon as you see her, you're going to fall in love with her. Trust me."

"But what if I don't? What if I'm really as heartless as my own mother?" My pride flew out the window and I began sobbing in earnest now. "What if I can't love her? What if she turns out to be a terrible daughter, just like me?"

Lee lifted my hand in his great big paw and squeezed it. "There are no terrible daughters. Of either gender," he said softly. "There are only terrible mothers."

"That's what Spot's teacher said the first day of class," I told him, still holding his hand. "He said, 'There are no bad dogs. There are only bad dog owners.'"

"Exactly," said Lee. "And the good news is, you were trained by the best. You know exactly what kind of mother you don't want to be."

"Yeah, but the problem is I also don't know what kind of mother I *do* want to be."

"You'll figure it out. What's that saying: Mothers are the invention of necessity?"

"I think it's 'Necessity is the mother of invention.'"

"Whatever."

I smiled, and Lee did too. I had a feeling we were going to be friends. "Hey," I looked into his eyes, "maybe Lark will need an uncle."

"Maybe," he said. "But I don't know if I'm man enough for the job. I think I'd be better as her fairy godmother."

I laughed. "I think she has enough mothers as it is," I said, surprising myself.

"Sounds like you're ready now." Lee let go of my hand. "Do you want me to come with you?"

"No, I think I want to go it alone," I said, getting to my feet.

"Ah, the stoic butch. Now I know you'll be all right."

I nodded, left the room, and headed down the hall before Lee had a chance to point me in the right direction of the nursery. But I flew to it like a homing pigeon, my breath and steps both quickening as soon as I turned the correct corner.

I stood outside at first, gathering my courage as I peeked through the window. There were several babies there, all sound asleep, but I knew Lark instantly. I don't know how I knew her, but I did. Mother's intuition maybe, or maybe something else. *She's already tamed me,* I thought, as I stepped inside and tiptoed up to where she lay on her back, to study her hands, her feet, her face, her tiny, closed eyes. She was no bigger than a puppy, but still, even with her eyes shut, it was clear she was the most beautiful girl in the world. I couldn't wait for her to wake up, and when she did, the nurse led me to a rocking chair and showed me how to hold her. I still had her on my lap the next morning when Phoebe entered the nursery, stopped dead in her tracks, and then ran toward us, laughing and crying, her arms open wide.

Yiddish and Hebrew Glossary

Hebrew words are designated with (H). Yiddish spellings are not "official," as the only correct way to spell a Yiddish word is with Hebrew letters. Instead, the words are transliterated according to the author's ear. Likewise, the usage of Yiddish words may vary according to where one is from. Lastly, many Yiddish words have adopted English suffixes (i.e., shmoozing*), as Jews who came to America learned to speak English and sprinkled this new foreign language with words from the mama-loshen (mother tongue), which really do lose something in the translation.*

Ahnee Ze'ev (H): My name is Ze'ev.
aht (H): you (feminine)
Alav ha-sholom (H): May he rest in peace.
aliyah (H): to go up, to become a citizen of Israel
babka: a special kind of cake, often made with sugar and cinnamon
bar mitzvah (H): a formal ceremony to commemorate a thirteen-year-old boy's entry into manhood
bashert (H): destiny
bat mitzvah (H): a formal ceremony to commemorate a twelve- or thirteen-year-old girl's entry into womanhood
b'seder (H): in order
chai (H): two Hebrew letters representing "life"
challah (H): beautiful braided bread eaten on *Shabbos* and holidays
Chanukah (H): festival of lights lasting eight days and commemorating the Maccabees' victory over the Syrians and the rededication of the Temple at Jerusalem
chuppah: marriage canopy
dayenu (H): It would have been enough for us.
eppes: for some inexplicable reason
faygeleh: slang for gay man (literally, "little bird")

feh: ugh
gadol (H): big
Gottinyu: oh, my God
goy: person who isn't Jewish
Haggadah (H): the narrative read aloud at the Passover *seder* that tells the story of the Exodus of the Israelites from Egypt
halvah: a sweet made of sesame seeds and honey
he (H): she
hente(leh): hand (diminutive)
Kaddish (H): mourner's prayer
kibbutz (H): a community, often agricultural, organized under collective principles
kibbutznik: someone who lives on a kibbutz
kinder: children
knaydlach: matzo balls
kosher (H): fit to eat according to Jewish dietary law
kvetch: to complain
Lama lo? (H): Why not?
landsman: someone from the same hometown
latke: a potato pancake (traditionally eaten on *Chanukah*)
lila tov (H): good night
maidl, maideleh: a young girl
mameleh: endearment (literally, "little mother")
Ma-nish-ma (H): How's everything?
matzo: unleavened bread
matzo ball: dumpling made of *matzo* meal, eggs, oil, and salt, usually served in chicken soup
Mazel tov (H): Good luck!
me (H): who
menorah (H): candle holder used on *Chanukah*
mensch: person of character, someone you can count on
meshugeh: crazy
meshugeneh: crazy person
mezuzah (H): small oblong container holding parchment with biblical passages, affixed to the doorframe of many Jewish homes
Mogen David (H): **Star of David**
momzer: bastard

nosh: a snack
nu: so, well
oy: an expression of surprise, fear, sorrow, pain, excitement, etc.
oy vey: *oy* and then some
pardis (H): paradise
Pesach (H): Passover, the eight-day holiday commemorating the Exodus of the Israelites from Egypt
Rosh Hashanah (H): the Jewish New Year
sabre (H): a native Israeli
schlock, schlocky: junk, junky, something that is cheaply made
seder (H): the traditional meal eaten the first two nights of Pesach (literally, "order")
Shabbos: the Jewish Sabbath
shah: hush
shalom (H): hello, goodbye, peace
shanda: shame
shayneh: beautiful
shep naches: to reap joy
shlep: to drag or carry
The Sh'ma (H): a specific Jewish prayer (see below)
Sh'ma Yisroel, Adonoy Elohanu, Adonoy Echad (H): the most common Jewish prayer. Many Jews try to die with this prayer on their lips. (Literal translation: Hear O Israel, the Lord our God, the Lord is one.)
shmaltz: excessive sentimentality (literally, "rendered chicken fat")
shmate: a rag
shmegeggie (Yinglish): a whiner
shmooze: to talk or socialize, to "make the rounds"
shmuck: a jerk (literally, "penis")
shmutz: dirt
shtetl: Jewish village
shuk: marketplace
shul: synagogue
shvartze: a black person (not complimentary)
spiel: speech
takeh: really
tallis (H): prayer shawl

tateleh: endearment (literally, "little father")
tchotchke: a knickknack
tochter: daughter
Toda raba (H): Thank you very much.
tov (H): good
tuchus: buttocks
ulpan (H): Hebrew lessons
utz: to nag, move along
Va-ka-shah (H): You're welcome.
Vey iss mir: Woe is me.
vilda chayah: wild beast
who (H): he
yarmulke: skull cap
yarzheit: anniversary of someone's death
yoffi (H): pretty (slang)
Yom Kippur (H): Day of Atonement
yontiff: holiday
zaftig: plump, juicy
Ze'ev (H): male name (literally, "wolf")

Credits

"A Letter to Harvey Milk" and "The Gift" © 1988 Lesléa Newman, from *A Letter to Harvey Milk* (Firebrand Books, Ithaca, NY).

"Right Off the Bat," "What Happened to Sharon," and "A True Story (Whether You Believe It or Not)" © 1990 Lesléa Newman, from *Secrets* (New Victoria Publishers, Norwich, VT).

"Of Balloons and Bubbles," "With Anthony Gone," and "Comfort" © 1994 Lesléa Newman, from *Every Woman's Dream* (New Victoria Publishers, Norwich, VT).

"A Femme Shops Till Her Butch Drops," "PMS: Please Menstruate Soon!" "Butch in Training," and "The Butch That I Marry" © 1997 Lesléa Newman from *Out of the Closet and Nothing to Wear* (Alyson Publications, Los Angeles, CA).

"The *Babka* Sisters," "What Ever Happened to Baby Fane?" "Homo Alone," and "Eggs McMenopause" © 2000 Lesléa Newman from *Girls Will Be Girls* (Alyson Publications, Los Angeles, CA).

"Keeping a Breast," "*Bashert,*" and "Mothers of Invention" © 2002 Lesléa Newman from *She Loves Me, She Loves Me Not* (Alyson Publications, Los Angeles, CA).

About the Author

Mary Vazquez

Lesléa Newman is an author and editor whose forty books include *In Every Laugh a Tear* and *Good Enough to Eat* (novels); *Signs of Love* and *Still Life With Buddy* (poetry); *Girls Will Be Girls* and *She Loves Me, She Loves Me Not* (short stories); *Out of the Closet and Nothing to Wear* and *The Little Butch Book* (humor); *The Femme Mystique* and *My Lover Is a Woman: Contemporary Lesbian Love Poems* (anthologies); and *Heather Has Two Mommies* and *Too Far Away to Touch* (children's books). Her literary awards include fellowships from the National Endowment for the Arts and the Massachusetts Artists Foundation; a fiction-writing grant from the Money for Women/Barbara Deming Memorial Fund; two Pushcart Prize Nominations and second place finalist in the Raymond Carver Short Story competition. Nine of her books have been Lambda Literary Award finalists. A native New Yorker, she makes her home in western Massachusetts. Visit her Web site at www.lesleanewman.com.